An Extraordinary Woman
An Extravagant World

Everyone was on a party in the heyday of that long cocktail party that was the 1920s. Particularly Claudia Trenholm. Then she met Philippe, *le comte de Boissevain,* a dashing blueblood with a fatal attraction to blue-collar causes.

Hellbent on happiness, heedless of the consequences, she threw herself into a tempestuous love affair that outlived two stormy marriages and spanned three unsettled decades. The Roaring Twenties collapsed in Black Tuesday and a grim Depression sent the world careening toward war, but still The Rich Girl pursued a dizzying, dazzling love affair as wildly romantic as the era that spawned it.

"Elizabeth Villars out-Fitzgeralds Fitzgerald in casting this . . . with scores of glittering personalities from among the very rich of the 1920s. Complex and sympathetic characters and a fast-moving plot."

—*The Houston Chronicle*

ELIZABETH VILLARS

THE RICH GIRL

PUBLISHED BY POCKET BOOKS NEW YORK

POCKET BOOKS, a Simon & Schuster division of
GULF & WESTERN CORPORATION
1230 Avenue of the Americas, New York, N.Y. 10020

Copyright © 1977 by Elizabeth Villars

Published by arrangement with Coward, McCann & Geoghegan, Inc.
Library of Congress Catalog Card Number: 77-5347

ISBN: 0-671-81838-4

First Pocket Books printing December, 1978

10 9 8 7 6 5 4 3 2 1

Trademarks registered in the United States and other countries.

Printed in the U.S.A.

For
W. C. B.

They were careless people . . . they smashed
up things and creatures and then retreated
back into their money or their vast care-
lessness, or whatever it was that kept
them together, and let other people clean
up the mess they had made. . . .

F. Scott Fitzgerald

Book One

1922

1

Claudia stood in a creamy satin chemise, her forehead pressed to the rain-streaked window. Outside the small flat on the Rue de Tilsit dusk was gathering. All up and down the Champs Élysées, which she could see if she stood far to one side of the window, the lights were going on. Each streetlamp cast a perfect arc of light on the glistening wet pavement. With the heavy draperies pulled aside Claudia could hear the shrill sounds of a hundred taxi horns piercing the autumn twilight.

"Do you mind if I borrow your Chanel Number Sixteen? I've had enough of Mitsouko for a while." Katherine, Claudia's sister, older by two years, did not wait for an answer. She took the stopper from the bottle and crossed herself reverently, one earlobe, the other, her forehead, the décolletage formed by the deep V of her dress.

"I know what you mean. It seems to be the only scent anyone wears anymore." Claudia had turned from the window and was rifling through a pile of pale silk stockings. "The same scent, the same parties, the same people. Sometimes I wonder why we ever bothered to leave New York.

"Do you think there'll be anyone different there tonight? Anyone besides Harry and Anson and Bill Jarris and the rest of that crowd we've seen every day since we got here. Just more and more of the same faces. To think how worried Mother was. All the instructions to Aunt Louisa. And all those warnings about foreign rakes—blackguards Daddy still calls them. And the

3

fortune hunters. That was Daddy's real worry. I swear, sometimes I think he'd rather see us *ruined*"—she pronounced the word with a faint air of mockery—"than married for our money."

"Claudia! What an outrageous thing to say!"

"Oh, Kate, I'm only teasing. Besides, I don't see much danger of either. A month in Paris and the closest thing I've seen to a rake since I've been here is that lounge lizard Anson Hagerty. And he was every bit as wild back in New York. I'd give a closet of new Chanels and Poirets for one slightly suspect Frenchman. Just so long as he hadn't gone to Yale or Princeton and didn't think the number of cocktails he could put away before dinner was his most manly trait."

"I'm sure Mother and Daddy would be delighted to hear that. Why don't you put an ad in *Figaro*? 'American heiress desires disastrous affair with slightly suspect Frenchman. Purpose: ruination. Money is no object and impoverished aristocrats especially welcome.'"

Claudia thought of the man she had met at Auteuil two weeks ago. Well, not actually met. She had wandered out of the enclosed area, the *pesage,* and when she tried to get back in she had discovered she had no ticket stub. The republican guard, resplendent in his red cockade, was polite but adamant. No ticket, no admission. Her explanation in proper Spence School French made no impression. Indeed, the guard seemed not to understand what Claudia had always considered her impeccable accent.

Just as she had begun to despair, a young man in a sweater and beret had come to her rescue. His English was flawless, but his dark eyes under a thick fringe of lashes seemed to be laughing at her even as he helped her purchase a new ticket. As they walked back across the field, he had taken her arm. He was outrageously forward. He was also, she thought, the most attractive man she had met in the month she had been abroad. He was tall and, except for broad shoulders, slender, and he held himself well. His face had a hollow-cheeked ascetic cast. Were it not for the sweater and beret and the fact that she had met him in the field rather than the paddock, Claudia might have taken him for a gentleman.

"No one said anything about aristocrats, Kate. But don't be such a stick. After all, this is 1922, and things have changed since the war. At least that's what they tell me. As far as I'm concerned, it might as well be 1892. And Paris might as well be New York. Where's all the excitement? That's all I'm asking for—just a little excitement. Before I go home and marry some nice banker and grow old in the Junior League, I'd like to see a bit of the world, the real world I mean, not that microcosm we live in. Honestly, Kate, just once haven't you ever wanted to do something different, something just a tiny bit wicked?"

"No. No, I haven't. And I don't think you ought to want to either. You think it would be romantic, but it wouldn't. It would just be . . . well, bad. No, I don't think you ought to want anything of the sort. At least you oughtn't to talk about it if you do."

"Oh, Kate, I don't mean really wicked. Just a little different. Here we are thousands of miles from home, and what are we doing on this perfectly glorious evening? We're going to dine with twenty of the Kelways' closest acquaintances, who just happen to be the same people we had tea with today and yesterday and the day before that. What a bore!"

"Well, it may be boring to you, but it's better than spending the evening sitting here in your chemise complaining. Which is exactly where I'm going to leave you if you don't hurry. We're already late."

"All right, I'll hurry. Just wait till I get this scarlet A straight on my chest." Claudia adjusted the long rope of Cartier pearls nestling in a single knot between her firm young breasts and examined herself in the mirror. As usual she was pleased with what she saw. Her high, prominent cheekbones had been powdered fashionably pale, the same fragile hue as the chiffon frock that accentuated the subtle curves of her slender body.

She smiled at the image behind her that was almost a carbon copy of her own. Katherine was pretty in much the same way Claudia was beautiful. The two girls had the same tall, slim body, though Kate was less slender by a hair's breadth; the same fine-boned features, though Kate's were a shade less delicate; the same erect carriage, though Katherine was stiff while Claudia was infinitely graceful.

An hour later the two sisters, their evening capes butterfly bright against the somber dinner clothes of their escorts, passed through the gold and white entrance to Ciro's. Without a glance at the larger dining room, where the tourists who did not know that eight o'clock was too early for dinner clustered around sparkling white tables, they headed for the small private room at the rear.

Claudia followed Kate in. Her senses took in the room before they recognized the people who filled it. Tall candles shimmered in every corner, and the air was heavy with perfume and the scent of the orchids running the length of the table. The smoky mirrors lining the walls reflected a hundred Claudias, each one smaller, more remote, but no less beautiful than the one before.

Paula Kelway detached herself from a small group in one corner and hurried over. She greeted the two young women effusively and swept them toward her husband. Paula was a peripatetic hostess, never happy unless she was pushing one group here, shuffling another there, keeping everyone in constant circulation.

"Larry, look who's here." She seemed to invite surprise at their appearance, though the lack of it would have been more unusual.

Lawrence Kelway turned to his wife and the two girls, and the man to whom he had been talking followed suit. Claudia gasped, a small, involuntary sound she covered immediately by coughing politely into her lace handkerchief. She hoped no one had noticed, but as she looked at the man who stood at Lawrence Kelway's side, she knew that not only had he noticed, but he had been vastly amused as well. The sweater had been replaced by impeccably cut evening clothes, but the eyes under their heavy fringe of lashes were as sardonic as ever. And the scar that ran down one cheek—how had she forgotten the scar?

It was jarring, just like the maimed and crippled young men Claudia saw on the streets every day. She had mentioned it to Harry Van Nyes one day when they were having tea at the Claridge. She had known Harry since she was a child, and the fact that he was in Paris made him no more exciting to her now than he had been back in New York. "Don't they bother you?" she had asked him when a young man with a single arm had taken a table a few feet away. "I don't understand how everyone can go on so about the gaiety of Paris. Not with all those veterans around."

"Don't you see, Claudia, their tragedy merely sharpens our pleasure."

"Harry, what a horrible thing to say."

"Not at all. They intensify the atmosphere. They're a constant reminder to us that we'd better live today because yesterday—the Great War, all that—was awful and tomorrow is likely to be worse. You might say they lend an edge of desperation, and what could make pleasure more intense?"

"Katherine, Claudia, how good to see you," Lawrence said. "May I present le Comte de Boissevain. *Monsieur le comte*, Mademoiselle Katherine Trenholm, Mademoiselle Claudia Trenholm." The count bent over Katherine's hand and brushed it lightly with his lips. Then he repeated the homage to Claudia. As he straightened, he looked directly into her eyes. With a single look he undid all the formality of his manners.

"Mademoiselle Trenholm and I have already met," he said.

"Already met! But where?" One could tell from her voice that Paula felt cheated.

"I believe it was at Auteuil."

"But who introduced you?"

"Actually I introduced myself."

"Actually"—Claudia recovered her composure—"you didn't introduce yourself at all, *Monsieur le comte*. You merely bought my ticket to the paddock."

"The count bought your ticket to the *pesage*. Without an introduction. I don't understand."

"I had wandered outside the enclosed area. The count

7

was good enough to help me get back in. I'm afraid I would never have succeeded without him. My French simply wasn't up to the incident, and the guard's English was even worse."

"But that's just what I've been saying." Lawrence was eager to resume the discussion his wife had interrupted. "We mustn't expect republican guards or anyone else to speak English. That's precisely the sort of attitude that has ruined Paris. It's a hopeless problem since the Armistice. Wherever one goes, one meets Americans."

"I don't find it a problem at all."

"Of course, I don't mean Americans like Claudia. It's all the others. Everywhere one goes there are people one knows or worse yet, people one doesn't want to know. Cafes crawling with bohemians, show people at the Ritz, and the Crillon looks like an outpost of Harlem on a Saturday night. Why, my old swimming coach at New Haven—you remember Bob Kuphuth," he said to his wife, "has even opened a gym at the Claridge. If the Elis must have their own gym, why don't they stay in New Haven instead of coming over here and ruining Paris for the rest of us?"

"The problem with you"—the count laughed—"is you're a snob. You must learn to share Paris—even with people you don't like."

"Just as you've learned to share it with us?" Katherine asked coldly.

"I'm always delighted to share Paris with a beautiful woman." The count smiled and bowed ever so slightly.

"A bit smarmy, don't you think?" Kate whispered to her sister as Paula spirited them toward the table. Claudia remembered the afternoon at Auteuil and thought that was the last word she would use to describe him.

Claudia sat predictably between Harry and Anson Hagerty, and she glanced jealously down the table to where the count was helping Lucinda Ardsley into her chair.

What a waste, Claudia thought as she chatted absent-mindedly with Harry and Anson. And then dinner was over, and she found herself crushed into a taxi between

Anson and the count. Her spirits soared. Claudia was glad she hadn't let Anson's presence deter her from joining the group headed for Montmartre. Lawrence Kelway had refused to go. Montmartre with its jazz nightclubs and black performers was the epitome of the Americanization of Paris that he deplored. He had tried to lure Claudia to a chic nightclub on the Left Bank, and she had almost gone, if only to get away from Anson. But at the last moment the Kelways' group seemed even duller than more of Anson's inanities, and she had opted for Montmartre. So, at that point, had the count.

The taxi bumped over the wet cobblestones, tossing Claudia back and forth between the two men. Harry sat on one of the jump seats, and he and Anson were engaged in a heated argument over their destination.

"Smith's has the best jazz," Harry insisted.

"And the worst champagne," Anson added.

"Perhaps La Note Bleue," the count suggested.

"The French don't know anything about jazz," Anson said.

"The musicians there are American," the count answered.

"I wasn't talking about the musicians," Anson growled.

"La Note Bleue," Harry directed the driver. He didn't much care about the argument brewing behind him, but he was annoyed *he* hadn't thought of the club.

To reach La Note Bleue they climbed to the top of a steep cobbled street, then descended a steeper flight of stairs. The club was a single small dark room. A minute dance floor was surrounded by miniature tables, some of them scarcely larger than a checkerboard, encircled by rickety chairs. Men in elegant evening clothes lounged precariously. Women turned into slender little boys by their sleek bobs and straight frocks smoked, drank, and flirted.

The count cut through the confusion caused by Anson's demands for a certain number of tables in a certain location with a few words to the man with carefully pomaded hair who stood at the door, and Claudia found herself wedged into a corner once again between the

count and Anson. Katherine and several of the other
guests were at the next table, and Anson was making
a great fuss trying to move the tables closer together. He
was more than a little drunk by this time and had to do
something since that French fellow had already spirited
Claudia off to the tiny dance floor.

As they moved about the floor, he held her a little
too close. But after all, Claudia reasoned, La Note
Bleue was scarcely the place to worry about propriety.
Each time she looked up at him she found he was
studying her closely from under that fringe of lashes,
but the blare of the music made conversation impossible.

They returned to the table, and Anson immediately
claimed her for a dance. "It's too crowded, Anson. I'd
rather sit this one out."

Anson was drunk, but not too drunk to remember
that Claudia had spent more than one night dancing
through worse crowds than this. He turned away in annoyance.

"It's taken a month, but I finally tracked you down."

"I didn't know you were looking." Claudia answered
the count coolly. "And anyway, it's been only two
weeks." She laughed.

He joined her. He had a nice laugh, deep and very
quiet.

"You were terribly rude that day, you know."

"Rude! I thought I was quite helpful. If it weren't
for me, you'd still be standing there arguing with that
guard."

"Well, you might at least have said who you were."

"But who am I?"

"You know what I mean. I thought you were a stable
hand."

"Are you certain now that I'm not?" His eyes were
a little too teasing.

"You might at least have mentioned you were a friend
of the Kelways."

"But I didn't know you were until I watched you
walk back into the paddock. Besides, I wasn't much of

a friend of the Kelways then. But after I saw you with them, I decided to cultivate them. And I assure you I did a thorough job of it. Do you think you're going to be worth all those deadly cups of tea I had to consume with Madame Kelway?"

His directness unnerved her, and she tried to make her tone impersonal. "That's no way to talk about poor Paula. Especially after the way you scandalized her tonight."

"I scandalized Madame Kelway!"

"All that talk of meeting at Auteuil. You made it sound so . . . well, so *fast* I'm sure it's more than poor Paula can cope with."

"Do you think she'll be saying terrible things about us?"

"You know how it is, *Monsieur le comte*—"

"Philippe," he interrupted.

"She'll be saying terrible things about me, not about you."

"Which, I suspect, you rather enjoy." Claudia was startled. He seemed to know too much about her too quickly. "From what I've read," he went on, "that's what being a *flapper*—that is the proper term, isn't it? —is all about. Scandal."

"I think that's going a bit far. Besides, I've never called myself a *flapper*."

"Rather *déclassé*—like my sweater." She colored and looked down into her champagne glass, hoping he hadn't noticed.

"All the same, I think you enjoy shocking people, giving them something to talk about." She started to look away, but his eyes held hers. There was still humor in them, and now a challenge as well. "What do you say, Claudia? Should we give them something to talk about? *Toi et moi, devions nous leur offrir de quoi parler?*" he repeated in French. The way he pronounced her name and the personal *tu*—her French was not too academic for her to know when she had been tutoyered—startled her. She had never met anyone like him. She had known boys who had tried this sort of thing, to will her into an intimacy, but there had been no force behind

11

them. They had been merely boys playing at being men. Here was something different. The count, Philippe, seemed to assume her compliance, her willingness to go along with whatever he wanted. For the first time in her life Claudia was not in control of the situation.

"Then we'll lunch tomorrow. I'll come by at two." There was no question in his voice.

At eleven thirty the next morning Claudia, still flushed with sleep and wrapped in a pale lawn negligee, stood in the doorway to the small dining room. She raised one hand lazily to cover a yawn.

"Morning, Aunt Louisa. Morning, Kate." The two women were seated at the small table beneath the windows that opened onto the Arc de Triomphe.

They had been lucky to find this flat on the Rue de Tilsit. Many of their compatriots opted for apartments at the Ritz or the Claridge or the Carlton, but both girls and their chaperone had shunned the tone of transiency that a hotel apartment implied. Instead, they had taken this small but well-appointed flat on an attractive crescent of a street reaching around the Arc de Triomphe to lead directly, and conveniently, into the Champs Élysées.

"Did you have a nice time last night, dear?" Louisa asked.

"Wonderful." Claudia yawned again. "I had an absolutely wonderful time."

"Someone else must have had a wonderful time as well." Louisa nodded toward the long florist's box on Claudia's chair.

"Probably just old Anson again," Claudia said, praying it was not.

"Not old Anson again," Kate said. "Not after last night. Even old Anson has feelings, Claudia."

"You're just being difficult, Kate. When I'm nice to Anson, you ask me how I can stand him, and when I'm not nice to him, you tell me I'm being cruel. Anyway, who cares? It's much too nice a morning to worry about Anson Hagerty. And if I know Anson, he was probably too tight to remember. He'll be calling to apologize for being rude to me last night."

"Honestly, Claudia, you think you can get away with anything, don't you?" But Claudia was too busy untying the long white box to answer.

"Marvelous," she cried. "Absolutely marvelous."

"What is it, dear?" Louisa asked.

Claudia held up a single red rose.

"Is that all there is?" Claudia nodded, and her aunt looked suddenly alarmed. "The young man isn't terribly poor, is he?"

Claudia laughed. "Yes, Aunt, he's terribly poor. Absolutely impoverished. He can't even afford admission into the *pesage,* and now he's after Daddy's millions to save the ancestral home."

"Really, Claudia, I don't know what you're talking about, but I wish you'd be serious for a moment. Your parents put their trust in me."

"I'm sorry, Aunt. I don't know whether he's poor or not. And I don't really care." Louisa looked disapproving, but Claudia went on. "Anyway, I doubt that the single rose is in the interest of economy."

"Then what is it?" Katherine asked.

"It's romantic. Don't you see? Everyone sends flowers, dozens of flowers. It doesn't mean anything. But a single red rose. That's original."

"I've always thought"—Louisa sniffed—"being different was a much overrated trait."

"Oh, no, Aunt Louisa. Never. At least not for me. I'm so *tired* of everybody's being the same, thinking the same things and doing the same things. What's the point of coming all the way to Paris if it isn't going to be any different from home?"

"The point of coming to Paris is that it is the proper thing for a young lady of your position to do. You will have seen good pictures and been to the best couturiers and finest restaurants. You will also improve your French. When you return home, you will have acquired taste, and taste, my dear, is what the right people agree upon. Taste, in fact, is *not* being different. Now to return to the rose, tell me something about the young man who sent it."

Claudia refrained from saying he was unlike any young man she had ever known. "He's charming, absolutely charming, but you'll find that out for yourself. He'll be here soon." With that Claudia jumped up from her untouched cafe au lait and headed for her room.

"Aren't you going to have any breakfast?" Louisa called after her.

"I couldn't eat a thing."

At fifteen minutes before two o'clock Claudia sat in a corner of the small sitting room, an open book untouched on her lap. She was dressed in a cream-colored suit with a pleated skirt. The pale crepe blouse called attention to the brilliant crimson of her cheeks. The more she had tried to will her complexion into a fashionable chalkiness, the higher her color had risen.

"My, my." Kate came striding into the sitting room. "I've never seen you so prompt. Are you turning over a new leaf, or is it just the excitement of all that forbidden French fruit you were talking about last night?"

"Oh, stop it, Kate. I was just talking last night."

"Well, apparently someone was listening. Your prayers have been answered—one fortune-hunting Frenchman, made to order."

"What makes you so sure he's a fortune hunter?"

"Why else would a French aristocrat be at one of Paula Kelway's dinners?"

Claudia refrained from blurting out he had been there only to meet her. That would merely confirm Katherine's suspicions: He had spotted his quarry and now was moving in.

"And besides," Kate continued, "all French nobility is impoverished since the war. Paris runs on American money, and I have a feeling *monsieur le comte* would be only too happy to run on, or perhaps off with, Daddy's. Or was he just swept away by you? Oh, I *am* sorry, Claudia. I should have realized. It was love at first sight."

"And of course, you think that's impossible."

"I think you've bowled over so many college boys that you think it *is* possible."

"But he's different."

"And that, *ma petite soeur,* is precisely the point. I think your friend the count has been around a bit. A bit too much for my taste, but that's something else again. I don't think he's as easily impressed as Anson Hagerty, the steel heir of Pittsburgh, Pennsylvania. At least not with the belle of the Pump and Slipper at New Haven. With her father's money, perhaps, but not with her."

Kate let her voice trail off. There was no point in trying to convince Claudia. If she wanted to act like a little fool, that was up to her, but certainly Katherine wasn't going to be taken in. She'd been here a month, and as far as she could see there wasn't a man on the Continent who could hold a candle to Sam Beaumont. She only hoped Sam was missing her half as much as she was him. That was part of the reason Katherine had come to Paris. To make Sam Beaumont miss her. To make him realize how much he needed her, how much he wanted her. To make Sam Beaumont stop taking her for granted.

To be fair, and Kate always tried to be fair to Sam, it was logical that his behavior should be casual. They'd known each other for so long. Kate remembered Thursday afternoon dancing classes and a twelve-year-old Sam who was careful not to step on anyone's shiny high-button shoes and always kept his gloves on.

Not that Sam had ever been a sissy. Far from it. He was wonderful at riding and sailing, golf and tennis, any sport he put his mind to. That was how he and Kate really found each other. Not in Mr. St. John's dancing classes but sailing on Long Island Sound and riding over the green hills sloping down to its edge. Kate could still remember one afternoon when they had taken out Sam's small sloop and got lost in a fog. Sam hadn't been frightened for a moment, and when he saw Katherine was about to cry, he had laughed her out of her fear. Then he quickly set her to work so she wouldn't have time to be afraid. He had been cool and commanding and protective. As a grown woman Katherine still cherished the memory of that afternoon.

When America entered the war, Sam had gone off to Europe, and Kate had waited and worried and written proper, friendly letters once a week. She was sure they would be married as soon as Sam returned. But things hadn't worked out according to plan, at least not according to Kate's plan.

She could still remember the first time she had seen Sam after the war. In mufti he had cut quite a figure; in uniform Kate found Sam irresistible. If she hadn't already been in love with him, that afternoon would have done it.

They had gone to a tea dance, and everyone had treated Sam as the conquering hero. Not that he played the role in the least. Sam was the first to say he hadn't even got to the front. He had an air about him, nevertheless, and every girl there had been as taken as Katherine. But Sam had spent the afternoon with her. Even Claudia, who seemed to make a habit of taking the spotlight and everything else Kate ever wanted, had not been able to spoil that. Claudia was still a child, and Sam, a man of the world and a veteran of the Great War, had barely noticed her. When she had tried to get his attention, he merely ruffled her hair and teased her about finally being in long skirts. This last was a little inaccurate since Claudia's new grown-up skirts were barely longer than the childish pinafores she had been wearing when Sam went off to war.

Things had looked so bright that afternoon. Katherine had been optimistic about their future. But Sam turned out to be more interested in the present. The war, even his quiet corner of it, had changed him. There was now in that very proper young man who played hard but always by the rules a determination to, as the slang went, "live it up." He liked Kate, and he liked spending time with Kate; but he liked other girls, too. Someday he'd settle down, probably with Kate, but not yet. Now was the time for fun. The war had taught him that much.

In the meantime, all Katherine could do was wait.

But she didn't have to wait in full view of Sam and the rest of New York society. Kate was proud. She would have no snickering among her friends and no sympathy from the older women who observed these things so closely. A year abroad would give her the perfect edge, put her on an equal footing with Sam, who had already seen more of the world. It would also give Sam a year to miss her.

The doubts Katherine had sown in Claudia's mind had no time to germinate. Philippe arrived, all charm and serious good manners, and Claudia could see Louisa was impressed—despite the single rose. Claudia chalked up a point for her side. Kate was merely being contrary. It was not the first time Claudia suspected her sister of jealousy.

And who wouldn't be? she thought, stealing a glance at Philippe. That day at Auteuil she had thought him attractive. Today he was clearly the most desirable man in Paris. *I must be drunk,* she thought. On this, the first sunny day in more than a week, the Tuileries had exploded in a riot of color, of bright blue ageratums and pale pink dahlias stealing a last afternoon of life before the chill frost of autumn. The park was a maze of children suddenly liberated after long confinement.

A large red ball hit Philippe's foot, and a dark, curly-headed boy tumbled over it. Philippe righted the child and placed the ball solemnly in his hands. *"Merci,"* the boy whispered and scampered off.

"I imagine that's what you looked like as a little boy."

"And that formidable lady looks just like my English nanny." He indicated a poker-faced woman in stiff white and a navy blue cape. She returned their gaze sternly as if they were plotting to wrestle the red ball away from her charge.

"I don't think she likes us very much." Claudia laughed.

"That is the secret of the profession. Nannies don't like anyone very much, especially nasty little boys. Or so a series of them told me."

"I don't believe it. I suspect you were doted upon."

"Proper little French boys, especially proper little French boys destined to inherit a proper French title, are taught responsibility, the importance of France and *la gloire* and, in my case, the Boissevain heritage. They are never doted upon."

"I'd say from your tone that they weren't very successful with you."

"Let's just say I think some of those values are a little outdated. But that's all too serious and boring. I'd much rather talk about you. Now I imagine *you* were truly doted upon. And thoroughly spoiled."

"Not a bit. I was brought up very properly."

Philippe hooted with laughter, drawing disapproving glances from more than one observant nanny. "Was there ever anything you wanted, really wanted, you didn't get?"

"Of course, many things."

"Name one."

"Well. . . ."

"You see, you can't. You're accustomed to getting anything you want, Claudia. I know that from your mouth."

"My mouth?" she repeated incredulously.

"Your mouth. It's very inviting, but it's also very practiced at pouting, I think. You've been given everything. The interesting thing," he added slyly, "is what will happen if you are ever denied something you really want. What do you think you'll do?"

"Fight for it," she answered without a moment's pause.

"And will you win?"

"Of course."

"You know," he said, looking at her closely, "I think you just might. But enough of this. I promised you lunch."

"I'm not hungry," she said quickly. She was enjoying herself immensely and did not want to spoil things by going into some stuffy restaurant.

"I'm surprised at you, Claudia. You just told me you were brought up properly. Surely you know lunching has nothing to do with being hungry. If we don't have lunch, how can we be seen? Why, without lunch, society would perish."

"Then let's help bury it."

"I have a rebel on my hands. At your service, *mademoiselle*. Where would you like to go?"

"Any place. Only not the same old places. Not the Ritz and especially not the Claridge. Take me somewhere I've never been."

"How about Les Deux Magots? It's a cafe on the Left Bank."

"Is it very wicked?"

"Far from it. It is very serious, or so its habitues like to think."

"Are there many Americans there?"

"Some." He saw her face fall. "But none you'll know."

"Well, I was hoping for apache dancers, but I can see they're out of the question. Les Deux Magots it is." *Even the Claridge,* Claudia thought, *would be new and different with Philippe.*

Les Deux Magots sat on a tree-shaded corner. It was crowded at this hour, and most of the people were not, Claudia noticed, particularly well turned out. Several of the women were chic, but none was expensively dressed. Few of the men carried a stick or wore gloves. It was the sort of place, Claudia thought, Harry Van Nyes would discover in a few months and rave about for the rest of his life.

A slight, well-dressed man, one of the few with cane and gloves, sat alone at a table near the sidewalk. He nodded to Philippe as they passed, and Philippe bowed slightly in greeting. He did not seem to notice Claudia, but Claudia could not help remarking him. There was something in his bearing at once proud and sad, perceptive and dismissive.

"Who was that?" she asked when they were seated at a small table some distance away.

"André Gide, a rather well-known writer."

"I know who André Gide is," she said impatiently. "Why do all Frenchmen assume Americans are totally uneducated? Do you know him well?" She was curious. This was a new side to Philippe. She suspected there were many, and so far she had seen only the most superficial.

"We share certain interests."

"What sort of interests?"

"Mostly political."

"But he's a writer, not a politician."

Philippe laughed. "In France the pursuits are not mutually exclusive."

"What sorts of political interests?" she pursued.

"Oh, just politics," he said with elaborate casualness. "What would you like to drink?"

"Well, I certainly don't want tea."

"Absolutely not. And I forbid a cocktail. I drink them with Americans, but they're a disreputable habit. Besides, they make them dreadfully here. Perhaps a Pernod?"

She agreed, and he ordered two.

"Well, how do you like it?"

"I do. But I'm not sure it's the sort of place I'd expect to find le Comte de Boissevain."

"Why, Claudia, what a little snob you are!"

"I am not," she said hotly, guiltily.

"Then, like all Americans, you have a most misguided view of nobility—I mean the class, not the virtue. You think a count has no right to drink with a bohemian in a sweater or a workingman in a beret. Or to wear either, for that matter."

She blushed. "That's not it at all."

"But you're right. A proper count doesn't do that sort of thing. My father the marquis would not, as the saying goes, be caught dead here. But you see, I'm not a proper count at all."

Now she was confused. "I don't understand. Do you mean you're a younger son or something like that?"

This time his laughter was directed against himself. "No, I mean I'm an improper count. If my father were here, although the thought would horrify him, he could explain it to you. I don't have the proper respect for tradition, prerogatives. For example, I was educated at the École Normale Supérieure. Do you know what that means?"

"No."

"It means that I've betrayed my heritage. The *École,* you see, is thoroughly bourgeois. It's a school for writers and thinkers and politicians. It's not a school for noblemen. And do you know why? Because," he continued without giving her a chance to answer, "it does not teach how to fight. It teaches how to reason, and there are few things a count or a marquis or any of the others finds more useless. They sit at St. Cyr and look down their aristocratic noses at us Normalians, and most of all at me, who could have gone to St. Cyr and chose not to."

"Is that so terrible?" she asked.

"Nothing worse." He laughed. "You see, it isn't merely a question of schools. It's a question of a way of life. I didn't want to be a soldier."

"But you were in the war."

His hand touched his cheek almost involuntarily. "Yes, I was in the war. I don't suppose my face will ever let anyone forget that."

"I'm sorry." She was embarrassed at her lack of tact. "I didn't mean that."

"Of course you did. How else would you know I was in the war? But don't worry, I'm not vain about it. A scar like this, ugly as it is—"

"It's not."

He ignored her. "It's nothing compared to what most of the others came through with. And those were the ones who did come through. What about those who didn't? It makes me wonder, what right I had to get off so easily." His voice was low and bitter, and there was a bleakness in his eyes.

"What a terrible thing to say."

"Terrible? It's merely just. What right have I to live when so many died? Was it because as a Boissevain, a count, the son of a marquis, I was given preferential treatment? How much more just if that shoemaker's apprentice in my company had lived and I had been killed in his place. He was only sixteen. He had so much before him, had had so little in the past. I'm sure that if he had lived, he would have been a far more useful person than I. At least he would have been a good shoemaker. If someone has to die meaninglessly, why not the older or the more useless?"

He saw the shock on Claudia's face. "Do I offend you? Perhaps you don't think his death was meaningless. Or the war. Perhaps you think we won an important victory."

Claudia nodded, astonished at his sudden intensity.

"Well, I guess I believed the same thing at one time. Certainly it was what we were all taught to believe. Your American President told us we were making the world safe for democracy. Our own politicians were less idealistic, but they still claimed right was on our side. *Revanche* they called it. We had to get the Boches. Eighteen seventy, you see, was still vivid in their memories. Well, we won, but as far as I can see, it hasn't made much difference. The world isn't any safer for democracy than it was ten years ago. Oh, certainly there are fewer kings left on their thrones, but what difference does that make? Do you think a single German who lost an arm or a leg or had part of his brain blown away thinks it was worth that much to trade in old Kaiser Willie for a new republic?

"And as for beating the Boches, all our politicians are very proud of that, but do you think life in Paris is any better now than life in Berlin? All over Europe soldiers are out of work. Right here in Paris there are thousands of unemployed men, and they can't feed their wives and children victory any more than the Germans can feed theirs defeat."

Claudia had never heard anyone talk this way. Once or twice she had read the word "unemployment" in the paper, but she had never heard anyone use it in polite conversation. She had heard political cynicism from some of the young men at home. And she had heard about charity since she was a child. But what Philippe was saying seemed to go far beyond that. He seemed to dismiss the whole system, charity and all.

And the way he spoke about the war. All the American boys she knew were utterly romantic about it. One day, after she had first arrived in Paris, Anson and Harry had taken her to visit some of the battlegrounds. They had spent the afternoon tramping over innocuous-looking fields while the two of them fed her information in hushed tones.

"This land cost fifteen lives a foot."

"It took the Allies three months to gain these thirty yards."

And finally Harry had said there would never be a holocaust like it again and looked melancholy. Then they had gone to a nearby inn for sausages and cheese and some very good local wine and become quite gay.

"But what about the war itself?" she asked Philippe.

"What about it?"

"I've always heard about glory and honor and all that sort of thing." She felt silly and naive, and let her voice trail off.

"I'll tell you about glory and honor. They're talked about a lot on the home front, but they have a funny way of disappearing once the battle starts. I don't know. I've never really got it straight in my mind. Maybe they get lost in the mud. Or maybe they're asphyxiated by the mustard gas. That's it—you breathe in glory with the gas and then cough it right back up with your lungs. Because that's what men around me were doing, coughing up their lungs and I, as an officer, you understand, tried to convince them it was a glorious and honorable thing they were doing. Somehow they didn't believe me."

He saw the fear in her eyes, the fear of someone who had never heard such stories. "I'm sorry. I didn't mean to be brutal. It's just that when I remember battle, glory and honor are the last things I think of."

"What do you think of?"

He hesitated for a moment. "Well, confusion for one thing. That's another name for victory and defeat. It's a little like glory and honor. On the home front everyone talks about victory or defeat. At the front no one dares talk about it. That's because nobody can tell one from the other. At least most of the time. Oh, there are exceptions. If your company is wiped out, you can be pretty sure you've been beaten. But most battles aren't that clear. Like the Battle of the Marne, the second one. That's where I picked this up." He touched the scar on his cheek. "We took Soissons. It was supposed to be very important. Stopped Ludendorff from attacking Flanders, fouled up all the German plans, a major victory or so the papers said. I learned that in the hospital afterward, but out there in the trenches we weren't so sure. Oh, we knew well enough when we had to move back and dig a new trench or when we had to try to advance. But that was just staying alive. For the rest of it, not one man in my company could have told you if we were winning or losing. So much for victory, and so much for the glory of battle."

"I'm sorry," she said quietly.

"No, no. I'm the one who should be sorry. The war's been over a long time. It's all past history and very bad conversation." Silently Philippe cursed himself. He had gone too far. References to the war were all right. Girls liked to hear war stories, especially American girls. But not these war stories. They wanted amusing anecdotes or tales of heroism—glory and honor, she'd said. They did not want to hear about confusion or fear or lungs coughed up. They especially did not want to hear that the war had been meaningless. America had hesitated to enter the conflict, but when it did, it was with religious fervor. Its citizens did not want to learn now that perhaps it had not been the greatest and most successful moral crusade of the ages. And why try to tell them? Why bother to try to make this pretty little American understand any of that? Philippe doubted he could even if he wanted to. The greatest hardship she had ever known had probably been having to wait an extra five minutes for a table at Foyot's.

Philippe was usually careful about keeping the separate areas of his life distinct. First there was the familial side. He was, to a point, a dutiful son and heir to the Boissevain title. Then there was the lighter side. Neither his family nor his more serious friends knew or would have cared much about that. He took his pleasure with the hordes of Americans and English and Argentines who had descended on Paris since the war. With them he need establish no ties, feel no responsibilities. He could live at a nice hedonistic hum. That was where Claudia was meant to fit in. He had seen her, wanted her, and tracked her down. He had not lied about any of that. But it was not important, and it was not serious. The serious things belonged to another part of his life, a part that must be kept private. He vowed to be more discreet.

"No more lectures today, I promise. Now where would you like to go? Is there anything you'd like to see? We can go to the Bois and watch all the deposed kings and your cinema stars parade about? Or would you like some tea? We could go to the Claridge and scandalize all your friends by telling them you've been drinking Pernod in a cafe on the Left Bank. Or we could just walk back to your flat. We can go along the river. It's the perfect hour for it."

"*L'heure bleue.*"

"Now you've become a native. Shall we walk then?"

"By all means." Claudia wanted to savor the moment. She had never known anyone like Philippe. She did not understand half of what he said. And half of what she did understand she wasn't sure she liked. Why spoil their afternoon with talk of death and misery and hunger? But even as she thought that, Claudia knew she didn't really mean it. Part of Philippe's attraction was his dark passion. He was a mystery to her. She didn't understand what pained him so or gave rise to the flashes of anger she had seen this afternoon, but she knew it was real. Anson and Harry and the rest of the boys she knew aped adult ideas and habits and thought it made them men. Philippe was a man. He knew what he thought and what he wanted. He would be difficult at times, she suspected, brooding, even a little frightening, but he would never, ever be boring.

2

In no time at all the Count de Boissevain and Claudia Trenholm were the talk of her set. One night they went with a small group to a gambling club. Claudia found it wonderfully wicked and smiled to herself when she thought what Aunt Louisa would say if she knew. Well-dressed men and women, the women wearing some of the most dazzling jewels Claudia had ever seen, sat rigid in concentration. The only sound was the quiet clinking of chips and murmurs of *banco, rouge, noir* from here and there around the room. But Aunt Louisa would be impressed, Claudia thought, by Philippe's behavior. Although some of the men in their party gambled and lost heavily, Philippe merely observed. Claudia mentioned this particular virtue to Katherine later in the dressing room. In case Aunt Louisa did find out about the evening, Claudia thought it would be well to have erected a defense in advance. After all, Philippe would be blamed for taking them.

"Of course he doesn't gamble," Kate said in that impatient tone that implied there was no end to her younger sister's stupidity. "He can't afford to. At least not yet. But I could see that gleam in his eyes every time someone won."

"You're absurd, Kate. That was pleasure in Philippe's eyes. He likes to see people have fun." And once more Claudia wondered if her sister might be jealous. Whatever else was she doing watching Philippe's eyes?

But as much as Claudia loved her evenings with Philippe, it was their afternoons together she really cherished. Only then were they free to go off alone. Most of the men they knew were at the races, and the women went shopping or to fittings. Certainly no one had any interest in the sorts of things Claudia and Philippe did. He was showing her Paris from top to bottom, and that was not thought to be a very chic thing to do. It would have been all right if they had chosen to lounge beneath the chestnut trees in a cafe along the Champs Élysées or stroll down the Rue de la Paix past Cartier's and Worth's, Paquin's and Coty's to the Place Vendôme, where Mr. Morgan's bank and the Ritz stood as twin bastions of the American presence. These were the socially acceptable places where one met one's friends. According to Philippe, these were the *only* places Americans met their friends—banks and hotels.

Not for Claudia and Philippe this carefully circumscribed city. He introduced her to the old Paris, a steepled and domed city still entrenched in the last century. For hours on end they walked the winding cobbled streets, alive with the clatter of small children in their high wooden-soled boots and black aprons. In these same neighborhoods, solid, working-class, family neighborhoods, less than a mile and more than millions of light-years away from the worlds Claudia and Philippe had grown up in, they would stop at a modest cafe. There Claudia, like the other women, would drink a lemonade and Philippe would order a beer. The French, he assured her, made the worst beer in the world, but it was *de rigueur* to drink beer in these cafes. "After all, we don't want to stand out, do we?" Yet stand out they did. Her clean-lined beauty, his dark good looks, their delight in each other, and their joy in the simplest pleasures around them assured that.

One warm afternoon they took a *bateau mouche* up the Seine. They sat on the hard wooden benches and laughed all the way up to St. Cloud. How Lawrence Kelway would sneer if he could see them now, acting just like tourists.

On the ride back they watched the setting sun turn

the Seine purple and the air a heavy, smoky blue. "Why, *l'heure bleue* really is blue," Claudia cried in delight.

"Now you know Paris. In fact, once you've recognized that, you're entirely French—spiritually, if not legally."

"It's always been my favorite hour, especially here. I remember one night, it was the night we met, really met, that is, and I had been watching it for what felt like hours and thinking how beautiful the city was and how exciting it was supposed to be and how it was all passing me by. I tried to explain it to Katherine, but she refused to see it."

Philippe laughed. "She doesn't trust the French. Me, in particular, I imagine."

"Oh, it isn't that. Certainly not you at least."

"You're a terrible liar, Claudia. Katherine did not like me very much when we first met, and her antipathy has grown with time. Only. . . ." He let his voice trail off slyly.

"Only what?"

"Well, I'm not suggesting she doesn't have good cause to dislike me, but perhaps her feelings have more to do with her jealousy of you. Sometimes I think it's you she really doesn't like."

"What a terrible thing to say! Kate and I have never been as close as some sisters—our interests are so different—but surely you can't think she doesn't like me."

"I don't think you've come up against much dislike in your life. Not with a face like that." He ran his finger over the perfect contour of one cheek. "But jealousy, surely you're an expert at recognizing that."

"But how could Kate be jealous of me—at least not of my appearance? We look so much alike."

Philippe let out one of his hoots of laughter. "Claudia, if ever there were two sisters who did not look alike, it is the Mademoiselles Trenholm. Oh, there are certain similarities between your features, but you do not, I repeat, do not look alike."

"Everyone says we do."

"That is simply because most people don't bother to look beyond those perfect noses."

"In that case, you're merely being vain. What could Kate possibly be envious about except you? Tell me, do you think she has designs on the dashing Comte de Boissevain?"

"You think you have me with that argument, but you're wrong again. I have no suspicions there. I think Katherine's dislike of me is sincere. Almost as sincere as her dislike of you."

She pulled away from him. "There you go again. Why, Kate and I have never even had a serious quarrel."

"Never?"

"Well, not since we were children." She was thoughtful for a moment. "Kate always thought I was spoiled."

"Another of my theories substantiated."

"I guess I was at times. Though, of course, it wasn't really my fault."

"Claudia, you're marvelous!"

"Well, it wasn't. Not really. I remember one time— I was just five, I think, so Kate must have been seven. We had a new nurse. Lizzie was her name.

"I liked Lizzie as soon as she came to us, but Katherine didn't feel the same way. She hated Lizzie from the first day and kept accusing her of favoring me. I guess she did a little. I mean, I know she did. That was the whole point.

"One night—it was winter I think—it was my bedtime, and I didn't want to go alone. I insisted Kate come along with me. I thought the dark wouldn't be nearly so scary with someone else there. Kate refused. She said—and she was right, of course—that she still had an hour to go before her bedtime. Well, Lizzie— I guess she felt sorry for me—said Kate must go along with me. She insisted she made the rules and Katherine would go to bed when she said and not a minute later. Kate still refused—even then she could be stubborn when she wanted to—and, it was so awful, Lizzie took Kate's head in both her hands and began beating it against the wall of the playroom. I can still see the tears

running down her face and her braids swinging back
and forth against the little violets on the wallpaper.
Kate didn't utter a sound. I don't think she ever cried
about it, not even later when we were alone in our
room. And she never told Mother either. I did that
the next morning. I think I was more frightened than
anything else. If I hadn't insisted Kate go to bed, none
of it would have happened. I thought it was all my fault
and, if I didn't confess, something terrible would happen
to me. Of course, Mother dismissed Lizzie that very
morning, but no one ever mentioned the incident again.
Once or twice I tried to apologize to Katherine, but
even when we were older, she wouldn't talk about it.
She acted as if it had never happened."

"If that little story is typical of your childhood, it
isn't exactly surprising your sister doesn't like you."

"Of course the story isn't typical. That's the reason
I told it. Because it was so unusual—what's the word,
atypical?"

There were less conventional outings as well. One
afternoon Philippe took her to an exhibition of paintings by German artists. It was in a small gallery just off
the Rue de Rivoli, and they had to cross a line of men
picketing the entrance. The men shouted at them not
to enter. *"Traître,"* they spat at Philippe, but he merely
put a protective arm around Claudia and hurried her
inside.

"Perhaps we shouldn't have come." She had never
walked through a mob like that, and they had frightened her.

"Nonsense, the war's been over for four years. Besides, what does one's nationality have to do with art?
Once we begin letting one dictate the other, it's the
end of everything."

He led her to a small woodcut about a foot square.
It was the face of a man, and it contained more horror
and pain than Claudia thought possible in a single portrait.

"It's called 'Prophet' and it's by a German. Emil
Nolde is his name. Now do you think his nationality

really matters? Does it make any difference that he's German and I'm French and you're American?"

Philippe watched Claudia as she examined the portrait. "You don't like it, do you?"

"It's not that. It's just that it makes me sad." She hesitated for a moment. "There's something in it that reminds me of you." She thought he might laugh or tell her she had no eye for art. Instead, he merely turned away and walked to the next picture. She followed him.

"Perhaps this one will make you less sad. Kirchner's 'Five Women in the Street.' Surely that doesn't depress you."

"Yes, yes, it does. There's something . . . I don't know, ominous about all these paintings. Why aren't any of them in nice colors? You know, like Monet or Degas Why aren't any of them pretty?"

"Perhaps the artists don't find life pretty."

"But isn't that what artists are for, to make it look pretty?"

"Claudia, you're wonderful! Whatever you do, don't let me change you too much. Let me show you things, but don't let me change you." She refrained from saying what was in her mind, that she loved the way he was changing her.

Louisa was, for her part, pleased. Clearly this young Frenchman was a good influence on Claudia. If Louisa did not entirely approve of German Expressionism, whatever that was, she thoroughly approved of Versailles. Malmaison, the Louvre, and fine little Gothic and Romanesque churches. Yes, Louisa was pleased with the course their year abroad was taking. Or at least she thought she was until Paula Kelway called one rainy afternoon. At first there seemed nothing unusual in the visit. As a conscientious leader of the young married set Paula was careful not to forget the older members of the expatriate community.

A cold, driving rain pelted the windows, but the small sitting room was cozy. Light from the fire danced off the silver tea things and flattered even Paula's plain, blunt features.

"I'm delighted, Paula. I haven't seen you in weeks, though of course I get regular reports from the girls." Louisa was not overly fond of either Kelway, but she was grateful for company on such a bleak day. "You've been so kind to the girls."

"Perhaps we've been too kind." Paula seized the first opportunity to direct the conversation where she felt it must go. "You see Lawrence and I feel responsible. It was at our party that Claudia met young Boissevain."

"Yes, I believe it was. Well, then we must thank you indeed. He's a very pleasant young man."

"He is pleasant, isn't he? And from a very good family. It's so hard to tell with Europeans these days, you know. Practically every one of them claims a title of some sort, but Lawrence is careful about that kind of thing. He checked the count out. Before our dinner party, that is," she rushed to assure Louisa they had not been meddling. "Yes, he's from a fine family. But of course, they're just like all French families with titles these days. Not a sou left since the war. Absolutely penniless."

"Come now, Paula," Louisa answered with more assurance than she felt. "Surely things can't be that bad."

"All I know is that it's common gossip among certain people who know the family that the count *must* make a spectacular marriage. It's the old marquis' only hope."

"Well, I wish the young man well."

"Of course. We all do. But not at the expense of Claudia. Ordinarily I wouldn't say a word," Paula went on, clearly eager to say many more words, "but it's no secret how your brother, Mr. Trenholm, feels about these things. Some families would be only too happy to trade a large *dot* for a title, but as Lawrence understands it, that has never been Mr. Trenholm's view. That's why we felt we had to speak at this time. Before it's too late. You know how these things happen."

"All I know," Louisa answered with every ounce of

sternness her advanced years permitted, "is that you're making a great fuss about nothing. There has been no talk of marriage. Claudia is a beautiful and much sought-after girl. She has been pursued by young men before, and she will undoubtedly be in the future."

"But this time there *is* a difference. Until now Claudia has never cared. This time apparently she enjoys being pursued, positively encourages it."

"Are you suggesting Claudia's conduct is anything less than proper?"

"My dear Miss Trenholm," Paula cried in a tone of hurt and indignation, "how could you think I would ever imply such a thing! Of course the child is spirited but that's such a charming trait in youth," she continued quickly. "No, Claudia is perfect, just perfect. You know how fond Lawrence and I are of her. And that's the point. We feel almost as if she were our own, and we don't want to see her hurt in any way. It's simply that one can't be too careful. Paris isn't New York you know. And things have changed since the war. There's no doubt about that. Girls have so much freedom these days." For a moment the fierce glint in Paula's eyes softened to a wistfulness that seemed to regret a girlhood passed in sterner times. "It's so easy for them to have their heads turned here or make one little slip there. And then, of course, there's talk and all that unpleasantness one does so want to avoid."

Louisa drew herself up, the better to look down her long, sharp nose at Paula Kelway. Louisa might be a parvenue in society, there only by virtue of her brother's recently accumulated wealth, but she had dealt with stronger than Paula Kelway in her day and was not to be intimidated. "So far the only talk I've heard has been from you, Paula. And frankly I don't understand what you're getting at. You accuse young Boissevain of being a fortune hunter, and then you begin to prattle about heads turning in one direction and girls slipping in another. I would appreciate it if you would speak either plainly or not at all."

"Then I will speak plainly, Miss Trenholm. Lawrence and I have agreed it is our duty to do so. Though the count is a charming young man, there's every indication that he must marry for money. It's our understanding your brother will not approve of such a match for his daughter. Now, charming as he may be, the count is an unknown quantity. He's not one of us, and we haven't known him for long. Is it not possible that he might choose to place Claudia in a, shall we say, compromising position in order that she must marry him?"

At this last sentence Louisa was on her feet and Paula shrank back into the sofa. "We only wanted to warn you of any possible danger," she said quietly.

"I would like to say I appreciate your warning, Paula, but I do not. I would like to say I feel you have Claudia's interests at heart, but unfortunately, I think you are merely interfering. We will forget we ever had this absurd conversation. I will mention it to no one, and I am sure you will not be foolish enough to refer to it again. Now would you care for some more tea or must you be going?"

Louisa was as good as her word. She mentioned the conversation to no one, not even Claudia. It would, she reasoned, do no good.

She could of course forbid Claudia to see young Boissevain, but on what pretext? Paula Kelway's gossip must not be given such credence. Besides, Louisa doubted her niece would obey such a stricture.

There was, then, nothing she could do. And wasn't that precisely the problem of a chaperone in this day and age· She occupied a position, but held no power. All around her Louisa saw things she disapproved of. Kisses in the backseats of taxis, for example. In her day no nice girl would have kissed a man to whom she was not engaged—especially in a public conveyance. She had said as much to Claudia, but the girl had merely laughed. "But, Aunt Louisa, boys *do* dance most with the girls they kiss most. They even marry them. Things are different these days."

The only thing Louisa could see that was different were the young people themselves. They did exactly as they pleased and justified it in the name of progress.

Heavens, but Louisa was tired of hearing about progress, just another word for bad manners and worse morals. It was all a result of the war, that dreadful war that had put an end to the world as Louisa had known it and ushered in this reckless new age.

3

Claudia felt no despair about the age she lived in, especially on the November morning following Louisa's confrontation with Paula Kelway.

She got up to ring for her croissant and cafe au lait and pushed the heavy brocade draperies aside for a peek at the day. It had stopped raining, and the sky was a vast high canvas crossed with bold streaks of bright blue and white. She swore that this afternoon they would take that long-planned drive to the country. They had been talking about it for more than a week, but the days had been so dark and rainy they hadn't been able to pull themselves away from the cozy charcoal-burning *bracieri* in the cafes.

When the bell rang, Claudia, looking as brilliant as autumn itself in a swirling suit of russets and golds, ran for the door and threw it open. Before Philippe could speak, she was telling him that they must go to the country.

"Even better than that." He laughed as he walked through the foyer into the sitting room. "At considerable expense, to say nothing of extreme effort, I have arranged for France to stage, in your honor, Mademoiselle Trenholm, one of its greatest, most colorful, most historic, et cetera spectaculars."

"What are you talking about?"

"St. Hubert's Hunt at Chantilly, of course."

"Who is St. Hubert and what is he hunting and why is he hunting in my honor?"

"Who is St. Hubert! St. Hubert is the patron saint of

ravishing American girls who like to dance till dawn in Montmartre and then sleep till noon. He is," he added in a hushed voice "a very decadent saint."

"In other words you have no idea who St. Hubert is."

"Can't remember for the life of me, but please don't tell the good brothers who saw to my early education, or who knows what the penance will be?"

"Well then, what is this decadent patron saint going to hunt in my honor?"

"A stag, of course, and not the sort that follows us around every time I try to take you across a dance floor."

"Oh, the poor dumb beast."

"Now which sort of stag are you talking about?"

"No nastiness about my compatriots. Anyway, I don't like hunting and killing."

"I couldn't agree with you more, which is why we won't participate. But it is a sight you must see before you return to America." At this Claudia turned away, and Philippe's hand involuntarily touched the scar on his cheek. It was a nervous habit, his only one, and he seemed now to want to cover the jagged red line, as well as his faux pas. Claudia's return home was a subject they avoided, and Philippe, cursing his tactlessness, went on quickly. "No, we won't participate. We will merely drive behind the hunt with a mass of spectators, and with any luck we won't get to see the blood part at all. Now enough of these explanations, or we'll miss the whole thing."

The ride to Chantilly was glorious. The countryside sped by in flaming colors, punctuated by neat little farmhouses and cleanly painted barns. The wind threatened to make off with Claudia's hat—all for the best, Philippe teased her—so she tossed it on the seat and let the breeze whip through her hair.

When they arrived at the chateau, Philippe drove immediately to the small stone church. "We're just in time for the blessing of the hounds. Pagan, but colorful."

From the car they could see the hunters assembling on the chapel steps, their scarlet coats vivid against the autumn foliage, their gold braid glistening in the afternoon sun. "If you don't mind waiting in the car, I'll try to find Father."

"Your father?"

"It wouldn't be St. Hubert's Hunt without a Boissevain. He's as much a part of all this as the stag. I'll be right back," he called over his shoulder as he disappeared into the crowd milling about before the church.

The marquis was standing with a group of huntsmen before the massive carved doors of the chapel. His military bearing set off the traditional *Rallye-Vallière* costume perfectly. Like his son, he was tall and slender. They shared the same dark hair, the marquis' now flecked with gray, and the same brown-black eyes; but the father's had never held sorrow or pain, and the son's had never flashed with a pride that made peasants quake and the entire regiment quiver. And the face of the marquis, the real warrior of the family, was not slashed by any visible sign of war. When he caught sight of his son, he excused himself from the men and turned toward him. It was typical of the marquis that he waited for Philippe to reach him.

"Ah, Philippe, what a delightful surprise. Have you changed your mind and decided to ride with us?"

"No, Father, I'm just one of the spectators."

"Well, that's up to you, my boy, though I can't see why you decline to ride in your rightful place."

"We've been through all this before, sir."

"I daresay, yet I keep hoping that one of these days you will grow up."

Philippe declined the bait. "You've good weather this year."

"Yes." The older man's eyes lit in anticipation of a hunt in the brisk open air followed by several whiskeys, a fine dinner with good wines, and who knew what other pleasures.

"In fact, it's such perfect weather I've brought a friend along to watch. Would you care to meet her, Father?"

"I'm always happy to meet your friends, my boy."

Philippe saw no need to remind his father he had many friends whom he would refuse to acknowledge under any circumstances. "Who is the young lady? Do I know her family?"

"I doubt it, sir. She's an American."

"Ah, then she's rich. I hope for your sake she's pretty as well."

"She's very pretty, Father. As for money, I assume it's there, but I don't really know."

"Don't know, my boy. Then whatever are you doing with her? Surely if it's no more than an affair, you would prefer a civilized woman, or even an English-woman, to an American. They're such barbarians. But unfortunately, or perhaps fortunately for you, Philippe, they tend to be rich barbarians. Well, I'm a realist. If some American wants to trade her *dot*—provided it's a sizable one—for an eight-hundred-year-old name, I'll not stop her. Just make sure the *dot* is sizable, my boy. Remember you'll have a lot of expenses."

"Aren't you anticipating, Father. I merely asked you to meet a friend."

"And I'm merely giving you some paternal advice. I know you prefer to deal in dreams; but someday the title and all its responsibilities will fall on your head. You try to keep up the château, to say nothing of the *hôtel* in town, on those fine ideals you and your friends sit around discussing till all hours."

"All right, Father, all right. In the meantime, will you forget the falling franc and try to be pleasant?"

"Pleasant." The marquis chuckled. "Of course, I'll be pleasant. Have you ever known me not to be pleasant to a pretty face, my boy?" The marquis prided himself on neglecting no side of the noble military character. If his ancestors had at one time been fearless warriors and great tacticians, they had also been given to prodigious whoring. Not for nothing had they fought at the side of Henri IV.

The marquis was as good as his word. If Claudia had not been swept off her feet by Boissevain *fils,* Boissevain *père* would have accomplished the feat. He flattered her, amused her, entirely captivated her.

The marquis' canny eye missed nothing—her perfect features and the expensive hat that shaded them, the long, slim legs that reminded him of the prize colts he had owned before the war and the couture dress that swirled about them as she strolled back and forth beneath the old oaks in front of the chapel. Philippe was right: She was a beauty. As for the rest, it was always difficult to tell with women, especially during the day when the ones with taste left off their jewels, but if the expensiveness of her attire had anything to do with the size of her father's holdings, Philippe had done well indeed. There was a definite ring of approval in the marquis' voice as he bade good-bye to the young couple, a ring as clear and sharp as the bell of a cash register being pushed securely closed.

"You liked him, didn't you?" Philippe asked half in pride, half in annoyance at his father's hypocrisy and the simplicity with which Claudia had accepted it.

"I think he's charming, and now that I've met him I'm convinced you've exaggerated all those stories about his displeasure with you. You're very much alike, you know."

Philippe's laughter was almost a bark. "Don't ever say that to the marquis. He'd take it as a grave insult."

"There you go again. Perhaps you and he have disagreed over minor points in the past, but your father clearly adores you."

"Let's just say I'm all he has to work with." There was an air of finality in his tone that stopped Claudia from pursuing the subject. Just one more of Philippe's closed doors.

As they drove toward the sunset, the reflections of the trees formed a dark mosaic on the windshield and she felt the warmth of his body as a shield against the autumn wind. From the way his arm held her tightly to him and the tenseness around his mouth she could tell he was as aware of her body as she was of his. Suddenly she understood those young men who had pursued her in the past. She had never comprehended what they wanted from her, why had they trembled when she was close and schemed for moments alone with her. Now it all came clear. For the first time in her life Claudia understood desire.

They were silent most of the way back to town, but as the countryside gave way to the crowded streets of Paris, Claudia began to chatter about places they planned to go and invitations they ought or ought not to accept. The season was in full swing.

The Kelways, despite their insistence that they were more French than American, were planning an old-fashioned Thanksgiving.

"I'd love to, Claudia, but that Thursday is impossible."

"Impossible," she repeated as if she had never heard the word. There was no annoyance in her voice, only incredulity. Once again Philippe was reminded she was very much accustomed to getting her own way.

"Yes. I'm afraid I've got into something I can't possibly rearrange." He gave her an affectionate hug with the arm that was still around her, then removed it to shift gears. He noticed she didn't move away, but she did stiffen almost imperceptibly.

"Oh, come now, Claudia. You're not going to be angry about one dinner. You've said more than once the Kelways give the dullest parties in Paris—though I've always suspected you thought that because you found me at one of them." Once again his arm went around her. "Honestly, darling, you know I'd go if I could."

In the thrill she felt at this new term of endearment— he had never called her darling before—Claudia almost forgot her annoyance. It was only later alone in her room that she returned to her brooding. It wasn't the dinner, of course. The point was not that Philippe refused to go, but that he would not tell her why. Didn't he see that was the real insult to her affections? He had missed the whole point. Or had he?

Claudia's anger did not last. She was too cheerful by nature to carry a grudge. And she couldn't believe that anyone, especially Philippe, would willingly forgo her company. Surely he must have a good reason.

Perhaps she would ask him right now. She was hurrying across the Luxembourg Gardens to a little cafe they had discovered just beyond. Because they had stumbled upon it together, she liked it almost as much as Les Deux Magots.

Claudia stopped a few yards from the cafe. Philippe's head was bent over a newspaper, and he had not seen her. Unnoticed, she stood for a moment watching him. She loved everything about him: the way he tilted his head forward over the paper, the fine veins that stood out in his temples when he was deep in thought, the way his long, slender fingers toyed absently with the half-empty glass on the table.

He had not known he was being watched, and when he looked up, his face was unguarded. She saw the sorrow in his eyes.

"Is something wrong?" she asked as she sat down. She did not expect an answer. Whatever Philippe's pain was, it was private.

To her amazement he said, "Yes." Then he added, "Marcel Proust died today."

Claudia felt as if she had been tricked. He had begun to speak, and she had expected, if not a heartfelt confession, then at least a glimpse into the darker reaches of his mind. Instead, he merely told her about the death of some writer. He *was* a writer, wasn't he? Claudia ransacked her memory.

"I'm sorry. Did you know him well?"

Philippe laughed, but there was no joy in it. "No, Claudia, I didn't know him at all. Though my parents did, before the war, when Proust was thought of as little more than a social butterfly. My parents were far more approving of him in that role," he added dryly. "No, I'm not grieving for a friend. I'm grieving for the death of an artist. Every generation has its heroes. I guess he was one of mine. You don't know his work at all, do you?"

"No." There was a defensive edge to her voice.

"Now don't be angry. There's no reason you should.

I imagine few Americans have heard of him yet, to say nothing of read him. And those who have, at least those you would know, are only the ones who live in Paris and are looking for a blueprint to French society. Well, I must get you a copy. It's really quite pretty, you know. Not at all like those nasty German paintings."

"There you go again. Just the same, you must get me the book. I won't have you thinking I'm completely frivolous."

"Very well, we'll be serious and proceed with your education. I will get you not *the* book, but all seven. But I warn you, it's a great undertaking. This may be your last outing till spring."

Then she remembered. She had meant to find out why he could not go to the Kelways, but it was too late. He had summoned the waiter and ordered two coffees and a *fine* for each of them and without missing a beat was deep into how he had discovered Proust just before the war and why she would love him and which parts she must read first.

Suddenly a woman appeared beside the table. She was tall, and her long neck and erect carriage made her appear even taller. Her hair was soft gray, swept back in a simple pompadour; her eyes were gray, too, and steel hard. Behind her stood a younger woman. The similarity of her features and bearing revealed a family bond, but the younger woman's presence paled before the older's arrogance.

"Ah, Philippe, *now* we know where you hide yourself. I was telling your dear mother only yesterday that we never see you anymore. Wasn't I saying just that to the marquise, Simone?"

Philippe was on his feet in a moment. "Aunt, how good to see you. Simone, how are you? Aunt, may I present Mademoiselle Claudia Trenholm. Mademoiselle Trenholm is spending the winter in Paris. . . . Claudia, this is my godmother, the duchesse de Chauvres and her niece—and my good friend"—he smiled at the girl—"Simone de Chauvres."

The woman barely glanced at Claudia. It was all that was necessary for her to classify and dismiss the little American upstart. "As I said, Philippe, we simply do not see enough of you. I plan to remedy the situation, however. I'm giving a dinner for Simone in a fortnight. You will come, of course." It was more a command than an invitation, but Philippe did not appear to demur. He simply bowed over the hand the *duchesse* had extended to him, and then both women were gone without so much as a glance at Claudia.

The *duchesse's* behavior had not escaped Philippe. "Don't let her manner offend you. It's her eyes. I'm afraid the *duchesse* doesn't see very well anymore."

"The *duchesse* sees perfectly well."

He laughed appreciatively. "You're right, Claudia. I have the honor of having as a godmother one of the greatest snobs in all France. Which brings me back to Proust. . . ."

He was off again, but Claudia was no longer listening. So that was the way Philippe defined her—"spending the winter in Paris." She wondered how he would describe Simone de Chauvres. Certainly she would be more than a line from a travel guide. *"Amie intime,"* he had said. How *intime?* What was the bond between niece and godson?

The girl was not what one would call pretty—her features were too sharp and spare for mere prettiness—but Claudia suspected men found her attractive. Her long dark hair had not been bobbed, and it made a soft frame for her oval face. Her eyes, large and almond-shaped, were the same color as her aunt's, but softer. They had turned luminous when they had fallen on Philippe.

"Amie intime," Claudia repeated to herself. There was much about Philippe she did not know.

Shortly after Thanksgiving Philippe took the Kelways and Claudia to dine. They were at the Golden Snail, rumored to be Edward VII's favorite restaurant, and the dinner was going well except for Lawrence's occasional muttering about how the Snail, like everything else in Paris, was "going to the dogs." "It's the Americans." He warmed to his favorite topic. "They spoil everything. Americans begin going to a place, and in a few months the cuisine has deteriorated. And you know why," he said angrily.

"No, why?" Philippe asked good-naturedly. He was enjoying his dinner with Claudia too much to let even Kelway spoil it.

"Because Americans don't know anything about food. Give them a superb sauce, and they'll salt it; offer them the perfect tournedos, and they'll smear catsup on it." Philippe made a face of mock horror, but only Claudia knew it was mock. "That's exactly it," Lawrence continued. "The Frenchman sees how his culinary art is made mock of, and he thinks *why bother?* And within months a four-star restaurant is . . . *poof!*" Lawrence gave his best imitation of a Gallic gesture.

"But that's not all," he went on, and Claudia and Philippe, who were about to turn to each other, were forced to direct their attention to Lawrence again. "Americans are not satisfied at merely ruining the food. They must undermine the entire restaurant, the very foundation of French life and business."

"Surely, that's going too far." Philippe laughed.

"No, it's all of a piece. You see, the American tourist has no interest in learning, in adapting his habits to French ways. He thinks he's too good for that. So he sweeps into the restaurant and wants to be a great man. And how does he achieve that end? The way Americans always do. With money. He tries to bribe the maître d'hôtel, gives the wine steward too much because he hasn't the taste or knowledge to choose his own wine, and overtips the waiter. And what's the upshot? The service is ruined forever! The maître d'hôtel no longer recognizes patrons of long standing unless they cross his palm with silver, the wine steward insists on choosing your wine for you and being paid to do so, and the waiters, they're the worst of all. Have you noticed how the service has deteriorated? Why, they just slam the plates down in front of us. No tact, no finesse. Just spilled sauce and rattled cutlery. They have no pride in their work anymore. Now all they have are grievances and rights. Why, I heard just the other day"—he lowered his voice and leaned forward conspiratorially—"that the waiters here, here at the Snail, are all a bunch of anarchists. They're trying to join a union."

Through most of Lawrence's diatribe Philippe had listened with only one ear. Now Claudia saw a glint of anger in his eyes and his facial muscles tightened. "Would that be so terrible?"

"Don't be absurd, my dear fellow. It would be the very ruination of the Snail."

Philippe caught himself. He was certainly not going to take on a fool like Kelway. "But you've just told us the restaurant is already corrupted."

Lawrence misunderstood the note of annoyance in Philippe's voice. "Oh, my dear fellow, you mustn't take me too seriously. You've given us a superb dinner. I couldn't have done better myself. You mustn't let my anger at my compatriots offend you."

"You haven't offended me, Lawrence. But of course, I can't speak for the waiters." His tone was light again, but Claudia noticed that his fingers were touching his scar uneasily.

As November turned to December and the winter rain grew colder, Claudia's affection for Philippe burned steadily brighter. For the first time in her life she had come to care in ways she had never dreamed. As sheltered as she was pampered, Claudia gave freely without fear of pain or rejection—how could she fear what she had not known?—and the more she gave of herself, the more she found she had to give. *This,* she thought, *must be what marriage is like, marriage for love at least.*

Philippe had no idea of Claudia's plans. Or at least he pretended so to himself. Claudia might be young and naive, but not that young and naive. He reassured himself that he was being perfectly fair, that his actions were carefully correct. He said nothing to imply that their relationship would outlast Claudia's stay in Paris. Surely she didn't think a few kisses stolen in the backseats of taxis or on her doorstep in the early hours of dawn meant any more. After all, this was 1922.

No, Philippe told himself more than once, there was no reason for Claudia to expect anything more than a casual flirtation. He was attracted to her, perhaps more than he had ever been to a woman. She was beautiful and a little reckless. She was at once clever and naive, headstrong and open to anything he might show her. He was attracted to all these things—and to one other. Beneath her cool, blond, almost ethereal beauty, Philippe sensed a dark sensuality. Not that he would ever take advantage of it. But he knew it was there, and the knowledge of its existence excited him.

On a rainy afternoon early in December they were sitting in Les Deux Magots, dawdling over their empty glasses. Neither wanted another drink, but neither wanted to part just yet.

Claudia recognized the well-dressed man she had seen on her first afternoon at the cafe. "Isn't that André Gide over there?" Philippe turned and nodded, and the older man, who was about to sit down, changed his mind and approached them.

"Claudia, may I present Monsieur Gide. Monsieur Gide, Miss Trenholm."

The author acknowledged Claudia politely but without interest and turned back to Philippe. "A nice piece in *L'Humanité*," he said in French.

"I'm glad you liked it."

"I did. I liked the piece on Drieu as well. I'll run it in the next issue, but I don't think Drieu will thank you for it."

"But then one doesn't write for thanks, does one?"

Gide smiled. "A good point, Boissevain. A good point." He bowed to Claudia and returned to his table.

"What was that about?" she asked as soon as he was gone.

"I'm sorry. Were we speaking too quickly for you?"

"You know that's not what I meant. What is *L'Humanité*, and who is Drieu?"

"*L'Humanité* is a newspaper, Drieu is a writer, and curiosity killed the cat. The last is, I believe, an American expression. And now we really must go or your

47

dear aunt will take me to task." Philippe signaled for
the waiter as smoothly as he had closed the conversation.

Claudia, however, was not so easily diverted. The
next afternoon on her way through the Ritz she stopped
at the little newsstand just beyond the lobby.

"L'Humanité, s'il vous plaît."

The girl laughed her pretty laugh—she was rumored
to be an exiled Russian princess—and told Claudia the
Ritz did not carry *L'Humanité.* "There is no call for it,
mademoiselle. Would you like *Figaro* or the Paris
Herald?"

Claudia made a mental note to ask Philippe why the
Ritz did not carry *L'Humanité.* When she did, he acted
as if she had just told the most amusing anecdote.
"That's marvelous, Claudia. Absolutely marvelous. But
why did you want a copy of *L'Humanité?"*

"I wanted to read the article you wrote."

"That's very kind of you, darling, and I'm flattered,
really I am, but stick to Proust. You'll find him more
rewarding. Besides, that piece was technical, full of
statistics. It would have bored you."

"You're just putting me off again, Philippe. I'd like
to read something you've written."

"Very well, if you insist, I promise I'll bring you the
other piece Gide spoke of. Though I warn you, that
will bore you, too."

Philippe was as good as his word. The following week
he turned up at the flat with a journal under his arm.
It was entitled *Nouvelle Revue française.* Late that
afternoon Claudia curled up before the fire with the
journal. She recognized André Gide's name at the top
of the masthead. *That explains the acquaintance,* she
thought and wondered why Philippe had been so mysterious about it the first time she asked him. "Politics,"
he had said.

Philippe's article was called *"Les Spiritueux Dangereux."*

In the poems and essays that have appeared
since the war, Pierre Drieu la Rochelle has claimed

that we are a generation. The experience of the war has forged a single consciousness in the young men who lived through it. No one who fought in the war could disagree with Drieu. We are, in fact, a generation with a special past and a collective consciousness. But what sort of consciousness is it that Drieu claims for our generation? That is the true issue at hand.

Drieu has written of "intoxicating violence" and the "grandeur of war." He has warned us that the war must not be looked upon as a catastrophe. It was, instead, the greatest event of our lives, of our generation. Has he perhaps seen a different war from the rest of us?

And the peace? Drieu does not like the peace. He finds it dull. He finds it lacking in glory and grandeur. He finds it bereft of spiritual values. "Is man to end his days as a retired shopkeeper?" he asks.

Drieu's reference to shopkeepers is no accident. It echoes Napoleon's description of the English as a nation of shopkeepers, and as such it evokes the Napoleonic mystique. War is good and glorious. A long and quiet life, no matter how useful, is to be despised.

There are many in France today who would not despise such a life. There are many in France today who yearn for the prosperity of that shopkeeper Drieu ridicules. . . .

The article continued for several pages. There were lengthy quotes from this Drieu, of whom Philippe so obviously disapproved, and there were many of the same thoughts Philippe had voiced that first afternoon. He spoke of hunger and misery and unemployment. He spoke of the horrors of war. He called for an end to hatred of Germany and a new era when the two nations would join together to combat the real enemy— social inequality. The words struck Claudia as admirable and uplifting, but they did not make much sense to her on a concrete level. She read the last sentences over.

> If Drieu is intoxicated by violence, I suggest that he has been drinking dangerous spirits indeed. I suggest further that we, as a generation. ban those spirits from France. Let us follow the example of our American allies. Let us declare our own pro- hibition—a prohibition of the spirit of violence that has already intoxicated too many of our gen- eration.

Claudia was not so naive as to think Philippe was advocating prohibition of the sort she was familiar with, and yet what *did* he want people to do? When she asked him that night, he laughed and told her not to bother about it. The article was merely literary infighting be- tween two young men of no importance.

"But surely it must have some importance to you or you wouldn't have bothered to write it."

"Oh, well, for me, yes, and perhaps for a few others, those of us who like Drieu's writing—he's quite a fine writer—but don't approve of some of his ideas. For us it is important, in a small way of course. But why would you want to bother?" He stood and held out his arms to her, and she went into them and forgot, in the music and the champagne and the closeness of Philippe, all about the article.

She forgot about the article, and she forgot about Thanksgiving. Or at least she thought she had until a week before Christmas.

They were in the small sitting room of the flat on the Rue de Tilsit. The room was festive with holly and greens, and the fire cast a glow over the heavy old fur- niture. Claudia and Philippe sat on the floor before the hearth, surrounded by calendars and lists and cards. She was organizing Christmas, she explained to Philippe, who laughed and said he thought that had been done almost two thousand years before.

"Don't be silly. There's so much to do, and Christ- mas is only a week away."

But Philippe insisted on being silly. He shuffled her lists and got them out of order, read sonorously from the cards she received and those she was sending, and kept hiding things behind his back so Claudia would have to wrestle them from him. The price of his yielding was always a kiss, sometimes two.

"Now be serious," she chided after the last two had turned to three or four.

"I *was* being serious."

"The embassy ball. Whose dinner should we go to before it?"

"Which embassy and which ball?" he asked without interest. He would have been much happier spending the holidays right here alone with Claudia.

"The American embassy, silly."

"I haven't received an invitation. Perhaps they think I'm a suspect Frenchman."

"Of course you have. If I know you, it's probably sitting at home with a pile of unopened invitations. Well, it's for the twenty-eighth, and even if it is a little stuffy, the parties before and after are supposed to be fun."

"Oh, darling, I'm sorry, but I won't be able to get away on the twenty-eighth."

Claudia had expected Philippe to have to spend Christmas with his family—he had warned her that the entire clan gathered in the old château—but what was so special about the twenty-eighth? "Won't you be back by then?"

"It isn't that. It's just that I'll be tied up. You go, darling, and have a good time. But not too good a time."

There was a pause. Claudia had never had to beg. Indeed, she was the one who made the decisions, bestowed her presence like a gift. What did he mean, "tied up"? But Philippe seemed to understand what she was about to ask and began talking quickly about other parties and what would she like for Christmas and then a long story about a childhood Christmas at the château, and there was simply no way to get back to the subject.

If Philippe had succeeded once again in manipulating the conversation, he was not so successful with Claudia's emotions. This time she was angry. But he was pleased to see that although she was good at momentary pouting, she was incapable of a sustained sulk. *By New Year's everything will be all right again,* he thought as he made his way to the flat on the afternoon of Christmas Eve. He was leaving for the country in a few hours and had come to say good-bye and give Claudia his gift.

Philippe had spent days contemplating the perfect offering. He had foraged around in shops for hours on end, but everything was either too banal or too outrageous, too personal or too impersonal. Then, as he sat reading in his room late one afternoon, it had caught his eye. A small marquetry box, just large enough for a rope of pearls or a few sets of earrings. It had been in the family since the seventeenth century, and the work was exquisite. It was the perfect gift, an impersonal object made intensely personal by virtue of its ownership. He held it now carefully wrapped in gold paper.

"Oh, Philippe, it's magnificent."

"I hope you like it. It's pleased many generations of Boissevains." For one crazy moment she thought he was going to propose, but he merely went on in answer to her expectant silence. "It's been in the family since sixteen something or other, fifty or sixty, I imagine, and I thought you'd like it. It looks like you," he added as he traced the delicate design with one finger.

"But, Philippe, I can't accept this if it belongs to your family." Her sense of propriety in giving and receiving, a subtle sense drilled into her since childhood, flared to life. If Claudia had a conventional side, this was it.

"It doesn't belong to my family. It belongs to me. Or rather it belonged to me and now it belongs to you."

"But it's too . . . too costly." She was embarrassed by the vulgarity of her argument.

"I don't know about that," he said, and Claudia thought she could detect a note of annoyance. "I only know that it's beautiful and it reminded me of you."

And then Philippe and the books she had given him

were gone, and Claudia was left alone to mull over the marquetry box and what it meant, if anything. It was a piece of rare beauty. There was no doubt about that. Even Katherine agreed it was exquisite as she turned it carefully in her hands. "Where on earth could he have found the money for something like this?"

"Oh, Kate, don't be vulgar. Anyway, he didn't have to find the money. It's been in his family for centuries and centuries."

"Selling off the old possessions? Or should we say gambling them for higher stakes? You know Mother and Daddy would never let you keep it."

"Why not?" Claudia tried to sound innocent, but she suspected her sister was right.

"Because, my naive little sister, a gift like this implies . . . well, *more*."

"Oh, Kate, are we going to worry about my ruination again?"

"No, I was referring to marriage. Perhaps I shouldn't have said gamble. Perhaps I should have said investment. This is the Boissevain capital, and I think your count is counting on big returns."

"Don't be ridiculous, Kate." Claudia pretended to be annoyed, but her sister's speculations pleased her more than she dared admit. Surely no one would casually give away something that had been in the family for centuries. There was only one explanation. Philippe must be planning to repossess the gift—and her.

4

Claudia's euphoria, like the excitement of Christmas, did not last. It waned with Philippe's absence and reached a low ebb on the day of the embassy ball. Listless, miserable with longing, she decided not to go. She knew well enough she wouldn't be a wallflower. All too many young men would be delighted at his absence. But despite their pleasure at having Claudia to themselves, they would wonder why—wonder and speculate. Claudia couldn't face it! She pleaded too much Christmas to Aunt Louisa and took to her bed.

Louisa did not entirely believe her niece but reasoned a day in bed and a good night's sleep would not hurt the girl.

"Aunt Louisa, that's absurd. There's *nothing* wrong with Claudia."

"Perhaps not, dear, but a little rest can't hurt her."

"But if Claudia doesn't go to the embassy ball, people are bound to talk."

"Now no one is going to talk, Katherine. If they ask about Claudia, simply say she's had too much Christmas and will be fine in a day or two."

"And have the whole American colony laughing at us. Not I. Claudia can make her own excuses. And I'll tell her that right now." Katherine pushed politely but firmly past her aunt into her sister's room.

"You're a fool, Claudia, a silly little fool. Well, you can make a spectacle of yourself, but you won't make one of me. Stay home from the ball if you like, but don't expect me to make your apologies. I can see it all now, everyone pretending to be so concerned about poor little Claudia and the moment I turn my back snickering about her tragic love affair."

"That's not fair, Kate! I just don't feel well."

"Rubbish!"

"Well, I don't. And anyway, what business is it of yours if I don't go to the ball? I'm sure *you* won't miss me."

"No, I won't. But I won't make your excuses either. You can let people laugh at you if you want, but I won't have them laughing at me. And make no mistake, Claudia, they're going to laugh. This will be the best gossip of the holiday season. Well, I'll be off before I tire you. I'm going to dress now, and," she called over her shoulder as she left the room, "I do hope you feel better soon, sister dear."

For several minutes after Katherine left the room Claudia lay staring at the ceiling, her hands clenched at her sides. Kate was right, of course. Everyone would know why she wasn't there. How they'd laugh! Or worse still, pity her. She wouldn't have it! She was on her feet and ringing for the maid. No one was going to laugh at Claudia Trenholm. And no one was going to feel sorry for her either.

By nine o'clock Claudia was ready. She examined herself in the mirror and decided no one could possibly guess at the pain in her heart. Despite her unhappiness, the thought made her feel terribly sophisticated. As did the dark satin dress that, in the latest style, had no back. The rope of Cartier pearls, knotted at the nape of her neck, swung gently against her naked skin.

She held her head up and looked her image coldly in the eye. "We'll see who has the last laugh after all," she whispered to her reflection.

The embassy was ablaze with lights and fragrant with Christmas greenery. Claudia did not sit out a single dance. Nor did she dance with any man more than once. She twirled from one pair of arms to another, her spirits soaring higher with each glass of champagne, every outburst of flattery. Claudia Trenholm was a flapper again. And for the moment the pain was dormant.

The embassy ball, staid and carefully chaperoned, was only the beginning of the evening. After all, this was Paris and it was almost 1923, and everyone was young and beautiful and very, very free.

"Let's go to Linda's. There's always a party there," Bill Jarris said.

"You mean Cole's," Harry corrected.

"No, he means Linda's." Anson laughed and shot Harry a look that said we men of the world know all about kept men and all the other wonderful, forbidden sins of Paris.

On the Rue de Monsieur a single house was alive with music and noise. Through the lighted windows Claudia could see men and women dancing with more abandon than the American embassy had ever permitted. The women were beautiful, and the men, who were not clever, were even more beautiful. There was champagne everywhere. One man in a grotesque pantomime was drinking it out of a spike-heeled slipper. Now that the war and its shortages were a thing of the past, high heels —and other excesses—were again permissible. Nearby a woman danced drunkenly in a single shoe. In corners couples clung to each other. Claudia had never seen anything like it.

She found a glass of champagne in her hand before she had even removed her cape. They strolled from room to room, and for once she did not resent Anson's heavy arm around her. He was a familiar presence in this strange world.

"This is really something, isn't it?" Anson exulted. "They give the best parties in Paris."

"Shouldn't we find the hosts to say hello?"

"Don't be so old-fashioned, Claudia. This isn't that kind of party," Harry explained in his most worldly manner.

She danced with Anson, then Bill Jarris, then Anson again, and then some sticky little man with beady eyes and a bristly mustache. She knew it was bristly because he kept trying to press his face close to hers. When the dance was over, she broke away immediately and returned to Anson and Harry, who had been watching her with amusement.

"The least one of you could have done was cut in."

They were clearly not in a protective mood. "Here we are showing you the world, Claudia, and you aren't even grateful." Anson smirked.

"Sometimes you really are impossible. I'm going to find the powder room. Is there any chance you'll still be here when I get back?" Claudia asked in a more conciliatory tone. She didn't want to be left alone.

"Wouldn't leave you for the world, Claudia. You can count on me," Anson said as he drifted off toward the nearest champagne tray.

Claudia mounted a wide circular staircase to the second floor. All the doors were closed, and there was no telling what lay behind them. She asked a woman who was leaning against a wall with her eyes closed, but the woman seemed not to hear her. She knocked on the first door. There was no answer. She opened it and peered in. In the center of a huge canopied bed lay a mass of what she at first thought were coats. Then she made out several, too many, arms and legs. Silently, she closed the door and walked quickly down the hall.

She knocked on another door. A sleepy voice said, "Come in." She opened the door and found two men and a woman strewn across one another on the floor. The room was heavy with smoke, but through the dimness she could see the woman was fair and very beautiful. She wore a black satin dress that had fallen off one shoulder. Both men had removed their coats. They seemed to be held up only by their stiff shirtfronts.

"Ah, new blood," the woman murmured languidly, lifting a heavy braceleted arm toward Claudia. In it was a long, elaborately twisted pipe.

"Sorry," Claudia mumbled and retreated quickly.

She found a maid sitting sullenly at the end of the hall. "Use Madame's boudoir," she said in annoyance.

Claudia followed her directions to an enormous bedroom. She was struck immediately by its opulence, but there was nothing in poor taste. Beyond it were a dressing room and then a bath almost as large as the first room. It was exquisitely appointed.

Claudia was accustomed to sumptuousness. Her parents' town house was, thanks to her father's money and her mother's taste, comfortably palatial. The country place in Glen Cove was rambling and elaborate without being ostentatious. Most of her friends had grown up in similar surroundings, and she was familiar with some of the best and certainly the most expensive architecture and interior decoration on the eastern seaboard. But here was something different. There was a finish, a sophistication, she had never seen before.

She returned to Anson and the others. "Come on, Claudia. Onward and upward, to the 'hill.' Nothing much happening here anyway," Anson said, helping her on with her evening cape and running a hand, by supposed accident, across her slender back.

Nothing much going on here. She laughed to herself. She could tell Anson and Harry and the rest of them a few things, but she merely smiled and tramped out into the cold December night.

They had picked up several new people at the last party, and it took four taxis to get them to Montmartre. Once there they crawled from one *boîte de nuit* to another, looking for *le jazz hot,* hotter, hottest. Then someone suggested Harry's Bar, and everyone was off for Bloody Marys. After all, it was almost breakfast time.

Claudia sat wedged between Bill Jarris and Anson. There seemed to be no escaping Anson tonight, but at this hour she scarcely cared. If her exhaustion hadn't dulled her distaste for Anson, the champagne would have. Her mind was as foggy as the predawn streets. She knew there was something wrong, a dull pain gnawing at her, but she couldn't focus on it.

Anson placed another drink before her and resumed the monologue he had been whispering for the last hour. At this point she could only giggle. To Anson it was sheer encouragement.

Suddenly she stood up. "Time to go home. S'time to go home."

Harry made a great show of looking at his wristwatch. Though he had owned it for several years—considerably before most of his friends had begun wearing them and only slightly after the Lafayette Escadrille had popularized them—he still delighted in its cachet. No pocket watch for worldly old Harry. "It's only four thirty, Claudia. Much too early to go home. Have another Bloody Mary. Best thing in the world for champagne."

"No, no more Bloody Marys. I want to go home."

"I'll take you home." Anson got unsteadily to his feet. "Never let it be said, refused you a sin'le wish, Claudia."

"You're drunk," Harry said. "We're all drunk."

"Right. We're all drunk and ought to go home." Anson looped an arm around Claudia and staggered to the door. He hailed a cab, opened the door for Claudia, then tumbled in after her.

"Anson, you're practically in my lap!"

"Ah, but what a lovely lap," he murmured sloppily into her hair and draped one dead arm around her shoulders.

It was all so confusing, Claudia thought. *If only the taxi would stop bumping and things would stop spinning for a moment.* She made an attempt to pull herself up and away from Anson, but his weight was too much for her. She felt like an underwater swimmer trapped in the tentacles of some huge, damp animal, and all the while Anson kept murmuring unintelligible words at her. She felt his breath, hot and sour, on her face and tried again to pull away. She struggled against him as his mouth searched drunkenly for hers.

"Stop it, Anson." He paid no attention. One arm was an iron bar around her shoulders, pressing her to him. His hand fumbled inside her evening cape. Through the satin she felt his hot, wet fingers on her breast.

"No more games, Claudia," he slurred, his face against hers. "Woman of the world, now, remember. French gigolos and all the rest. Fool the rest of the Yalies, Claudia, but not me, not old Anson. Come on, Claudia, come on. I know everything that French joker does. Wan' me to speak French, Claudia, that it? *Je parle français,* Claudia? *Je t'aime, je t'aime,* Claudia. That it?"

His words sliced through the alcoholic haze. She managed to raise both hands and, using every ounce of strength left to her, pushed Anson to the other side of the taxi. Then she flung open the door and, as the driver screeched to a stop, jumped from the car.

Blinded by tears, she began to run down the street. Anson sat slumped in the corner of the backseat mumbling to himself. "Sorry, Claudia, didn't mean it. Come on back, Claudia, come on back."

At the end of the second block she found an empty taxi and threw herself into it. She had stopped crying by the time she got home; but her cheeks were tearstained, and her gait was none too steady. She let herself in quietly, slid out of her dress, torn at one shoulder, and collapsed into bed. Her last vision before she passed out was of Anson's blurred and sweaty face pressed against her own.

Claudia awakened early. She had a headache from the champagne, and the recollection of Anson's hand on her breast made her cringe with shame and disgust.

How had it happened? She tried to piece the evening together, but it was an out-of-focus kaleidoscope of parties and people and smoke-filled nightclubs. She remembered standing in the center of that glorious boudoir and thinking how very much she had to learn. *But I didn't mean that,* she almost cried aloud and buried her face in the pillow.

Why was everything suddenly going wrong? Anson had been annoying her, but he had never behaved like this.

And then Philippe. The memory of last night's humiliation paled when she remembered what had haunted her all evening. The anguish was sharper than ever. She had set out to show Philippe. Instead, she had made herself miserable.

Why was Philippe behaving like this? Could there be

another woman? Claudia hadn't thought so, but after last night she knew anything might be possible.

She remembered the house on the Rue de Monsieur. Wild parties were anything but unusual in Paris these days. If Anson and Harry took them for granted, surely Philippe was far more familiar with them. She thought of the two rooms she had wandered into by mistake and shuddered. What was Philippe mixed up in?

Whatever it was, it was too terrible to tell her about— and too important to him to give it up for her. She didn't know which bothered her more, Philippe's secrecy or his refusal to yield an inch. No one had ever treated her this way before. By this time any other man would have proposed. Many had with far less encouragement. She had wanted Philippe to be different, but not this different.

It was all so confusing, and she was too tired and sick to make any sense of it. She dreaded the day ahead, but knew she had to go through with it. Kate had been right. People *would* talk. *Especially after last night,* Claudia thought. It seemed to her everyone must know about that shameful incident with Anson.

She permitted herself a few more hours of sanctuary, then a long hot bath. At eleven she emerged from her room red-eyed and pale.

Katherine sat alone at the table. In Louisa's place lay a huge florist's box. "Another conquest. Judging from the size of the box, I'd guess it's more than a single rose this time."

Claudia's spirits lifted. Philippe was thinking of her. She tore open the box. Inside lay two dozen yellow roses.

Katherine raised her eyebrows. "He certainly does go from one extreme to the other." But Claudia knew immediately they were not from Philippe. Philippe's would be red or perhaps white, but never yellow. White was pure love; red, passion; yellow was for friendship. And, in this case, apology, she guessed.

"They're not from him."

"Who then?" Katherine asked. Claudia tossed the card to her sister. " 'Please forgive me, Anson,' " Katherine read aloud. "Forgive him for what?"

"For behaving like an animal. After we left Harry's —in the taxi . . ." She began to cry.

"Really, Claudia, you must be exaggerating. After all, you've seen Anson drunk before, and Anson drunk is Anson amorous."

"But not like this. He kept pushing himself on me, and then he said the most awful things, ranting about Frenchmen and not being able to fool him anymore and all sorts of craziness."

"Won't you ever learn? First you're seen all over Paris mooning about with that slick count and you know the ideas people get; then you get drunk at a party and let Anson Hagerty, of all people, take you home. Anson probably did behave badly, but then Anson almost always does."

"Oh, Kate, stop being so holier-than-thou. I've seen you drink too much champagne, and no one ever attacked you in a taxi."

"I, my naive little sister, have not spent the last three months gallivanting around town with a great French lover, or so he fancies himself judging from the way he looks at women. Sweet little American girl, sophisticated French count, the two of you always so involved in each other. Of course, people are going to talk. And of course, some fool like Anson Hagerty is going to draw his own dirty conclusions."

"But why? Why is it Anson's business at all? Why can't people just leave us alone?"

Katherine was a less than sympathetic confidante. "That's very romantic, I'm sure, Claudia, but not very realistic. It's a pretty picture, I admit, you and Philippe and the family château, but after that, what? Will you live on love?"

"Why do you always have to harp on money, Kate? I don't care about money. I told you, I only care about Philippe."

"For once in your life, Claudia, try to understand. Philippe is not a pretty toy Daddy's going to buy for you. He doesn't have a penny, and he doesn't work. You know how Daddy will feel about that."

"Daddy's not marrying him! I am," Claudia snapped and then remembered in fact she was doing no such thing. Wasn't that the real problem? Not that her father would disapprove, but that Philippe seemed determined not to give him the opportunity.

Claudia remembered an afternoon early in December. She and Kate had gone to Coty's on the Rue de la Paix to select gifts to send home for Christmas. They were debating the advisability of a pair of long gray gloves for one of their southern cousins when Claudia looked up and saw the Duchesse de Chauvres across the shop. Again she was with Simone, who looked even lovelier than she had the first time they met. Much to Claudia's surprise the *duchesse* had recognized her. She had nodded curtly and gone back to her purchases.

"Who is that?" Katherine had whispered as the girl turned to wrap the gloves.

"The Duchesse de Chauvres."

"A friend of your count, no doubt."

"His godmother."

"And what about the girl, is she her daughter?"

"Her niece. She's a friend of Philippe's." *Amie intime. Amie intime.* The expression beat in her head.

"I have no doubt."

"What is that supposed to mean?"

"Nothing much. She's an attractive girl. I have no doubt your count knows many." They were outside the shop now, walking toward the Place Vendôme. "Oh, Claudia, when are you going to wake up?"

"To what, the fact that Philippe knows other women?"

"Don't you see? That girl is the sort he would be likely to be drawn to, certainly the sort he would be likely to marry. They're the same kind of people, from the same background. It all fits together."

"Yes, so terribly neat, isn't it?" Claudia had spoken with more confidence than she felt. "Did it ever occur to you, Kate, that two people might be drawn to each other for reasons other than a shared background?"

"Certainly, that's my point. Your Count, for example, might be drawn to you for Daddy's money."

"Here we go again."

"Well, if he isn't a fortune hunter, then I'd worry all the more about that Chauvres girl. After all, you have to admit she'd make a more appropriate wife for le Comte de Boissevain than an American. You've spent enough time with your count and his friends to see how they feel about us. And really, Claudia, the girl *is* lovely. . . ." Kate had let her voice trail off cruelly.

Claudia was startled from her reverie by that same note of cruelty in Kate's voice. "But that's just it, *are* you marrying Philippe? Has he ever mentioned marriage?"

Claudia said no more to her sister about Philippe, but now that her private fears had been echoed she found them inescapable. Philippe returned to a carefully aloof Claudia.

He was half relieved, half hurt by her reserve. Once again he cursed himself for letting things go this far. He had gambled on an infatuation, and the cards had turned up a full-scale passion. If only he had never pursued, if only she had never succumbed. Now there was nothing for it but marriage, and that, of course, was out of the question.

Often on these cold afternoons they sat in silence, a dirty rain pelting the windows of the winter-weary cafes. Each pursued his own thoughts. Philippe was more than ever preoccupied. The newspapers that hung on the wooden racks in the cafes absorbed him increasingly, and now, when Claudia arrived a few minutes late, she would find him poring over them, oblivious to everything around him. Once or twice she had asked him what he found so engrossing. He had tried to dismiss her question with a vague statement of "just politics," but she had pursued, and he had finally begun to explain to her something about the Ruhr Valley and German war debts and the occupation of French troops. Only the last words made any sense to her.

"Does that mean you'll be called up again?"

Philippe's presence might not be totally satisfactory, but anything was better than his absence.

"Unlikely. They have enough regular soldiers without recalling the likes of me." His pleasure at her concern mingled with annoyance at her refusal to see the larger issue. Philippe patted her hand affectionately and went back to his newspaper, and Claudia returned to her own thoughts.

Philippe's disappearance at Christmas still haunted her, and with it that awful night and Anson. With hindsight she had come to see that Anson's behavior, unpleasant as it was, had not been as extraordinary as she had thought at the time. She had known fast girls at home, and she was pretty sure some of them were becoming faster over here. The young men, for their part, made no bones about it. What had Harry called Paris? The Sodom and Gomorrah of the modern world. That was one of the reasons Mother and Daddy had worried. So far they'd had little enough cause. Paris had been no sexual awakening for Claudia.

The idea struck her with sudden force. She remembered an article she had read last year in *Metropolitan Magazine*. It was called "Eulogy on the Flapper." "I do not want to be respectable," the woman, the wife of a famous author, had written, "because respectable girls are not attractive." Was that her problem? Was she too respectable, too conventional, for someone like Philippe?

Well, if that was the problem, there was an equally simple solution. She shivered. Of course, it was a risk, but it was worth it. If she won, she'd have Philippe. And if she lost—but Claudia Trenholm had never lost.

There was no time to waste. That evening they were going to a small dinner and the theater. Claudia dressed in a new ivory satin from Vionnet. It clung closely and, like the dress Anson had ruined, had no back. Philippe thought he had never seen her more beautiful.

In the foyer of the small flat they had been saying good-night for the last twenty minutes. "I really ought to leave," Philippe whispered. His lack of movement belied his words.

"Don't go yet," Claudia said, taking his hand and leading him toward the sitting room.

"It's almost morning." He let himself be drawn to the sofa.

Claudia half sat, half lay across one end and pulled Philippe down next to her. Her arms went about his neck, and she lifted her face to him. He had never wanted her so much, and knowing that, he removed her arms gently and stood up. "I think I'd better go." His voice was strained.

"There's no need."

"Your aunt. . . ."

"She's sound asleep."

He was surprised at her directness. "Claudia, what are you up to?"

"I should think that would be obvious."

"In some women, yes, but not in you."

"Am I so different from other women?"

"You're different to me."

"Then why don't you want me?"

"You little fool, if you only knew how much I wanted you."

"Then it's all right, darling, really it is." She could not stop now. She had already risked too much. "I want you to love me . . . to make love to me." Her voice was almost a whisper now.

"No, you don't, Claudia." Philippe's voice was even. "You think you do now. You think it would be exciting and forbidden. But that's not for you, Claudia. You want more."

They were standing only inches apart, and he turned to the window to put his back toward her. He knew as certainly as he knew his own desire that if he gave in to Claudia now, he'd be married to her within months. It was the only thing that kept his passion in check. "Be fair, Claudia. For God's sake, be fair. Don't you think I want you? I want you so much I don't let myself think about it. But I can't marry you." *It was out,* he thought. *He had finally said it.*

"Why not?"

"For one thing, I'm poor."

"What does that matter?" She swept the issue away like so much dust. "I have enough money for both of us, more than we'll ever need."

"That would be charming. Shall I write to your father immediately? 'Dear Sir, may I have the honor of your daughter's hand in marriage? And a yearly income as well?' "

"But it's done all the time. Nobody thinks anything of it."

"I do."

"You're just being stubborn."

"Perhaps, Claudia, but I'm not going to live off a woman."

"You'd rather throw away everything for your pride."

"It's not only my pride. There are other things, impossibilities. There are parts of my life you wouldn't like, wouldn't fit into."

"That's ridiculous!" Her voice had mounted steadily with her anger and frustration. They heard Louisa rattling about just beyond the sitting-room doors, and Philippe seized the pretext.

"Now we've disturbed your aunt. I'm sorry. I'll go before we bother her anymore." And he was out the door before Claudia could say another word.

And then, a week later, Philippe again begged a previous engagement. He was contrite but unyielding. He offered no explanation. This time Claudia's anger was too painful to reveal. She met his apologies with silence. *Perhaps a clean break would be better,* she thought and wondered how she would find the strength to shut Philippe out of her life. Philippe had become her life.

5

The morning after the dinner that Philippe had declined
to attend, Claudia was awakened early by Marie, one
of the elderly Frenchwomen who seemed to belong
more to the flat than its occupants.

"Mademoiselle Claudia, *je regrette,* I'm so sorry,"
she stuttered half in French, half in English. "I said
that you were not to be disturbed, but the young man
insisted."

"What young man?" Claudia asked sleepily.

"The young man on the telephone. He said you
would not know him. He said he is a friend of *monsieur
le comte.*"

Without taking time to tie the cashmere robe Marie
held out to her, Claudia ran down the hall to the telephone.

"*Mademoiselle,* I am sorry to disturb you." He
spoke formal English with a heavy French accent.
"Boissevain does not know that I am calling. He would
say no, but I think he would want me to."

"What is it? What's happened?"

"Philippe is in the hospital. The doctors say he will
be all right, but he has been hurt."

"How? What happened?"

"I cannot say more. I thought you would want to
know. He is at St. Gervais. That is all I can say."
Claudia heard a click and knew the man had severed

68

the connection. Within minutes she was dressed and out the door.

The night before, while Claudia had dressed for the Simpsons' dinner, Philippe had been making his way through the dark back streets of one of the shabbier quarters of the Left Bank, and while Claudia had wrestled delicately with a perfectly seasoned ortolan, Philippe had been brought to his knees in a brutal fight. He did not know his attackers personally, but he knew them by reputation. Before the war they had called themselves *camelots du roi*. In years to come they would be called fascists and then collaborators. In the early months of 1923 they had no name.

Philippe had gone, as he always did on these clandestine nights, to a meeting of a small underground group. Like its opponent at the other end of the political spectrum, it had no name and many names. Its enemies called it at various times anarchist, socialist, even communist. It was actually none of these, but merely a band of men, mostly young, mostly veterans of the Great War. Some were workers. Others were intellectuals. Some were devoted to world peace; others, having fought in the war, merely wanted a peacetime job. It was an amorphous group that rarely agreed on any single idea or plan of action. Its members united only in their hatred of the war and their anger that a better society had not sprung from its ashes. They printed a small newsletter, read by few outside their own group, and wrote heated articles for other journals. They were, until recently, a peaceful and, despite the government's ban, law-abiding group. In the last weeks, however, some of the younger members had become dissatisfied with theory. It was time to fight. They made stirring speeches harking back to 1789, 1830, 1848, and 1871. Parisians, they argued, had always manned the barricades to get what they wanted. Now it was their turn.

Philippe and some of the others tried to reason with them. Violence would achieve nothing. It would merely

69

ensure their imprisonment—if it did not kill them first. While Philippe and his friends reasoned, their opponents began collecting weapons, and storing them in the small room behind the large office where they printed their paper. Neither Philippe nor his colleagues knew of the arsenal. They knew only that they were meeting to determine what stand they should take in response to the government's invasion of the Ruhr. The occupation was an act of aggression. It could lead only to another war. Moreover, the peasants and workers of the Ruhr were their brothers. Protest must be made, but what form should it take? There were as many answers as men in the room. It was a typically French gathering.

Philippe had taken the floor. He had been listening to his colleagues debate for almost two hours and thought he could effect a compromise. He stood facing the group of men sprawled about the room on straight-backed wooden chairs. His back was to the plate-glass window with the printer's name in large block letters PEIGNUY ET FILS. Suddenly Philippe heard glass shatter and felt a dull pain in his right shoulder. He turned to see a dozen men, some with stocks and lead pipes, others with knives and guns, rushing through the broken window. He realized dimly that the rock that had shattered the glass had struck his shoulder.

Chaos! Men jumped to their feet. Some picked up chairs to ward off the attackers; others ran to the back of the office and returned with the weapons they had stored there. A brawny man in a cap bore down on Philippe. He picked up one of the toppled chairs, but a rifle butt crashed through it and came down heavily on his shoulder. Unable to move his right arm, he raised his left to ward off further blows, but he was helpless against the huge man and his weapon. The overhead light had been smashed, and in the darkness Philippe heard shouts and curses. He could barely see the figure bending over him, but he felt the rifle butt crash down on him again and again and tasted the blood pouring down his face. His body, no longer something he controlled, slumped to the floor. He heard what sounded like a shot, then another.

Claudia made her way down the long bare corridor. The girl at the desk had not been helpful. She seemed bored and angry with Claudia for bothering her at this hour of the morning, and the directions she gave were mumbled in rapid French. It seemed to Claudia she had been wandering the winding halls for hours.

Suddenly a young nurse, very dark and very pretty, was at her side. "Can I help you, *mademoiselle?*" she asked in French.

"I'm looking for Room Thirty-seven. The Count de Boissevain."

The nurse smiled as if in recognition. "Oh, of course, *monsieur le comte.* Right this way."

Philippe was propped up in an iron bed along one wall of the darkened room. His head was swathed in bandages, and one arm was in a cast. His eyes were rimmed with black and swollen into slits, his face was discolored with bruises and slashed by cuts, and there was a bandage over his nose with a thin tube running out of it taped to one side of his face.

"Philippe! What have they done to you?" She was kneeling beside the bed, and the tears were streaming down her face.

"Now, Claudia, I'm all right. Really I am." Philippe tried to raise his free hand to stroke her head. "How did you know I was here?" He attempted to sound stern, but he was clearly overwhelmed by her presence.

"A friend of yours called this morning."

"A friend? Which friend?"

"I don't know. He wouldn't give his name. He merely said he was a friend of yours and you were hurt."

It must have been Pierre, Philippe thought. He had known Pierre since the war, and though their lives were different now—Pierre worked as a waiter most nights to be able to afford to study during the day—they had retained an affection for each other. Once after a meeting they had sat for hours over bottles of wine that Philippe had bought and talked less and less about politics and more and more about themselves. He remembered the night and silently thanked Pierre for remembering it, too.

"But what happened to you?" Claudia's voice called him back to his bruised body. "Who would do this to you?"

"It's a long confusing story. Don't let's talk about it now. It's enough that you're here, Claudia. You shouldn't have come, but I'm glad you did."

"We have to talk about it now, Philippe." She had stopped crying, and her voice was very serious.

He thought of the police prefect, who had been in this morning, and the newspaper reporters, who were bound to come and sighed. There was no point in secrecy now. "I went to a meeting, a very dull political meeting. Or what was supposed to be a very dull political meeting."

"I don't understand."

"I belong to a group, Claudia. I have ever since the war. I guess politically you'd call it left wing, but mainly it's just against war and for jobs for veterans, for all workers who want to work and can't. There are groups like it all over the world—even in New York."

"But why didn't you tell me about it?"

"Well, darling, it isn't exactly the sort of thing one discusses in polite society. Besides, technically, it's illegal. The government has outlawed certain organizations."

"Are you a . . . a Bolshevik?" Claudia was shocked. She thought of the posters she had seen here and at home since the war. They showed a ghoulish half man, half monster about to spring and warned of the "Red Menace." She remembered a terrible incident—it must have been almost three years ago, right after those bombs had been mailed to J. P. Morgan and several others. Her father had received a threatening letter, and although he and the police who had come to the house that afternoon dismissed it as the work of some crank in his employ, Claudia knew her father had worried. She also knew, though no one had told her, that for months a private detective had stood patiently across the street.

Bolsheviks, Claudia repeated to herself now. *Could Philippe possibly be mixed up in something that terrible?*

"What does the name matter, Claudia? Bolshevism, anarchism, socialism, none of them really means anything. The only thing that means anything is a better world."

"And is this your idea of a better world? Blood and bandages and . . . and bombs."

"No, this is the failure of everything we were working for. This is the war all over again."

"But how did it happen?" Philippe was like mercury. She asked for concrete answers, and he slid away in vague generalities.

"We were meeting, just an ordinary policy meeting, but fellows who apparently don't like our policies decided to break it up."

"But who would do a thing like this?"

"Their name doesn't matter any more than ours does. They're simply men who hate. But that was the terrible thing, Claudia. They weren't the only ones who fought. I saw friends, men I've known and respected, turn to their own weapons. I didn't even know the guns were there," he said in amazement. He seemed to be talking almost to himself now. "I thought it had all been just talk. They were young—some of them too young for the war—so they talked of barricades and action. I never dreamed they meant it."

She covered his hand with hers, and his eyes came back to her as if from a great distance. "They killed a boy last night, Claudia." She gasped half in fear, half in relief that Philippe was all right. "We killed him, everyone who was in that room. He was only sixteen. Oh, he was on their side, so we're supposed to think it doesn't matter. But how can a sixteen-year-old be on any side? It was my fault as much as anyone else's. I should have known the guns were there. I should have paid more attention to their threats. If I had, maybe none of this would have happened."

The sixteen-year-old boy had no reality for her. Nor did anyone else. Only Philippe. *What if he had been the one?* "You must promise me, Philippe, you *must* promise that you'll give up these secret meetings. You have to . . . . If anything ever happened to you . . . ." She was crying again, and she buried her face in the blanket, half to hide it, half to feel his hand against her cheek.

"Don't worry, Claudia, there'll be no more meetings." His voice was bitter and full of pain, but Claudia felt a flash of exultation. It was over. No more mysterious disappearances. Secretly, guiltily, she thanked the sixteen-year-old boy for putting an end to it. Philippe would be well again, and anything was possible. They could even marry. Before she had time to think about it, she blurted out the suggestion. "Don't you see, darling, nothing stands in our way now."

He laughed bitterly. "We've only traded one problem for another. There's bound to be trouble. The police were here this morning. A boy was killed, Claudia."

"But you didn't do it," she insisted.

"But I was a member of an illegal group that did." Even as he spoke, he knew he was exaggerating. The police were too impressed by his name, his family's name, to take his membership in the organization seriously.

At least Pierre had got away before the police arrived, he thought with relief. The *flics* did not treat a penniless student from Toulon with the same respect they accorded the son of a marquis.

"Surely they won't send you to jail for going to a few meetings," Claudia said.

"No, darling, you're right. They won't do much more than talk to me, but even that could be embarrassing for you."

"No one cares about that sort of thing, Philippe. Everybody gets in trouble sometimes—drinking, or speeding, or something. Even Mother and Daddy pass it off with a 'boys will be boys.'"

That's what it all amounts to, he thought ruefully.

"So you see, darling, there's absolutely no reason why we can't be married," she repeated.

"One thing hasn't changed, Claudia. I'm still poor, and you are still, apparently, quite rich. I haven't changed my mind about that. I won't let you support me."

"Then I'll let you support me—very, very modestly. Oh, don't you see, it'll be such fun. I'll learn to cook, and we could get a small flat. . . ."

"The one thing we don't need is a small flat." He laughed. "We already have too many places to keep up."

"But we can manage somehow. I know we can. I'll learn to live simply. You'll see. I can sell my jewels and wear simple dresses. . . ."

"Marie Antoinette playing milkmaid."

"You know that isn't what I mean at all."

"I can see you now in your threadbare Chanels." Philippe was still smiling, but his eyes looked sad. "You'd be miserable, darling, and I could never stand to make you miserable."

"I could never be miserable with you, Philippe. Besides, you make some money from your writing, and you could do more. Honestly, I'd be quiet as a mouse and we'd never go out so you'd have plenty of time to work. And we'd be together. That's all that matters, isn't it?"

Philippe looked at her as she sat beside his bed. Her eyes bright with hope and her face flushed with excitement. Through all his pain he knew that he wanted her very much. And maybe, he thought as exhaustion began to weigh down his limbs and close his eyelids, maybe she was right. Perhaps money wasn't that important to her. "Yes, darling," he closed his eyes and gave himself over to Claudia and to sleep, "that's all that matters."

Philippe was home in two weeks. Toward the end of the third week Claudia received an invitation to lunch with his family. It was to be an intimate gathering. Just the marquis and marquise, Philippe and Claudia. Anything more elaborate would have been too much strain on Philippe, or so the marquise maintained. In fact, anything more elaborate was more than the marquise was ready for at this point. She was not averse to having her son marry an American. A French girl of his own class would have been preferable, but, in most cases, not nearly so profitable. Of course, Simone de Chauvres was the woman Philippe ought to marry. While not rich by American standards, the girl stood to inherit what was still a respectable fortune. And if Simone's brother's energy and ambition were any indication, the family holdings would increase rather than decline in the coming years. Simone would have been the perfect choice, but trust Philippe to be contrary. So a rich American it would be. But not just any rich American. The marquise wanted an opportunity to look the girl over in private. If she passed muster, as the marquis might have put it, then she would launch the girl into French society. With the Boissevain name and Claudia's money it would not be a difficult task, provided the girl had some style and as much breeding as one could hope for from that side of the Atlantic.

Claudia did not guess at these Byzantine subtleties of the marquise's mind as the taxi pulled up before the red and white brick Louis XIII *hôtel* on the Avenue Bois de Boulogne, but she was nervous nevertheless. She stood for a moment before the large iron gateway. Over it, emblazoned in black marble, was the Boissevain coat of arms. Claudia felt a twinge of insignificance. It was a fleeting feeling, immediately dispelled by the reassuring sight of her own reflection in the large gilded mirror of the foyer.

The house was even more splendid than she had expected. She must remember it all for Louisa: the Louis Quinze and Seize furniture with its original petit point, the buhl tables, the old porcelains and tapestries, the rugs from India and China, and in every room portraits of noble ancestors. There was no need to mention, Claudia thought later that afternoon, that the well-worn splendor of the *hôtel* was in marked contrast to the simple meal she was served and that the marquise's pearls, the most lustrous and perfectly matched Claudia had ever seen, only made her expensive but outdated dress look shabbier. There would be plenty of time for her family to learn about that sort of thing.

The marquise, like the home she presided over, was splendid and only slightly faded. She received Claudia in the small second-floor sitting room. The glistening gilt and pale blue silk of the furniture, made originally for Madame de Pompadour herself, were the perfect setting for the marquise, whose blond hair, only slightly touched by gray, rose in a smooth arc from her high, unlined forehead and whose icy blue eyes took in every inch of Claudia with a canniness that was not entirely unkind. The girl had beauty and a certain bearing. She had spirit but was clearly eager to please. She would benefit from the marquise's tutelage.

Claudia's behavior on subsequent meetings confirmed this first impression. The marquise and her husband agreed: Philippe had not done badly, considering. The girl had style and taste—for an American. She seemed healthy and strong, which bode well for future generations of Boissevains. And she was rich. Her father, the marquis had learned through certain discreet inquiries, was worth many millions. The marquis congratulated himself that the Boissevain lands and possessions were safe for another generation, and the marquise breathed a sigh of relief that her jewels would not have to be sold. She indicated as much to Claudia one evening several weeks later.

Philippe and his father were lingering over brandy in the library, and the marquise and Claudia were left alone in that same second-floor sitting room where they had first met. The marquise was wearing a gown that was clearly prewar—not even the cleverest alterations could disguise those lines—and a brilliant necklace of beautifully cut emeralds.

"My mother-in-law, the twelfth marquise, never wore them." She touched the gems lightly. "She thought they made her look sallow, and she was right, my dear. Emeralds are for fair women with high coloring." She looked down her aquiline nose. "Women like us."

During the weeks of Philippe's convalescence

Claudia's admiration for the marquise and her husband grew. It would be perfectly all right to be poor in the way *they* were poor—to wear shabby dresses with expensive jewels and an air of superiority, as if anyone who chose to wear the latest style were simply in bad taste, to know that it was all right to scrimp on the fish course because the wines that accompanied it came from a superb, if rapidly dwindling, cellar. Poverty with Philippe would be ever so much more fun than wealth with anyone else.

Of course, Claudia did not really believe she would have to live in poverty. Philippe said he would not take Daddy's money, but surely he would not stop her from taking it—if only for an occasional luxury. And as time went by, distinctions of that sort would dwindle. They would live comfortably. Of that Claudia was certain.

Louisa was not so optimistic about her niece's future. It wasn't young Boissevain's suddenly disreputable appearance, though heaven knows that was unpleasant enough. Still, one could only feel sorry for him after that unfortunate accident. Claudia had presented her aunt and Katherine with a carefully whitewashed version of some terrible street melee in which Philippe had been innocently swept up. Since neither her aunt nor her sister read French newspapers, Claudia felt certain her small white lie would not be discovered. But Louisa worried nevertheless. Claudia was clearly seeing too much of Philippe. She knew the futility of forbidding her niece, yet she could not resist a small confrontation.

"Do you think, dear," Louisa began rather hesitantly one morning, "that it's proper to spend so much time alone with Philippe?"

"Oh, *proper*, Aunt Louisa. Don't bother about that. No one does anymore. Anyway, there's nothing improper about my spending so much time with Philippe. Nothing *happens*, you know."

Louisa looked shocked. "Of course, Claudia. I never for a moment suspected anything like that."

Claudia laughed. "Then whatever are you worrying about?"

"Well, dear, whether you care about propriety or not, others do. I'm not sure that it looks quite right for you to spend so much time alone with a young man to whom you are not engaged." Louisa was startled by the look that flashed across her niece's face. "I am right in assuming that you are *not* engaged?"

Claudia was silent for a moment. She had been through this with Philippe a dozen times since that morning at the hospital. Philippe insisted on a cautious policy. He agreed their marriage might be possible. It would, however, never be easy. Even if Claudia could live without money—and he still had doubts about that —he was certain her father would not approve. And even if her father was willing to overlook Philippe's lack of fortune, he was not likely to be so understanding about a questionable political past. The least Philippe could do was to put those scandalous newspaper headlines behind him and present an impeccable appearance. And if he could not yet ask Claudia's father for permission to marry her, there could be no talk of marriage before anyone else.

Claudia looked at her aunt carefully. Surely Philippe could not object to her confiding in Louisa. "Well, not exactly. In fact you're entirely wrong in assuming we're not engaged." She rushed on before Louisa could speak. "I'm sorry, Aunt Louisa, I know I should have said something to you, but Philippe insisted we mustn't say anything until he wrote Daddy and asked him properly."

Louisa brushed aside the young man's fastidiousness. "But, dear, you can't be serious about marrying him."

"Of course I'm serious. And so is Philippe. Why shouldn't we be?"

"I've heard he hasn't a penny."

"Where did you hear that?" Claudia shot back.

Louisa's spirits plunged further. So Paula Kelway had been right after all. "It's of no importance how I learn things, Claudia. It matters only that the young man has no money. How can you consider marrying someone like that? You, who have known nothing but comfort and luxury all your life." Louisa's eyes flashed in memory of her own childhood poverty.

"But Daddy will take care of all that, Aunt Louisa."

"Your father will never approve such a match."

"Perhaps not at first, but you know Daddy. He'll come around. When he sees how wonderful Philippe is—and how happy *I* am—he'll approve. You know he will."

Louisa did not share her niece's certainty, but she had to admit the girl had an uncanny way of "bringing her father around." Perhaps it would be better to leave the financial arguments to her brother. "There will be other problems as well, Claudia. With all the young men in New York—and you can take your pick, dear, you know that—with all those fine young men, it seems so unnecessary to choose a foreigner."

"But, Aunt Louisa, isn't that precisely the point? I can do the easy thing, the expected thing, and live happily ever after—in stifling boredom. I want more than to spend the next fifty years shut up in the same tight little world."

"You know my feeling about that sort of thing quite well, Claudia."

"Please try to understand, Aunt Louisa. It isn't just a question of being different for the sake of being different." Above all, she must not sound like a romantic child. "You approved when Philippe showed me Paris, didn't you? You said it was grand that I was learning about good pictures and architecture and all the rest. You said I'd develop good taste and that's what we had come to Paris for."

"And I still feel that way."

"But don't you see, Aunt Louisa, it's more than a question of developing good taste. Philippe has shown me so much more than that. He's opened my mind—made me see people differently and events and everything. He's made me see just how little I knew or saw or thought before. How can I give that up now? How can you expect me to?"

"But's that's exactly my point, dear. You needn't give up any of it. What you're saying is that you've discovered a new viewpoint, which is only another way of saying you've developed taste, that you will return home a more . . . shall, we say *finished* young lady."

"But why should I have to return at all? Why can't I stay here with Philippe? You're telling me I've come this far, but must go no further. Well, I want to go farther. As far as Philippe will take me." Suddenly it was too much for Claudia. She'd been reasonable, and it had got her nowhere. "And besides"—her tone was petulant now—"I love Philippe. That's all there is to it. I love Philippe, and he loves me."

"Oh, love," Louisa murmured and turned her eyes, if not her attention, to the social page of the Paris *Herald*. She was not going to argue that point with her niece.

Louisa would have to write her brother. She told Claudia as much the next morning. Claudia agreed but was determined not to be beaten to the mark.

"You're perfectly all right now, Philippe, so there's no need to wait any longer. It's time to tell Mother and Daddy."

Philippe noticed Claudia never spoke of asking, only of telling. He suspected she was in for a surprise. A penniless husband, one with a recent history of questionable judgment, was a far cry from a Shetland pony or a Poiret.

Dear Mother and Daddy,

I have the most wonderful news! At least I think it's the most wonderful news, and I don't see how you can help thinking the same. I'm in love, and I'm going to be married. To Philippe, of course! I know my letters have been full of him, so perhaps I've already made it clear how wonderful he is and how much I love him and how much you are going to love him, too.

I can just see Daddy saying, *"Hrmp, get to the facts!"* Here are the facts, Daddy. He is Philippe de Boissevain, more accurately Charles Henri Philippe Claude Monceau Montifiore, le Comte de Boissevain. Quite a mouthful, as you would say,

Daddy. It took me an entire afternoon to memorize them in the proper order. He is twenty-seven years old and was an officer, of course, in the war. And most important of all, he is warm and kind and wonderful. He is wonderful-looking too, Mother, and has beautiful manners. He can even pass your test of walking into a room full of people without smoothing his hair or fixing his tie, so you see he really is a gentleman. If you don't believe me, ask Aunt Louisa. She has promised to write to you about him. And of course, Philippe will write. He's frightfully old-fashioned about these things. He insists that before we make a single plan or any announcements, he must write you formally and ask for my hand. You will give it to him, Daddy, won't you?

Philippe won't even tell his family until you give your consent, though I suspect they already know. They're a wonderful family, very old and noble and charming. The *hôtel* here in Paris is marvelous and I've seen photographs of the château. So you can see we're going to be quite happy and splendid.

I must dash now or I'll never be dressed in time for dinner. Mrs. Priestly-Soames' party at Ciro's again. I'll write more tomorrow, but I couldn't wait to tell you this much. I'm so happy, and I know you'll be happy for me. I miss you both terribly.

Love,
Your devoted daughter Claudia

Claudia hummed happily as she sealed and stamped the envelope. There was nothing to do now but wait.

Dear Elizabeth and James,

I'm afraid I have some startling news for you. Claudia has announced to me that she considers herself engaged. She has asked me to write you in support of that engagement. I told her that I would tell you about the young man in question but that I could not in good conscience lend my support to an engagement you have not yet approved. I will try to impart an objective view, but the responsibility of the decision is, of course, entirely yours.

I have mentioned the Count de Boissevain often in my letters. Claudia has spent a good deal of time with him, and I have always regarded him as a suitable companion for her. As you well know, I do not take my responsibility to the girls lightly.

I believe that Claudia and young Boissevain care for each other deeply. I am not, however, a romantic. I realize that there are more important issues. I am not familiar with the details, but I believe Boissevain is, if not poor, then certainly without a fortune. He is of an old and noble family, but like so many in Europe these days, their responsibilities outweigh their assets.

As for his prospects, they are for you to judge. Claudia has told me he intends to write to you, and I am sure you will have many questions for him. As you know, life here is very different from life at home. Boissevain's father, the marquis, has, of course, never engaged in commerce. The war, however, has wrought many changes, and Philippe does not seem to share his father's fastidiousness in that area.

I understand you cannot welcome this match with unmitigated enthusiasm. You have not met the young man, and I'm sure we all agree that it would be more pleasant and easier for Claudia if she were to marry closer to home. I am afraid, however, that Claudia has her heart set on this match.

I trust I have made the various obstacles to the marriage sufficiently clear. I would therefore like to add that I believe Boissevain to be a man of honor. I think he will do all in his power to make Claudia happy.

I realize there are many questions I have not answered. I regret to say that I do not have those answers. I only hope I have not disappointed the trust you placed in me when you put your two cherished daughters in my charge. I await your instructions.

Fondly,
Louisa

Louisa did not hum as she sealed her letter. If she did not entirely disapprove of the match, she had sufficient reservations about it to cast some doubt on her success as a chaperone. The only comfort Louisa could find was that the girls were sufficiently independent and the times sufficiently advanced for it to have made little difference whether it was she or someone else who had been sent abroad with them. Even James Trenholm himself could not have hoped to stem the tide of the times.

James Joseph Trenholm and his wife sat in the small morning room where they had breakfasted almost every day for the last twenty-five years. It was a sunny room with a bay window that afforded a sweeping view down Fifth Avenue. The house owed its grandeur to James Trenholm, but this room, like all the others, owed its warmth and charm to his wife, Elizabeth.

James had not been a young man when he married. He had been too busy making money in his youth to think of marriage. When he had finally deemed himself ready, he had chosen carefully. Elizabeth's social position had been as attractive to him as her delicate features and restrained good nature. He had admired her, but he had not at the time thought he loved her. Love was for the young, particularly the young who did not have to make their way in the world. And then he had discovered, to his delight, that just as his well-bred wife had furnished the rooms of his imposing mansion on the corner of Fifth Avenue and Sixty-ninth Street with quite good taste, so she had filled the empty corners of his life with warmth and affection.

Elizabeth Trenholm was no less pleased with the match. If James hadn't been the romantic figure she had dreamed of during those long sleepy afternoons on the veranda of the decaying house in Virginia, he had been a forceful and strangely attractive suitor. For

Elizabeth there had been little choice in the matter. Her family was very old and of late almost as poor. James Trenholm would be their salvation, as well as hers. Yet she found to her surprise and delight that this unexpected Yankee made up in vitality and decisiveness what he lacked in southern charm. And she knew now, with the wisdom of middle age, that those traits had worn better than the more superficial attractions of the young men she'd grown up with.

They sat across from each other now with the silent ease of two people who cannot remember a time when they did not breakfast together. James as usual was buried in the financial pages of the *Times*. Elizabeth leafed through the morning mail, heaped on the silver tray beside the informal breakfast china. With the exception of letters from the girls, there was little that interested James in this delivery. This was his wife's mail. His was being sorted at this moment a hundred blocks south at 120 Broadway.

Elizabeth was halfway through Claudia's letter, and James saw her usually pale skin go white. "Is there something wrong, dear?"

"I'm not sure. There might be something wrong—or perhaps quite right. It seems Claudia plans to marry—a count in fact." Elizabeth's voice held none of the admiration for the title that might be expected. She considered her own ancestors every bit as important as some obscure French family. The Sheridans were known throughout the South, and there was never any need to explain that there was no connection with General Phil Sheridan, thank you very much. And she had met too many European noblemen married to American wealth to retain a blind admiration for them. She held her daughter's letter out to her husband.

When they finished the two letters, husband and wife sat for several moments in silence. If James Trenholm was a decisive man, he was also a deliberate one. Finally he spoke. "I don't like it, Elizabeth. I don't like it at all."

"Louisa says he's a young man of honor."

"*Hrmp.*" He imitated the sound his daughter had

predicted. "I daresay. Knowing Claudia, he's probably a good enough sort. She may be a beauty, that girl, but she's got a healthy amount of common sense. But what does the young man *do*? That's what I want to know. In fact, the more I think about it, the less I like this count idea. If he were a penniless stockbroker or lawyer, that might be all right. He'd have a future. That's what I care about—not a fortune, but a future. But a *count*. What does that mean? Besides I don't like the idea of my little girl spending the rest of her life being condescended to by some threadbare bluebloods."

"You're jumping to conclusions, James. There's no reason to think anyone is going to look down his nose at Claudia." Secretly she thought her husband too sensitive on that point. The memory of his treatment at the hands of his wife's family was still vivid.

"I'll say no one is going to condescend to Claudia. Especially not some fortune-hunting blackguard." James watched his wife, suddenly busy with the coffee urn. "I know what you're thinking, Elizabeth, but it isn't the same thing. I didn't mind being married for my money. I'm a man, and with some men that's to be expected. But it's different with a girl. Especially a girl like Claudia. I won't have some good-for-nothing foreigner marrying her for her money and abusing her for the rest of her life."

Elizabeth chose to ignore the references to their own marriage. "But, James, we know nothing *about* the young man."

"That, my dear, is the point."

"I don't suppose you could get away now?" Her voice was hesitant. She had suggested joining the girls in Paris at Christmas, but her husband had maintained he was too busy.

"Well, it will be difficult—but not impossible. I'll find the time. I'll have to. I certainly don't intend to sit here in New York while some ne'er-do-well runs off with my daughter and picks my pockets as well. I'll have Roberts book passage first thing this morning. We should be able to leave by the end of next week."

James Trenholm left New York before Philippe's letter arrived. It would not have changed his mind.

Mr. and Mrs. James Joseph Trenholm arrived in Paris early one Thursday morning, but it was only after a simple lunch at the flat that James was ready to talk. As the meal drew to a close, he announced he and Claudia would take their coffee in the small library alone.

"So you've found the one, eh, Claudia?" His tone was all good nature, and Claudia's spirits soared. She'd been right all along. Her father *would* agree.

"Yes, Daddy, I've found the one. Now that I know Philippe I can't imagine life without him."

"No doubt, child, no doubt. But tell me, how do you envision life with him? We assume you'll live happily ever after, but where and on what?"

"Oh, Daddy, I knew that's what you'd be worried about. Kate said you'd think Philippe a fortune hunter, but it isn't true. He doesn't want a penny of your money. He wouldn't hear of it."

"What do you mean he wouldn't hear of it? Did you suggest it?"

Claudia realized she'd gone too far. "Well, in a way. You see, Philippe said he was too poor to marry, and I said it didn't matter since I had enough money for both of us, or rather you did, and he got very angry and said he would never live on my money," she finished proudly.

"And whose money does he plan to live on?"

"On his, of course."

"But you've just told me he has none."

"Well, he doesn't exactly have money, Daddy, but his family has lots of, well, possessions, and of course, there's the *hôtel* here in Paris and the château, so we won't have to worry about a place to live, and he does make a little money."

"How?"

"Oh, he writes articles and things," she said airily.

"That is scarcely a profitable profession."

"Now, Daddy, don't be an old bear. We won't need much money. . . ."

"Claudia! I've been paying your bills for twenty years."

"But, Daddy, you should see the way Philippe's parents live. They have so much style on so little."

"Did it ever occur to you, child, that these people were merely keeping up appearances until you, or someone like you, came along?"

"But I've told you, Daddy, Philippe refuses to touch your money."

"I daresay he'll allow himself to be persuaded—if I should choose to persuade him, which I very much doubt. I tell you honestly, Claudia, I don't like the sound of the whole thing. In fact, I'm very much opposed to it."

"But, Daddy, you can't be. I love Philippe. And he loves me. We have to marry."

James saw the color mount in his daughter's cheeks and felt a stab of anxiety. "What do you mean, you have to marry? Tell me the truth, Claudia. If that young man has taken advantage of you—and I think you know what I mean—I'll have his hide. Young men today, they've got no morals. And these Europeans with titles, they're the worst of the lot. I've seen them operate. Standards of a guttersnipe. Now you answer me, young lady, just what has been going on here?" By this time the color in James' heavy, florid face matched his daughter's.

"Oh, Daddy, don't be silly. Absolutely nothing has been going on here or anywhere else for that matter. Philippe isn't like that. He wants to marry me; he doesn't *have* to marry me."

"Philippe isn't like that," her father mocked. "What about my daughter?"

"I thought we were discussing Philippe, Daddy." Claudia could not lie to her father, and she remembered too vividly the night she had offered to become Philippe's mistress. James saw his daughter turn his question aside and guessed what had happened. He knew something about the romantic notions of young girls and a great deal about the spirit of his younger daughter. Well, at least the man was not a cad.

James relit the cigar that in his rage he had allowed to go out. After several puffs he spoke quietly. "Other problems as well. Problems besides money. You'll be far from home and entirely on your own. Won't have your mother or me to turn to if anything goes wrong."

"Oh, Daddy, you know I'll miss you, all of you; but I'll have Philippe to rely on, and surely that's what marriage is all about." It was the one argument he could not fault.

"Well, I'm glad to see you still have some sense left."

"Oh, Daddy!" She threw her arms around his neck. "I knew you'd say yes."

"Now I haven't said yes. I just haven't said no. I agree to meet the young man, and I'd like to make some inquiries about him. Then we'll see."

James was still not happy about the match, but he had always found it painful to disappoint Claudia when she wanted something. And she obviously wanted this very much. Perhaps there would be a way to work things out. Why, if the young man had get-up-and-go, there might even be a place for him in James' business. Just because he was a count didn't mean he couldn't be a good businessman as well. James thought of the vast tracts of land he'd recently bought outside New York. His holdings were extending far beyond Manhattan, and he'd need someone to look after them, someone he could trust to look after the family's interests. He wasn't ready to say yes, but perhaps he'd been too quick to say no.

"Ask the young man to dine. Let's say next night but one—I'd like a little time—and we'll take a look at him."

Claudia sat before her mirror, singing quietly to herself as she brushed her hair. Her voice was low and husky, but she carried a melody lightly.

> Love will find a way,
> Though the skies are gray.

> Love like ours can never be ruled
> Cupid's not schooled that way. . . .

The song had been popular in New York when she left. Mother hadn't let her see the show it was from. It was the first black Broadway show, and she had deemed it too risqué for Claudia. There was nothing risqué about the song, however, and she had bought the sheet music and learned to play it on the piano. The lyrics were sentimental, she knew, but they seemed especially apt these days.

She started to sing again. "Love will find a way." She heard the front door slam, heard her father's voice in the next room, then pounding on her door. She covered her chemise with a pale satin robe. James exploded into his daughter's room, his face crimson. "What is the meaning of this?" He flung several newspapers on the bed. Claudia recognized the picture of the print shop with the broken window and a smaller photograph of Philippe. The sudden whiteness of her skin belied the calm in her voice.

"Now, Daddy, there's nothing to get excited about. It isn't at all the way it looks."

"You mean you *knew* about this!"

"Of course I knew. There's nothing to hide. If you'll just give me a chance to explain."

"Explain! What is there to explain? It's all there in black and white. To think my own daughter could be such a fool. I've always given you credit for good sense, Claudia, but I see now I was wrong. If the scoundrel had misled you, that would be one thing. But to think you knew about this—knew about it and thought it didn't matter."

"Please, Daddy, just give me a chance to explain."

A dozen perfume bottles danced in the air as James brought his fist down on the small vanity table. "What is there to explain?" he shouted. "That you planned to marry a Bolshevik. A Bolshevik with a police record for fighting and killing—yes, killing. It says that a young boy was killed. That's the kind of man you want to marry!

90

"Now I know why he didn't want my money. Oh, no, that's too honest for *his* kind. No, he'd like to burn down every building I own and turn the land over to the 'people.' Well, he won't get the chance. He'll not get into my family, and if I have anything to say about it, he'll not get into my country either. Send him back to Russia, where he belongs."

"Daddy, you're being ridiculous."

"*Ridiculous*, am I?" he thundered. "No, by God, I knew from the beginning it was wrong. *There will be no marriage, Claudia.* I forbid you ever to see the man again."

"Daddy, you're not being fair. You won't give me a chance to explain. You haven't even met Philippe."

"No intention of meeting your Bolshevik. Or of letting any member of my family see him again."

"But you can't do that. I won't let you. I won't listen to you. I'll run away."

"You will stay right here and obey me. You're still my daughter, and I'm responsible for you. I can have you watched, or I can lock you in your room; but I have no intention of doing either." His voice, now quiet and even, was deeply frightening to her. "There is no need for that, Claudia, because I know you will obey me."

"But, Daddy, I love him. I love him so much."

His voice was still quiet, but now the edge was replaced by kindness. "Claudia, child, you think you're in love now, but what do you really know about love? Love isn't gallivanting around Paris. It isn't even passion—that burns out after a while. Love is something you share—like interest and habits and"—he hesitated for only a moment—"backgrounds. I don't expect you to admit it now, but someday you will. Someday after you've married some fine American fellow—someone like that Hagerty boy or Harry Van Nyes—and raised a family of your own, you'll laugh at this, and you'll know I was right."

"No"—she sobbed quietly—"I'll never laugh at this. And I'll never marry anyone else. If I can't marry Philippe, I won't marry."

"I daresay you believe that now." James was willing to concede the point for the moment. Claudia was no longer defiant. It was enough that she should accept his dictates. He could not expect her to see their rightness as well. At least not yet.

"I tell you what, Claudia, why don't we just forget this whole unpleasantness? We'll go away—all of us. You've been abroad for months, and you haven't seen anything of the rest of Europe. Your mother and I haven't been over here since before the war. We'll do Italy—oh, you'll like Italy, Claudia—and Spain and stop on the Riviera for a while. Maybe Antibes or Juan-les-Pins. The important thing is we'll get away and have a real holiday. For the next few months, Claudia, I don't want you to worry at all. I don't want you to think about anything except how nice the sunsets are in Venice or whether the Mediterranean is warm enough for you to swim." He took her chin in his hand and turned her face toward his. "That is Dr. Trenholm's prescription, and I'm going to see that it's followed."

James left his daughter's room wondering if there were still time to drop around to Cartier's before it closed and pick up a little something.

The next morning Claudia slipped out early to call Philippe. They agreed to meet at Les Deux Magots at noon. Both were early, and by the time the bells of the little Romanesque church down the street struck noon Claudia had told Philippe the whole story.

"And is this your reward?" Philippe touched the fine gold chain encircling her neck. From it was suspended an antique ivory heart. It reminded Philippe of a shrunken head, a grotesque parody of the real thing. It had cost James several hundred thousand francs at Cartier's, but the clerk had assured him it would be twice as dear in New York.

"Oh, darling, you're being unfair."

"Not at all, Claudia. I'm just looking out for your interests. I should think you could have traded me in for something a bit more splendid. Diamonds perhaps or emeralds. But I guess the value of everything French has fallen since the war."

"Stop it, Philippe. I haven't changed my mind. It's just that I've come to see that you were right. It won't be easy. It will take time to bring Daddy around, but I can do it. I always have."

Suddenly the anger was gone. He was merely tired, more tired than he had been at any time since the war. He'd always known it would end like this. He'd fooled himself for a while, let himself believe they could beat the whole damnable society that conspired against them, but he had always known it was only a dream. The irony of the dream was that he had begun by worrying that she might be hurt and ended up by being wounded himself.

He sat quietly while Claudia chattered on about her strategy. She would bring her father around in no time. Philippe began to interrupt her and then thought better of it. He had been about to say that the only wedding they could look forward to was one they might run off to secretly right now, but he knew that was no answer. He knew as he had always known that he couldn't afford Claudia Trenholm.

6

In late October the society column of the Paris *Herald*
reported that Mr. and Mrs. James J. Trenholm and the
Misses Katherine and Claudia Trenholm had returned
from their travels on the Continent and taken up resi-
dence at the Ritz. Invitations began to flow in, and the
girls went out constantly. After two weeks of dinners
and parties that bored James and several afternoons at
the races he found neither emotionally nor financially
rewarding, he decided a trip to London was in order.
The fact that one of his business associates, now an
expatriate who made his home in London, owned three
Fifth Avenue properties that made an unpleasant and
alien dent in a two-block stretch of Manhattan James
called his own promised the trip would be profitable,
as well as pleasant. He and Elizabeth could hop over,
transact the necessary business, and be back in ten days.
By then the girls would be ready to sail. They'd all had
enough of travel for a while. James was fairly certain
his prescription had worked. Months passed in exotic
watering places had distracted Claudia. She seemed almost herself again.

James had no idea how carefully Claudia had worked
at pleasing him. Only by behaving exactly as he wished
could she prove to him that she was a determined but
also a dutiful daughter. Never had Claudia and her
father been more concerned—or more deluded—about
each other's feelings.

"Pleasant to be back in Paris, isn't it?" James alone
with his daughter at breakfast, was clearly on tenter-

hooks. Though he was fairly certain she was over her infatuation, the mere idea of the young man's proximity made him uncomfortable.

"It has been a long time." Claudia kept her voice carefully neutral. "I wonder how everyone is? I wonder how Philippe is getting along?"

James struggled to make his voice as impersonal as his daughter's. "He's making out for himself, I daresay."

"Oh, Daddy, he really isn't such a bad sort, you know. You never even met him."

James debated his answer for a fraction of a moment. Berate the man again, and he might just challenge her. His daughter was made in his mold. Hand her something easily, and she dismissed it. Tell her she could not have something, and she'd fight twice as hard for it. "Well, dear, I'll take your word he wasn't such a bad sort—your word has always been good enough for me," he added pointedly, "but enough about old flames, tell me about last night. Who was that young fellow on your right at dinner, the one who kept making those mournful eyes at you all evening?"

Both father and daughter left the table satisfied that a point had been scored. James was sure Claudia would have forgotten all but the young man's name by the time they returned to New York. Claudia was convinced she was making progress. Her father had not even said a harsh word about Philippe, at least not a really harsh word. Everything was going according to plan. Everything, that is, except Philippe. He was nowhere. She hadn't heard from him while she was traveling, of course. She hadn't expected to, but once back in Paris she'd been certain they would meet. Surely their paths would cross at a party or she'd catch a glimpse of him in a restaurant or cafe. Or perhaps he'd hear of her return and find some way to see her. But Philippe did not seek her out, nor did they meet accidentally, and by the time James and Elizabeth left for London, Claudia had made up her mind. If she were going to see Philippe—and there was no doubt in her mind that she must—she would have to act.

She dared not go to his house. She could not face

meeting the marquis after all that had happened—or worse yet the marquise. Even the idea of a telephone call unnerved her. It had been so long, perhaps too long. As the months passed and Philippe drifted farther into the past, she'd begun to worry about losing him in another way. Paris was full of beautiful women, women who would be only too glad to console Philippe for the loss of some silly American who had allowed herself to be bought for the price of an ivory trinket and carried off for a few months of forgetfulness. What if he were to dismiss her politely but indisputably?

A note. That was the answer. It was much easier to write than Claudia had imagined. There was so little to say, or at least so little in a letter. Simply, "I am in Paris. Will you meet me at Les Deux Magots tomorrow at two." Her heart pounded as she posted it. Her mother would be scandalized; her father outraged. Claudia felt only exhilaration.

The next morning Claudia discovered an undreamed-of talent for deception. There was a Post-Impressionist exhibit at a new gallery she was dying to see. Secure in the knowledge that Louisa's preferences in art stopped midway through the last century, Claudia even invited her aunt to join her.

With no more than a twinge of guilt, she set out alone for the Left Bank. She wore her new beige silk suit with the skirt that swung gracefully as she walked. The sleek little cloche made a pale frame for her flushed face. Even the weather seemed to conspire, and the sun shone brightly through the chestnut trees that had just begun to turn.

As she neared the cafe, her excitement turned to fear. What if he weren't there?

With quick, nervous steps she approached the corner. Half the tables at the cafe were filled, but her cursory glance did not find Philippe. Without slowing, she walked past and down the block to the small Romanesque church at the end of the street.

The church was empty, and grateful for the sheltering dark, she slipped into a pew. On the street the bright sunshine seemed to reveal her shame to every casual passerby.

What a fool I was. I should have known he wouldn't come. Damn you, Philippe Boissevain, she raged to herself, too miserable to care that she was in a church. *Damn you for making me believe in you.*

"I think it's very rude to invite someone to tea and then simply walk by without so much as a how-do-you-do." He was trying to be light, but there was no laughter in his tone or in his eyes, as Claudia saw when she whirled around.

"But you weren't there."

"Of course, I was there. If you hadn't raced by like one of my father's English colts, you would have seen that. Did you think for a moment I could stay away?"

"Oh, Philippe, I didn't know what to think. It's been so long. . . ." Her voice trailed off.

Silently he took her hand and led her out of the church. "Would you like a drink?" She shook her head.

They walked on in silence for a few minutes. It was not a peaceful silence. Finally, they found themselves in a small park. It was deserted, and they sat on one of the rough wooden benches.

Philippe looked at her closely. "How have you been? You look wonderful. But then you always do."

"I've been all right . . . I guess. We traveled a lot. . . ."

"Yes, I know. I ran into Paula Kelway once last July. . . ."

"Oh, did you stay in Paris?"

"No, I went to the country with the family. They're still there. . . ."

Their sentences drifted off aimlessly. These were not the questions they wanted to ask, not the things they wanted to say, but how could they speak? Where could they begin? Claudia had come this far, but could go no farther. Perhaps Philippe had come only out of politeness. Perhaps he'd found someone else. Had he come only to tell her that?

"I'm sorry, Philippe. I should never have tried to see

97

you." Her voice, timid and abject, shattered the strain between them.

"It's not that, Claudia. Of course I wanted to see you. I've wanted nothing else since you left Paris. It's only that nothing has changed. It's as hopeless as ever."

Nothing had changed! That meant he still loved her, still wanted to marry her. "But then it's not hopeless, Philippe, not in the least."

"Claudia, Claudia." He shook his head. "Your father will never allow you to marry me. Maybe there was a chance at one time, perhaps if I hadn't been involved in that incident, if he hadn't seen those papers, perhaps there might have been a chance. But not now."

"Then you're saying it's over."

"Darling, your father said it was over last spring. And you accepted it, just as you did that ivory heart."

"But I didn't. I haven't. Why, the other morning I mentioned your name and he seemed absolutely . . . well, absolutely moderate about you."

Philippe laughed, but there was no joy in it. "Claudia, what does 'absolutely moderate' mean?"

"Well, he didn't get angry or forbid me to mention your name or anything like that."

Philippe was tired of the argument. "Perhaps you're right, but let's not worry about that now. I refuse to spend our first afternoon in months arguing about your father. Let's just enjoy today. I've been without you much too long, you know." He did not add, though he felt certain of it, that he would be without her even longer in the future. "What would you like to do?"

"I don't know. Nothing. Everything. I want to walk all over Paris. I want to see everything all over again . . . with you."

Hand in hand they walked, over the Left Bank, across the Pont des Invalides, along the quai, and over to the Trocadero, cool and green in the late-afternoon sun. They sat on a bench, and Philippe told her about his summer in the country. He made it sound bucolic and witty, like a comic opera. And Claudia told him about Italy and Spain and the Riviera, about the end-less sightseeing and the hordes of Americans.

They walked along the river again, watching it turn purple in the shadows, just as it had that afternoon almost a year ago when they had taken the *bateau mouche* up to St. Cloud.

"We'll have a drink in the Bois, and then I'll take you back to your hotel," Philippe said quietly. In the twilight they began to walk in that direction, then suddenly they found themselves on the Avenue Bois de Boulogne. "I must be a homing pigeon." Philippe laughed uneasily, indicating the familiar red and white brick building still shuttered for the summer.

"I can't bear the Bois, Philippe. Not today. All those people so eager to see and be seen. Can't we have a drink here instead?"

"But, darling, it's closed up for the summer. I've been staying at my club since I got back to town. Even if we could find something to drink, the glasses would be dusty." Philippe hesitated to mention propriety, the real key that locked the door to the *hôtel*.

"Oh, bother the glasses. Don't be so bourgeois. I'll wash them. Or better yet, we'll drink straight from the bottle. Frightfully decadent.

"It's like a haunted house," she said. Heavy green baize covered the old portraits, and white dust covers hung over every table and chair. The tapestries had been removed, and the rugs rolled up. Their steps echoed on the bare marble of the foyer.

"Do you know what I'd really like, Philippe? I'd like to see the whole house. Every single room."

"Very well, the grand tour, *mademoiselle*."

He led her down a long dark hallway that opened into a vast kitchen occupying half the bottom floor. In contrast with the shiny steel and white facilities on Sixty-ninth Street this was hopelessly out of date, but there was something cozy about the room.

"At one time this was the happiest room in the house. There was a chef, and he had two or three women under him—that was before the war—and then, of course, the other servants used to congregate here when they had finished their work. They were all very kind to me

99

and there was always a cup of tea and a *madeleine* for
little Philippe."

"It all sounds so Proustian."

Philippe smiled to himself, thinking of how much he
had changed her. "All right, I can take a hint. I'll cur-
tail my memoirs from now on."

"You know that isn't what I meant. I love those
stories. That's one of the reasons I want to see the
house. It's part of you."

They climbed the service stairs to the main floor,
and Philippe led her through sitting rooms and libraries,
dining rooms and drawing rooms. For every well-
appointed room she was familiar with, there were two
no longer in use. Philippe had stories for all of them.
In one he used to hide from his tutor when he hadn't
prepared his Greek lesson; in another he'd been beaten
by his cousin Gaston for calling him the bully he was;
a third housed a vast collection of model soldiers, some
very old and very valuable. "I was thrilled when Father
finally decided I was old enough to play with them, but
he, unfortunately, was not impressed by my aptitude.
He wanted war games, and all I wanted to do was
admire them.

"And this," Philippe said, throwing open the doors
to a huge ballroom, "is the *pièce de résistance*. I believe
that's the way you Americans phrase it. This was
Mother's favorite room. She used it often before the
war."

The petit point of the chairs lining the walls was
worn and faded, but their gilt legs still shone, and the
crystal of a dozen chandeliers glistened in the late-afternoon light.

"May I?" Philippe bowed deeply and took Claudia in
his arms. He began to hum a Strauss waltz, and they
circled the room in great sweeping arcs. A hundred
other couples kept time with them in the mirrored
walls. *Such handsome couples,* Claudia thought, *the
young men so tall and slender and dark, the girls so
fair and graceful.*

They climbed to the third floor, where there were
more sitting rooms and many more unused rooms.

Finally, Philippe opened the last door at the end of the hall. "And this is where the son and heir lives."

Claudia walked into a large, comfortable sitting room, lined with books and pictures and scores of photographs. A small boy sat on a pony, stood with a lovely woman in white, with a stern-looking man in military uniform, with other children, with dogs and soccer balls and all the accoutrements of childhood. It made Claudia want to cry, for all the years she'd missed, for all those she might still miss.

"I chose the paintings—those photographs were put there by Mother."

Claudia laughed. "I suppose I'd be just as embarrassed if you saw my mother's collection."

Through an open door Claudia saw another room, about the same size and obviously Philippe's bedroom. She felt a thrill at the intimacy. There was a narrow bed, two bergères, a chest of drawers, an armoire, and more pictures and books.

Suddenly they were quiet. Philippe had opened the shutter to let in some light, and Claudia saw the last rays of afternoon sun slanting across the bare floor.

"I must go."

"I know."

Later she could not remember who had moved first, but suddenly they were in each other's arms. It was nothing like her dreams. There was no slow undressing, no elaborate dance of expectancy. She didn't know how she got out of her clothes or how Philippe had. It did not matter. What did matter were his hands, caressing her back, her breasts, her thighs, and his lips, which seemed determined to leave no part of her untasted. He drew her to the bed. They moved slowly; but there was an urgency in Philippe, and it aroused the same fierce response in her. She wanted this to go on forever, yet she found herself rushing precipitously toward an end. She felt a flash of delicious pain and clutched at his shoulders, holding him to her with all her strength. Then she felt his body relax on hers, and he buried his face in her hair.

They lay in silence for several minutes. Finally, he

spoke. "I know I should be sorry, but I can't. I can't ever be sorry for this, Claudia—for us."

"Why should you be sorry, darling?" She was amazed at how calm she sounded, how calm she felt. Surely she should be overcome with shame and regret, but search as she might for those emotions she could feel nothing but happiness. "Why should we ever be sorry for each other? And now we really do have each other, don't we? Now there are no silences and no secrets and no fears. Like this," she said, running her index finger slightly over his scar. "I was always afraid to touch it, afraid you might not want me to. And yet I love your scar, Philippe, just as I love you." Suddenly her voice became light and playful. "Besides, I always thought you'd be much too handsome without it."

"Oh, yes. That's always been my problem. I'm much too handsome for my own good. Why, you ought to be overjoyed to have caught me, you ugly duckling. Just look at you." He held her at arm's length, and for the first time Claudia felt a twinge of embarrassment. She reached for the chemise lying on the floor near the bed.

"Don't you dare. I want to look at you." His eyes were like hands on her body. Then he pulled her to him, and it was his hands beginning the same journey, but more slowly now, as if they had all the time in the world.

The square of sunlight on the floor had faded, and the room was almost in darkness. Claudia watched the end of Philippe's cigarette flare.

"There's only one thing for it," he said abruptly. "We'll go to the country tomorrow and be married. When your father returns, he'll be faced with a *fait accompli.*"

"But I can't do that to Daddy."

"If you don't, what you'll be doing to us will be worse. I was willing to go along with you before, Claudia, because I didn't think I had the right to ask you to give up your family, a fortune, everything you've known all your life, but all that's changed now.

I can't give you up. Not after this. You can't want me to."

"Of course I don't want you to, but running off . . . it seems so, well, drastic."

"It is drastic," he said, stubbing out his cigarette. Claudia could not help noticing the way the veins stood out against the smooth skin of his arm. "But it's the only way. We can't wait for your father to return. We can't take the chance. And surely you couldn't expect to use this afternoon as an argument."

He saw the panic in her eyes. "Don't even joke about that, Philippe."

"I wasn't joking. We must marry now, before your father returns."

"I suppose you're right," she said slowly.

"Wonderful! We'll go to the château tomorrow. You'll love it there."

"Not the château, Philippe. If we're going to . . . elope, then I think we ought really to elope. It doesn't seem right to be married in front of your family without even telling mine."

"Of course, darling. It was thoughtless of me. We'll go away." He was silent for a moment, and she could see his imagination scanning the map of Europe. "Why not Montreux? It's a beautiful little town. We won't know anyone, and no one will think of looking for us there. I'll take the train to the country and pick up the old Benz. Then I'll motor back here and collect you."

"Don't be foolish, Philippe. You can't simply drive up to the Ritz and carry me off."

"Of course. I guess I'm a little inexperienced in these matters. You see, it's my first elopement."

She finally laughed. "Just see it's your last."

"That," he said as he drew her to him, "is a promise."

By the time Philippe dropped Claudia at the Ritz later that evening their plans were made. Claudia would tell her aunt she had decided to accept Mrs. Priestly-Soames' invitation to stay with her in Italy for a few nights. A wire to Philippe that evening confirmed the older woman's complicity. Despite the dire outcome of her own elopement with a penniless English actor, Mrs. Priestly-Soames continued to view all runaway marriages romantically. Besides, it would be pleasant to be in the limelight for a while. She looked forward to meeting the astonished gossip over Claudia Trenholm's elopement with the Count de Boissevain with equanimity. "But of course," she would murmur, allowing just a tinge of boredom to creep into her voice, "I was the first to know."

Two mornings later, as Claudia boarded a first-class compartment in the Venice-bound car of the Orient Express, Philippe was heading south from Paris through a fine drizzle. The marquis' old Benz handled well. It was a superb machine and had weathered the years well.

Philippe thought of his father now with annoyance. Their interview the previous day had left him with a distinctly bitter taste. The marquis had yielded the car, the only one left to them these days, with grace, but the rest of his conversation had been anything but tactful.

"Off for a tryst, my boy?" The older man's voice had a distinct barrack's room edge to it.

"Not at all, Father."

"Have it your way, Philippe. If I can't stake you to this, as my father used to when I was your age, I thought I could at least lend a little advice, but as usual you're certain I couldn't possibly know anything of interest to you." The marquis turned abruptly and stood staring out the window at his wife's formal garden. Like her, it was impeccable. Philippe watched his father and could not help remarking that the older man's casual country tweeds did nothing to soften the stiff correctness of his bearing. He felt disgust at his father's indelicacy, but also pity at his repeated failures to establish what he considered a proper paternal relationship.

"It isn't a tryst, as you put it, Father. As a matter

of fact, it's a marriage, an elopement of sorts, you might say."

The marquis turned back in surprise. "An elopement? That's the most ridiculous idea you've had yet, Philippe—and heaven knows you've had your share."

"Well, ridiculous or not, our plans are made."

"It's that American girl, isn't it, the one who disappeared so abruptly last spring? You're running away from her family, aren't you?"

"As a matter of fact, we are. Do you find that immoral, Father?"

"Not in the least immoral, Philippe. Merely stupid. The marriage won't do you any good, my boy, if the girl's disinherited."

"It will do me all the good in the world, Father. It will bring me Claudia. That is 'that American girl's' name, in case you had forgotten."

The marquis ignored the sarcasm. "I think you've been spending too much time with Americans, Philippe. The next thing I know you'll be telling me you're in love. I believe that's what one marries for in America."

"There are those in Europe, even in France, who marry for love, Father."

"I daresay. Well, the lower classes may do as they like, but among people like us one marries for many reasons. Which is precisely why your mother and I have been urging you to consider Simone de Chauvres more seriously. It would be a perfectly satisfactory match."

"Satisfactory to you perhaps, sir, but not to me. I've told you before, I'm fond of Simone, but I could never love . . . excuse me, marry her."

"Certainly I would not urge you to select a wife for whom you did not feel affection, Philippe, but let's have no more talk about love or, more important, about 'living on love.' I believe that's another expression of your American friends. Very well, you say you intend to marry this girl. What financial arrangements have you made? Exactly what is the size of her *dot*? What does her father plan to give her a year? Have you drawn up any arrangements as to the improvements and upkeep on the *hôtel* and this house?"

"You sound as if you're on the floor of the bourse, Father. Why, if I didn't know better, I'd swear there was bourgeois blood in the family."

"Don't be impertinent, Philippe. I can't stop you from doing anything. In fact, in this case, I don't want to stop you. But for once in your life be sensible. It would be so simple to do this properly, even spectacularly. Why do you insist on doing it badly? Why not go to the girl's father, ask for her hand correctly, and have the agreements drawn up? Certainly the fellow can't object to paying a bit for a name like ours."

"What he objects to, sir, is not our name, but my politics."

"Your politics! My God, Philippe, don't tell me you've been talking politics—especially your kind of politics—with the girl's family."

"No, Father, I haven't been talking anything with them. It seems the old man got hold of newspaper accounts of that incident last winter."

"I knew that would haunt you. Well, there's nothing that can be done about it now. The incident's over. You'll simply have to convince the father it was merely a boyish prank. In fact, perhaps *I'd* better do that. I'll give the fellow lunch at Les Épatants and then see what he has to say about a financial settlement. There's more than one American millionaire trying to buy his way into the club these days. Leave it to me, Philippe. I'll bring the father around."

If the circumstances had been different, Philippe would have had to laugh at how much like Claudia his father sounded. "I'm sure that's very kind of you, Father, but I'd rather handle this myself."

"Very well, my boy. So long as you realize that there *is* a matter to be handled." The marquis was silent for a moment, and Philippe rose to take his leave. "One more thing, son." Philippe turned back to his father, expecting the older man's best wishes. "This girl, this Claudia, she's a pretty little thing, but be careful. Make sure you start out properly. American women

are different. They like to run things. And they expect
so much. Continual attention." The marquis coughed.
"Fidelity. That sort of thing. It's best to make things
clear from the start. Establish the balance of power.
Ensure your freedom. I trust I've made myself clear,
Philippe."

"Perfectly, Father."

The conversation had rankled Philippe all through
the previous evening, and it haunted him even now
as the suburbs of Paris fell away and the countryside
spread out before him.

By the time he reached Lyons it had stopped raining; but the air was still heavy, and there was an un-
pleasantly warm wind from the south. Philippe was
glad they had chosen Montreaux. It would be fresh
and crisp, and there might be snow in the mountains.

The train wasn't due for half an hour, so he bought
several newspapers and seated himself directly across
from the track where the Orient Express arrived. The
minutes seemed to drag, and neither President Poin-
caré's demands for full reparation from Germany nor
the parliamentary debate raging around it could hold
his attention. Then Claudia was running toward him,
followed by a stoop-shouldered porter weighed down
by six Vuitton suitcases.

It was well after dark when they crossed the border
into Switzerland. The French guard examined their
papers for a long time, and Claudia felt herself flush
as he looked from the documents to the young couple
in the aging Benz and back again to the documents.
The Swiss guard merely glanced at their papers and
wished them a pleasant stay. The night had turned
cold, and a chill wind blew from the Rhone Valley.

"Here we are, darling. Switzerland, the land of
asylum." The road wound through dense pine for-
ests, and below them the lake lay blue-black in the
moonlight.

"It's beautiful," she said, trying to concentrate on
the scenery.

"It is that. It's also very clean and very straightforward. The Swiss judge nothing—or if they do they keep it to themselves. That's the way they've weathered the centuries—that and the mountains."

"I wish you'd stop talking that way, Philippe. Why do you go on about asylum and judgment?"

"I'm sorry, Claudia. I was trying to amuse you. You've been so quiet for the last few miles. Are you sure you're all right?"

"Of course I'm all right. Just a little tired. It's been a long day." The expectations of the morning, the exhilaration of the afternoon seemed to be evaporating in the chill mountain air.

"It won't be much longer now. Montreaux is just the other side of the lake."

Claudia began to feel better as they drove through the narrow streets of the town. The lights in the shop windows were out, but two large hotels seemed to extend a warm invitation.

"Which one are we going to? I think that one on the right looks more inviting. I don't like the gargoyles across the street."

"Neither. I think it would be wiser to stay outside the town. There's a little chalet up the mountain. It will be more private, and until we take care of the formalities, I think that might be best."

The practical problems had never occurred to her. Claudia had pictured the two of them occupying a luxurious suite overlooking the lake he'd described for her. It had never occurred to her they could not be married as soon as they arrived in Switzerland, and she had never concerned herself with the difficulty, or embarrassment, of checking into a hotel with papers that clearly identified them as not belonging to each other by any law but their own.

"It will be simpler to stay at the chalet. Frau and Herr Schwarzburgen know me. I've stayed with them several times, so they won't ask for papers. You'll find it pleasant, darling. You can see across the lake to France from the terrace, and Frau Schwarzburgen will take very good care of us. She and Herr Schwarzburgen ran a luxury hotel in Zurich before the war."

The chalet was a small rustic wooden building nestled into a hillside of pines.

"Herr Boissevain, how good to see you. You should have let us know you were coming. I would have had things ready for you. I wager you have not had dinner. I will get you your food after I make you comfortable in the room. In the meantime, Herr Schwarzburgen will make some hot spiced wine." Frau Schwarzburgen, tall and broad with heavy brown braids circling her head, had looked only at Philippe as she spoke, but Claudia knew she was acutely aware of her presence.

"Thank you, Frau Schwarzburgen. It's good to be back. And this time I've brought you my wife. Darling, may I present Frau Schwarzburgen, who runs the best chalet in all Switzerland."

"How do you do, Frau Boissevain. We are honored that you and Herr Boissevain have come to stay with us." Her tone was perfectly polite, but Claudia noticed that her eyes were cold, and her upper lip, shaded by a patch of heavy down, turned up almost imperceptibly as she pronounced the words "Frau Boissevain."

"Thank you, Frau Schwarzburgen. My husband and I are happy to be here." Claudia read the amusement in Philippe's eyes, but she found nothing funny in the situation.

Frau Schwarzburgen led them to two large rooms on the second floor. The rooms were sparsely furnished—a table and a few chairs in one, a chest of drawers, a standing closet, and a four-poster bed heaped with eiderdowns in the other—but immaculate. Frau Schwarzburgen immediately set about making fires in both rooms.

"This is fine, Frau Schwarzburgen," Philippe said. "Isn't it, darling?" He turned to Claudia.

"Yes, it's quite comfortable, I'm sure. . . ."

"You require something else?" Frau Schwarzburgen was still holding a pile of wood in her arms, and she spoke as if she were challenging Claudia.

"The bath," Claudia said quietly. *"La salle de bain."*

"Of course," Philippe said quickly. "It's right down the hall."

"Down the hall," Claudia repeated incredulously.

Frau Schwarzburgen, who was about to turn her attention to the fire, straightened again. "I will show it to Madame as soon as I have finished the fire."

"But, Philippe, isn't there a room with a bath?"

Philippe laughed. "This isn't the Ritz, Claudia. You won't mind. There isn't anyone else on this floor. Is there, Frau Schwarzburgen?"

"No, sir. You and Madame are alone."

When Frau Schwarzburgen left, Philippe went straight to the window and drew back the curtains. "Is it as perfect as I told you it would be? Of course, you can't see much of the view now, but just wait till morning."

Claudia, sitting on the end of the bed, seemed not to hear him. "Aren't there any rooms with baths, Philippe?"

He turned from the window, and the expression on his face was like that of a father dealing with a difficult child. "We won't have to share the bath, Claudia. We're the only people on the floor."

"But I don't like having to walk down the hall."

"Then I'll carry you." He laughed and took a step toward the bed, but at that moment Herr Schwarzburgen appeared at the door with two steaming mugs.

"That's what you need," Philippe said as the old man placed the tray on a small table next to the bed. "Some hot spiced wine will lift your spirits—and then," he continued in an undertone, "I'll carry you to the bath."

The wine did help, and the hot bath, and the thick sausage and potatoes steaming on a bed of sauerkraut which they consumed on the little table before the fireplace.

"I'm ravenous," she said as she helped Philippe and herself to more sausages.

"Frau Schwarzburgen will be scandalized when she comes back for the plates. She'll think I've starved you."

Claudia remembered the woman's reaction. "Frau Schwarzburgen is already scandalized, Philippe. Have you brought other women here? Have you introduced Frau Schwarzburgen to other 'Madame Boissevains'?"

He was around the table and had Claudia in his arms in a moment. "What a little fool you are! Do you think I would do that? Do you think I could humiliate you that way? I've stayed here twice alone and once with friends. That's why we came here, because they knew me and I could introduce you as my wife."

"All the same, Frau Schwarzburgen didn't believe you—the old cow."

"It doesn't matter. By tomorrow at this time it will be true. We'll show 'the old cow' the paper if you like."

"And have her know it wasn't true tonight."

"I'll hold my finger over the date. Now enough of this. I don't care what Frau Schwarzburgen or anyone else thinks. And you wouldn't either if you weren't so exhausted." He led her into the bedroom and held back the thick eiderdown for her. "I'm going to open the window just an inch," he said as he tucked the linens under her chin and kissed her gently.

Claudia stretched between the fresh sheets. The comforters were light and warm over her, and the pillows like a soft cloud beneath her head. She saw Philippe, a dark, slender silhouette against the mountains white and dry in the moonlight. Then she was asleep.

As he got into bed beside Claudia, Philippe was careful not to wake her. He could wait until tomorrow. In the meantime, he would hold her through the night.

"Marriage, especially marriage between aliens"—lids closed over two porcine eyes for a fraction of a second to indicate disapproval—"is a serious matter."

"I assure you we are very serious, *monsieur le préfet.*"

"Why have you left France to be married in Switzerland, Monsieur"—the round little man glanced at Philippe's passport on the desk before him—"Monsieur Boissevain?"

"We wanted to spend our first days together in your beautiful country, *monsieur le préfet.*"

"It is customary to journey after the wedding, not before."

"Be that as it may, *monsieur le préfet,* we chose to be married in Switzerland. Our papers are in order. I see no obstacles to our marriage."

"It is not up to you to discover obstacles, young man. That is *my* job." From the moment they entered his office the prefect had found something strange about the couple. They were well dressed. The young woman was wrapped in a cape of luxurious fox, but when she removed her gloves, her finger showed no trace of an engagement ring. The man was clearly a gentleman, yet he claimed he was a writer of pieces for magazines and newspapers. *Monsieur le préfet* trusted his instincts. There was something wrong here.

"Monsieur le préfet, we have come to your delightful city to be married. Our papers are in order. We have obtained the proper documents. Now you say you will not marry us. Perhaps the prefect in Locarno will be more accommodating." Philippe took Claudia's arm as if to lead her from the small, overheated office.

"Monsieur Boissevain." The prefect did not have to consult Philippe's passport this time. "I did not say I would not allow you to marry. I merely said this is a serious matter, not something to be hurried into in a single morning. Documents must be checked. My assistant must draw up the proper papers."

"I understand perfectly, *monsieur le préfet.* Perhaps I can compensate you and your worthy assistant for the amount of work involved."

A fat white hand scooped up the bills and secreted them in a waistcoat pocket so rapidly that Claudia was not certain she had seen them on the desk.

"Monsieur Boissevain, I will do my best. May I suggest you return in a few days, and perhaps we can make the final arrangements then?"

"A few days!"

"Monsieur, marriage lasts a lifetime. What are a few days in a lifetime of happiness?" He stood and executed what would have been a bow had his stomach not made such a move impossible.

They walked across the square to the hotel Claudia had chosen last night. Philippe ordered two vermouths.

"Don't look so glum, darling." He tried to make his voice sound more cheerful than he felt.

"How can you say that, Philippe, when that horrible little man refuses to marry us?"

"He hasn't refused. It's just the bureaucratic way. The longer he hesitates, the more money we'll give him to hurry. He'll marry us in the end."

"In the end!" she snapped. "And when is the end? When we're forty or fifty and too old to care. When we've wasted most of our life sneaking from one shabby hotel room to another."

"Don't you think you're exaggerating? I'm as disappointed as you are, probably more so. Every day I have to wait gives you another day to change your mind." He laughed as he spoke, but there was no humor in his eyes. "We'll go back to his office Friday morning, pay the necessary bribes, and be married by nightfall."

"Do you think it's really possible? Do you think if you pay that horrible little man enough he'll agree to marry us?"

"Why wouldn't he? That's his job."

"Perhaps if you had given him more now, he would have done it today."

He laughed. "That isn't the way it works. No matter what I gave him today, he'd assume he would get the same amount Friday."

"What a terrible man!" she said, but Philippe knew he had reassured her. He only wished he were as confident. He knew bribes were not the prefect's only interest. If he suspected something wrong—and he obviously did—he would guess he could make more than Philippe's paltry bribes by revealing this secret marriage to someone, anyone, who might be interested. Philippe thought of leaving this afternoon, but he knew it would be the same in Locarno or Geneva or Zurich. He should have realized that before they left Paris, but it was too late now. All they could do was wait and hope the prefect turned up nothing. After all, Philippe reassured himself, it was unlikely that this obscure Swiss functionary could cast his line as far as London.

"The snows will come early this year," Frau Schwarzburgen observed as she removed their lunch things.

"The old cow was right," Claudia said as they started down the mountain. The first flakes were beginning to fall. It was a light, dry snow, but it came quickly, and by the time they were halfway down the ground was covered with a thin white film.

"I'm glad. The mountains are never more beautiful."

"They may be beautiful, but they're cold." She pulled the fox cape closer around her and took Philippe's arm with both hands to keep from slipping. Her spectator pumps were too fragile for hiking in the snow.

"The first thing we're going to do is get you some sensible shoes. Galoshes, I think."

When they reached the village, Philippe steered her past the fashionable shops to a small, cluttered store. She balked at the unattractive rubber boots, but he was obstinate.

"You only like them because Frau Schwarzburgen will approve." She pouted.

"I like them because they're sensible."

"Sensible. Philippe, when have you ever been sensible?"

"When it's snowing and I want to walk in the mountains. They'll keep your feet warm. Besides they call attention to your ankles."

That settled it. Claudia went stomping out into the fresh snow. Every few steps she executed a little dance that left large, patterned prints on the still-untrampled roadway.

Halfway up the mountain there was an inn. "Would you like some *Glühwein?* That hot red wine with spices and lemons Herr Schwarzburgen made us last night."

"I'd adore it."

The inn was dark and smoky. In a few hours it would be crowded with woodcutters, but it was empty now. The woman brought them two steaming mugs and disappeared. They were alone in front of the fire. Claudia stretched her feet toward the hearth. "Very chic."

"But they work."

"More or less."

Philippe slid from his chair to the hearth rug. He unlaced the boots and drew them from her feet. Then he sat with his mug in one hand, staring at the fire and absentmindedly rubbing her toes. His head lay against her knees, and she stroked his thick dark hair in time with his own movement. Neither of them stirred when the woman returned and replaced their empty mugs with fresh ones.

When Philippe finally spoke, Claudia did not know if it had been minutes or hours. "Do you think you're warm enough for the climb now?"

"Warm enough, but far too lazy."

"I know, but the workmen will be coming in soon." He began to lace up her boots.

The cold air stunned them. It was snowing harder and faster now, and the wind blew the flakes in their faces. The wine and the weather turned Claudia giddy. She ran a few steps back, grabbed a clump of snow, and tossed it at Philippe.

"Now you've done it. That's a declaration of war!" She began to run up the road, and he followed, pelting her with snowballs. She was laughing and taunting him, and Philippe followed with war cries. The road turned, but Claudia kept running straight through the pine trees and Philippe was behind her, and then they were rolling over and over in the snow. His lips were warm and tasted of the spiced wine.

"Surrender," he commanded.

She shook her head back and forth in the snow. "Never!"

His mouth was on hers again, and she could feel the wine pulsing through her veins and see the snow white and fragile against his hair.

"I'd better get you back before frostbite sets in." His voice was quiet as he helped her up, and they were silent the rest of the way up the mountain.

Frau Schwarzburgen had laid both fires, and Philippe had only to light a match. Claudia sank down on the hearth. The waves of heat were a welcome assault on her body, and she shrugged the furs from her shoulders.

"Would you like some more wine?"

She shook her head. The room was as silent as the snow falling in the twilight beyond the window. He sat beside her and once again began unlacing her boots. The back of his neck looked so vulnerable in the firelight she could not help touching it. Her fingers were cool against his skin, and he lifted his face to hers. Each time he kissed her it was as if she were tasting wine again. His tongue was sharp with the lemon and spices. He unbuttoned her sweater and the challis blouse beneath, and they lay back on her cloak, and she felt the fur soft against her skin. Philippe's body was hard and lean in the firelight, and his skin smelled of smoke and snow and pine needles. His hands traveled slowly, kindling exquisite little flames of pleasure. He was above her, and she could see the fire reflected in the dark pupils of his eyes. Then the room was black but full of fire, and her body shocked her in a convulsion of ecstasy.

She lay very still for a moment with her eyes closed. When she opened them, she saw Philippe's face only inches from hers. He was watching her closely and almost, but not quite, smiling.

She turned over and buried her face in his chest. "Don't ever let me make you unhappy again, darling. Don't ever let me sulk or behave like a spoiled child. I've been such a fool. I don't care about baths or Frau Schwarzburgen or *monsieur le préfet*. I don't even care if we're married. As long as we're together. You're all I want, Philippe, all I need. You won't ever let me forget that, will you, darling? Ever."

He stroked her hair that lay like a thick curtain over his chest. "Not if I can help it, Claudia. Not if I can help it."

The snow continued to fall through the evening. They dressed and Frau Schwarzburgen brought dinner and they ate and drank and talked a little before the fire and Frau Schwarzburgen came and took the things away and they undressed and made love again. He kissed her shoulder, and she saw his lashes black against the snow beyond the window; he kissed her breast, and she felt his teeth hard and teasing against her skin. She had known nothing of love, and sometimes she had worried about it; but she felt him inside her full and complete and surging, and she knew why she had known nothing. How could anyone have told her?

When the prefect had banished them until Friday, Claudia thought the day would never come, but the hours passed as a single hour. When she thought about this time in years to come—and she often would—the days became a collage of snow and pine trees and the two of them clinging together in the small, firelit room. She remembered the warmth of Philippe's body against hers as they lay together in the morning and watched the sun melt the crystals of ice on the window, the sound of his voice in the darkness, the taste of his skin, the look in his eyes after they had made love. She had thought she loved Philippe that first night in his room, but as the days passed in the chalet on the mountainside, her pleasure in him deepened and swelled until she thought she would burst with wanting and knowing him.

Claudia arose early Friday morning. She left Philippe sleeping and crept quietly down the hall to the bath. When she returned, he was sitting up in bed, smoking a cigarette.

"It's freezing," she said as she began to gather her clothes to take them into the small dressing closet.

"You'll be warmer if you dress in front of the fire." She stood for a moment feeling awkward. "For me," he said quietly.

Her back was to him as she stepped into the white satin chemise. She felt him behind her, and his arms went around her and his fingers were buttoning the tiny mother-of-pearl disks that ran down one side. His beard was rough against her skin. "My wife," he whispered. "Ma femme."

The prefect's assistant showed them into the stuffy little office as soon as they arrived.

"Ah, *monsieur le comte,* I have been waiting for

you." So it was no longer Monsieur Boissevain. The prefect had made his investigation. "You should have established your identity immediately. *Monsieur* Boissevain, indeed." The prefect chuckled to himself at the futility of anyone's attempting to escape his net.

"Would it have facilitated matters?"

"Perhaps, perhaps."

"Well, there's no point in arguing about that now. We're here; the papers are in order; I trust you can marry us without further delay." Philippe began to reach into his pocket, but the prefect had more than money on his mind this morning.

"Ah, youth, ever in a hurry. Not so fast, *monsieur le comte*, not so fast." He opened a folder on his desk. "About this matter with the authorities . . . in Paris . . . last January . . ."

"That matter is closed."

The prefect's face was a mask of sympathy. "To be sure, *monsieur le comte*, to be sure. All the same, one can't be too careful."

"But that's absurd!" Philippe's fist, empty this time, came down with a bang on the prefect's desk.

The prefect drew himself up to all of his five feet three inches. *"Monsieur!* You are in an office of the government of the Swiss Republic. Histrionics are pointless. The French authorities have assured me this little matter"—he tapped his thick finger against the folder —"has been taken care of. I am now waiting for reports from the Swiss government. Once it is clear that you are in good standing in our country, that this unfortunate little incident has not had far-reaching repercussions, I see no obstacles to the marriage. That is assuming, of course, the reports on Mademoiselle Trenholm are in order."

Philippe felt Claudia stiffen. "Mademoiselle Trenholm is an American citizen."

"So I see." The fat fingers turned the passport over and over. "Still, one must always be ready for a surprise. Take you, for example, *monsieur le comte*. I was not surprised to find that Monsieur Boissevain was in fact le Comte de Boissevain, but I was surprised to discover this unusual chapter in your past. Who knows what surprises Mademoiselle Trenholm has in store?"

"*Monsieur le préfet,* you are being insulting."

"Not at all, *monsieur le comte,* not at all. A lovely lady should always have a bit of mystery about her." He turned to Claudia. "Is that not so, *mademoiselle?*" Claudia turned away from the leering little eyes.

"You must not be impatient, *monsieur le comte.* Now that the snow has come, the sports will be good. Have a pleasant weekend and come back sometime next week." He held up his hand. "But not Monday. On Monday I must escort *madame le préfet* to Geneva. My son studies there. Perhaps Tuesday or even Wednesday."

Philippe's reassurance echoed in Claudia's ears all the way back to the chalet. She heard his words, but they had no meaning for her.

He tried to prove to her with logic that once the Swiss reports were in, the prefect would be happy to marry them. He tried to tease her out of her mood. Later, alone in their room, he tried to show her with his hands and his mouth and his body what he had not been able to convince her of with words, but Claudia drew away from him in the darkness. Perhaps it was the one argument she knew could win her, and she did not want to be won now. Time was running out.

"No!" She got out of bed. In the darkness she was a pale silhouette that disappeared into a velvet dressing gown. Philippe sat up and turned on the small bedside lamp. He lit a cigarette and waited for her to speak.

"Daddy will be back in Paris tomorrow night."

"And think you're in Italy."

"What if he goes to Italy?"

"I think that's unlikely, Claudia."

"He's certain to call."

"Mrs. Priestly-Soames can say you're away for a few days with friends."

"What if the prefect refuses to marry us on Tuesday?"

"I doubt that he will, but if he does, then we'll go back to Paris and be married there. Or at the château if you prefer."

"But it will be too late then."

"Too late?"

"What if Daddy finds out before we're married?"

"As I said, I think it's unlikely, but if he does, we'll simply marry anyway. In fact, if you think about it, he'll probably call me a swine and insist we marry."

"Oh, Philippe, don't be horrid."

"I'm trying to be rational. Things haven't worked out as we planned, and I'm deeply sorry for that, Claudia. I'm sorry for every minute of disappointment or unpleasantness you've had to endure, but nothing has changed. We still have each other. Isn't that what you said that night in my room? It was true then, and it's more true now. Trust me, Claudia."

"I did trust you, and look where it's got us."

"It's got us a week together. It will get us a lifetime if you'll only be patient."

"But don't you see, it's too late. Tuesday will be too late to be married. Daddy will be back before then, and he's bound to find out and . . . and I couldn't bear that."

"Could you bear not being married now, after this?"

"I'm not talking about not being married, Philippe. It's just that . . . well, I don't want Daddy to know about this week. I can't bear to think he'll find out. If we go back now, he won't have to. He'll think I've been in Italy, and we'll have gained a little time, and then I'll be able to bring him around to a proper wedding."

He could not believe his ears. After the last week, she could still say the same foolish things. "Claudia, we've been through this a hundred times. Why won't you understand? Either you stay here now, either we marry here as soon as possible, or we won't marry at all."

"Are you giving me an ultimatum, Philippe?"

"I'm merely trying to make you see things as they are. Your father will never consent to our marriage. Not tomorrow . . . not next month . . . not next year. Our only hope is to present him with the accomplished fact."

"That's what you said that night in your room—a *fait accompli*. That was your idea, not mine," she snapped. "You never stopped to think how it would hurt Daddy or . . . or what he would think of me after this week."

"And that's more important to you than anything else." She saw his eyes flicker in anger and was around the bed and in his arms.

"Of course not. Nothing is more important than us, but the point is it doesn't have to be one or the other." She thought of that breakfast conversation with her father when they had first returned to Paris. "You leave Daddy to me. If we start tomorrow, we can be back in Paris before he is, and no one will ever have to know anything about this week."

"No one except the two of us."

"Of course, darling, the two of us. *We'll* always have this week."

She lifted her face to him expectantly. She had won her point. She would have Philippe *and* Daddy. She would have, she thought as he drew her down beside him and she felt his hands beneath the velvet robe, everything. But Philippe knew they would have nothing and his hands moved as if he were committing something to memory.

The morning after Claudia returned to Paris, two days before they were to sail, she lingered behind when Elizabeth and Katherine went to Poiret's for a final fitting. She found James hat in hand in the foyer.

"Daddy, there's something I'd like to talk to you about."

"Of course, Claudia, anything." He waited expectantly.

"I mean really talk."

"Well, of course we'll really talk, child. We'll have days to talk on the ship, but right now I have an appointment. Of course, if it's something important, something that can't wait. . . ."

"No, Daddy, it can wait." He was right. There would be plenty of time to talk on the ship. Or so it seemed in Paris. But somehow the days of the crossing slipped away without that crucial conversation. Claudia had never wanted anything so intensely in her life—and had never feared asking for it quite so much.

7

The skyline of Manhattan glistened in the early-morning sun. The steel buildings rose like spikes against the blue sky. Claudia remembered a softer Paris skyline of domes and steeples, a skyline where churches still towered.

She began to pick out familiar streets and scenes. There was the Woolworth Building and farther uptown a roof garden where she had danced more than one night away. She had never danced there with Philippe, nor had she walked these streets with him.

The Brewster town car laden with hand luggage— the rest would be sent along later—inched through the early-morning traffic. As Henry, the chauffeur, turned the car off Fifth Avenue and onto Sixty-ninth Street, Claudia felt a surge of familiar pleasure. How she would miss this house when she was married. She had been born in it, grown from infant to child to young woman in its rooms.

The small brass plate beside the front door sparkled in the sun like a homing beacon, a sign that nothing had changed. The rest of New York could go on reaching toward the sky, but the little house on the corner of Fifth Avenue and Sixty-ninth Street held its ground. James Trenholm saw to that. He had been offered a good deal more than the house was worth several times since the war, but he had no intention of selling. This was the home he had built for himself and his family. It was more than a monument to his wealth; it was a sign of his stability.

James had built it in the nineties. He could have

afforded a house before that, but not the sort he wanted. It was one of the most sumptuous town houses to be built in the area—and one of the last. Even before the war they were becoming too costly to construct or to run. Materials had become expensive and then, during the war, impossible to obtain. And these days who had the servants to run a four-story town house? Even if one could find servants, they were never properly trained. There was no question about it, the day of the New York town house was past. Since the war the trend was to those tall apartment buildings that lined Park Avenue. James owned several. He didn't mind owning them, but he was damned if he'd live there. All right for young people, perhaps, but not for him.

Claudia recognized every stone and pillar of the familiar Renaissance façade. She could climb the few steps to the huge iron grille door blindfolded. Hadn't she skipped up and down them thousands of times in the past?

Inside everything was just as she remembered it, including the servants assembled in the foyer to welcome them. The damask draperies of the large reception room on the first floor were closed against the early-autumn sunshine. The big curving marble stairway seemed to draw her upstairs. The formal living room was exactly the same, the Duncan Phyfe and Sheraton chairs, the Hepplewhite tables, the portrait of her mother over the marble mantel. It was one of the last portraits Sargent had done before he gave up painting the wives and children of the rich.

James was proud of the portrait and careful to call a visitor's attention to it. He always pointed out the fine technique of the oils, a subtle coup since the artist had not been strictly faithful to his word and had gone on sketching certain chosen women and children. It was not especially significant to have a drawing of one's wife by Sargent, but it was becoming increasingly rare to have a portrait of her in oil.

Claudia would miss the house, there was no doubt about that. But she could live with any deprivation so long as she had Philippe. Even without her father's approval? Philippe had asked once. Well, she supposed she could, but why should she have to? Daddy would let her have what she wanted. Now if only she could muster the courage to ask for it. But of course, asking outright gave Daddy the chance to refuse outright. It was a chance she knew she had to take, but somehow she was having a hard time finding the right moment to take it.

Samuel Livingston Beaumont was a sportsman. It was evident not only in the breadth of his shoulders, the wide expanse of chest, the powerful arms and legs, but also in the grace with which he carried himself. He stood now leaning against the bar in the Yale Club, and there was an ease about him equaled by few men in the room. He was perfectly at home in his body. It was the instrument of his pleasure from tennis to golf, polo to sailing. There was about Sam none of the big man's clumsiness. Indeed, except on the playing field, he appeared smaller and slimmer than he was. His perfectly tailored clothes saw to that. Sam's jackets never strained against the massive bulk of his back; his sleeves never pulled against his well-developed biceps. Samuel Beaumont was a sportsman, but he was a gentleman as well.

There was none of the professional athlete's intensity about Sam. That would be bad form. Good form, bad form, right and wrong—all were clearly defined in Sam's mind. Not that he would ever speak openly of that sort of thing. That in itself was bad form. There were more subtle ways of expressing one's standards.

One could, for example, speak about drinking, provided one did not brag about it. Whiskey was okay, Sam liked to say, as long as you controlled it. A highball or two before dinner was expected. An occasional binge acceptable. If you went too far, you simply went on the wagon for a few days or a week. By that time your game was back in shape and you were all the better for the spree. After all, no one liked a fellow who worked too hard.

This was Sam Beaumont's attitude, one might even

say his philosophy. It was also the philosophy of the young men with whom he stood drinking. It took more than family and money, more than Groton and Yale to make a gentleman. It took the right attitude toward things—be it work, women, or polo ponies. And the right attitude, of course, meant moderation. Respect must be colored by a touch of sophisticated cynicism, competitiveness hidden under a veneer of sportsmanship. There was no place for idealism, and ambition was bad form. This was the creed of their fathers, and it would be the creed of their sons. It was the adhesive binding their class together, and surely they had to keep together. Like old Anson Hagerty, who had just entered the bar. No one really liked Anson, but he was one of them and he played by the rules—most of the time. So long as he did he deserved to belong.

Anson worked his way down the bar, greeting the men he knew, and joined Sam's small group. "I saw an old friend of yours today, Anson." Grant Walbridge had been graduated the same year as Anson, and though he liked him little more than the others did, he felt a special bond, however slight. "I ran into Claudia Trenholm on Forty-fourth Street. She was coming out of Delmonico's with Alicia Sibbington, and she really bowled me over. She was something before she went away, but she's sensational now."

"It must be all that old-world charm—maybe I should say experience—she picked up in Paris," Anson said.

"What's that supposed to mean?"

"Just that there was some talk. Nothing really, only that she was supposed to marry some French guy, a penny ante count, and then she didn't. Suddenly old James Trenholm himself shows up, and Claudia is spirited off to Italy. The whole thing sounds a little fishy if you ask me."

"Are you trying to tell us something, Anson?"

"Well, Grant, old boy, you're the Phi Bete. You put it together. Girl's supposed to get married; girl doesn't get married; girl disappears for a few months. Now I'm not saying our little Claudia wasn't soaking up culture in Italy and Spain, but then again I'm not saying she was."

"Drop it," Sam cut in. Sam had his standards, and one of them was that you did not talk that way about the girls you grew up with. Not unless they gave you some pretty good reason to, and even then you were better off keeping it to yourself. "A joke's a joke, but that isn't funny. Besides, she's only a kid."

"She isn't a kid anymore," Grant said. "That's what I was trying to tell you."

"Whether she's a kid or not, it's pretty sordid gossip, Anson, and I don't want to hear it." By virtue of his family, his money, his reputation as a sportsman, and his membership in Skull and Bones, Sam Beaumont could afford to take this tack with Anson. Nobody could ever call Sam a prig, and everybody knew Anson was a boor.

"Okay, Sam, okay. Forget I mentioned the whole thing. Who's driving up to New Haven for the game Saturday?"

"I've got to look at some ponies on the Island."

"I hear you have quite a string these days, Sam."

"Anytime this spring you want to come out and play, Anson, I'll be happy to let you ride. Provided you treat the pony with more consideration than you do the reputations of most ladies." Everyone laughed appreciatively. Sam Beaumont was a good fellow. He had put Anson in his place with a minimum of bad feeling. It was the way things ought to be done.

Elizabeth Trenholm sat at the Chippendale writing desk in her small sitting room. "I think we ought to have a dinner before Alicia Sibbington's dance. Don't you think so, dear?" She was speaking to Katherine, who was stretched out on the silk-covered chaise, leafing through the latest issue of *Town and Country*.

"If you like, Mother."

It was one approach to the problem, Elizabeth thought, for Katherine was showing every sign of becoming a problem. Elizabeth was fairly sure her daughter's low spirits had nothing to do with leaving Paris.

More likely they could be traced to Samuel Beaumont. He'd come to call a week ago, and Katherine had seen him twice since then. Once they had gone dancing, and once she had driven with him to New Jersey to look at a polo pony. Both times Kate had gone off radiant with expectation, only to return home silent and sullen.

Katherine could not ask for a better match than Sam Beaumont. His family was impeccable. His father's people were bankers who traced their fortune back to the old China trade, and the slave trade as well, Elizabeth suspected with her southern sense of such things. His mother had been one of the New York Livingstons, one of them, moreover, who had the sense not to sell the land owned so early in the city's history. Yes, Samuel Beaumont's credentials were every bit as good as Elizabeth's own, even if they were Yankee, and what was more, the Beaumonts still had the money that went along with those credentials. There were many in New York who speculated on the size of James Trenholm's fortune. The Beaumont holdings, old and carefully diversified, defied popular accounting. Even James, who knew a great deal about the real and imagined wealth of many New York families, could not guess whether the Beaumont fortune was twice or twenty times his own. Had he been forced to make an estimate, however, he probably would have chosen the latter figure.

There were other indications the match would be a good one. Sam and Katherine seemed to share that passion for horses and sailing and all those pursuits Elizabeth Trenholm lumped vaguely together. *How I ever had a daughter like that I can't imagine,* she had thought more than once. Certainly, they were the sorts of things young girls were expected to be proficient in, but not the sorts of things one took very seriously after the age of fifteen, except, of course, to admire a man who excelled in them. *No,* Elizabeth thought, *in that respect Claudia is more like me. We're more delicate. But all the same, if it makes Kate happy and it certainly seems to, and Sam seems to like having her interested in those things . . . yes, it would be a spectacular match: background, breeding, wealth, and shared interests.*

What mother could want more for her daughter? What girl could dream of more for herself?

All the same, Elizabeth suspected Sam might need a little push. He'd been having too good a time since the war—all the young men had—to be overly eager to settle down. And he was a little too popular with women for him to fall head over heels in love with Katherine. But if lots of girls, and their mothers, pursued him, he had shown no special interest in any of them. Kate had the inside track if anyone did. Elizabeth was sure of that.

"A dozen people, perhaps fourteen. No more than that. A dinner before a ball should be intimate. Now let's see, the young men, we'll do them first. They're always so much harder to find than young women. . . . We'll invite the Winston boy, maybe both of them. How old is the younger one, Kate?"

"He's still an undergraduate."

"Well, your sister is only twenty-one, dear. But perhaps you're right. Only the older Winston boy then. And Grant Walbridge. And Sam Beaumont, of course. We couldn't have a dinner for you and Claudia without Sam."

Katherine looked at her mother sharply but said nothing.

"And I think Anson Hagerty. He has the advantage of always accepting."

"What about Anson Hagerty?" Claudia asked. She had been walking in the park, and her pleated skirt and long sweater carried the woodsy smell of the last autumn leaves.

"Kate and I are making a list, dear. I thought we'd have a small dinner before Alicia Sibbington's dance."

"If you like, Mother."

"If I like! It's for you and Kate, not for me. I must say both of you have been acting strangely since you've come home. I'm trying to arrange a party, and neither of you is particularly enthusiastic."

"Perhaps Claudia finds American dinner parties dull," Katherine said casually, still turning the pages of her magazine.

"Oh, Kate, why can't you leave me alone?"

"Yes, Katherine, that was not a kind remark. Now I want both of you to stop bickering and to help me with this list."

It did not, Elizabeth thought as the three women began to toss names back and forth, look like an easy season ahead.

Despite Claudia's apathy and Katherine's edginess, the dinner went well. It was a crisp early-winter evening, the sort that put color in the cheeks of the young girls. Everyone was in high spirits, including Elizabeth, who ran the party with a quiet firmness, never intruding on the young people, but making sure each stage of the evening flowed smoothly into the next.

Early on that was no easy task. More than one of the young men would have preferred to linger longer over cocktails. Elizabeth, however, had her rules, even if they were never stated as such. One highball was quite enough. There would be wine with dinner, a superb wine that was not easy to get these days with bootleggers pasting all sorts of labels on heaven only knew what kind of liquid. There would be champagne at the ball as well, and more than one cutaway bulged unbecomingly at the breast. Even Tiffany's slimmest silver flask was too bulky for a well-tailored tailcoat.

Sam Beaumont had arrived early with a bouquet for Katherine and a preoccupied air. Kate had noticed the air even before the bouquet, but the arrival of more guests fast on Sam's heels made it impossible for her to do more than guess at what it was that made Sam, always so at ease in society, suddenly uncomfortable.

Just an hour earlier he had held a long, albeit silent conversation with himself in his shaving mirror. Now that Kate was home, he told himself, looking sternly into eyes so clear they dared distrust, he had to make a choice. He had either to stop seeing her or to ask her to marry him. Anything less would be less than fair to Kate.

Sam wasn't vain, but he didn't have to be to guess Kate's feelings. She would marry him in a minute. She would also wait months and years. That was precisely why Sam had to make up his mind. To keep Katherine dangling while he played the bachelor-about-town was not cricket.

Could he give her up completely? he asked himself as he drew the blade neatly across the bottom of his left sideburn. She had been part of his world for so long, he'd come to think of her as existing for the sole purpose of complementing his pleasures. If he hadn't missed her as much as he had expected the year she was abroad or for the time he was in the Army, it was only because he knew these separations were temporary.

It seemed to Sam as he washed off the last traces of lather that he had made his decision years ago, that he had known the outcome of his life at age twelve. He would ask Katherine to marry him. Time he settled down. His father never mentioned it, but Sam knew the old man wanted grandchildren. His wife's death had made him conscious of his own mortality.

Sam flashed an appreciative parting smile at himself in the mirror. He would like being a father. He'd had enough of the bachelor life. A wife, a home, a couple of sons he could teach to ride and sail, and maybe a daughter, a pretty thing to spoil. This new image of himself delighted Sam. He would speak to Katherine that night.

Sam had been so absorbed in his plans when he arrived at the Trenholms he had not at first noticed Claudia. She was standing in a far corner of the room, talking to Grant Walbridge and a younger man Sam had seen at the Yale Club but whose name he did not know. Now, as she turned to greet other guests, he was struck by the reality of what Grant had told him that afternoon last week. Claudia was a beauty.

Sam remembered vaguely that Claudia had been touted as the belle of the season when she first came out. Each time he heard the report, three more proposals had been added to the tally of her conquests. Sam had paid little attention. Stories like that followed all the more popular girls the year they came out, and though he had admitted she was a pretty little thing, she had struck him then as young and undeveloped. There had been something missing in Claudia that first season. It was as if her girlish slimness had been the outward sign of an emotional thinness.

All that was changed now, Sam realized as he took in the young woman across the room. She moved differently. She was no longer a coltish, unripe girl. She was a woman. Every gesture, every stance proclaimed that.

It had nothing to do with the silly story Anson Hagerty had told that afternoon at the Yale Club. Sam had been around enough to know the old wives' tale about a woman's being changed by a sexual experience was just that, a myth and nothing more. He had known mothers of large families who struck him as icy and virginal, and he had met innocent young girls whose mere presence aroused him. It was nothing obvious or intentional. That would have been cheap, and Sam had no taste for cheapness. It was simply that some women had a sensual presence and some did not. Claudia Trenholm did. And it excited Sam enormously.

As he started across the room toward Claudia, he felt a restraining hand on his arm. "I was beginning to think we'd never have a moment to talk." Kate indicated the room full of guests with a toss of her head. "How did the race go on Sunday? I wanted to get up for the weekend, but I had the tiniest sniffle, and Mother insisted that a day on Lake Placid would turn it into pneumonia. I saw you came in third."

Katherine had expected a detailed account of the race. Bobsledding was not Sam's favorite sport—it couldn't compare with sailing or polo—but it was competitive, and that would be enough to make Sam dissatisfied with third place. Normally he'd have given Kate a detailed account of the heats and why he hadn't won. He would take full responsibility, she knew. Sam was not a man to blame failure on another member of the team.

The fact that Katherine had heard it all before—the detailed accounts of the polo match, the regatta, the tennis match, the bobsled race—made it no less interesting to her. As long as it was Sam telling the story, she could listen endlessly. She had certainly expected a full report tonight. Instead, he merely shrugged and said, yes, they hadn't done too badly.

Third place not too bad for Sam Beaumont! *I was right,* Kate thought as she took Sam's arm to go into dinner. *Something is wrong.*

Sam stood in the foyer of the ballroom of the Ritz Carlton with two dozen other young men. The conversation was general and noisy, and more than one flask made a brief appearance. As each girl emerged from the dressing room, freshly powdered and smoothly combed, a young man, sometimes more than one, would detach himself from the crowd and spring to her side. Several of the girls greeted Sam warmly as they passed. They knew he was waiting for Katherine, but the evening ahead was a long one with many dances. Anything might happen.

Claudia appeared in the doorway to the dressing room, swaying a bit in time to the music, and Sam saw half a dozen men surround her. She smiled at them absently. They seemed to have no more individuality for her than the line of perfectly matched orange trees adorning the entrance to the ballroom. For the second time that evening Sam remembered Anson's story. It was a nasty story, and Sam gave it no credence; but he was sure of one thing. Something had happened to Claudia during her year abroad. It took more than a mere glimpse of life on the Continent to make a girl, even a very popular girl, that blasé.

Sam danced with Katherine until they were cut in on, did a brief turn around the ballroom with Alicia Sibbington, who had just been freed from her responsibilities on the receiving line, then made his way toward Claudia. He tapped the dark shoulder of another indistinguishable admirer, who rewarded him with a black look, and took Claudia politely but securely in his arms. It was a brisk fox-trot, and he led her lightly about the room, expertly avoiding other couples, as well as any stag who looked as if he were about to cut in.

"Do you realize this is the first time we've seen each other since you've been home?"

"Mmmm," Claudia hummed half in answer, half in time to the music. "Who's sorry now, who's sorry now?" Sam had the distinct impression he was another orange tree. Claudia seemed to be looking through him.

"You look swell, just swell." Suddenly Sam felt more like an undergraduate than he had at any time in the last five years. "You certainly have changed."

Suddenly Claudia laughed, not an absentminded smile, but a real laugh. "That sounds as if I looked pretty terrible before I went away."

What was wrong with him anyway? He was no child.

"You know that isn't what I meant. It's just that you seem to have changed . . . grown up, if you like."

"You only think that because you thought I was such a baby before." She pouted a little, pleased at the fact that Samuel Beaumont had finally taken notice of her—and was impressed. Sam wasn't Philippe, but at least he wasn't Anson or that flock of dullards who kept cutting in on each other endlessly. Sam's success in steering around the stags hadn't escaped her.

"Well, you were a baby."

"Who's sorry now?" Claudia hummed along. *"Whose heart is aching for breaking each vow?"*

"Hair in pigtails and as I remember it, you always seemed to have ice cream or something sticky on your face."

"Sam Beaumont." Claudia stamped her foot without losing a beat. "I never in my life looked like that!"

"But what a pretty face." The music came to an end. "Next time I'll have to bribe the orchestra."

"And be arrested for cradle snatching," Claudia tossed over her shoulder as she danced off in another pair of arms. No, he wasn't Philippe, Claudia thought as she smiled absently at the young man who was replacing the one who had taken her from Sam, but he was the first conquest she'd enjoyed in ages.

Toward the end of the evening Sam cut in again. This time there was definite recognition in her smile.

"I think what I was trying to say before"—he resumed the old tack—"was that you look terrific to-night."

"It's my new Molyneux. Terribly chic, you know."

"I doubt very much it's your new Molyneux. But even if it is, you're not supposed to tell me."

"I know. That's why I told you." And then without missing a beat: "You're a marvelous dancer, Sam. I didn't think all that coordination carried over to the dance floor."

"It doesn't usually. It's you. I'm simply rising to the occasion. What did you do, tango your way around Paris? The tango craze was just coming in when I was sent home."

"Actually I didn't tango very much." Claudia remembered all the times she and Philippe had chosen to sit and talk instead.

"Somehow I find the idea of you as a wallflower a little hard to swallow."

"I never said I was a wallflower. I merely said I hadn't danced much in Paris."

"In that case we have some catching up to do. Kate and I are going dancing tomorrow night. Why don't you and one of that swarm of stags that follow you around join us?"

"I'm going to a play with Grant . . . or with George Talbott tomorrow. I'm not sure which."

"I'll bet Grant and George are sure."

"They always keep track."

"Well, in that case, you bring Grant or George or whoever it is along and meet us at the Stork afterward."

"Aren't you afraid I'm a little young for a speakeasy —even one called the Stork—with my hair in pigtails and all that sticky stuff on my face?"

"Well"—he laughed down at her—"I know it's dangerous, but I'll take my chances."

It was only after Sam was back in his room in the old Federal house on Washington Square, leafing through a catalog of sailing equipment and finishing the last inch of a tumbler of scotch and milk, his usual bedtime tonic after a night on the town, that he realized he had never had that conversation with Kate. Well, he reassured himself, there was no rush. He could speak to her just as well tomorrow night or, even better, at that house party this weekend. Yes, that was a much better idea. He didn't want to propose in a speakeasy. He'd wait till the weekend when they were in the country. After all, the setting was important. He planned to do this properly.

Sam never got around to speaking to Kate that weekend or for several weeks after that, although it wasn't for lack of opportunity. Since the evening he had decided to marry Kate, Sam seemed to be seeing more of her than ever. He dined and lunched at the Trenholms' as often as he was invited, which was as often as Elizabeth thought proper prior to an official engagement. More often than not they went out with a group of young people, including Claudia and one of any number of young men who had become almost as indistinguishable to Sam as they were to Claudia. And on the weekends there were house parties in New Jersey or on Long Island. If Kate found their time together too crowded by other people, she never said anything.

Elizabeth, for her part, was heartened by the turn the season was taking. She was expecting a proposal any moment now. Why else would Sam be around day and night? Not that she minded his presence. Indeed, she enjoyed it almost as much as both of her daughters did. And that was another thing. Sam was so wonderfully kind to Claudia. Elizabeth guessed that he'd heard about her experience in Paris. Gossip, even transatlantic gossip, travels easily in limited circles. What a fine young man Sam was to take such an interest in Katherine's younger sister. Sam Beaumont would make a good husband.

James Trenholm did not share his wife's optimism. "Why isn't he ever alone with Kate? Does he think marriage—and I assume it's marriage he has in mind—is a group effort?"

"Now, James, don't be unreasonable. If he and Katherine did spend a great deal of time alone, you'd be complaining about that. Just be happy that the young man and Katherine have some sense. So few young people today do. Just because they fought a war, they think they're entitled to do anything they want in peacetime. I don't suppose young people acted that way after the War Between the States. Certainly Daddy never did."

James ignored this reference to the late colonel and his heroic past. "I hope you're right, dear. It's just that half the time I can't tell whether it's Kate he's after or Claudia."

"What an absurd thing to say, James! Why, it's always been Sam and Kate. He's merely being kind to Katherine's younger sister. Just as he's polite to you and me. Sam Beaumont has beautiful manners, and that's all there is to it."

"Maybe, but I don't think it's natural. Now I know I never had 'beautiful manners,' dear," James went on quickly, ignoring his wife's attempt to contradict him, "like all those southern gentlemen I had to sweep off the veranda to get to you, but I knew what I wanted the minute I saw you, and it wasn't a long or crowded courtship. The point is that Sam ought to be trying to find ways to get off alone with Kate even if we don't want him to."

"Well, dear, I don't think you'll have to worry about that much longer. I suspect it's only a matter of weeks now, perhaps even days, before Sam proposes."

It was not, however, Sam Beaumont who knocked on the heavy oak doors to James' study the next evening. James was surprised to see his younger daughter dressed in a pair of wide-legged crepe de chine pants and a long matching top.

"What are those things you're wearing?" James had little time for fashion—twice yearly his tailor sent him fabrics from London and he sent back his order—but he enjoyed keeping his three women in the latest styles. They carried them off so well.

"Lounging pajamas, of course. Don't you know anything, you old bear?"

"Then you're not going out tonight?"

"No, I had a sniffle this afternoon, and Mother

thought a night at home would be good for me. Besides, Mother's playing bridge at the Cabbots' and Kate's off with Sam so that leaves the two of us. I'd much rather spend a quiet evening with you, Daddy, than go dancing with some callow youth. Why, I just love older men."

James was delighted. This was the daughter he remembered, the one he'd sent off to Paris more than a year ago. Now that she was back, he realized how much he'd missed her.

"Well, I may not be up to your style"—he indicated his comfortably worn smoking jacket—"but I'm still the best old at-home companion around. What will it be? Backgammon, cards, or just talk? It seems to me we haven't done that for a while."

"Much too long a while, Daddy," Claudia said, curling up in the big wing chair on the other side of the fire and preparing her attack. She had waited long enough. It was time to speak—more than time. She did not know how she had let things go this long.

"Actually, Daddy, I do want to talk to you."

"Does it have anything to do with the fact that you and your mother were down on Thirty-seventh Street at Tiffany's this afternoon?" He looked forward to buying her whatever bauble had taken her fancy.

"No, Daddy, it has nothing to do with Tiffany's."

"Something more serious than Tiffany's. Let me guess." He chewed on his cigar thoughtfully. "An affair of the heart?"

Claudia nodded eagerly. This was going to be easier than she'd dared hope.

"Well, I guess I've been remiss as a father. There's been such an army of young men in and out of here in the last few months, I guess I haven't noticed the important one. *The* one, I should say. I know! That Walbridge fellow. What's his name? Grant, that's it. Don't know the family. Father's a minister, isn't he? Well, not much money there, I imagine, but that's not important. The boy's a go-getter. I can see that. Down on the Street, isn't he?"

"No, Daddy, it isn't Grant."

"Well then, who is it, child? No point in guessing games. We'd be here all night."

"It's Philippe." Claudia spoke very quietly, and at first James thought he had not heard correctly.

"Who did you say?"

"Philippe."

His fist came down heavily on the arm of his chair. "I forbade you to see him, Claudia. What's been going on behind my back?"

"Nothing, Daddy, nothing's been going on behind your back." Claudia lied and tried to force Montreux from her mind. "But nothing has changed either. I still love him. And he still loves me. We've just been waiting. . . ."

By this time James was pacing back and forth, his cigar clamped in his teeth. "I forbade you to see him. Not for a few weeks or a few months, but forever. I don't know how to make that any clearer."

"But, Daddy, you've never let me explain."

"There is *nothing* to explain. The young man is no good. I suspected it from the beginning. Events proved me right. Damn it, Claudia, do you need any more than those headlines, those pictures in the paper to prove that to you?"

"Yes!" she said hotly. She was frightened—she'd never heard her father swear before—but she was angry and determined as well. "Yes, I need more than that to convince me Philippe is no good. I know what he's really like. He has ideals and principles. He's kind, and he cares about things—things and people. He cares about me." She looked her father in the eye. "Which is more than you seem to do." She saw the hurt flash in his eyes.

"Claudia, I could let you marry him tomorrow. That would be the easy thing. Don't you know that making you happy has always been the easy thing for me? But it isn't right. You'd be happy for a month and miserable for the rest of your life. Can you see yourself living in a cold-water flat, an outcast?"

"Oh, Daddy, now you're the one who's talking like a child. All that's behind Philippe. He's changed."

"People like that never change, Claudia. I know. I've been fighting them all my life." He thought of that threatening letter he'd received four years ago and shuddered at the danger to his home and family. "And no daughter of mine is going to marry one of them."

James stopped pacing and stood towering over Claudia's chair. He spoke deliberately. "I see now that you didn't believe me, Claudia. You thought you could bring me around." He saw the embarrassment in her face. "As you always have. Well not this time. I'll never give into you on this. Never. The matter is closed. Now will you ring for some tea or would you like a brandy? Perhaps we both could use one."

"Nothing, thank you, Daddy. I think I'll just go to bed."

Claudia went straight to bed as promised, but she did not sleep. Instead, she lay awake until the early hours of the morning planning.

Philippe had been right. Her father would never consent. Yet marry Philippe she would. She remembered that first afternoon when Philippe had asked her what she would do if she wanted something, really wanted it, and it were denied her. "I'd fight for it," she had answered without a moment's hesitation.

"And would you win?" he had asked.

She almost hadn't. Through her own blindness she'd almost lost what she wanted more than anything else in the world. Well, she'd come to her senses now. No more ploys, no more stratagems. With or without her father's approval, she would marry the man she loved.

She started the letter shortly after dawn. She wrote several drafts and, after she had completed each, tore it into small pieces, small enough that not even the most interested maid could piece it together again.

Claudia was surprised at how difficult the letter was to compose. The months and miles had separated her from Philippe more than she had known. What if he hadn't waited? What if he'd suffered enough of Claudia and her stubborn insistence that things be done her way? Why should he cross an ocean to fight her family and all the resources their society could muster? France was full of girls who would be his without a moment's hesitation. With less resolution than she had opened it, Claudia closed the little Sheraton writing desk and began to dress for lunch.

As she entered a small private dining room of the Ritz Carlton, crowded with a dozen chattering women, she wondered what Philippe would make of it all. What would he with his fine humanitarian sentiments, as Harry had once called them, say about all this elegant charity, all these girls and young matrons eager to get through the business at hand in order to turn their attention to matters nearer and dearer to their hearts—the most recent engagement, the latest hint of a breakup, who had gone where and been seen by whom?

At her right Lucinda Ardsley, her auburn hair sleekly marcelled, her pale eyes glinting with malice, sat like a sly little fox, and Claudia had the uncomfortable feeling Lucinda had spent the holidays abroad and returned barely a fortnight ago.

"Don't you just hate being home?" Lucinda crooned. "Everything is so dull—after Paris, I mean. And the men, they're all so . . . so provincial."

"You'll get used to New York again."

"Never. I never want to. New York is so . . . so provincial after Paris." Apparently Lucinda's education had included a new word. "It's all so dull after what I've seen. I saw the real Paris. The Paris of the Parisians." Claudia couldn't help smiling at how much like her cousins the Kelways Lucinda sounded. "Most Americans don't, you know, but I did. Just before I left, I went to the most wonderful masked ball. Out of hundreds of people, I don't think there were a dozen Americans." It occurred to Claudia that Lucinda was getting at something after all.

"The French know how to do these things, you know. They have so much style, such flair. One woman, for instance, but then, what am I saying, you must know her. The Marquise de Boissevain. She was simply stupendous. There were any number of women in Louis Quatorze costumes, but hers, well, it was just different. But it wasn't only the costume. It was the way she carried it off. I wanted to curtsy every time she looked at me. But of course, you of all people know how grand she is."

Claudia kept her head down, suddenly intent upon her lunch. She would not ask if Philippe had been there. She would not give Lucinda the satisfaction. Besides, she did not trust her voice.

"And of course, the count was there, too. He's so dashing. And so original. He and the woman he was with were dressed as. . . ."

Claudia couldn't hear another word above the pounding of her heart. She was sure Lucinda, everyone at the table, must be able to hear it. She didn't care. Nothing mattered now except the awful fact she had been right. Philippe had not waited. She clamped her jaw together to fight back the tears. There would be time for those later.

Still Lucinda chattered on. "Perhaps lovely isn't the right word for Mademoiselle de Chauvres. You know, the duchesse's niece. Striking. Yes, that's it, she was simply striking. A definite *type* and so much style. More than style, chic."

Claudia wanted to scream. Instead, she sat silent and unblinking, a small, tight smile on her closed lips.

"But then you know what Frenchwomen are like," Lucinda continued. "Why, she couldn't have been more than twenty, and she made me feel an absolute baby."

Claudia turned two cold green eyes on her companion. "That should not have been difficult to do, Lucinda." She knew the turmoil was under control now. She would be all right until she got home.

Later, locked securely in her room, Claudia stared bleakly out the rain-washed window. The park that had been white with snow a few hours ago was a sea of dirty slush, a grim reminder of the high hopes she had started the day with.

She must think clearly. But how could one think clearly thousands of miles from the facts? What did Lucinda's story mean? Did it mean anything at all? Certainly Philippe's appearance at a ball signified nothing. All the parties and dances Claudia had gone to proved that. After each one she had gone to sleep with dreams of Philippe.

But what about Simone de Chauvres? She, not the ball, was the real problem. *"Amie intime,"* Philippe had said. Just how good a friend had she become? The image of Philippe and Simone de Chauvres locked in each other's arms made her want to scream out in agony. She shook her head as if to drive away the thought.

She was being absurd. Philippe had gone to a ball. And he had gone with an old friend. What could be more logical? Claudia told herself she ought to be happy he had been there with Simone and not some woman she knew nothing about. How much more secure an old, childhood friend than someone new who might have supplanted her in Philippe's affections.

Claudia thought of the scores of men with whom she'd gone here and there since she'd come home. Why, if anyone saw her laughing and flirting with Sam Beaumont, they'd assume it was more than just a casual friendship. And surely her feelings for Sam were not in the least romantic. Why couldn't the same be true of Philippe and Simone de Chauvres? If only he were here to reassure her now, to take her in his arms and tell her that *amie intime* did not mean *amour*.

But Philippe wasn't here, and perhaps her doubts weren't silly at all. She didn't know what to think, but one fact was clear. After what she had heard this afternoon, she could not bring herself to write that letter. Claudia didn't know whether to curse Lucinda Ardsley for snatching away the happiness that had seemed so close only hours before or to thank her for saving Claudia from a terrible humiliation. She didn't, it seemed as she watched the gray slush of Central Park regain its apparent whiteness in the gathering dusk, know anything.

8

To Claudia's credit few people could have guessed at her pain. The society columns described Miss Claudia Trenholm as one of the most popular members of the young set, and she played the role with a vengeance. She was seen everywhere with all the most eligible bachelors. And her presence made news. If she chose to frequent a restaurant, others followed. If her picture was taken at the opening of a new nightclub, its success was assured. When the *Times* or the *Tribune* covered a party, her name was listed first among the younger celebrants, and *Town and Country* ran her photograph twice in three months. If Elizabeth felt her daughter attracted more publicity than was seemly and if James worried about the pace at which she drove herself, they hesitated to say as much to Claudia. Hadn't they been urging just this sort of life on her since her return from Paris?

Each night brought another party and another young man, yet to Claudia they all seemed curiously the same. Only Sam, who as Katherine's escort was Claudia's constant companion, stood out.

Claudia liked Sam. He seemed older than the others, but he wasn't a stuffed shirt. Not really. Oh, sometimes he was a little stiff, but at least he never pretended to be what he wasn't. And Sam Beaumont, kind, straightforward, and attractive, if somewhat lacking in imagination or wit, was a perfectly nice thing to be. Claudia told him as much one night at Charlot's, a speakeasy on Forty-ninth Street.

Claudia had suggested the spot, and everyone immediately agreed. Everyone except Sam. The best people went there all right, but unlike most places the best people went, they did not go there to be seen. More often than not, they went there not to be seen. The last time Sam had been at Charlot's he had run into an old Groton/Yale chum with a woman who was not his wife. Sam knew that immediately, although he had never met the man's wife.

"Why don't we go to the Villa Venice? Emil Coleman's there."

"Oh, Sam, don't be such a stuffed shirt. Charlot's can't be that bad. Besides, I've never been there, and I want to go." That obviously settled it. If Claudia wanted something, the other men in the party were determined to give it to her. He and Kate might as well go along. At least that way he could keep an eye on things.

He was dancing with Claudia now, and feeling just a little sorry about teasing him before, she told Sam that, yes, he was a very nice person indeed.

"Even if I am a stuffed shirt?"

"Well, at least you never pretend to be something you're not. Like the rest of them."

"They're not such bad fellows, Claudia. At any rate, they've got good taste. They all flock after you, don't they?"

"Oh, they're not bad fellows at all. That's just the point. Take George, good old George." She tossed her tawny bob in the direction of the young man who sat alone at the table watching their every step and trying not to. "Why does he have to pretend to be a wild and wicked parlor snake when he's nothing but a dull old pussycat at heart?"

"Maybe that's why."

"What do you mean?"

"Maybe he thinks you'll find him more exciting as a parlor snake."

"George Talbott exciting," she scoffed.

They returned to the table laughing. "Honestly, Claudia," Kate hissed across the table, "I don't know what's so terribly funny, but try to keep your voice down. Everyone is staring."

"As far as I can see, Kate, you're the only one who's staring."

"What about those people?" With her eyes Katherine indicated a table to their left. Claudia followed her gaze.

"Yes, I suppose they are staring. Well, at least I can be polite." She flashed her most dazzling smile at two overdressed women and three men. Like peeping Toms, they turned away in embarrassment, all except one of the men. He rose and walked to where Claudia sat.

"Would you care to dance?"

There was a stunned silence at the table. Claudia looked at the man carefully. He was handsome, in a raw, unpolished way. His tuxedo—she was sure that was what he would call it—was a little too small and much too new. She felt the eyes of the group on her. "Why, yes, I'd like to very much."

The man danced politely, if a little unsteadily. Claudia suspected he'd had a good deal to drink. Well, they were in a speakeasy. Who hadn't had a good deal to drink?

"Name's O'Hara. My friends call me Billy."

"How nice for your friends, Mr. O'Hara."

"What?"

Claudia did not answer, but Mr. O'Hara was capable of carrying the conversational burden alone. "I didn't think you'd say yes. I was watching you, and I thought a girl like that, she isn't going to dance with a strange guy in a speak, at least not a guy like me. Not that there's anything wrong with it," he hastened to reassure her. "I just didn't think you would."

She looked idly over his shoulder.

"Well, it just goes to show, you never can tell, can you? I always say. . . ." But the music ended, and Claudia turned her back on Mr. O'Hara and what he always said and returned to her table.

"I hope you're satisfied. You made a spectacle of yourself."

"Oh, Kate, that's overstating it, don't you think?"

"Well, you did. It was scandalous."

"Scandalous," Claudia repeated. "George, do you think I was scandalous?"

"Of course not."

"See, Kate, George doesn't think I was scandalous. I bet George will even dance with me. You don't think I'm too scandalous to dance with, do you, George?"

"Not for a minute."

A half hour later Mr. O'Hara returned. He stood over Claudia's chair, a little more familiarly this time. "Like to dance?"

"No, thank you," she tossed over her shoulder as she went on talking to George.

"Oh, come on, just a dance."

Sam was on his feet in a minute. "The lady does not want to dance."

Mr. O'Hara looked at Sam, who was exactly his height. He took in his broad shoulders and powerful chest. He also took in the icy stare and commanding tone. "Okay, okay. No need to make a fuss. Just a friendly little dance. That's all I wanted," he mumbled as he backed away.

"Are you satisfied now?" Kate snapped.

"I know, Kate. I was scandalous. Again."

"You might at least think of other people. If you want to get mixed up with types like that, it's up to you, but you don't have to entangle the rest of us."

"You mean Sam, of course. Poor Sam. I'm sorry, Sam. I'm sorry I entangled you. Will you still dance with me? I promise to behave."

"Of course, I'll dance with you." He excused himself from Katherine and led her sister onto the small dance floor.

"You know, I am sorry, Sam. I didn't mean to embarrass you."

"You didn't embarrass me, Claudia." He was silent for a moment.

"But?" she said.

"But what?"

"You were going to say something else."

"Well . . . why? Did you really want to dance with that fellow?"

"Of course not."

"Then why?" He paused for a moment. "Just to shock everyone?"

"Oh, I don't know. Maybe. Maybe I did want to shock everyone, shock them out of their nice smug little seats. Is that so terrible? Do you think I'm a terrible person, Sam?"

He paused again. "I think you're a very unhappy person, Claudia."

Her eyes, so defiant a moment ago, suddenly filled with tears. "Oh, Sam, Sam. Now I really will make a scene—crying in public."

He pulled her to him, and she buried her face in the dark privacy of his dinner coat. Through all the shame and misery she noticed Sam had a nice smell about him, a nice, clean, masculine smell. She also noticed that his heart beat very loudly beneath that proper dinner coat.

It was pity he felt for her, Sam told himself as they finished the dance, but later that night alone in his room with a nightcap and a sailing journal, he found it less easy to fool himself. He'd been through the problem scores of times in the last months. Shortly after he'd seen Claudia that first time last autumn he'd admitted to himself he was infatuated with her. Well, that was all right. He'd been through enough infatuations in his day. Either you did something about them and they passed, or you did nothing and they still passed.

His infatuation with Claudia, however, did not seem to be passing. Of course, there was another problem as well. In this case it wasn't an infatuation with just anyone. It was an infatuation with Katherine's sister.

He hadn't entirely given up the idea of marrying Kate. The old images of himself as an upstanding family man with a brood of children could be summoned at a moment's notice. And Kate was a good, logical choice. She just wasn't an exciting choice. Sam remembered that night he and Katherine had sneaked away from the club dance and gone down to the dock. Little enough had happened—*at my age,* Sam thought, *a man doesn't get all worked up about a few kisses*—but even less had happened to Sam's feelings for Kate. He hadn't liked her any less after that evening, but he hadn't liked her any more either.

Claudia, on the other hand, was something else. He had never even kissed her, yet she fanned a fire in him that Kate barely ignited.

But there was more to marriage than sex. Sam was the first to admit that. Not that he believed in marriage without sex. He had often wondered about his own parents' relationship. Not that anyone could have thought them unhappy. Until his mother's death four years before they had got along well enough by the standards of the day. Sam had never heard either of them utter an unkind word to the other. But that was precisely the problem. They had been perfect with each other, polite, like two strangers.

Which merely brought him back to Katherine and Claudia. If there was no excitement in his old friend Kate, were there enough real bonds with Claudia? She attracted Sam, she aroused him, but he wasn't sure she suited him. Like her behavior tonight. Sometimes Claudia seemed to like breaking rules just for the sake of it. It made Sam uncomfortable.

If the idea of marrying Katherine didn't excite Sam, the idea of marrying her sister alarmed him. If only there had been one Trenholm daughter with the attributes of both. He'd marry her in a minute.

The society columns may have been taken in by Claudia's appearance at every party and social event of the season, but James Trenholm was not. Since the night of their discussion, he had been quietly but constantly observant of his daughter. He was not pleased with what he saw.

True to form, he tried all manner of treats and surprises. Every absentminded word of thanks, every routine kiss of gratitude drove a nail in the coffin of the daughter he had loved, the daughter who seemed no longer to exist. The course of action James decided on was determined as much by his own discomfort in the presence of this new Claudia as it was by any benefit he thought she might derive from it.

"I'm going to make arrangements for you and Louisa to take the girls south for a month or so," he announced to his wife one grim February morning. Even the breakfast room, normally cheerful, had a gloomy winterized air. "It seems to me you could all use some sun."

Elizabeth knew from her husband's tone, from the way he seemed more concerned with his coffee and the *Times* than any information he was imparting, that he had considered the matter and made up his mind. He said they would go south and south they would go. She knew the futility of argument, yet she could not refrain from a small struggle.

"Do you think it's wise, James? Just at this time?" Her voice was still casual. "Do you think it's wise to take Katherine away from Sam now? He isn't going south at all this winter. It seems he's having a new boat built—a yawl, Kate says, though I never can keep them straight. It's almost finished, and he won't leave New York until it's commissioned. Katherine says he's fanatical about it. Spends all his days out at City Island, supervising every detail. Thank heaven there's no work in the evenings, or we'd never see him."

"That settles it." James closed his paper with an air of finality. "Just one more reason for you to go south. Maybe if Sam Beaumont looks up from his new toy one afternoon and finds Kate isn't there, he'll get some sense in his head. Stop taking her for granted and start acting like a man. The very idea. A grown man—how old is Sam anyway?—spending all his time building an elaborate toy.

"Well, be that as it may. . . ." He rose from the breakfast table. "I'll have Roberts book your staterooms on the Florida Special as soon as I get to the office."

The following week James delivered his women to the new Pennsylvania Station. There had been much fanfare about the terminal's fidelity to its model, the Baths of Caracalla, and as James stood waving good-bye, he was very much the twentieth-century emperor. As the train gained momentum, so did James, and he was up the stairs and back in the Brewster within minutes. He told Henry, who would have known without being told, to take him straight to the office and sank back into the dark upholstery with a satisfied air. The holiday was exactly what they needed. He was already looking forward to seeing his daughters' relaxed, sun-blushed faces in a month's time.

Once in Palm Beach, securely established at the Royal Poinciana, each girl set about getting through the month in her own way. Katherine, longing for Sam, swam and sailed, played lawn tennis and golf, all with a grim determination to make the interminable hours pass as quickly as possible. Claudia's approach was more passive. She brooded. For long hours she sat on the white sand, gazing across the azure water wondering if she dared write Philippe. At night both girls played bridge at the Everglades Club with assorted and admiring young men. The cards were hot and stuck to their fingers. The girls, sleek and tanned in their printed chiffons, were cool, as if determined that the young men, unlike the cards, would not stick.

Then Sam Beaumont arrived, and everyone's spirits soared. At first it seemed what Katherine had dreamed of and Elizabeth hoped for had finally come true: Once Kate was gone, Sam had realized how much he missed her and had followed her south.

Sam had missed Kate, just as he had Claudia, but there was more to it than that. His days had been filled with purchase orders and exacting measurements. He hadn't gone near his office in several weeks—one of the advantages of working for a family banking firm—and spent every day at Minneford's Boatworks on City Island. It was doubtful Sam would have taken off for lunch had the workmen not done so, and more often than not he spent that half hour climbing and crawling among the tools and sawdust, inspecting every inch of this magnificent thing he was creating.

Sam's yawl—it was his first real boat since the others had been gifts from his father—had been many years in the making. Work had begun only ten months before, but ever since Sam had returned from the war, the plans had been germinating in his mind. His requirements were simple and exacting. His boat must be beautiful, its lines clean, sleek, and graceful. It must also be fast. He planned to win as often as he raced. It must also be small and carefully equipped. He estimated that between forty-one and forty-six feet would be the perfect length. Sam had no intention of being chained to a large crew. If he did marry Katherine, they could get away entirely on their own. It would make an ideal wedding trip. He could count on Kate to appreciate that.

The boat, originally Sam's dream, had become his passion. It is doubtful that had a shipment of fittings and winches from England not been delayed, he would have decided on two weeks in Palm Beach. As it happened, they were delayed, and he sat now on the breeze-swept terrace of the Breakers with Kate and Claudia and Elizabeth. It was tea time, and behind them a dozen couples swept energetically back and forth in the double shuffle. Dusk was gathering, and the girls' chiffon bodices were pale blurs against their partners' dark blue jackets.

"I've decided to call her *Mistress*," Sam said. Elizabeth thought she had never heard a more appropriate name for a vessel. "I went through all the traditional names—*Adventurer, Windsong, Sea Witch*—I even tried name names. I thought of Katherine for a while and Claudia, but I couldn't fit both names on the transom and"—he flashed a brilliant, healthy smile—"I didn't want to play favorites."

Elizabeth shuddered at his last profession of fair-mindedness. Had James been right after all?

It was late afternoon, and the beach was nearly deserted. Claudia sat at the water's edge, hugging her knees to her chest and savoring the warm foam lapping her toes. She wore a navy woolen suit with stripes of white around the hips and legs. The wisps of hair that had escaped from her turban formed a halo around her face, and the band of pale freckles the sun had sprinkled across her nose made her look like a child. Sam felt very protective as he dropped down next to her on the sand.

Claudia started. "I didn't hear you."

"Judging from the way you looked, you wouldn't have heard an approaching hurricane. You were miles away."

"Was I? What are you doing here anyway? I thought you were playing tennis with Kate."

"That was this morning. She's in the women's singles this afternoon, and I don't qualify for that one."

"No, I don't suppose you do." She smiled at him. He looked strong and attractive in his rumpled tennis whites, his shoulders straining against the soft shirt, his hair sun-bleached. *Mother's right*, Claudia thought. *Sam is "a fine figure of a man."*

"What do you do here all day anyway? Don't you get bored just lying around on the beach?"

"Honestly, Sam, you make me sound like a sea slug. I do move occasionally. I played tennis yesterday, and I swam twice today. But don't let the information get out. It might ruin my reputation."

"Your secret's safe with me."

"But what about you, Sam? Don't you ever stop? Even for a while. What's the point of coming to the beach if you never look at the sea? Do you know it's a different color in the afternoon from the morning? There are all sorts of things to see. I could sit here and watch for hours. Sometimes I do. Just sit and watch and think."

"And what do you think about?"

"Oh, nothing . . . anything . . . everything, I guess."

"That French fellow?"

She looked at him sharply. "Sometimes."

"I'm sorry, Claudia. I had no right to say that."

"Don't be silly. I'm surprised you never mentioned it before. After all you are my friend. I guess that's why you never did. Tell me, what do people say?"

"Not much. Nothing really. Anymore."

"Then what did they say?"

He hesitated for a moment. "Only that there was talk you were to marry some Frenchman and then you didn't."

"Well, I guess that much is true."

"He was a swine!" The harshness in his voice startled her.

"No, Sam, he wasn't. It was my fault, not his."

"Of course." He was suddenly embarrassed. He hadn't meant to suggest she had been jilted.

"It was, really, Sam. He told me Daddy would never allow the marriage, and I wouldn't believe him. I wanted everything. Him and Daddy's blessings—everything. I wanted it my own way. And now it's too late."

"Do you still love him?" Sam seemed to be looking off at the horizon, but he was acutely aware of every movement Claudia made. She nodded. "And you still want to marry him?"

"Yes."

"Even if it means being cut off from your family for the rest of your life?"

The words rang harshly in her ears. "I think so."

"Then why don't you?"

"Because I'm not sure *he* wants to."

"Claudia, I'm a fool for saying this. For one thing it's none of my business. For another, I can't imagine why I'm so eager to send you halfway around the world to marry some Frenchman, but my guess is that he still loves and wants you. Love doesn't die that easily." His voice was husky, and he went on quickly. "At any rate, there's only one way to find out. Write to him. Ask him straight out."

"I tried to once, but it was more difficult than I thought it would be. I felt so . . . well, forward. What would you think, Sam, if you received a letter like that?"

"Pretty darned swell."

"But that's just the point. You'd feel good. You'd feel flattered. But that's all about you. How would you feel about me? I mean how would you feel about the girl who wrote the letter?"

"Good enough to grab the next boat for New York."

"But that's you, Sam."

"Well"—he tried to make his voice light—"next time have the sense to fall in love with someone like me."

"That"—Claudia laughed—"is the best advice you've given me all afternoon." His laughter, joining hers, was a little self-conscious, but Claudia was too absorbed in her own thoughts to notice.

A quarter of an hour later she was sitting at the desk in her room when Katherine burst in. "Really, Kate, you might knock." Claudia slid a copy of *Vanity Fair* over the letter she was writing.

"Oh, yes, we must all be so terribly considerate of Claudia. But what about Claudia, does *she* ever consider anyone else? Or would that be too much to ask? Well, you won't get away with it this time. I swear to that."

"What are you talking about, Kate?" Caught in one forbidden act, Claudia racked her brain to think of other trespasses. Surely she couldn't know about the letter. Surely Sam hadn't been foolish enough to tell her.

"You know exactly what I'm talking about. You've ruined your life with that French gigolo, and now you want to ruin mine. Mine and Sam's. I saw you on the beach with him just now."

It suddenly came clear to Claudia. "We were only talking, Kate."

"You're always only talking. And when he's not talking to you, he's talking about you. 'Do you think Claudia's all right?' 'Do you think we ought to ask Claudia along?' 'Isn't Claudia coming?' It's gotten so I hate the sound of your name."

"Sam's only being polite. We're friends, Kate. It is no more than that."

"It wasn't any more until you decided to make it more. You couldn't stand to let one get away, could you, Claudia? Or did you need another notch in your belt after that Frenchman threw you over."

Claudia kept her hand over the magazine. "He never 'threw me over,' Kate, and just because you're having trouble with Sam, don't come storming in here and blame it on me. Maybe if you weren't such a harridan, you wouldn't *have* trouble with Sam. Maybe if you weren't so destructively jealous, you'd be better off. I don't know what your problem is, Kate, but it doesn't have anything to do with me, so why don't you just go chase Sam and leave me alone?"

"The way you've been leaving him alone. 'Oh, Sam, I'm so bored, why don't you dance with me?' 'Oh, Sam, please drive into town with me or I'll have to go with that awful Nick Tokely.' Is *that* what you call leaving him alone!"

"I can't help it if he offers to do things for me."

"I wonder if Sam would want to do so much for you if. . . ." Kate walked to the French windows and stood looking out over the beach.

"If what?"

"Nothing much. I was just wondering if Sam would think you were so wonderful if he knew about Montreux."

Claudia was suddenly on her feet and face to face with her sister.

"How do you know about that?"

"Just because you're a fool, Claudia, don't take me for one. I guessed where you'd gone, and it didn't take long to get it out of Mrs. Priestly-Soames."

"Does anyone else know?"

"I haven't told Mother or Daddy if that's what you mean. What an idiot you were, Claudia! Going off that way."

"You don't know anything about it."

"Oh, no, only you know about it. I know you think it was a *grand amour*—of course, it sounds better in French—but it wasn't. It was a cheap affair, no more. And where has it got you? All you're left with is tawdry memories."

"Shut up, Kate. Just shut up. You don't know what you're talking about."

"Tawdry memories—and now you want Sam. You think having Sam will make everything all right. But I warn you, Claudia, I'll fight for Sam, I'll fight you every way I know. And if I have to tell him about Montreux, I will."

"Now you're the fool, Kate. If you tell Sam, it may make him like me less, but it certainly won't make him like you more. In fact, knowing Sam, he'll probably think less of you for talking about it than he will of me for doing it."

"I'm willing to take that chance. Or at least I will be if you keep after him. If I can't have Sam, I'll see that you don't either."

"But I told you, Kate, I don't want Sam."

"And I don't believe you."

Claudia thought for a moment. Katherine already knew too much. It would be worth wagering one more secret to keep her quiet. "What if I could prove it to you? If I could convince you I'm not interested in Sam, would you promise never to tell anyone about Montreux? Especially not Daddy or Mother."

Katherine was silent. She had worked herself into a rage and was unwilling to be conciliated so easily.

"Would you?" Claudia repeated. Kate nodded. "All right, Kate, but you have to promise not to tell. The reason I was annoyed when you walked in without knocking was that I was writing a letter—to Philippe. You see he didn't throw me over. We were going to marry in Montreux, but we couldn't, and then I got frightened that Daddy would find out, and I ran away. But I realize now I was wrong. In fact, that's what I was talking to Sam about on the beach."

"You were talking to Sam about Montreux!"

"I was talking to Sam about Philippe, and he said if I still loved him, I should marry him. No matter what. And that's what I'm going to do. At least I am if you don't breathe a word of it to Daddy."

"But how? Are you going to go back to Paris? Is Sam going to help you?"

Claudia laughed and started to ease her sister toward the door. "Don't worry about how it's going to happen. Just remember that it is. Now get out of here, or I won't get my letter written and you won't get Sam."

As Katherine closed the door behind her, she thought she had never been so fond of her sister. Of course, Claudia was a fool for running off with that French-

man, but that was her problem. She could marry Jack
the Ripper, for all Kate cared, just so long as she left
Sam Beaumont alone.

The return of the Trenholm women was far more
cheerful than their departure. Sam had arranged for his
father to send the private railroad car for them. From
the moment it pulled up on the tracks next to the Royal
Poinciana, there had been an air of festivity. Kate was
glad to be going home with Sam. Claudia was eager to
get back to New York. Elizabeth watched her daughters'
happy faces carefully and was grateful for Sam's presence. On the brief trip home the four women pampered
him almost as much as the Beaumont staff pampered
them, and they arrived in Pennsylvania Station bronzed,
relaxed, and cheerful.

James was delighted. "You see, my dear," he whispered to his wife while the luggage was being loaded
into the Brewster, "I was right. You're all much the
better for a month in the sun."

James would have been less sanguine had he known
of the cable that lay waiting for his daughter at home.
In the excitement of reunion neither he nor his wife
noticed the yellow envelope lying with a pile of mail
on the Hepplewhite table in the foyer, and Claudia was
able to make off with it to the privacy of her room.
Her heart pounded as she closed the door behind her
and tore open the envelope:

ARRIVE NEW YORK ABOARD PARIS SATURDAY
MORNING STOP WILL TELEPHONE IMMEDIATELY
STOP PHILIPPE

The days till Saturday dragged, but if Claudia saw
the world through a thick haze, the world saw her as a
bright beacon of light. Never had she been more radiant.

It would have taken a less observant admirer than
Sam Beaumont not to notice the change. He sat next
to her now in the orchestra of the New Amsterdam
Theater acutely aware of her presence. The actresses
on the stage held no attraction for him next to Claudia's

tangible beauty. He was scarcely aware of Katherine, who sat on his other side, or of Grant Walbridge, against whose dark dinner coat Claudia glowed. When she leaned forward to get a better view of the stage, Sam felt her arm brush against his, heard the silk of her dress rustle against her body, smelled the special fragrance perfume assumed on her skin. Every time she crossed and uncrossed her legs he was aware of their pale sheen against the blackness of the seat before her. During the intermission, when she held her glass of ginger ale out for Sam to pour whiskey, his hand shook, and laughingly she placed her fingers on his to steady the flask.

It took more than his usual before bedtime scotch and milk, more than the latest issue of *Pound and Paddock,* more than a careful going over of the latest changes in the plans for *Mistress* to put Sam Beaumont to sleep that night. No matter where he turned, what he tried to read, Claudia was there. She filled his mind and senses.

For the first time Sam admitted to himself the impossibility of marrying a girl whose sister attracted him so fiercely. And then he came face to face with that other problem. If he did not want to marry Kate, did he want to marry Claudia? Could he marry Claudia? He might rationalize his own doubts out of existence, but he could not dismiss Claudia's reasons for refusing him so easily. She was in love with another man. And stupidly, thoughtlessly, he had encouraged her to marry that man.

Claudia was up and dressed before dawn and out of the house without breakfast. She left a note saying she had gone for an early-morning walk and would probably lunch with a friend and shop later in the day. That would prevent them from worrying for the next few hours. After that, well, she'd worry about that later. With Philippe. He'd know what to do. He'd have some plan in mind. Philippe would take care of her.

Claudia stood at the end of the pier and felt the March wind whipping around her. She remembered a similar day just a year ago and an ocean and a lifetime away when she'd stood on the pier waiting for her parents to arrive. She shivered and drew her fur-lined cape closer. She could go inside, but there was a chance she might meet someone in the first-class area.

Suddenly men were rushing back and forth, tying lines and securing gangplanks. The wind—or was it the wind?—brought tears to her eyes, and through the blur she scanned the passengers who crowded the deck.

Then she saw him. He had lost some of his boyishness. From under a soft gray hat Philippe's dark eyes scanned the pier. He had wired he would telephone, but he knew she would come to the ship to meet him.

Claudia began to jump up and down and wave wildly. She knew she was making a spectacle of herself and didn't care. Philippe saw her, and his face broke into the grin she loved.

It seemed an interminable time before the custom officials would permit them near each other. Then suddenly he was holding her close, and she was crying, and all he could do was whisper "darling" over and over into her hair.

Somehow through the tears and excitement they managed to get themselves and Philippe's few pieces of luggage into a taxi. Philippe directed the driver to take them to the St. Regis. When they arrived at the hotel, Claudia insisted on going with him to see his room. "But what will they say?" he whispered when the desk clerk turned his back in the tiny gilt cage.

"All sorts of terrible things, I'm sure."

The bellboy seemed to take an interminable time showing them through Philippe's suite, opening curtains, calling their attention to the fine view of Fifth Avenue, and pointing out assorted bells and buzzers. Finally he was gone, and Claudia was across the room and safe in Philippe's arms.

His response was not what she had expected. Slowly, reluctantly, he took her arms from around his neck and held her a little away from him. "Claudia, we must talk." His eyes grew dark, and she felt a stab of fear.

But why had he come all this distance if not to marry her?

"But, darling, there's plenty of time for that. The rest of our lives. Now I just want you to hold me, to make me know we're together again—that everything is all right."

Claudia saw a shadow move across his face. Then it struck her. His behavior now, his distance in the taxi. It was his old sense of honor. Philippe felt he had behaved badly once. He was determined to keep her at a distance until they were safely married. She laughed in delight and relief.

He read her thoughts as he had so many times in the past and colored. "No, darling . . . Claudia, it's not that."

"Then what is it? Why are you acting so strangely?"

She had never seen him look more defeated. "Because I have no right to act differently."

"But you have every right . . . every reason. I want to marry you. I should have listened to you last fall. I should never have left you then. I thought Daddy would come around, but you were right. He won't. But that doesn't matter. All that matters is that we're together again."

"No, Claudia, that isn't all that matters."

She brushed aside his protest with a wave of her hand. "You're not going to talk about money again. We've been through all that. Even you agreed after . . . before I left that we had to marry."

"I did. And I meant it. We should have."

"Then I don't understand. What has changed?"

"It's too late, Claudia, but not because I no longer love you. I have no right to say it, but I still love you, more than ever. When I saw you this morning, jumping up and down on the pier like a beautiful little fool, I knew all over again how much I wanted you." He hesitated for a moment. "But I no longer have any right."

"But why not?"

"Because I'm married." He had spoken so quietly that for a moment she thought she had imagined the words. Then she realized he had spoken. The expression on his face told her so.

"How could you, after . . . after Montreux? How could you marry someone else after Montreux?"

He looked at her miserably. "Claudia, I'm a man." They were silent for a moment, and then he went on. "I can't tell you why or how it happened, but it did."

"Why or how. There are no whys or hows to marriage." She was moving around the room quickly now, gathering up her cape and hat and gloves, trying to hold back the tears streaming down her cheeks. "I'm the one who should apologize. I'm sorry. Sorry for embarrassing you . . . for embarrassing us both."

"Please, Claudia, please don't sound like that."

She whirled on him, too hurt to care about her pride. "How do you want me to sound? In one breath you tell me you love me, in the next you're married. I don't understand. Or maybe I do. Maybe I was too American to see it before. Is that the French way, Philippe? You love me, but she's your wife. It's Simone de Chauvres, isn't it? Simone is Madame, excuse me, the Countess de Boissevain, and I'm your mistress—your tart."

At the last word he was across the room, his hands on both her shoulders shaking her into silence. "Stop it! Stop it this minute."

He released her as if afraid of her closeness, and she sank into a chair, her anger spent.

"It isn't like that, Claudia. You must believe me. I never wanted to hurt you."

Claudia was quiet as if waiting for more, but there was no more. There was nothing that Philippe could say. Even if he could, would the truth make any difference? Would Claudia hate him less if she knew the conditions of his marriage, if she knew he had betrayed her not a month ago when he married Simone de Chauvres, but two months earlier when he had first made love to the woman who was now so strangely and distantly his wife?

How could he explain any of it to Claudia? Could she understand the loneliness and misery, the aching longing for her that had made him ripe for another woman? He had given himself over to a momentary desire, and his crime, for he had come to think of it as such, had been compounded only by his choice of victim. Had it been another woman to whom he had turned perhaps he would not be married now. But in his loneliness and need he had turned to Simone. His choice had been his old friend, and now the child would be Simone's, Simone's and his. Once he knew that, there had been no question of not marrying her. And now there was no question of trying to explain any of it to Claudia. It would be the final betrayal of both women.

Claudia stood with one hand on the door. She turned to him for a moment, and the look in her eyes tore Philippe's heart. "Just one more question. Why didn't you simply answer my letter? Why did you have to come all this way to tell me you've married someone else?"

"I guess it was selfishness. I couldn't give up the chance of seeing you one last time."

"But your wife, didn't she object to your coming here alone? Or is she more understanding than that?" There was a new hardness in her voice.

Philippe looked away, as if he could not meet Claudia's eyes in this final admission. "I've come ostensibly on her behalf. Her family has business interests in America. They asked me to look after a few things."

So even this, Claudia thought, their final parting was sullied by his new life. "Then I didn't put you to all that much trouble after all. I'm so glad." She flashed a bright, hard smile, one Philippe had never seen before.

"How you must hate me," he said miserably.

"How I wish I could."

9

Claudia sat before the fire in her father's library. It was her first afternoon out of bed in a week, and she had chosen this room because it seemed more comforting than any of the sitting rooms.

At first she had welcomed the cold she had caught that morning on the pier. It provided the perfect excuse to retreat from the world. But now she was well again, and the days and weeks ahead yawned before her. All her plans, every hope had hinged on Philippe. Her future had revolved around him like a planet around its sun. Now her sun had gone out, and there was nothing but darkness.

There was a knock at the door, and Sam came striding into the library. "They told me I'd find you in here. How are you feeling?"

"The patient will live."

"You don't sound terribly happy at the prospect."

Claudia turned back to the fire. "Kate isn't home. I don't think she's due back for an hour or so."

"I know. I came to see you."

"That's kind, Sam, but you didn't have to. I'm not that much of an invalid. I'll probably be out of here in a day or two."

"I didn't come because you were sick, Claudia, I came because I wanted to see you."

"Thank you." Her tone was polite but uninterested. Sam did not notice. He was preoccupied. He had pondered the meeting carefully, ever since that night at the

163

theater before Claudia had fallen ill. He had made up his mind.

"Remember that conversation we had on the beach a few weeks ago, Claudia?" His voice was elaborately casual. "Did you take my advice?"

She was silent for a moment. When she spoke, her tone was dry. "I'm not going to be married if that's what you mean."

He was too elated to hear the strain in her voice. "You're not?"

"I said I wasn't going to, Sam, and I'd rather not talk about it." She had told no one she had seen Philippe, and she was not going to confide in Sam now. How could she admit to anyone that the love that meant everything to her had meant nothing to Philippe? She hadn't been enough to hold him. It was that simple—and that painful.

"I'm sorry, Claudia. It's only that I had to know. Before . . . before I said anything."

For the first time that afternoon Claudia looked at Sam carefully. Instinctively she knew what was coming. She wanted to laugh and cry. It was so absurd. And so cruel. Why were people always wanting to marry people who did not want to marry them? She liked Sam well enough, better than any one else, in fact, but marriage was another matter.

Or was it? The idea struck her as absurd because she had never considered it. Now that she did, it seemed far from preposterous. She had to marry someone. She wouldn't spend the rest of her life mourning Philippe! Why not Sam? She *was* fond of him. Certainly marriage to Sam would be better than marriage to George or Grant or any of the others. In more than one way, she mused; not only did she genuinely like Sam, but she also felt a certain cold satisfaction that he was the most eligible bachelor in her set. It would be a spectacular match.

And what about Kate? cried a small voice. But surely Sam did not belong to Kate. Oh, she wanted him, but wanting was scarcely enough. Claudia had her own proof of that.

Besides, if Claudia refused Sam, it did not follow he would turn to Katherine. No, Claudia decided, she was not taking anything from Kate. This was a matter between her and Sam. Kate had nothing to do with it.

"Before you said anything about what, Sam?" Her voice was all innocence.

"This may seem unexpected, Claudia, but I've thought about it for a long time. And I've made up my mind. I love you. I've loved you ever since I saw you that first night last fall. I didn't know it then, but I do now. And I want to marry you. If you'll have me. I know you were in love with that other fellow—or at least you said you were—but you tell me that's over now. I don't know how you feel about me, Claudia, but I think I could make you love me."

She was silent for a moment. It was not a girlish ploy but a moment of real indecision. Then the moment was gone, and everything fell into place. "I think you could, too, Sam. Of course I'll marry you. Why on earth wouldn't I marry you?" Her tone was light and slightly teasing.

He was across the room and on his knees before her chair. "I think you're a little late with that pose." She laughed, but for Sam this was no time for jokes. His arms were around her, and he was holding her to him. "I'll make you happy, Claudia. I know I will."

"I'm sure you will, Sam," she said easily and disengaged herself. "And now perhaps we ought to be practical for a moment."

They agreed Sam would return the next morning, Saturday, and speak to James. They talked about the wedding and the wedding trip and where they would live. Claudia was wonderfully acquiescent. It seemed there was nothing Sam wanted she would not agree to, including a short engagement. "It's just that I'm so darned eager, Claudia. I've waited this long, and I don't want to wait a minute longer. I'd elope this weekend if you said yes."

"Well, perhaps not this weekend," she teased, "but as soon as you like." A short engagement suited Claudia perfectly. Less time for second thoughts.

"There is one problem, though, Sam."

His look was full of concern. Whatever Claudia wanted she must have.

"Kate."

He looked away quickly. "I know."

"We'll have to be very kind."

Claudia was alone in the library when Katherine came in. "Was that Sam's car I saw pulling away? Why didn't you tell him to wait? You knew I'd be back early." Kate poked furiously at the fire.

Claudia's voice was quiet. "Sam came to see me, Kate. To ask me to marry him."

Katherine whirled to face her sister. She was still holding the poker, and for a moment Claudia felt sure she was going to strike her. "You bitch," she snarled. "You lying little bitch."

"I'm sorry, Kate."

"You're sorry? What do I care whether you're sorry or not? And to think I believed you in Florida."

"What I said in Florida was true—then."

"So this time your Frenchman *did* throw you over."

Claudia said nothing.

"I knew it! You're a fool, Claudia. You've made a mess of everything. First you run off on your sordid little tryst, and when he's willing to marry you, you don't want to. An affair is all right, but when it comes to marriage, you come running home to Daddy. Daddy's little girl. Then you decide perhaps you want him after all, and you think all you have to do is snap your fingers and he'll come running. Only he didn't, did he? What happened Claudia? Did he find someone else to go to Montreux with him?"

Claudia was ice cold. "Be quiet, Kate. You know nothing about it."

"I know all about it, about the lies and the fairy tales you tell yourself. True love! It looks more like sex from where I stand. Well, you were a fool then and you're a fool now. But you'll never marry Sam Beaumont. *I'll* see to that."

"If you're talking about Montreux again, it won't do any good. I've already told Sam," she lied.

"You told Sam about Montreux! And he still wants to marry you. I don't believe it."

Claudia held her sister's eyes. If she looked away now, it would be fatal. "It's true. We're going to be married as soon as possible. I'm sorry if we've hurt you, Kate, but that's the way things are. Sam loves me and . . . and I love him. I hope you'll wish us well, but if you don't, it won't make any difference. We'll be married with or without your approval."

There was nothing more to say. Claudia started for the door, but Katherine held her back. Claudia could feel her sister's nails digging into her arm as she spoke. "I called you a bitch before, Claudia, but that's too good for you. There isn't a word that describes you and your filthy selfishness. You don't love Sam, and you know it. You may want to marry him—for all I know you're pregnant and you have to marry him—but you don't love him. Well, you're right. I can't stop you. But you're both going to suffer. I promise you that. And the beautiful part of it is I won't have to lift a finger. You'll do it all by yourselves. You'll make yourself miserable, and you'll make Sam miserable, and when he's had enough of you—and someday he will—he'll come back to me. Remember that, Claudia."

Saturday lunch was festive, the more so for Kate's absence. She had decided to make that long-postponed visit to her cousin Amanda who had begged her to come. "You'll adore California," she had written. Kate doubted that; but it was three thousand miles from her sister and Sam Beaumont, and that was attraction enough. She would leave within the week, and there was last-minute shopping to keep her from the house whenever Sam might be there.

Not even Elizabeth objected to Katherine's departure on the eve of her sister's wedding. It might make things simpler for everyone.

"I do wish you'd give us a bit more time," Elizabeth pleaded with Sam as they sat down to lunch. "After all, there's Claudia's trousseau to take care of and the announcements. I'd much rather they be invitations. I've always wanted the girls to have large weddings."

"Of course, you're right, Mrs. Trenholm. And if Claudia wants a big wedding, we'll have one. It's just that I'm so eager I don't have the patience to wait." Sam looked across the table at Claudia. She smiled back but said nothing. The bride-to-be was curiously silent while the wedding plans were being made.

"And that's as it should be, my boy." James was pleased that Sam had taken some step, even this one. "If you weren't in a hurry, I'd worry about you. No Elizabeth, we can do without the frippery. Let the young people be married in the eyes of God. You can give all the parties you want for them afterward. And I daresay Claudia has enough clothes to get by. It isn't as if the stores will close down the day she's married. You'll have all the time in the world to take her shopping after the wedding."

"But what about the wedding trip? We must get you some things for that, at least, dear. Have you decided where you'll be going? All the young people seem to head for Europe these days. . . ."

"There are plenty of other places to go," James broke in. "Plenty of fine places on this continent." He did not think Europe, Paris especially, a propitious setting for the beginning of his daughter's marriage.

Elizabeth saw her mistake immediately. "Of course, why travel all that distance?"

James and Elizabeth needn't have worried. Sam had his own ideas. He had already suggested them to Claudia, who agreed amiably.

Sam was delighted. He'd thought Claudia might want a grander, more social wedding trip than the one he had in mind. It was the dream he'd carried for years, the dream in which Katherine had once played a part. Now that he could picture Claudia in the role of the bride he knew it was the perfect wedding trip. Isolated, romantic, intimate. No museums and stuffy hotels for them. Just Sam and Claudia exploring deserted islands by day, making love under the stars at night. Once again he congratulated himself on designing *Mistress* for just over forty feet so there would be no need of any crew or other interlopers in their paradise. But how could Sam possibly explain this dream to Elizabeth? And Claudia was no help. Surely that faraway look must indicate her happiness.

"I can promise you, Mrs. Trenholm, our wedding trip won't be a problem in the trousseau department. All Claudia will need is some sailing togs." It was one way, Sam thought, to approach the problem.

"Some sailing *togs?*" Both men smiled at the distaste with which Elizabeth pronounced the last word.

"*Mistress* is ready, and I plan to have one of the men sail her down to Florida in the next few weeks. We can take Father's railroad car and pick her up there. Then we can cruise for a month or so. Nothing strenuous, just some cay hopping. Claudia and I think it's the perfect wedding trip. I have to admit I had it in mind when I built *Mistress*. I just never thought it would happen so soon."

"Now that's a delightful idea, Sam," Elizabeth began carefully, "and very romantic. But perhaps that sort of holiday is better left for a little later. After all, you can't expect a girl to rough it on her wedding trip. If you're determined to cruise, why don't you charter one of those steam yachts? It would be so much more comfortable for Claudia—and more appropriate as well."

Sam had not expected Elizabeth to welcome his plan, but he hadn't anticipated real interference either. "Claudia seems to like the idea of roughing it, Mrs. Trenholm." All eyes turned toward Claudia. "You did say that, didn't you, Claudia?"

"Yes, I like the idea."

"Really, dear," her mother broke in. "I know you always favor the unconventional, but don't you think this is carrying it a little far?"

"Now, Elizabeth," James said sternly, "the young people have made up their minds, and it's none of our business. It's their wedding. Let them do it in their own way." James had begun to see Sam in a new light. The young man had more spunk than he had thought. Now if only he would apply some of it to his business. Not that the Beaumonts needed the money, of course, but it was the principle of the thing.

The next day Sam took Claudia to lunch at his father's. Sam had broken the news as soon as he returned home Friday evening, and early the following morning the older man had gone down to the bank and had the watchman let him into his own vault. There he had opened several satin-lined boxes and brooded over which of his wife's jewels to bestow. Claudia would get them all eventually, except for a few minor pieces that might go to an affectionate niece, but the problem now was to decide in what order she would get them. Tobias thought of saving the emeralds, easily the most exquisite and costly of the collection, for the birth of the first Beaumont grandchild but decided against it. Who knew if he'd be around for that event? Better to give the best now with meaning than have them all go in a lump after his death. If he were still alive when the grandchildren began arriving, well, then sapphires and diamonds would have to do. Besides, he was pleased with his son's choice and wanted to express his approval. The emeralds it would be, he decided, and slipped the long flat velvet box into the breast pocket of his coat.

Just before he turned to go, Tobias remembered the other, more important stone. He took the heavy diamond his wife had worn for fifty years of her life and slipped it in his other pocket. Sam could buy his bride all the jewels he wanted, but surely this all-important one signifying their engagement, the beginning of their life together, ought to be one that had some tradition.

Claudia's reaction to Tobias' gift the next day at lunch was everything he had hoped for. At first she was rendered speechless, and neither father nor son knew the tears that welled up were in memory of those other emeralds she had lost. When Claudia regained her composure, she rose from the table where all three canvasbacks sat untouched and walked around to kiss the old man.

"You're too good to me, both of you. I don't deserve it."

"Nonsense," Tobias said, obviously pleased. "He doesn't deserve you. Though I must say I'm mighty pleased he got you."

The emeralds seemed to mark the beginning of the furor. The next morning at nine one of the tabloids phoned to inquire if it were true the necklace and earrings Mr. Tobias Beaumont had presented to Miss Claudia Sheridan Trenholm on her betrothal to his son, Samuel Livingston Beaumont, were really valued at two hundred thousand dollars. Elizabeth said she had no idea and hung up immediately. She instructed the butler that neither she nor her daughter was at home to newspapers, magazines, or society columnists. The announcement of the engagement would appear in the proper manner.

Nevertheless, the public or at least that segment of it that followed "society" was kept informed. Old pictures suddenly reappeared in newspapers and magazines. There was the Bachrach portrait of Claudia in her coming-out dress, a candid photograph of Sam holding a polo trophy, Claudia at someone else's ball, Sam holding a tennis trophy, Claudia strolling in Palm Beach, Sam holding a sailing trophy. There were no photographs of the happy couple together.

Each morning Claudia arose to stacks of elaborately wrapped boxes. Each evening Sam arrived to inspect the contents that had been carefully unwrapped and arranged during the day. There were the usual silver and crystal and china from Tiffany's, mostly from acquaintances and younger friends. Then there were the special pieces, the full set of Lowestoft from one of Sam's aunts, the George II silver tea service from a Sheridan who no longer had the money to purchase such heirlooms but had the style to give them away, the George III fish forks and knives from a Beaumont cousin, an extraordinary Ming vase from another of Sam's aunts. The Beaumonts, it appeared, were very happy with the match. If they found James Trenholm something of a parvenu, the Sheridans were fine old stock and the girl herself was delightful.

Claudia proved that on any one of a dozen or more visits to assorted Beaumont relatives. There she sipped tea, listened to stories of Samuel's childhood, and exclaimed over the photographs that a host of Beaumont and Livingston aunts seemed to have been hoarding for just this occasion. After the first two or three afternoons Claudia found she could look at these photographs—Sam on his first pony, Sam in a Groton football uniform, Sam and his father on a small sailboat, Sam with his mother on the lawn of a large country house—without the wrenching memory of similar pictures scattered around Philippe's room.

And then there was the shopping. Elizabeth, who had bemoaned the lack of a proper trousseau, was assembling the most splendid makeshift one imaginable. There were satin chemises ranging in subtle degrees from a virginal white to a deep rich coffee. There were nightgowns of silk and crepe de chine and lawn, all trimmed with fine and fragile lace. There were negligees and dressing gowns, morning dresses and evening dresses, handbags and hats and shoes. And there were the things for the wedding trip, or sailing *togs* as Sam still teased Elizabeth: bathing suits and turbans, middies and pleated skirts, and simple little frocks for evening.

For the first time in his life Sam was thankful for his responsibilities at the New York Bank and Trust Company, formerly the Beaumont Bank and Trust Company.

Hour after hour he sat in his comfortable office high above Wall Street and dreamed of their life together. The murky Hudson churned up by the late March winds became a deep azure sea ruffled by gentle tropical breezes. Stacks of financial reports lay untouched before him, while he charted their wedding trip and mapped out the rest of their life.

He had already taken the top floor of one of the new apartment buildings springing up along Park Avenue. It was only a block and a half from the express stop on the new Lexington Avenue subway. Its convenience to Wall Street did not impress Tobias. After all, what was more convenient to Wall Street than Washington Square? He suggested the young couple come live with him, at least till they had a proper house of their own. There was plenty of room in the old Federal mansion—too much, in fact—and once children began arriving, there was the small park right across the street. Sam would not hear of the idea. Of his many rules about marriage, one of the first was that a young couple did not start out in the presence of either set of parents.

Tobias' next suggestion was for a brownstone of their own. There was one for sale just across the square. He offered it as a wedding gift, and once again Sam refused. Brownstones were old-fashioned and difficult to run. Moving into the drafty old house across the square would put too much of a burden on Claudia. Might as well move into the old Astor mansion, Sam joked, calling his father's attention to the headline on the front page of the morning's *Tribune.*

ASTOR MANSION TO BE RAZED:
NEW SKYSCRAPER TO RISE ON SITE.

"Well, my boy, I'm sure it's the wave of the future, but I'm not sure it's one I approve of. Then again, it's not up to me to approve or disapprove. What does Claudia think about living in an apartment?"

"She likes the idea. It'll be small—not more than a dozen rooms—and modern, and she can do it up exactly as she pleases. And she won't have the servant problem. A man, a cook, and a couple of maids. That's all we'll need."

"Well, you've obviously given it a good deal of thought, but that leaves me the problem of a proper wedding present. Claudia has her emeralds, but I wanted to give the two of you something concrete, significant."

"If you insist on land or buildings, Father, there is something. The apartment is just a temporary thing. Oh, we may keep it up later as a sort of pied-à-terre, but our real home, that will be in the country. Probably on the North Shore."

"But what about Tarlton? That will be yours one day. Now if you like. I rarely go to Newport anymore, and if I do, I trust you and your wife will put me up for a few weeks."

"That's just the point. No one gets to Newport anymore. Besides, we don't want a summer house; we want something for all year round. I can commute to town easily enough, and Claudia will be able to get in whenever she wants. But we want to *live* in the country."

"Well, if that's what you want. I guess I can keep Tarlton as well. You might still want to get away during the summer."

"I doubt it. Anyway, Tarlton needs a lot of work, and I'd much rather concentrate on a new place. I want the most up-to-date stables and I'd like to build tennis courts. Not lawn tennis, but court tennis."

"You building a country club or a home for you and your wife, Sam?"

"It'll be a home all right. Claudia will see to that. I'll give her a free hand. I want her to love the place as much as I will."

"Well, I can see your mind's made up. Do you want to build, or have you found something you like?"

"I'm not sure. I'd like to take my time. We'll look around after we get back."

"Then that takes care of that. You find what you want and send me the bill."

"Thank you very much, Father. From both of us."

"Least I can do. After all, I don't say much, but you know I'm happy about this, don't you, Sam? It's about time you settled down. It's not good for a man to be a bachelor for too long. He gets used to it."

"You mean he might begin to like it?" Sam laughed.

"Well, I guess that's part of what I mean. But only a small part. A man thinks he's happy as a bachelor, but he *is* happy when he starts raising a family. And I'm selfish, I guess. I'd like to see some grandchildren before I go."

"Any other requests?"

"No, that's it. Oh, maybe another suggestion. The Yale Club and the Racquet are fine for a young man, but now that you're settling down don't you think it's time you joined the Union League? Those other clubs are all right in their place, but when you have a family, you'll want something, well, more solid."

"You know, Father, you make it sound so bleak. If it weren't Claudia I was marrying, I'd think it was the end of my life."

"Ah, but that's just the point," Tobias said with an appreciative smile that took ten years from his age. "It *is* Claudia you're marrying."

March slipped away, one frantic day after another. There was so much to do and so little time to think. If occasionally during a fitting Claudia was pricked by doubts sharper than any dressmaker's pin, if sometimes she sat listening to aged relatives' tales of Sam's childhood and felt no affection for the remote little hero of their stories, she did not have the time to follow those feelings to their source.

Not even Lucinda Ardsley could imagine that any girl lucky enough to win Sam Beaumont might still be grieving over some childish romance that probably had more to do with the magic of Paris than with any particular person, Claudia told herself during those hectic March days. But the nights were a different story. It wasn't that anything was wrong when she was with Sam. They never quarreled. He was considerate to a fault. If Claudia's spirits did not always match his own, he excused her on the grounds of wedding jitters. And if her ardor did not match his own, how could it be expected to? She was a nice girl, properly brought up. He had been around a bit. Surely it was this very contrast between them that made Claudia nervous. She was frightened and didn't know what to expect. Well, there was no need to hurry her. There would be plenty of time after the wedding. *And that's as it should be,* Sam thought. It was all very well to say things were different since the war, but not for his wife. He was almost glad when Claudia seemed nervous or shy during the brief moments they had alone. It proved she was as innocent as Sam had always thought her, as innocent as he wanted her to be.

Claudia could not excuse herself so easily. She knew the real reason for her coolness to Sam. In her feelings for him there was admiration and a very real affection, but none of the desire she had felt for Philippe, none of the passion she had known with him. It was a terrible way to feel about the man you were about to marry. Each day Claudia resolved more fervently that she would learn to love Sam, and each evening, when he took her in his arms, she prayed affection would blossom into passion. But there seemed to be a demon within Claudia, a recalcitrant soul that led a life of its own, for the more she resolved to love Sam, the more she recoiled from his touch.

Then it was the eve of the wedding, and all of Claudia's minor doubts suddenly coalesced into a single stifling terror. She must cancel the wedding. It would be a scandal, but what did that matter? The only thing that mattered was that it was not too late. Twenty-four hours from now she would have passed the point of no return. She and Sam would be bound together—legally, religiously, and socially. They would have a history, measured only in hours, but a history all the same. Twenty-four hours from now she and Sam Beaumont would belong to each other.

Despite the fire in the hearth and the mildness of the evening, Claudia shivered. If only she had taken the time to think things out. If only they hadn't given her this last night for second thoughts.

It was the first night Claudia had been alone since she and Sam had decided to marry. Sam had gone to his bachelor dinner. A dozen young men would start the evening off in high spirits in the bar of the Yale Club and end up innumerable speakeasies later in raucous and maudlin camaraderie. The young lady to whom many polite toasts would be drunk during the evening was expected to stay at home, dreaming of the happiness before her, and perhaps, though this was no longer thought entirely necessary, having a quiet talk with her mother. Last-minute nerves were permissible, but not last-minute doubts, and she was certainly not supposed to be dreaming of a lost lover.

Like his daughter two floors above, James sat staring into the fire. There was a glass of brandy at his side, and a newspaper lay unheeded in his lap. "How is she?" he asked as his wife entered the library.

"As nervous as might be expected."

"Well, there's nothing wrong with a mild case of nerves on the eve of a wedding." James spoke as much to reassure himself as to comfort his wife. A month ago he had welcomed his daughter's engagement to Samuel Beaumont. He had known the match brought pain to Katherine, but better one happy daughter, he reasoned, than two miserable girls. His thinking was much like his daughter's: Discouraging Claudia from marrying Sam would not make the young man propose to her sister. Beaumont had dragged his feet long enough to leave no doubt. No, James hadn't regretted the match, but during the last month he had begun to wonder. He wasn't at all sure his daughter was in love with Sam. Not that James thought love the most important prerequisite to marriage. But just the same he didn't want Claudia to make a major mistake. A year before he had prevented her from going all out for love. Now he wanted to stop her from veering to the other extreme. If only he knew what her real feelings for Beaumont were. When she'd returned from Florida, there hadn't been any doubt in his mind. Obviously Sam's presence had had a salutary effect, but since the engagement she seemed more distracted than anything else.

"Perhaps I'll stick my head in and see how she is." He climbed the stairs slowly, thoughtfully. "How are you, baby?"

"I'm all right, Daddy." Claudia's tone belied her words.

"All set for the big day? You know, I'm going to miss you. But you've made a good choice, Claudia. Sam will be a fine husband to you. Nobody could love you more than he does. Except me, of course, but that's another matter. Just the same, Sam's crazy about you. Can see it in his eyes every time he looks at you. As it should be. You deserve the best."

"No, I don't Daddy. I don't deserve the best, and I certainly don't deserve Sam." Suddenly without any warning she began to cry. "Sam is so good to me, and I don't deserve him."

"Now that's foolishness. You're just nervous, child, and darned well in love too, I'd say. Why else would my little girl think she wasn't good enough for someone?"

"But that's just it. I'm not in love. At least not with Sam."

"Claudia, do you know what you're saying?"

"I'm saying that I don't love Sam Beaumont. The man I'm marrying tomorrow morning."

"Here, use this." James handed her his handkerchief. "Now let's look at this without tears. You may know about romance, Claudia, but how much do you know about love? Love, the best kind of love, grows. In fifty years you'll look back and know you didn't love Sam now, not the way you will then."

"Oh, Daddy, I've told myself that over and over. But what if it doesn't grow? It hasn't so far, and the harder I try, the worse it is. Sometimes I try so hard I don't even like Sam anymore. That's how horrid I am."

"Now you're not horrid, Claudia. I won't hear that kind of talk." James was silent for a moment, and the hand that had been stroking Claudia's hair lay lightly on her head. "Just the same," he spoke, carefully weighing each word, "if you honestly feel you're making a mistake, it isn't too late. Oh, people will talk. But what does that matter? The important thing is not to ruin your life or Sam's for that matter. If you feel real affection for him, and I think you do, then marry him. Love *will* grow. I promise you that. But if you have no real affection for him, then don't go through with it. Sam's a fine man, but perhaps he isn't right for you. You're young, Claudia, still so young. There'll be others."

"That's just it, Daddy." The tears were flowing faster now, and her words were interrupted by sobs. "There'll never be another. Not after Philippe. I'll never love anyone the way I loved him."

James recoiled. There was fury in his eyes, and his voice was icy. "I thought you had more sense, Claudia. I thought you'd grown up, but I find you're still a spoiled foolish child. Determined to ruin your life for some fast-talking Frenchman."

"Don't speak that way about Philippe."

"I will speak whatever way I wish in my own house. And I will make one last statement about that good-for-nothing count of yours. I don't think it's love you can't get over, Claudia. I think it's loss. The only loss you've ever known. For the first time in your life you wanted something you couldn't have. I guess that's *my* fault. Mine and the good Lord's. I bought you anything you asked for—and He gave you the beauty and the charm to get what couldn't be bought. Along came the first exception, the first toy you couldn't have, and you're ready to throw away your life over it. That's childish, childish and weak. Tomorrow morning, you will marry Sam Beaumont. If you have any sense, you will make that marriage work, though heaven knows you'll have little enough to do in that department, the way Sam loves you. Now I have nothing more to say, except to add my best wishes."

James looked at his daughter, small and vulnerable in the oversized chair. Childlike, she clutched the wet handkerchief in a ball and dabbed at her eyes. All the harshness went out of him, and he felt a stab of pity for her pain, however misguided. "Now I think it's time you tried to get some sleep. I'll have some brandy sent up. It will relax you. And remember, no more tears. We don't want a red-eyed bride tomorrow morning." He kissed the cheek she raised to him and was gone.

A dutiful child, Claudia drank the glass of brandy her father had prescribed. Then she drank three more. When she finally fell asleep, there was barely an inch of amber left at the bottom of the decanter. It was a heavy, drugged sleep, and for the first time in weeks Philippe did not invade it. Neither, however, did Sam.

The season's chosen couple could not have asked for a more perfect morning for their wedding, even if each of them did view it through red-rimmed eyes. Spring had made its debut. A warm breeze ruffled the tender green leaves just beginning to sprout, and an occasional hearty crocus even showed its colors. Claudia sat staring out the window at that tiny patch of Central Park that was hers, that small corner of the city where for the past two decades she had watched the seasons turn. *By the time I get back the trees will be green and all the flowers will be out.* Then she realized with a start she wouldn't be coming back here at all. She'd be going to that shiny modern apartment with Sam. No longer could she retreat to the security of her own room. Now her room would be Sam's room. A shudder ran through her, and she wondered for the thousandth time how she would be feeling if it were Philippe she was marrying instead, if it were Philippe's bed she would share.

She pushed her untouched breakfast tray aside and noticed the bottle of brandy at her bedside. That was one way to get through the morning. By the time Elizabeth and two of the maids arrived to help her dress she was in light spirits. And thanks to Pebecco, which promised a blissful love life, as well as whiter teeth, not even James suspected she had drunk anything stronger than tea for breakfast.

Indeed, he was delighted with his daughter this morning. She was once again the carefree girl he adored. And she looked exquisite. Never had he seen a more beautiful bride, or at least not since Elizabeth had worn the Sheridan satin lace with her own special flair a quarter of a century ago.

Claudia was a beautiful bride. Everyone agreed: the onlookers who crowded the canopy of the new St. Bartholomew's on Park Avenue hungry for a glimpse of a "society" wedding, the guests whose heads turned and eyes lit up in open admiration as she sailed down the aisle on James' proud arm, and especially Sam.

Sam had wilted three collars in the last hour, clocked close to a mile pacing the vestry for the last thirty minutes, and asked his best man about the ring no less than a dozen times. But now, as he turned to see Claudia coming toward him up the aisle, her step so light she seemed almost to be floating, her veil a fragile halo around her golden hair, all nervousness drained from him. He had what he wanted.

The next few hours were interminable. It was technically a small wedding, yet the reception line seemed endless. Cheeks touched in mock kisses, best wishes and good luck were murmured over and over, and cries of "What a beautiful bride!" echoed through the air heavy with smoke and Chanel and good fellowship. Then there was the interval with the photographer while Claudia sat impatient, eager to be off and enjoy the party—after all, it was hers, wasn't it?—and innumerable relatives and friends were summoned, posed, then swept summarily away. And there was a fresh glass of champagne to revive her from the ordeal of the camera. Then Sam's arms were around her and they were circling and circling in a waltz and everyone was saying yes, weren't they the handsomest couple ever and she was laughing and thinking that they were, of course, the handsomest couple ever and wasn't Sam the best dancer in the whole world. And then she was dancing with Daddy, who had tears in his eyes, the lovable old bear, and then with Tobias Beaumont, who said she had to call him Father now, and then with Sam's best man and what seemed like a hundred other young men in identical cutaways with indistinguishable faces—all the bachelors out of her party-going past. And every few steps or every few men—it was the same thing really—someone was kind enough to hand her a glass of champagne because dancing was such terribly hard work and she was so thirsty.

Then suddenly Mr. and Mrs. Samuel Livingston Beaumont were alone in the new Rolls-Royce—a token from Tobias until they had chosen their house—that would take them the ten blocks south to the Plaza. The suite was filled with roses, and there was champagne cooling in the bucket. Sam had ordered a light supper for later.

"You've thought of everything, Sam," Claudia said, twirling around the room, dropping her cloche on one chair, her cape on another, plucking a blood red rose from the dozens clustered about the room, and ending in Sam's arms. He bent to kiss her, and she accepted his kiss briefly, then twirled off again. "We must have some champagne!" She was feeling a pleasant warmth, and wanted to keep that feeling as long as possible, certainly for the next few hours.

Champagne was not a bad idea, Sam thought as he sent the cork skyward and felt the cool foam bubble over his hands. It would relax Claudia.

So they sat and drank two glasses of champagne each and laughed about the wedding and hadn't this fellow been funny and hadn't that girl looked pretty and Sam said yes, but no one had been nearly so pretty as his beautiful wife, and his eyes took on that special look she'd seen more than once in the past month and he asked Claudia if she'd like him to go downstairs for a few moments, and she laughed, but a little less lightly than before, and said no, she'd go inside and wouldn't he follow her in a few minutes.

She stood staring at herself in the white lawn nightgown trimmed with fluted Val lace. Of the dozens she had bought, this one was the most virginal. "What a hypocrite you are," she snarled to the mirror and prayed that when she felt Sam's hands on her body, she would not think of Philippe. Then she saw Sam's reflection behind her in the mirror, and his arms went around her, and she was no longer thinking of Philippe. It took every fiber of her being, every ounce of will to keep her body from stiffening in revulsion, her arms from pushing him away. He picked her up and carried her to the bed, and then his powerful body was above hers. For all his strength and size he was enormously tender.

Afterward, as he lay beside her trying to regulate his uneven breathing, Claudia looked at him and realized with what effort he had transformed his urgent passion into tenderness. And she hated herself for the responses she should have been able to give, had wanted to give, but had not given. But she hated Sam a little too, for having, no matter how kindly and gently, taken her.

Book Two

1924

1

At the end of the dock a dark-hulled yawl bobbed gently in the water. "Oh, Sam, it's beautiful." Claudia hadn't expected to be much impressed by Sam's boat. One vessel was much like another to her—a convenient vehicle for an afternoon's pleasure. Nothing more. But Sam had built something special. Even Claudia could recognize that.

He took her arm and hurried down the dock. As they walked, he began to single out the vessel's finer points. Claudia laughed. "I've told you I don't understand any of that."

She knew the specifications. Sam had told her over and over. Forty-three and a half feet overall with a beam of twelve feet. Double planked with Honduras mahogany over three-eighths-inch Oregon spruce. A main salon paneled in Brazilian rosewood, a comfortable captain's cabin of the same paneling forward, a small but sparkling galley aft, and an open fireplace like a truncated obelisk for cold nights off Bar Harbor or the Cape. But all the specifications meant nothing to Claudia. She knew only that the boat was sleek and graceful and the dark teak decks glistened in the late-afternoon sun. The waves made delicious little noises as they slapped against the hull.

"I laughed when you named it *Mistress,* but I think I'm going to be jealous."

"Not it, Claudia, she. Boats are always she."

"Now I know I'm going to be jealous."

Sam beamed with pride. "Much as I would like to

185

accommodate you, I can't change the name. It's bad luck. And this boat was made for good luck. I can feel it."

"Then I guess your *Mistress* and I, *she* and I, will just have to learn to be friends."

He smiled at her gratefully. He had everything he wanted, or almost everything, he thought as he watched Claudia climb aboard, her long legs flashing in the sun.

The rest was only a matter of time, he told himself, as he had so often since their first night together. What had he expected? Had he really hoped to transform an innocent virgin into an accomplished mistress on their wedding night? It would take time, he knew, time and tenderness. And he had plenty of both where Claudia was concerned.

That of course was the point. Claudia was well worth waiting for. He was sure of that. Just as he was sure her icy beauty camouflaged a deeply sensual nature. He'd recognized it the first time they met after her return from Paris, and he'd seen flashes of it any number of times since. Sam knew, as certainly as he knew his own passions, that another side to his wife existed. *Just wait until we're at sea,* he told himself. *Things will be different then.* Sam was counting on a more primitive existence to bring out Claudia's darker nature.

The next morning, while the sun was still low in the east and the sky a pale blue, they set out. There was a fresh wind from the northwest, and Sam was sure they could make the small island he had in mind by lunch.

In less than an hour the shoreline had dropped away, and Claudia could barely make out the roof of the Royal Poinciana. Suddenly she wanted very much to be back there. She wanted to doze away the afternoon on the palm-shaded beach and look forward to tea and dancing and the company of other people.

There was something ominous about the two of them sailing off into the empty horizon. She wasn't exactly frightened. She'd spent too many afternoons on the Sound or in the bay separating Palm Beach from the mainland to feel fear, but somehow this was different, different enough to make her uncomfortable. Now there was no party on board to divert her, nor could she look forward to the post-race dance at the yacht club. All she could look forward to was day after day, night after night alone with Sam. Alone with her husband. It was more than a little unnerving.

"Take the tiller for a minute while I trim up, will you, Claudia?"

"What do I do with it?"

"What do you do with it?" Sam laughed. "Why, you steer, of course."

"I know that, but how?"

"Do you mean after all the times you've been sailing you still don't know how to skipper a boat?" His voice was good-natured but incredulous.

"Well, it was never necessary. There were always so many people around who wanted to work, and it was more pleasant just to lie in the sun."

"Of course, I shouldn't have assumed. Well, first lesson right now. . . ." And Sam proceeded to explain in the simplest terms possible how to run the boat. The tiller moved one way and the boat turned the other, but then it all depended on how the sails were set. Claudia tried to concentrate on Sam's instructions, but her mind kept wandering. Should she put more lotion on her legs? Was her nose getting freckled?

The moment they dropped anchor in the tiny cove Claudia's spirits rose. The water was brilliant blue and crystal clear, its glassy surface broken only by an occasional fish as it leaped through the air. As *Mistress* swung at anchor, Claudia watched the crescent of white sand dotted with dark palm trees come closer and draw farther away.

"Oh, Sam, this is paradise."

"And we're Adam and Eve. How about a swim before lunch? You don't even need a fig leaf."

He saw her face darken for a moment, and then she disappeared down the hatch. "I'll be in my bathing suit in a minute."

Silently Sam cursed his clumsiness. He hadn't meant to say that, didn't know he was going to until he saw Claudia looking so suddenly free and happy. Patience, he reminded himself, and swore for the hundredth time since their first night together that for the moment at least he would learn to control his desire.

After dinner they sat in the cockpit and watched the stars move overhead as *Mistress* described a perfect arc on her anchor.

"I think if I reached up, I could touch them."

"The only time they seem closer is when you're flying."

"I didn't know you had ever flown, Sam."

"Only once and that wasn't at night. There was a time when I wanted desperately to fly. I dreamed of running off to join the Lafayette Escadrille. But then I guess half the men at Yale that year were dreaming the same thing."

"What stopped you?"

"Father talked me out of it. Discretion is the better part of valor, and first finish Yale. And then we were in it, and the infantry seemed the fastest way to get a commission and get over there. Not that I got very far once I was there. I'd give a lot to have seen some action —just one battle. Then I'd know I'd done something."

"Made the world safe for democracy?"

It was too dark to see her face, and Sam couldn't tell from her tone whether Claudia was mocking him. "Well, not single-handedly, perhaps, but I wouldn't have minded putting in my two cents for freedom."

"Whose freedom?"

"Why, ours, of course. The whole world's. The Kaiser had to be stopped someplace. But it's more than that. I don't suppose you can understand this, Claudia. I don't suppose any woman could, but there's something . . . well, almost uplifting about war. A man finds out things about himself under fire—what he's made of and how much endurance he has and whether other men can count on him."

"And what it's like to die."

"That too, but that's part of the glory of it—giving your life for something you believe in."

"No matter how you dress it up, it's still death. And murder."

"I told you you wouldn't understand. But then you're not supposed to." He reached an arm around her shoulders, pulled her to him, and felt her shiver against him. "I'm sorry. I've been so busy talking I didn't realize how cold it had gotten. Why don't we go below and turn in?" He pulled her closer, and Claudia shivered again.

Claudia smelled coffee before she was awake. When she opened her eyes, she didn't at first know where she was. Then the kerosene lamps swinging above her head and the sight of Sam in the main cabin made everything fall into place.

She stretched in the narrow bunk. "That smells good. What time is it?"

"After eight. And it is good. I've already had a cup."

"After eight! I haven't been up this early in years. But then again I guess I haven't been to bed that early in years."

"One of the advantages of sailing. No nightclubs or speakeasies." He sat on the edge of her bunk and handed her a cup of coffee. A small cloud of steam hung over it. "Better bundle up this morning. It's nippy."

"But it's April—in Florida."

"Well, I didn't mean furs, but there is a strong wind. It's blowing at least twenty-five, and we may hit a line squall or two before the day's out."

Claudia turned and looked apprehensively through the porthole at the sky. Thin clouds raced overhead.

"There's nothing to worry about. But chances are we'll find some strong wind and rain sometime today. You'll like it. It puts some spice into cruising. You don't want to laze in the sun every day, do you?"

She did, of course, but she couldn't admit that to Sam. Claudia thought of pulling the covers around her and sinking back into the warm bunk, but she knew Sam would interpret her actions as an invitation. She sat up and took another sip of the hot coffee.

"One sweater ought to be enough if you stay below, but when you come up, better put on your oilskin. We're bound to take on spray in this sea."

Claudia had planned to stay below—she found no romance in salt spray in her hair—but the pitching and tossing of the small boat made her uncomfortable. She had never been seasick in her life, but she felt unmistakably queasy now.

Sam peered down the hatch. "You look a little pale. Do you feel all right?" She nodded unconvincingly. "Maybe you'd better come up here after all. You won't feel it as much."

Sam was right. The fresh air blew away her nausea, but the cold spray stung her face. She couldn't decide which was worse, to be warm and sick below or chilled and wet up here. Then the wind came up, and she knew.

The boat seemed to be sailing on its side. She braced her feet against the seat on the opposite side of the cockpit and tightened her grasp on the backstay, but still she felt as if she were going to be tossed over the low side of the boat into the sea. The deck on the port side was completely submerged. She considered pointing it out to Sam but she doubted he would care. Like her, he sat with his legs braced against the opposite seat, but he was holding onto nothing but the tiller, and he greeted each new dousing with a howl of exultation.

"I think I'll go below after all." The wind snatched her words away.

"What did you say?" he shouted.

She repeated herself and crawled below to a dry corner of the forward cabin. It was darker here than the main cabin, but the spray could not reach her. She lay on the port side, looking out the starboard porthole. At least that way she could see the sky. As mean and overcast as it was, it was preferable to the foaming water covering the other porthole.

She could feel the sea pounding the hull, and the pitching motion tossed her mercilessly. She wrapped herself in a blanket, as much to soften the blows when she was hurled against the sides of the boat as to keep warm.

After half an hour the boat began to pitch more

gently, and the porthole gave an occasional glimpse of the horizon. In another half hour she heard Sam stomping around overhead and then the noise of chain and line running out as the anchor was dropped. She looked out the porthole and saw a beach. The palm trees were heavy with water, but it had stopped raining.

Sam came below. His hair was plastered to his face, and he was laughing. "Wasn't that something?" He peeled off his oilskin. It had provided little protection, and his shirt and trousers were soaked. He began to unbutton his shirt. "I bet it was gusting up to forty-five for a while there. That's why I love these waters. You can wait all summer for something like that on the Sound, but here we are, second day out, and wham." He sounded as if he had managed to find her exactly the gift he had been searching for. When she said nothing, he looked at her in surprise. "You weren't frightened, were you?"

"Well, not exactly frightened. . . ."

He dropped his wet shirt on the floor and sat down next to her on the bunk. For once Claudia did not stiffen as his arm went around her. She welcomed any comfort. "There's nothing to be afraid of, Claudia. I wouldn't take you out in anything dangerous, and I know these waters pretty well. I knew it would only be a squall, and that's no problem. I can handle it."

He went on reassuring her quietly, and as he spoke, he began to stroke her arm. He was whispering comforting words into her hair, and then she felt his lips against her ear and his hand beneath her middy. She started to pull away, but Sam held her tight and turned her face to him. He was still exhilarated from the storm, and his feelings of tenderness at her fear and helplessness had swelled to desire.

She felt like a child as she watched him unbutton her blouse and then her skirt and drop them on top of his wet things on the cabin floor. She closed her eyes, and through the thin silk of her chemise she felt his body on hers. Then the chemise too was gone. She could taste the salt on his mouth and feel his hands trying to knead her body to life. The storm was long past, but Sam was still in its thrall, and there was nothing she could do but wait it out.

"I think," Sam said, looking at his wife who had that maddening air of not being there again, "the crew could use some shore leave. Perhaps this has been a little hard on you." He had no right to be disappointed, he told himself. He couldn't expect Claudia to love sailing or its isolation as he did. Certainly she'd never complained. And yet Sam knew she'd been frightened during that storm and occasionally uncomfortable, and he suspected she missed the festivities associated with a holiday in the South.

"Oh, Sam," she said, returning from whatever thoughts had taken her so far away, "hard on me, indeed. I don't lift a finger. You spoil me shamelessly."

It was true. He was a one-man captain, crew, and steward. Claudia's duties were no more strenuous than an occasional moment at the helm while Sam raised sail or weighed anchor. Even galley duty, which Claudia realized was hers by right, had been usurped by Sam. Claudia knew, he had learned their first day out, as little about preparing a meal as she had about sailing a boat.

"But, Claudia, you *must* be able to fry a steak." His voice held that same blend of kindness and incredulity.

"Now where on earth would I have learned that?"

"Where everyone learns it."

"But that's just the point, Sam. Everyone *doesn't* learn it. You did because you like to hunt and sail and do all those sorts of things, but I've never gotten that far from a proper kitchen, and a proper kitchen usually has a proper cook in it. I don't suppose there's a decent restaurant hiding under one of those palm trees. I'm awfully good at reading menus."

"Ah, I knew you must be good at something," he said, taking her in his arms.

"I'm also very good"—she kissed him lightly and eluded his embrace—"at mixing rum cocktails according to your specifications. Two more coming up." A few cocktails before dinner and a few highballs after, Claudia had discovered, made that inevitable moment when Sam extinguished the kerosene lamps and turned to her in the darkness just a little more bearable. And if he chose to stay the night in her narrow bunk as he often did, the alcohol brought at least a few hours of sleep.

"Yes, I think you're due for shore leave," he repeated. "If the wind holds, we can be back in Palm Beach by five or so, and it's the Everglades Club for you tonight."

"Oh, Sam, you mean I can have a bath and get dressed up and dance and see people." She stopped abruptly. She hadn't meant to blurt out that last.

Sam heard but pretended not to. He refused to blame Claudia. It was more his fault. He had asked her to rough it, as Mrs. Trenholm had put it, and was that really fair to a girl on her wedding trip? Later, when they were more accustomed to each other, it would be different. He could teach Claudia to sail during the summer, and by next winter she'd be as avid to go to sea as he was.

If life was no better in Palm Beach, it was no worse. Sam missed sailing but contented himself with what he referred to as getting the kinks out of *Mistress*. He golfed and played tennis and swam. Occasionally Claudia joined him. More often she lazed away the hours on the beach or the veranda of the Breakers and played an occasional desultory game of bridge. They met for lunch and tea and dinner—always with other people—and each night, when they closed the door to their suite, Claudia was, if not affectionate, at least acquiescent. Her conscience and Sam's bootlegger saw to that.

The wedding trip hadn't been exactly the one Sam had planned, but it had been good enough for all that. In fact, when Sam thought about it, the trip was a most auspicious beginning to their married life. It had been a compromise, and wasn't that what a good marriage was based on?

Mr. and Mrs. Samuel Beaumont returned to all the furor and celebration their brief engagement had precluded. The summer passed in a sunny haze of long country weekends blending into one another. Since Sam had not yet found the proper house or land, they spent a month in Glen Cove with the Trenholms, three weeks in Newport with Tobias—once again Sam admitted it wasn't quite so bad during Race Week—and any number of long weekends with friends. On those rare summer nights that found them in town there would be impromptu cocktail parties in some of the big houses closed and shuttered against the New York summer. There among the cretonne throws and slipcovers the girls would sip orange blossoms and the men whiskey in preparation for dinner at some small French restaurant that stubbornly remained open during all but the dog days of August.

The slightly musty rooms darkened against the brilliant summer sun reminded Claudia all too vividly of the Paris *hôtel* shuttered against the September heat. She had only to close her eyes to be back in Philippe's room, in his arms, to feel his hands, his body on hers once again.

It was not Philippe's hand she felt on her shoulder now. They had been married four months, and Claudia still stiffened at Sam's touch. She knew Sam sensed it, and she was sorry. But pity was not love.

"What about it, Claudia? Is the Park Casino all right?"

"Since it's the only thing open, it will have to be." She was bored. Bored with parties where everyone drank too much, bored with her own attempts not to be bored. Claudia's rebelliousness hadn't subsided with marriage. In an era when all the most beautiful young women rode on the roofs of taxis, jumped into fountains fully clothed, and stowed away on luxury liners to be gently but spectacularly removed by tugboat in New York Harbor, Claudia indulged in her share of romps. It had been *de rigueur* that Claudia convince George Talbott and Schuyler Mason to kidnap the headwaiter at Liat's and that she lead the two of them and Harriet Ardsley Mason in an attempt to commandeer a Fifth Avenue bus over to Madison Avenue. It had been *de rigueur,* but it hadn't been much fun. And the fact that Sam put up with it patiently, good-naturedly, and a little sadly hadn't helped. If only he had got angry, it might have made the whole farce worthwhile. But Sam said nothing. If he didn't approve of some of his wife's escapades, he did enjoy, with a certain pride of ownership, the admiration she aroused in other men. Her popularity was all the more pleasing to Sam because she did nothing to encourage it. If Claudia were not as warm to Sam as he would have liked, he could not fault the coolness with which she treated other men. In that sense she was scrupulously fair to Sam, and Sam was scrupulously fair in return. He would not protest her behavior so long as it was harmless, so long as it did not involve another man.

"Then the Park Casino it is." Sam's arm was still around her as they walked to the door. Once out on the street Claudia shrugged herself loose. She felt Sam move away from her and knew, without looking, that there would be pain in his eyes. "It's unbearably hot tonight," she murmured.

Dinner at the Park Casino was a desultory affair. Too hot to eat much, too hot to dance at all. The talk was chiefly on Lucinda Ardsley's forthcoming wedding to, of all people, Anson Hagerty. For all her dreams of conquering Paris Lucinda was settling for the son of a Pittsburgh steel baron. Anson's reasons for marriage were less clear. There were those who suspected he would never marry. Harrison Hagerty numbered himself among that group. He therefore reverted to type and made a simple business deal with his son. Mr. Hagerty wanted Anson to return to Pittsburgh. Anson recoiled at the thought of life beneath the dark clouds of a western Pennsylvania sky. If he could not remain in

Paris, he would at least live in New York. Mr. Hagerty would permit that. He would buy Anson a seat on the Stock Exchange if, and only if, Anson married and settled down. Not even Harrison Hagerty believed he could enforce the second part of that edict, but he could at least hold his son to the first. Anson weighed his alternatives and found the prospect of life in New York with Lucinda preferable to freedom in Pittsburgh. The wedding would take place just before Christmas, and Lucinda and Harriet could talk of nothing else.

"Lot of fuss about nothing," Anson said, pouring more gin into his glass of ginger ale. "If we had any sense, Lucinda, we'd go down to city hall and get married."

Lucinda turned to Claudia. "Aren't you sorry you didn't have a big wedding, Claudia? I mean a *really* big wedding?"

"I'm not sorry in the least. Besides, we didn't want to wait. Did we, darling?" She turned to Sam.

"What was the hurry?" Lucinda's voice was as innocent as a child's, but there was a malicious glint in her eye.

"I was afraid she'd change her mind." Sam laughed.

"I guess Anson doesn't have to worry about me."

"And Sam never had to worry about me. But he didn't know that." She turned to her husband. "Dance with me, Sam. Very slowly in deference to the heat."

"Don't let her irritate you," Sam whispered when they were some distance from the table.

"She doesn't irritate me," she snapped.

"Have it your way."

"I'm sorry, Sam. It's just the heat. And she is a horrid little thing. So vicious."

"Well, console yourself that she's getting her just reward. Can you imagine spending the rest of your life with Anson Hagerty?"

"Can you imagine spending the rest of your life with Lucinda Ardsley?"

"A marriage made in heaven." They laughed together. It was a rare moment.

Claudia returned to the table with her guard up, but Lucinda had focused on a new subject. "Who is that dancing with Sybil Chesney?"

"You never can tell with Sybil Chesney."

"Why is it, Anson, that you always have the nicest things to say about people?" Sam asked.

"I'm only saying what everyone knows," Anson said defensively. He was recalling a similar conversation with Sam some months ago. "First she was fired from Foxcroft for smoking, and then there was that business with Bill Winston in the sun porch that afternoon at Alicia Sibbington's. Sybil Chesney's always been a little wild, and everyone knows it."

"Everyone may know it, Anson, but somehow you're the one who always feels obliged to mention it."

Anson looked sullen but said nothing.

"I've never seen him before," Lucinda persevered.

"I didn't see him," Claudia said without interest.

"His name is Joe Denbigh," George chimed in.

"Denbigh," Harriet said. "Do we know any Denbighs, Sky?"

"I doubt you know this one."

"What does that mean, George?"

"Nothing much. Only that nobody seems to know him or much about him. I met him at Sybil's house. Didn't say or do anything wrong, but there's something peculiar about him. It was as if he had just been created —out of thin air."

"Where does he come from?" Sam asked.

"No one seems to know."

"You mean no background, no family, schools, anything?" Sam pursued.

"Not a Yale man? Not even Groton or Choate? Shocking." There was only a little humor in Claudia's voice. *"Listen* to all of you. Sybil Chesney dances with a man no one knows, and within five minutes you've condemned him and labeled her."

"Why, Claudia, I never knew you were so broad-minded." Lucinda's eyes were wide with feigned innocence.

"Oh, what does it matter? The conversation is getting dull. So is this place. There must be something else open."

"Charlot's hasn't closed for the summer."

"There's a new speakeasy over on Forty-sixth Street."

And the evening, if not saved, was at least not thrown away at once.

Sam looked across the room at his wife. She was sitting at her dressing table brushing her hair, and the twin arcs of her arms were continuations of the graceful curves of the black basalt and white tile table that, like the rest of the apartment, was in the fashionable *style moderne*. Sam was lounging in the white upholstered chair Claudia had informed him was the modern equivalent of the wingback chair he had expected in his bedroom. It was comfortable to the body, Sam admitted, but stark to the eye. Unlike his wife, he thought as he watched her slender body move beneath the thin satin of her peignoir.

"That was quite a defense of Sybil Chesney *and* her friend you put up tonight."

"Not much more than yours of Sybil." Claudia addressed her husband's image in the mirror.

"But that's my place. Someone has to see to it Anson Hagerty minds his manners."

"We all ought to thank you for that." She seemed willing to let the subject drop.

"But why were you so incensed? Do you know anything about the fellow? Has Sybil said anything to you?"

"I haven't seen Sybil Chesney in weeks, and I don't know anything about the man."

"Well, you certainly did champion his cause."

"It had nothing to do with him. It was the idea. All of us sitting there, questioning his background and breeding as if he were a horse or a dog. 'Who are his people? Where did he go to school?' It was all so vicious."

"I was the one who asked where he came from," Sam said quietly.

"Well, then I was annoyed with you, too. For all we know he may be a perfectly nice man."

"Or he may be a not-so-nice man."

"That's just as likely."

"But don't you see, Claudia, that's the point. He's an unknown quantity."

"Maybe we should all take the terribly dangerous step of discovering that quantity for ourselves, instead of trying to tag and pedigree the man. Perhaps that's what Sybil Chesney is trying to do."

"You know Sybil."

"Now *you* sound like Anson."

"For pete's sake, Claudia, a man can say things to his wife he doesn't want to say in public."

"Well, Sybil Chesney is beside the point anyway. It's the man she was with, or rather our judgment of him."

"But Sybil Chesney isn't beside the point. In fact, she is the point. That's why we judge. I don't mind for myself. I've known all kinds of men, many I wouldn't want you to know. There are men I've liked that I still wouldn't want in my house—our house."

"In other words, if we were to meet Sybil Chesney's friend, you would be civil so long as I was not."

"You know that isn't what I'm saying."

His voice clawed at her conscience. She never meant to hurt Sam, yet she did, repeatedly. She set the silver-backed brush on the table and turned to him. "It's just that the conversation tonight seemed so petty and snobbish, Sam. It doesn't lead anywhere—except further and further into some tiny restricted world. I don't want to live in that world. I don't want *us* to live in it."

There was more kindness in her eyes and voice than Sam had become accustomed to, but for once he knew enough not to let Claudia see how overwhelmed with love and gratitude he was. "I promise"—he raised his right hand in mock solemnity—"I will not judge Sybil Chesney's new beau. I promise I will be civil, polite, even friendly to him. He is welcome to dine in my house, ride my horses, even sail on my boat. The admirable fellow, whoever he may be, may have my fortune, my worldly possessions, anything," he said, walking to the dressing table and putting his arms around her, "anything but my wife."

Harriet Ardsley Mason sat in the Rolls-Royce between Sam and Claudia. "It's good of you to give me a lift out. Schuyler always seems to get tied up at the office on Friday afternoons, and I just hate sitting around waiting for him. You're lucky, Claudia. Sam is so considerate."

There was little envy in Harriet's voice. Schuyler Mason was a good catch—better than Harriet deserved, more than one young man had observed on the announcement of the engagement. Harriet was not unattractive. Her small, regular features had a certain classical symmetry, and her figure, too round to be fashionable, was nevertheless alluring. Unfortunately, Harriet hadn't the wit to make the most of her attributes. The fact that she had pursued and won Schuyler Mason was a source of amazement to everyone but Harriet.

It wasn't that Schuyler was particularly handsome. Nor was he a raconteur or a spectacular sportsman. Schuyler was pleasant-looking with sharp, straightforward features and a ready smile. He was enthusiastic without being zealous and threw his small, wiry body wholeheartedly, if somewhat ineptly, into the sport at hand. Schuyler Mason was perfectly moderate in all areas except two. His ancestors—mostly Philadelphians with the exception of some distant New York Schuylers on his mother's side—were very good indeed. And his financial situation was exactly the opposite. Schuyler's father had lost the little he had inherited early in his legal career and then proceeded to lose the career as well by helping himself to small amounts of the various trust funds that constituted the bulk of his practice. Not even his powerful Main Line relatives could prevent the disbarring of this most un-Philadelphian of lawyers.

Fortunately for Schuyler his father's disgrace had occurred early in his career and, if not forgotten by the time Sky reached manhood, was at least no longer mentioned. A maternal uncle, not a Schuyler, saw him through Choate and Princeton and into the investment firm of Winett, Barton, and Winett. The uncle had gone to Princeton with old man Winett and reasoned that the cloud of his father's misbehavior would cast a smaller shadow over Schuyler in New York than in Philadelphia.

From the first day at Winett, Barton, and Winett Schuyler had worked diligently and visibly. Old man Winett was satisfied. And finally after a year in New York he had married Harriet Ardsley and her yearly income of twenty-five thousand dollars. It wasn't much by the standards of Sam Beaumont or many of the men Sky had cultivated at Princeton, but for the first time in his life Schuyler did not feel like a poor boy in a rich boy's school.

"Now don't blame Sky, Harriet," Sam said easily. "He can't help it if old man Winett runs that place like Simon Legree. According to Sky, he just about stands at the door and clocks his men out on Friday afternoons. I'm lucky. All I have to worry about is Father, and he thinks there's something sinful about spending afternoons like this"—Sam indicated the brilliant autumn foliage speeding past the windows—"in a stuffy office. And I couldn't agree more." He rolled down the window an inch and took a deep breath. "It's a good weekend for the hunt. Don't you think so, Claudia?"

"It's a good weekend for the country." She was determined to be as affectionate as possible this weekend, but he knew her feelings about hunting.

"It should be a marvelous weekend," Harriet said. "Polly promised there would be all sorts of fascinating people there. You don't suppose she snared the Prince of Wales, do you? I read in the paper he plans to do some fox hunting on Long Island while he's here."

"I wouldn't count on it." Claudia laughed. "But then again I wouldn't put it past Polly either. She does have a way of collecting unusual people."

"Yes, but they're usually the wrong unusual people." Claudia shot Sam a warning look, and he turned back to the passing scenery.

"That reminds me," Harriet, who had noticed nothing, went on. "The funniest thing. Remember that man we saw with Sybil at the Park Casino last summer. Jim Denbigh? No, Joe Denbigh. Well, he's going to be there. It seems Charles didn't want Polly to invite him—he doesn't like the idea of his little sister Sybil getting mixed up with someone like that. But Polly and Sybil have always been thick, so Polly asked Joe Denbigh anyway, and Charles was furious."

"Well, then he can't be such a bad sort after all," Sam said. "If Charles had really disapproved, he would have put his foot down. I know that much about him."

"You're suddenly very broad-minded, Sam."

"Whatever made you think he wasn't?" Claudia said, looking directly at Sam and smiling.

"Yes, Harriet, whatever made you think I wasn't?" Sam and Claudia laughed, and Harriet looked from one to the other. Now *there* was a happy marriage.

Charles and Polly Chesney had a dozen people for the weekend and another ten for dinner on Friday night. Claudia knew everyone in the room except one couple, attractive but obviously out of place, who clung to each other and the fireplace in the chilly gathering, and a tall, dark man in a far corner. He was standing with his back to Claudia, but she knew most of the men there well enough to recognize even their backs. The man was talking to Sybil Chesney, and she guessed he was the infamous Mr. Denbigh.

Polly Chesney fell upon her. "Claudia! You look marvelous, darling. You know everyone here, except Mr. and Mrs. Dedwin." She swept Claudia past the couple in front of the fireplace. "Deadly dull people," she whispered, "but Charles insisted. Very important client, or so says Charles. I told him one doesn't necessarily want clients, no matter how important, in one's house, but you know how headstrong Charles is. Anyway they're here only for dinner. And of course, you haven't met Mr. Denbigh, have you?" The man turned, and Claudia was struck by his good looks. She was struck also, shockingly, painfully, by his resemblance to another tall, dark man. His eyes were almost black under long, thick lashes, and he was tall and lean. But his face had none

202

of Philippe's sensitivity. His features, though similar, struck Claudia as crude and a little too dramatic. He reminded her of that movie star Rudolph Valentino. She suspected he had been told of the resemblance and prided himself on it.

Claudia said a few words to Sybil and Mr. Denbigh and excused herself. He didn't actually look like Philippe, not really, but there was sufficient resemblance to make her uncomfortable. She wanted badly to get away.

"Well, after all that, you don't seem much taken with Mr. Denbigh." Sam was at her side. He had watched his wife closely, and even across the room he could recognize the familiar iciness with which she dismissed people.

"Did you meet him?"

"And kept my promise. I was perfectly polite. Which" —he laughed—he was delighted with his wife's behavior —"is a good deal more than I can say for you."

"Don't be silly, Sam. I was perfectly polite, too."

"That's funny. I could have sworn you didn't like him. In fact, I could almost feel the chill."

As Claudia approached the dining room on Saturday morning, she saw that it was empty except for Joe Denbigh. She thought of turning back and ringing for coffee in her room, but he had already seen her.

Denbigh rose and bowed a little awkwardly. He was wearing a tweed jacket that looked too new and too obviously expensive and flannel trousers. "Good morning, Mrs. Beaumont. I guess it's only the two of us for breakfast. Everyone else is after the fox."

She turned her back to him and busied herself at the sideboard. "Ah, yes, the poor fox. I don't suppose a weekend in the country is very pleasant for him."

"Then you don't share your husband's passion for blood sports."

"It has nothing to do with my husband," she said too quickly. She cursed herself. They were talking about the hunt. He had said nothing about her marriage.

"I meant only that your husband has a considerable

reputation as a sportsman. I wondered if hunting were one of your passions too." His smile was a little too familiar, belying the formality of his speech.

"I don't enjoy killing small animals if that's what you mean." She sat as far down the table from him as she could without being rude. "But of course, you must feel the same way, Mr. Denbigh. After all, you chose not to hunt this morning too." She suspected he rode poorly or not at all and would make some absurd excuse to cover his lack of expertise. She wanted very much to humiliate him.

"Not at all, Mrs. Beaumont. I have no scruples about killing—animals, of course. I'm simply a bad horseman. And"—he looked directly at her—"there's one other thing. The doctors tell me I'm allergic to horses." It was an outrageous admission for him to make, but it worked. For the first time that morning she smiled.

"You ought to smile more often, Mrs. Beaumont. If not for your own sake, then for mine."

Sam sat in their room with a whiskey and soda, watching his wife get ready for dinner. She was still flushed from her bath and was trying to hide her high color with powder.

"What did you do all day? I hope you weren't bored."

"Just because I wasn't chasing around on horseback all morning, Sam, doesn't mean I was bored."

"I wasn't trying to convince you to come along, Claudia. I merely said I hoped you weren't bored."

"I'm sorry, I didn't mean to snap. I took a long walk and read a bit. This afternoon I played bridge with Harriet and George and that Mr. Denbigh."

"Oh."

"Why do you say 'oh' that way?"

"No reason. I'm surprised, that's all. I could have sworn last night you didn't like Denbigh very much."

"He was the fourth for bridge. We couldn't very well play without him."

"Did Denbigh have anything interesting to say for himself?"

"I must say you're taking an extraordinary interest in the man."

"I'm only following directions. Trying to keep an open mind and find out something about him. Define the unknown quantity. Especially since the unknown quantity spent the afternoon with my wife."

"And Harriet and George."

"George can take care of himself, and Harriet is Schuyler's problem."

"Well, since you're so interested, I can report that Mr. Denbigh had absolutely nothing to say. Except that he rides badly and is allergic to horses."

"He has a peculiar sense of humor."

"He wasn't being funny."

"What a thing to admit!"

"I don't think he finds it especially embarrassing."

"Fellow sounds a little queer to me." He saw the look Claudia shot him. "I'm not saying there's anything wrong with him. He just sounds a little strange."

"I don't think he's strange, but I don't think he's terribly interesting either, and for an uninteresting man we seem to spend an awful lot of time talking about him. Don't you think you ought to start to dress?"

"In a minute." He stood behind her at the dressing table, and she watched him in the mirror as he reached into the pocket of his silk foulard robe and pulled out a chain of diamonds. "Happy anniversary, Claudia." His voice was very quiet as he fastened them around her neck.

"Oh, Sam, they're beautiful, but why?"

"I told you; it's our anniversary. We've been married six months today."

She had forgotten, but Sam hadn't. Wasn't it supposed to be the woman who remembered these things? "You're too good to me, Sam. You really are." She stood and kissed him lightly in thanks.

"There's another reason, Claudia." His arms tightened around her. "Because I love you." She felt him fumbling with the tie of her dressing gown, and then his hands were warm against her skin.

"We'll be late for dinner, Sam."

"No one will notice."

"Don't be ridiculous, everyone will notice."

"Do you care?"

"I thought you did."

"Not particularly."

"You usually do."

"Not now."

But the bargaining had gone on too long. He let her go, and she turned away from him, tying the robe tightly around her.

Later that night, when they were alone again in their room, Sam was more persistent. He had been drinking heavily all evening. Claudia had watched him closely. It wasn't like Sam.

She had taken her time undressing, brushing her hair, removing her jewelry. She dropped the diamonds into the small marquetry box. "Thank you, Sam. The necklace is beautiful." She spoke very quietly. She hoped the whiskey had at least put him to sleep.

"I hope you like it." His words were slurred, but his eyes were two sharp lights watching her move about the darkened room.

On her way to the other bed she bent to kiss him good-night. She owed him that much. Before she could slip away, he pulled her to him. She could feel him tugging at her nightgown, and then his hand was rough against her breast. Her legs were twisted in yards of satin, then freed only to be caught again by Sam's. Above her in the darkness his movements were abrupt and his breathing quick and shallow.

It's almost as if he were on the playing field, Claudia thought. It was a side of Sam she had never seen.

Joe Denbigh was born Giovanni Daivone in the hills outside Messina in 1892. He had, however, no memories of the barren Sicilian countryside. At the age of six months his father had died in a vendetta. Maria Teresa Daivone had lost her husband to the laws of vengeance. She was determined to save her sons. At the age of twenty-three she arrived in New York with her five children. The oldest, Salvatore, was eight. The youngest, Giovanni, had not yet been weaned.

The Daivone brothers flourished on the Lower East Side. They were tough and quick and became smart in the ways of the street. And Giovanni became the smartest of all. He also became the most Americanized. By the time he was ten Giovanni had become Joe.

Like his brothers, Joe eked out a meager existence doing odd jobs for the local families of Little Italy. But unlike his brothers, Joe went to school as well. Maria Teresa Daivone could neither read nor write, but she could understand with pride and wonder the high school diploma her little Giovanni brought home one day.

Despite the promises America had made to Joe Daivone, education did not bring him success. True, he had a better standing in the local organization than did any of his brothers, but he was still small time. No one knew that better than Joe himself. Then three years in the infantry—his brothers said he was crazy to risk his life for anything but his family, but Joe still believed in America—made him a second lieutenant and gave him his first taste of a world he had dreamed about since childhood.

Joe did not speak badly. If there was a hint of New York in his speech, at least he had freed himself from the cadences of Sicily. Moreover, he cut a figure in uniform. Back on Mott Street in his shabby civilian clothes he had been a success with the girls. In Texas, where he spent two and a half of his three years of service, his accent was no more offensive than any other easterner's and his dark, liquid eyes and knowing way with women cut a swath through the local belles. True, they were never the real belles of the town, never came from the best families, but neither were they the easy girls an officer could pick up on the street or buy for the price of a movie and an ice-cream soda. He wasn't at the top of the ladder, Joe knew, but he had started the climb.

Late in 1919 Joe Daivone ceased to be, by act of Congress, an officer and a gentleman. He returned to New York, and for a while it looked as if his story would be that of hundreds of other young men who had been lifted suddenly and spectacularly above their station by the war and then tossed cruelly away. But the United States government did not abandon Joe Daivone. On October 28, 1919, Congress passed the Volstead Act. It might as easily have awarded Joe Daivone ten million dollars.

By 1921 Joe and his brothers had made enough money to move an ailing Maria Teresa out of the tenement and into a house in Brooklyn, a house with a yard in back and another in front. And that was only the beginning. By 1923 they controlled three-quarters of the bootleg traffic in Connecticut and New York and were moving into New Jersey. It was then that Joe, the youngest and the real head of the Daivone brothers, announced he was getting out. He wanted nothing more than his share of the profits—and legitimacy.

"What will you do?" Salvatore demanded.

"I'm going into the stock market."

"That's a good one, Joe. You think people are going to give you their money—little Giovanni Daivone from Mott Street. You crazy, Joe. Stay in the business. We're making good money."

"I won't need other people's money. I've already got enough in the market to keep me busy."

"You'll never make as much as you're making now."

"Maybe not, but I'm going to do it anyway."

The first thing Joe Daivone did was to change his name again. He went to the library and read through all the names in the social register beginning with D. None of them seemed to fit. Besides, Joe didn't want one of those names with a pedigree. When he met the people who belonged to those names rightfully, as he knew he would in a year or so, he didn't want to be looked on as a thief or an impostor. He merely wanted to make people, the right people, sit up and notice him.

The name, when it finally came, was not Joe's idea. Mae suggested it. Mae was a showgirl. Her dream was to become a Ziegfeld girl. And her name was not Mae but Mabel. She called herself Mae after Mae Marsh. She had another dream besides the one that involved

Mr. Ziegfeld: it was to make her relationship with Joe Daivone legal and permanent.

Mae had no idea she was to play no part in Joe's future. In fact, in the words of the theater, her show was about to close.

Nevertheless, she had been a pleasant playmate for the past year, and Joe liked her. He confided none of his plans to her, but he did allow her to share in his search for a new name.

"You ought to have a name with a Latin sound, Joe." They were in a speakeasy on West Forty-fifth Street, celebrating Mae's promotion to the front line in the chorus of *The Dream Girl*. "It's sexier." The lashes she had left on after the show fluttered over her round baby-doll eyes. "Look at Valentino, and all the girls say you look just like him."

"I don't want a Hollywood name. I told you, I want a name that's dignified."

"What's not dignified about Hollywood?"

Joe ignored her. "It has to be American-sounding. And it ought to start with a D. That way it really belongs to me."

"Denby. You can't get more American than that."

"Where'd that come from?"

"It's the street I was born on. The most two-bit American street in the most two-bit one hundred percent American town in the country. Honey, you don't know what America is until you spent fifteen years in Indiana. I mean on Denby Street there were these . . ."

Joe had ceased listening. "And spelled with *gh,* it sounds almost English. D-e-n-b-i-g-h. Joseph T. Denbigh. Joseph T. Denbigh, Esquire."

That was the first and last Mae saw of Joseph T. Denbigh. He bought an apartment on Park Avenue, a house in Westchester County, dropped all his old friends except those who would be helpful without being incriminating, and took into his employ the aging, penniless younger son of an English viscount. In six months Joe could speak, if not the King's English, then a passable eastern dialect. He learned how to address servants, which forks to use in what order, and how to select a wine. His colored shirts were replaced by fine white silks and cottons, and his snugly tailored suits gave way to roomier tweeds and flannels. He had become the perfect second-rate imitation of an English gentleman. But to give Joe Denbigh his due, if he didn't realize the imitation was second-rate, he never forgot that it *was* an imitation. He was careful to provide no information about himself or his past, but he was equally scrupulous about not pretending to a background that was not rightfully his. The sort of people he was interested in, he knew, would always recognize him as a self-made man. He was hoping they might accept the man he had made of himself.

Joseph T. Denbigh was launched in New York society by his aristocratic English tutor. Joe Denbigh made it possible for him to pay his social debts. When the Englishman asked a dozen friends to dine on the roof of the Ritz, which was, of course, not the roof at all, but the first floor, Joe Denbigh paid the bill. When the Englishman took a party cruising on his chartered yacht at the height of the Palm Beach season, Joe Denbigh occupied the owner's cabin. Joe knew that the people with whom he dined and cruised would not have accepted an invitation from him, just as his guests knew that he was the real host, but Joe didn't mind. He had great respect for tradition. He wouldn't have wanted his new friends to accept the invitation of an upstart. When he was one of them, in a year or two, *he* certainly would not.

As might be expected, Joe's success in his new realm was even more marked among the women. The polish Joe had so recently acquired had done nothing to dull the essential magnetism that had drawn the girls of Mott Street. Women liked him. Sybil Chesney adored him—for the moment. He was handsome, appealing, and forbidden. The combination delighted Sybil, who compensated for her commonplace looks with extraordinary behavior. Opinion had it that no one but a beauty would dare carry on as Sybil Chesney did, and Sybil had convinced a good many people that she was a good deal prettier than a close look at her features revealed.

Joe Denbigh had no illusions about Sybil's appearance, but the accidents of her birth and upbringing made her beautiful to him. She was wild, though. There was no doubt about it. And Joe wasn't sure that in his position he could afford a wife with a reputation. He wasn't even sure he wanted one. At least he wasn't sure until he met Mrs. Samuel Livingston Beaumont. The moment he saw her across the room that weekend at Charles and Polly Chesney's he gave up any idea of marrying Sybil.

Mrs. Beaumont had more than beauty. She had what Joe would have called, a few years earlier, class. The way she moved, the way she talked, even the way she had dismissed him that first night proved that. It was an aura he had seen in only a handful of women, even among his new friends, but Mrs. Beaumont went those women one better. She might be a lady; but she was a woman as well, and Joe Denbigh knew women. This one would be worth fighting for.

The fact that there was a Mr. Beaumont did not bother Joe in the least. He had only to watch them together for five minutes to decide that Mrs. Beaumont cared very little for her husband. It was clear Beaumont was crazy about her, but it was also clear he didn't know what to do about it. Joe Denbigh watched Mr. and Mrs. Samuel Livingston Beaumont through the prism of his experience and was almost glad he had not been better born. At least he knew how to fight for what he wanted.

Claudia had, for her part, made up her mind to avoid Denbigh. When she encountered him a week later at a dinner party, she kept her distance. At two subsequent dinners she was able to get away with only the barest greeting. Then at a large charity ball he tracked her down. She was dancing with Schuyler Mason when he cut in.

"I'm a bit tired," she said quickly. "I think I'll sit this one out."

"That's even better. We can talk."

"No," she snapped too quickly. "I must find my husband. It's terribly late."

"Until now, Mrs. Beaumont"—he pronounced her name with a faint air of mockery, as if they knew each other too well for him to be addressing her so formally —"I had the impression you were avoiding me. Now I'm sure you're trying to get rid of me."

"Not at all, Mr. Denbigh. It's getting late, and my husband will be wanting to leave."

"You're a very considerate wife, Mrs. Beaumont." She looked at him sharply. "So few women today are, or so the magazines tell me."

"Ah, yes, the decline of morals since the war." She pounced on the familiar topic.

"I take it you don't think there has been a decline. Well, I believe in maintaining certain standards." They were still dancing, and he watched her carefully as he spoke. There was admiration in his eyes, but it was not the blind admiration of a George Talbott or her husband. "You're laughing, Mrs. Beaumont. Is the fact that I believe in standards really so amusing?"

"Not at all. I was merely thinking that there are people who would be very glad to know of your feelings."

"Your husband perhaps."

"At the risk of being rude, Mr. Denbigh, I don't think my husband has troubled himself very much about your beliefs. And now I really must find him."

"I'll let you go if you'll promise to lunch with me."

"That's impossible."

He was still watching her closely, and now his eyes turned cold. "If there is one thing I've learned, Mrs. Beaumont, it is that nothing is impossible."

"I hate to contradict you, Mr. Denbigh, but our lunching *is* impossible."

"Because of your husband?"

"Because of me."

"You never lunch with friends?"

"You're purposely being difficult."

"Not at all. I'm trying to be as easy as possible. I want to make it as easy as possible for you to lunch with me."

"I told you, it's impossible."

"Why don't you simply say you don't like me?" He was fairly certain this was not true.

"I didn't say that."

"Then why don't you say what you do mean, Mrs. Beaumont, that you don't trust me?"

She looked at him closely. "All right, Mr. Denbigh, I don't trust you."

"You should have said that at the start. I assure you I'm quite harmless, but to be on the safe side, I'll invite you *and* Mr. Beaumont."

"My husband lunches downtown at his club."

He laughed. "It needn't be lunch. We could dine or you could come out for the weekend."

She caught sight of Sam, finally. "Perhaps . . . sometime . . ." she murmured and disappeared into the crowd.

Three days later Claudia sat in the stark white living room watching Sam at the cocktail wagon.

"Who's coming tonight?" he asked as he mixed drinks for them.

"Schuyler and Harriet, and George is going to bring Lucinda."

"Where's Anson?"

"Heaven knows. I'm sure Lucinda doesn't." They let it drop. The prospect of another unhappy marriage did not warm their own.

Sam walked back and forth across the room with his drink in his hand. "Please don't pace, Sam. You know it makes me nervous."

He stopped at the edge of the foyer and turned to her like a small boy caught with his hand in the cookie jar. "I wasn't pacing, Claudia. I was going to look at the mail." He scooped up the pile of envelopes on the ebony and ivory table and carried them back to the living room.

"What's this?" He held up a heavy white envelope, indistinguishable from several others.

Claudia did not recognize the handwriting, but she knew which one it would be. "That man Denbigh—you

213

know, the one we met at the Chesneys—invited us for the weekend."

"You'll refuse, of course."

"Probably, but you needn't make such a fuss about it." She tried to make her voice sound casual.

"I'm not making a fuss. I'm merely saying I don't want to go."

"Of course. He's not one of us. He isn't a Livingston or a Beaumont. He hasn't gone to the right schools or grown up with the right people. He can't even sit a horse properly. We couldn't possibly think of spending a weekend with him."

Sam's voice when he answered was even, far more even than Claudia's. "Everything you say about the man is true, Claudia. And perhaps you're right. It doesn't mean that we can't spend a weekend with him, but neither does it mean that we have to spend the weekend with him. We barely know the man, and you said you didn't find him very interesting. Or have you changed your mind? You did talk to him for some time the other night."

"Oh, Sam, don't be absurd. I danced with him for a minute. Just like everyone else. Anyway, Denbigh isn't the point. I keep telling you that. I don't want to go for the weekend, but I don't want to think we refused for the wrong reasons."

"Then let's refuse for the right reason. Let's refuse because I decided I want to spend a weekend alone with my wife. Do you realize we haven't even dined alone more than twice in the last six months? I think that's a darned good reason for refusing Mr. Denbigh's invitation—and a few others as well. Like tonight. It would be a perfect night to stay home—or go out—as long as we were alone."

"That's a wonderful idea, Sam, and of course, you're right, but it's a little late now. Harriet and Schuyler will be here any minute. In fact, I think I'd better check the pantry to make sure Wilfred has the cocktails ready and enough ice."

She was on her feet and out of the room in a minute. This was one conversation she did not want to pursue.

As autumn progressed, Joseph T. Denbigh's invitations became more and more difficult to refuse. Mr. and Mrs. Beaumont regretted that they could not weekend, they were sorry they were not free to dine on Thursday or Tuesday or the following Thursday, but finally they could not avoid Denbigh's large cocktail party after the Yale-Columbia football game. All their friends were going.

"Why is he throwing a party?" Sam asked. "He isn't a Yale man. The game doesn't mean anything to him." The usual group was gathered in the Mason's living room before a small dinner at the Ritz Carlton in honor of Lucinda and Anson.

"Maybe he's a Columbia man," Lucinda suggested slyly.

"Someone has to throw a party after the game. It might as well be Denbigh," George suggested.

"Why might it as well be Denbigh? Why doesn't one of us give it this year?"

"Oh, Sam, *no*," Claudia wailed. "We'll give all the parties you like, but not this one. It's so uncivilized. Everyone drinks too much, and there are always stray people bringing other stray people. It would be as if someone brought all those hulking, dirty football players into my living room."

"Weren't you captain of the football team at Yale, Sam?" Lucinda asked.

"Might as well settle for Denbigh's," George broke in quickly. "It's too late to do anything else anyway. His invitations went out a week ago, and it would look funny if we tried to get up something now."

"I think the idea of a party at Joe Denbigh's is amusing," Lucinda said.

"Like slumming, you mean." But there was no anger in Claudia's voice. She was remembering a time when they had gone slumming, when Philippe had taken them to Père Tranquil's and Claudia had not been amused, but frightened. How they had laughed at her that night. But they had laughed at everything then.

Lucinda's voice called her back to the present. "I keep forgetting. We mustn't be unpleasant about Mr. Denbigh in front of Claudia. She's his champion."

"I'm not anyone's champion, Lucinda. I simply think we make a lot of fuss about nothing. We go to hundreds of parties. Why should Denbigh's be any different?"

"Because Denbigh is different."

"How inexcusable of him!"

The day was uncommonly warm for late October, and they stood uncomfortably in front of the stadium waiting for the cars that crawled slowly through the post-game traffic.

"Does anyone remember where this Denbigh fellow lives?" Charles Chesney asked.

"You going too, Charlie? I didn't think you approved of him," Schuyler Mason said.

"Oh, he's not such a bad fellow."

"You mean now that Sybil has given him up."

"As a matter of fact, that's exactly what I mean. Denbigh's not a bad sort, but I wouldn't want him in the family."

"I can see your point there."

"Whatever he is, he's certainly more interesting than the Dedwins," Polly said, remembering the weekend.

"Polly thinks he's a *sheik*." Lucinda giggled.

"Well, you have to admit he does look like Valentino," Polly said.

"He's probably just the sort of fellow who would use slang like that," Schuyler said. "I can just see him calling himself a *sheik*."

"As a matter of fact, he speaks quite correctly," Charles offered. "No accent of any sort."

"Looks like a foreigner to me," Anson mumbled.

"He is. He's Italian."

"How do you know he's Italian, Sam?" Claudia was determined not to enter into the conversation, but her husband's statement surprised her.

"A fellow at the bank knows him. Took care of some transactions for him."

"What kind of transactions?" Charles asked. Everyone was suddenly interested.

"Shady?" Schuyler asked.

"Of course they were shady," Claudia said. "Mr. Denbigh couldn't possibly be honest like the rest of us. We're all so terribly honorable—tearing to pieces a man whose party we're about to go to. But I guess it's all right, we're not actually under his roof yet."

Joe Denbigh occupied the penthouse of a new apartment building at Park Avenue and Seventy-third Street. It had, predictably, been *done* by Elsie de Wolfe. "Done to a fare-thee-well," Polly sneered in a large bedroom so spanking new even the authentic Empire table and chairs looked as if they had just been made.

"This is Mr. Denbigh's heritage." Lucinda giggled. "His family heirlooms. We must remember to ask him if the Joseph is after Josephine. Have you ever seen so much *Empire* in a single room in your life?" She pronounced it with a French accent.

Claudia turned away and tried to concentrate on her reflection in the mirror. She hated their viciousness, but she hated herself for recognizing the truth in their words. Everything was obviously expensive and in perfect condition. It all matched. And nothing blended. Joe Denbigh had learned thousands of tiny lessons in style, but he had not comprehended the meaning of taste.

She left them to their gossip and began to wander from room to room. Each was more correct and slightly more ostentatious than the last. The apartment made her tired. She found a chair in a quiet corner of the living room.

"Mrs. Beaumont, alone in a corner. I find that hard to believe." She stood quickly as Denbigh approached. She did not want to be caught alone in conversation with him again. The greeting at the door had been difficult enough, and Sam had listened carefully and weighed each word.

"Not alone in the least, Mr. Denbigh. I was just

217

waiting for Mrs. Chesney, and there she is now." As she started across the room to Polly, she felt a restraining hand on her arm.

"I thought you were different, Mrs. Beaumont, but I see I was wrong. You're exactly like them."

"I don't know what you mean." She stepped back from his grasp, hoping Polly and Lucinda hadn't seen.

"You know exactly what I mean. Your little circle of friends don't think I'm good enough. Oh, they're polite to my face, but I thought you were different. I don't know why I thought so—maybe because I wanted you to be—but I see now you're not."

"If you dislike us so, why did you invite us?"

"Do you really want to know?"

She did. She'd forgotten her uneasiness of a moment ago. Denbigh intrigued her. She hadn't thought he knew the things they said about him, but she'd underestimated him. He might be many things, even some of the things her friends said he was, but he was not stupid. "Yes, I would."

"Let me show you my garden, and I'll tell you." He held open the door to the terrace that ran the length of the living room. She hesitated for a moment, then stepped outside. The last rays of afternoon sun slanted across flagstone paths winding through the carefully manicured shrubbery. The heat of the day had lifted, and a gentle breeze ruffled Claudia's hair. Through the windows she could see people talking and laughing, but the only sound on the terrace was an occasional horn from the street eighteen floors below.

"It's lovely out here."

"Yes, it is, isn't it? I'm very proud of my garden."

"You sound as if you miss the country, Mr. Denbigh."

"Not at all. I've lived in the city all my life. Except for the war."

"In New York?"

"Yes, in New York." He laughed. "But not the parts of it you know. I was a rather poor boy." He did his best to inject a note of impoverished gentility into his words.

"Oh, money," she murmured. "Why do people care so much about money?"

"I quite agree with you, Mrs. Beaumont. People care too much about money. One ought not to care. But then one must have money in order not to care about it."

"And that's why you invite all these people—because they have money?"

"Not at all. In fact, some of these people don't have very much money. I probably have a good deal more than half of the people in that room." He looked through the windows at his guests. "No, it's more than money."

"Background and breeding? The right credentials?"

"You're laughing at me, Mrs. Beaumont."

"Not in the least. I'm trying to understand you. It seems you want something very badly, badly enough to invite people like us to your house. I'm merely trying to find out what it is you want."

"Not us, them. I was right after all. You're not like them."

"We were talking about you. What it is you want so badly."

"I'll tell you a story, Mrs. Beaumont, a story I've never told anyone. When I was a boy, I found the Metropolitan Museum of Art. That doesn't sound particularly important to you, but I assure you it was quite an event in my life. I never knew things—objects—like that existed. Not so much the paintings, but all the rest. The things that people lived with and used. Pieces of silver and crystal and china. And the rooms, oh, how I loved those rooms. Once I sneaked into one—you know how they close them off with a velvet cord—well, I sneaked under the cord and sat in that room for half an hour before the guard found me. He threw me out, of course, but he couldn't take away that half hour. It was long enough. I decided someday I would have a room like that, a dozen rooms like that."

"And now you do," she said quietly. She remembered Polly and Lucinda in the bedroom and wanted to cry for Joe Denbigh, but Joe Denbigh found nothing sad in his situation. His voice was full of pride, and his eyes had grown darker as he spoke. There was a determination in the man that reminded Claudia of her father. He was rough around the edges and entirely too hungry, but he was undeniably dynamic.

"Yes, now I do. And I wanted you to see them."

She ignored his words and tone. "And everyone else, of course. Your rooms must be filled with the right sort of people."

"Exactly. Empty rooms are for museums. I want to fill my rooms."

"You could fill them easily. You know that. It isn't simply filling them that interests you."

"These rooms aren't meant for just anyone."

"Mr. Denbigh, I'm afraid you're a terrible snob."

"There's no one more devout than a convert."

"But you're a straightforward snob. I'll give you that."

"And I, Mrs. Beaumont, am grateful for anything you are willing to give me."

"Right now I'm afraid I must give you back to your guests. I've monopolized the host for much too long."

"For a man who doesn't interest you, you certainly spent enough time alone with him." Sam stood with his back to her while he mixed a tumbler of scotch and milk. "Do you want a drink?"

"No, thank you. I think I'll go to bed. I'm tired."

"You mean you don't want to talk about Denbigh."

"I said I was tired. I didn't say I didn't want to talk about Denbigh. What is there to say about the man? He was the host, and I talked to him. If you want to make a scene about that, then go ahead."

"I'm not the one who's making a scene, Claudia. I'm not the one who was alone with him on the terrace for half the party."

"Don't you think you're exaggerating, Sam? I don't think I spoke to him for more than ten minutes."

"It was longer than ten minutes. I know. I was watching."

"I won't have you spying on me!"

"And I won't have you disappearing from parties with strange men!"

"I didn't disappear. I was standing on the terrace— in full view of you and everyone else."

"Well, I won't have it!"

"What won't you have, Sam? My talking to other men? My having a conversation you didn't participate in? Why don't you get me a nanny? Or better yet, hire a private detective."

"Claudia"—his voice was full of misery—"you know that's not what I meant. It's just that I don't know the man, and I don't trust him."

"Do you have any reason not to?"

He was silent for a moment. "No."

"Then actually I'm the one you don't trust. Isn't that it? Why not admit it, Sam? You don't trust your wife. It's insulting, but it's the truth."

"It's not that I don't trust you. Please stop twisting everything I say. I'm not accusing you, Claudia. And I don't want to argue. Can't we talk without arguing. What's happened to us?"

His words shocked her. Did he believe something had happened to them? Did he believe they had ever been happy? "Nothing's happened to us, Sam. It's late, and we're both tired, that's all. We need some sleep." As she started for the bedroom, she prayed he would take her at her word, that it would be sleep he wanted and not her.

2

"Shall I get out the gray chiffon for tonight, ma'am?"

Claudia stared at her reflection in the mirror over the black basalt dressing table. "Not the gray, Ellen. I'm much too sallow for the gray."

"Nonsense, you look lovely as ever."

Most of Claudia's friends thought it perverse of her to have as a personal maid an elderly Irishwoman who seemed better suited to the nursery or kitchen, but Claudia enjoyed Ellen's maternal devotion.

"You always say that, Ellen, but you can't get away with it tonight. I look awful. Sallow and tired—and bored. My hair, my skin, my eyes—all bored. You don't suppose there's a beauty cream for boredom, do you?"

"What a lot of foolishness you talk! Why should you be bored? Married less than a year to as fine a man as I've ever seen. This lovely flat and all your friends. And in another six months I wager there'll be a small one on the way."

"Do you know something I don't, Ellen?" Sam walked across the room to where Claudia sat. "Good evening, Claudia."

"Excuse me, Mr. Beaumont. No, I was just talking—too much as usual. If there's nothing else, Mrs. Beaumont. . . ." Ellen backed out of the room in embarrassment.

Claudia raised a cool cheek to Sam.

"You're home early."

"The dinner starts early."

"Another of your award dinners. Do you really have to go?"

"Of course, I have to go. *Mistress* won, and I'm not going to let someone else accept for me."

"Not another cup, I hope. The library's overflowing. I swear one of these days I'm going to move them all down to your office."

"It isn't a cup; it's a cigarette box, I think. You can always use another of those, can't you?"

"I could if it were plain silver, but they're bound to put some awful enamel flag on it or something like that. The whole thing is so silly. I can understand your racing —or at least I try to—but why you want to spend an evening sitting around that stuffy old yacht club reliving old races is beyond me."

"Partly because it's a way to avoid still another dinner for Lucinda and Anson. Which one is this?"

"It's not for Lucinda and Anson. It's not for anyone —except the hostess. Alicia loves playing young matron."

"Somehow I can't get accustomed to thinking of Alicia Sibbington as married."

"She didn't give us much of a chance. . . ."

"That's true. It was all so sudden and . . . well, disorganized. She left for Newport engaged to one man and came back engaged to his cousin. Must have been messy for the family."

"I don't imagine it was too bad. After all, they weren't first cousins."

Sam looked at her sharply. Was there an intended rebuke in her words, or was he merely sensitive about his own behavior? "Was that supposed to be funny, Claudia."

"Why, yes, Sam, as a matter of fact, it was."

Feeling clumsy again, he turned away from her.

"What time would you like the car? I plan to leave at seven. Will that give you enough time?"

"Don't worry about the car. George promised to come by for me."

"Of course, good old George. I guess I should have realized before I married you that you came with a full

223

complement of old beaux. But I'm glad he's coming by for you. I don't like to see you go out alone."

"Of course, all those nocturnal dangers. You must protect me, Sam."

"What's wrong with wanting to protect you?"

"That all depends on what you want to protect me from. I'm not sure I'd like to have you protect me from life."

"What's that supposed to mean?"

"Nothing much, only that sometimes I feel I could do with a little less protection and a little more excitement."

"I don't understand you, Claudia. Are you saying you want to go away? Because if you do, you know we can go anytime you like. We don't have to wait till after the holidays."

"No, Sam, I wasn't saying I wanted to go away."

"Then what is it you do want?"

She turned back to the mirror. "Nothing, nothing at all. I have everything. That's what Ellen was just telling me. I have everything a woman could want."

Two hours later Ellen knocked at the door. "Mr. Talbott is here, Mrs. Beaumont."

"So soon! Have Wilfred see that he has something to drink." Claudia examined herself critically in the full-length mirror. She was wearing a white chiffon dress with crystal beading. "Then come back and help me change. Get out the black crepe de chine."

"The one with the small cape?"

"No, the new one with the handkerchief hem."

Dressed in the black crepe de chine, Claudia was no more pleased with herself. "Perhaps the blue velvet," she murmured at her reflection.

"This one looks lovely."

"It isn't right. But it will have to do." George was patient, but she was far too late even by his standards. He stood as she walked into the living room, a dark young man whose features were so bland that he looked no older now than he had five years ago. She presented a cheek to be kissed.

"Sorry I'm late, George. You're a darling to be so patient."

"You're always worth waiting for, Claudia. You look wonderful as usual."

"I'm afraid I don't feel very wonderful tonight."

"Is anything wrong? Can I do anything?"

"Good old George. No, nothing's wrong. I'm just a little sad."

"Then I've got my work cut out for me. I'll simply have to cheer you up."

"That's sweet of you, George, but I'm afraid it's a herculean task. Besides, there's nothing more depressing than *trying* to have a good time."

"Is that why you don't try anymore?"

"What do you mean?"

He was silent for a moment, seemingly absorbed in some truth in the bottom of his martini glass.

"It's none of my business, Claudia, but you've changed. You used to have so much . . . well, call it spirit. And now you don't seem to care."

"You make me sound dreary."

"Never dreary, Claudia. Just different."

"Nevertheless, if my moods are that obvious, it's time to do something about them, and I'm going to start right now. We're going to have a wonderful time tonight. It won't be easy if I know Alicia's guest lists—marriage may have made me boring, but it's made her stodgy—but we're going to do it anyway. Or at least we'll go down fighting."

"That's the Claudia Trenholm I know. Excuse me, Claudia Beaumont. I'm sorry, I just can't get accustomed to your being married."

"Well, George, darling,"—she laughed, pouring another martini for each of them—"neither can I."

"I was prepared to change cards, Mrs. Beaumont, but fortunately Mrs. Hallsby saved me the trouble. She had the good sense—and the infinite kindness—to seat me next to you."

"I seriously doubt, Mr. Denbigh, you would have changed cards at all. Certainly your respect for standards and tradition forbids anything so unconventional as tampering with one of Alicia Hallsby's seating arrangements."

"You're laughing at me again. Well, I'll permit it on one condition. You must call me Joe and I'll call you Claudia." It was a statement rather than a question, and Claudia turned gratefully to answer Schuyler Mason, who was sitting on her right. But dinner was just beginning, and Denbigh was in no hurry. It was not until a strawberry mousse had been set before each of them that he tried out their new intimacy. A man across the table had told an anecdote that was only mildly amusing, but Claudia laughed as if he were W. C. Fields himself.

"You're very gay tonight, Claudia." Her name on his lips sounded foreign.

"Yes, I am as a matter of fact. It's a resolution. George and I have resolved to be very gay tonight."

"Is it a private party or may anyone join?"

"Well, scarcely anyone, Mr. Denbigh."

"Joe."

"Scarcely anyone, Joe." She pronounced his name with difficulty. "After all, we have our standards, too."

"I can see you're not going to let me live that one down."

"Not down. You don't live standards down. You live them up, or rather you live up to them."

"At the risk of being discriminated against again, may I join the fun?"

"I'm afraid you'll have to ask George about that."

"I'm asking you. I know a speakeasy on a roof on Fifth Avenue. The air up there is as good as the view and the orchestra's even better."

"I'm afraid my resolution doesn't go that far, Mr. Denbigh."

"Joe."

"All right, Joe. Anyway I couldn't possibly go."

"Are you afraid of what people will say?"

"If you knew anything about me, you'd know I don't care a fig what people say."

"Then come with me. Unless of course you're afraid of something else."

"What could I possibly be afraid of?"

"Anything new or different. A place you don't know. People you don't know. Me. Yourself."

"You aren't half as frightening as you think, Mr. Denbigh . . . Joe."

"Then come with me." He saw her hesitate for a moment. "We'll take Polly and Charles along. The place just opened, and Polly said she's dying to see it. Please come. You won't regret the view. And the stars are very close."

"That is an inducement."

"Then it's settled," he said as they stood.

A short, swarthy man with a head like a melon that had been flattened at the top reached out to take Denbigh's hand. Then he caught himself and bowed slightly. "Good evening, ladies, sir. A table in front of the windows or on the dance floor, Mr. Denbigh?"

"Let's sit on the dance floor," Polly said. "Then we won't miss anything."

"The dance floor," Denbigh said coolly to the little man. He drew his chair close to Claudia as they sat down. "I'm sorry about the table, but we can go out on the terrace later. I did promise you the view."

"What a happy little party! All my old friends and my new friend, all having a friendly little evening out." Anson Hagerty stood unsteadily before their table. "So nice to see you all. Such a nice surprise. Dance with me, Claudia."

Denbigh leaned closer to Claudia. "You don't have to."

She turned quickly. "I assure you I'm quite capable of deciding whom I have to dance with."

"Excuse me. It's simply that Hagerty's been drinking."

"Excuse *me*," she said as she stood and stepped onto the dance floor with Anson. They began to move lightly around the floor. It always amazed Claudia that Anson

227

could dance long after he reached a point where he could barely walk.

"I didn't see you before, Anson. Is Lucinda here?"

"No, Lucinda's not here. I'm with those people over there."

He nodded toward a noisy group of two men Claudia knew vaguely and three women she definitely did not. "Now, now, Claudia. No raised eyebrows. Still got my freedom. Not like you. What are you doing out with that fellow anyway?"

"I'm not out with any fellow. You may have noticed there are several people at the table."

"Sure, Claudia, sure. If that's your story, you stick to it. Anyway, I don't blame you. Sam's always been a stuffed shirt. Just remember when you get tired of that Denbigh joker, I'm still available. That goes after the wedding, too."

She stopped in the middle of the dance floor. "You're obnoxious, Anson, obnoxious and drunk." As she turned she found herself face to face with Denbigh.

"I was about to cut in, but I see you saved me the trouble. Is anything wrong?"

"What makes you think anything is wrong?"

"Why don't you admit it, Claudia? Hagerty was too drunk to dance with. You didn't even want to dance with him until I tried to stop you."

"I can take care of myself, thank you."

"I don't think so."

"Now you're being as insulting as Anson."

"So Anson was insulting. Come now, Claudia." Very gently, with one finger, he raised her face to his. "That face is pretty enough to wear a little egg occasionally." His accent hadn't altered by a single inflection, yet suddenly he seemed very different.

Claudia laughed. "You win."

"Not yet, but I'm working on it."

The song ended, and the orchestra started up again in a slower tempo.

If you were the only girl in the world
And I was the only boy. . . .

"Wartime tripe." She laughed, but he ignored her words and pulled her closer to him. Every few steps she could feel the smooth cloth of his jacket against her cheek. Once she thought she felt his chin resting against her hair, but she wasn't sure, and another couple jostled them a moment later.

When the music ended, he began to lead her toward the terrace. "Let me show you that view I promised."

"Polly and Charles. . . ."

"Polly and Charles can take care of themselves."

"It will be chilly."

"If you really don't care what people think, you can put my coat around your shoulders." Once outside he removed his dinner coat and dropped it over her shoulders. They stood resting their arms on the high brick wall. Across from them was the Metropolitan Building and the clock that told half New York the time. Its face was darkened and illegible now.

"Look," he said.

A beacon at the top of the tower flashed red twelve times. "It doesn't chime at this hour."

"Of course. You're right. I never noticed before, but I never have heard it chime late at night. And I never knew about that light."

Claudia kept her eyes on the tower long after the beacon had ceased flashing, but she could feel Denbigh's eyes on her.

"That's much better," he said. "That red light doesn't suit you. It's too vulgar." He turned her face to him. "I prefer you in the moonlight."

She knew she should move away, but she felt transfixed. Then his arms were around her, and there was no question of moving. His mouth was warm against hers, and she was shocked by the desire she felt rising within her.

She took a step backward. "I think we'd better go in."

"I have a better idea. We can slip away."

"I couldn't."

"Stop playing games, Claudia. You know why you came with me tonight, and it wasn't for the view or the orchestra."

"That's not true. . . ."

He pulled her to him again, and she could feel his body hard against hers. His breath was soft against her ear, but the words were insistent. "I want you, Claudia. And you want me. I can feel it."

She lifted her face to his to say no, but his mouth on hers turned the word into a lie. She clung to him as if to a last hope.

Within five minutes he had made the appropriate excuses to the Chesneys, and Claudia found herself in the back of Joseph Denbigh's Bentley. His apartment was dark, and he switched on a single lamp in the huge living room. She was in his arena now.

"Would you like a drink?"

She nodded.

"Champagne?"

"Whiskey."

Her hand trembled as she took the glass from him.

His bedroom was large and somber and looked as if it had been imported part and parcel from an eighteenth-century English manor house. "Rather a stern setting for . . . for adultery."

He crossed the room and took the glass from her hand. "Some things are better left unnamed." His fingers were gentle but experienced at the buttons of her dress. Her own worked more slowly at the studs of his evening shirt. The touch of his skin against hers was electric. His hands traveled slowly, searchingly over her body. When she felt as if she could stand no longer, she clung to him, and he half led, half carried her to the bed. In the dim light his lashes were a dark fringe against the white arc of her breast. Then she closed her eyes and let his hands and his mouth hold her conscience at bay. And then there was no thought, but only her own body moving in rhythm with his and the waves of pleasure carrying her further and further into herself. It was only her own cry of delight that brought her back.

"The lady," he said, kissing her shoulder, "is a woman." She said nothing but turned away in search of a cigarette. She took one from the silver box on the table. He looked at her face in the flame from the lighter. "Pangs of guilt?"

"I'm a grown woman—as you pointed out—I make my own choices."

"All the same, I don't want you to be unhappy. This isn't just an affair to me. I've wanted you ever since that first weekend at the Chesneys. I love you, you know."

She was out of bed in a moment. In the large bathroom she turned on the shower. The sound would drown his words, the water wash him from her.

She stared at herself in the brightly lit mirror. He loved her. It was laughable. There had been nothing of love in what had just happened.

She watched as a curtain of steam fell across the mirror. At last she could see no more than her mouth. Her lips looked thin and cruel.

The hot water streamed down her. Unlike everything else in the apartment, the bathroom was not an antique. She reached up and turned the modern chrome shower head until the water pricked at her skin like hundreds of tiny knives. She would cut Joe Denbigh out of her.

Through the frosted glass door she thought she saw a figure. Then the door opened, and he was standing beside her. He reached up and turned the shower head until the water was a soft stream again. "Was that supposed to be penance?"

"Go away, Joe. Leave me alone."

"I don't think so. I don't think I'll ever be able to leave you alone again." He took the soap from her hands and began to lather her body. She closed her eyes and leaned against him. She felt drugged by the steam and the water and his hands, gentle and coaxing against her skin, but somewhere in the back of her brain was a single lucid point. Joseph Denbigh would not be easily washed away.

Through the open door Claudia could see Sam in his dressing room. He was so meticulous. The stiff collar, the somber Turnbull and Asser tie, the dark pinstriped suit, the carefully waxed black calf shoes. And then the

accoutrements—everything in its proper pocket: the
Mark Cross wallet, the watch and chain with the miniature football, fountain pen, handkerchief, cigarette case.
The order was always the same, and she turned back
to her breakfast tray as he deposited a handful of silver
coins, the last item, in his pocket. She did not want him
to know she had been watching.

He stood at the foot of her bed. This morning, as
every morning, the world would find Sam Beaumont a
very attractive man. Why was she so contrary?

"What are your plans for today?"

"Nothing much. I thought I might call Polly for
lunch," she lied. For the last two months she had been
in the habit of seeing Joe once or twice a week and
she hadn't seen him for five days now. If she lunched
anywhere, it would be at his apartment.

"Couldn't you put that off until tomorrow? If we're
going to have the house ready by summer, we ought to
go at it as soon as possible. They can't break ground
for the tennis courts yet, but you can get started inside.
And you have to decide what you want to do about the
greenhouse and the small cottage near the west edge of
the property. Mr. O'Rourke said he'd be happy to take
you through again any day you like. Why don't you
drive out today? I'll leave you the car and—"

"Don't bother leaving the big car, Sam. I'd rather
drive out myself in the Cord."

"You know I hate to see you drive by yourself—
especially all the way out to Oyster Bay."

"Then I'll take Polly." She could always say later that
Polly had been unable to go. "And drive very slowly.
I promise."

"Not over forty all the way?"

"Like a snail."

"All right, then, but be careful. And don't forget to
get those floor plans from O'Rourke. He was supposed
to put them in the mail last week, and they still haven't
arrived."

"Any other orders?"

"Nope, the rest is up to you. I'll take care of the
tennis courts and the stables, and you take care of—

what do they call it in *Vanity Fair?*—interior decoration."

"In that case we'd both better get going." Instead of the usual cool cheek, she dropped a light kiss on his mouth in passing. Claudia always felt fondest of Sam when he was properly dressed and on his way to the office.

As Sam watched her disappear into her dressing room, he thought he might change his plans and accompany Claudia to the country, but then he remembered a meeting that afternoon. Tobias made few professional demands on Sam, and the least he could do was to be there. All the same, Claudia was in high spirits this morning. It seemed a shame to waste them.

An hour later she pulled up in front of Denbigh's building. The doorman rushed to the curb. "Shall I park the car for you, ma'am?" He knew Claudia, but not by name.

"No, thank you. Just tell Mr. Denbigh that a lady in a yellow Cord is waiting. Tell him that she will wait for exactly seven minutes."

Denbigh was down in four. "I didn't know you had a yellow Cord. If I had known it was you, I would have been down sooner. I thought it was one of your rivals."

"Liar."

"I thought you weren't going to see me again."

"That was Thursday. Today is Tuesday."

"A logical explanation. Do you want me to drive?" She shook her head as she pulled away from the curb and narrowly missed two taxis.

"You're a rotten driver."

"That's what my husband thinks, but he's too much a gentleman to say it."

"Which I, of course, am not."

"Why, Joe"—she turned two eyes large with innocence on him—"I never said that."

"Just keep your eyes on the road. You may not think my life is worth much, but I do. Where are we going?"

"I'm taking you to Oyster Bay. I thought you'd like to see my new house. It's a wedding present, you know."

"Did it ever occur to you that I might not want to see it?"

"Never. But if you don't, I can drop you here. I'm sure you can get a taxi back to your apartment."

"Claudia, has anyone ever called you a bitch?"

"Yes, as a matter of fact. My sister."

"I guess to love you is to know you."

O'Rourke was waiting for them when they arrived. "I've taken the liberty of starting a fire here and another upstairs, Mrs. Beaumont. The house was bone cold, and I'll wager we're going to have snow before the day is out."

"Thank you, Mr. O'Rourke. This is Mr. Joseph, my interior decorator."

"How do you do, Mr. Joseph. You've got quite a job for yourself. Nineteen rooms without the servants' wing. But I guess Mrs. Beaumont has told you all about it."

"Well, almost all. Mrs. Beaumont does like to have her little surprises."

O'Rourke caught the tone and looked at Denbigh sharply. *Upstart,* he thought. The man wouldn't get many jobs the size of this one if that was the way he treated his employers.

"Now, would you like me to show you around, Mrs. Beaumont?"

"Thank you, Mr. O'Rourke, but that isn't necessary. I'll take the floor plans and you can be on your way."

O'Rourke's fist struck his forehead to reveal the extent of his anguish. "I forgot them again. Mr. Beaumont will be furious."

"He did mention particularly that I should get them."

"I tell you what I'll do, Mrs. Beaumont. I'll just drive back to my office and pick them up. I can be back within the hour."

"That's fine, Mr. O'Rourke. Mr. Joseph and I will wait for you here."

"I'd rather," Joe said as soon as he heard the door close behind O'Rourke, "not be Mr. Joseph, the interior decorator."

"What should I have said, 'Mr. Denbigh, the man I'm sleeping with'?"

"You can't say 'lover,' can you?"

"You worry too much about words, Joe. Isn't that what you told me that first night?"

He followed her into the living room where O'Rourke had laid a fire. "Well, I've seen your wedding present. What are we supposed to do while we wait for O'Rourke and your floor plans?"

"You could take some measurements and make some suggestions, you know, about draperies and rugs, things like that."

"You're not very amusing, Claudia."

"All right, I have a better idea. We'll have lunch. You see, I'm not all bad. I had them pack a picnic for us before I left. If you get the hamper out of the car, I'll put the things out. We can eat before the fire. A picnic before the fire. See how romantic I am, Joe."

When he returned with the hamper, there was a thin film of snow over his hair and shoulders. "It looks as if Mr. O'Rourke were right," she said, brushing the snow from his hair. She slid her arms around his neck, and her mouth teased at his. She felt his hands beneath her fur coat and pressed her body against his. His fingers were icy under her blouse.

"Not now." She pulled away. "Mr. O'Rourke could walk in at any moment." She kneeled with her back to him, opened the straw hamper, and began spreading the cloth. On it she placed the Lenox dishes, the silver, and two crystal wineglasses. "Here, you can open the champagne." As she turned to hand him the bottle, she saw his eyes dark with anger.

"I don't play games, Claudia. I'm not your husband."

"Why, I never said you were, Joe. I can keep the two of you straight. Now will you please open that bottle? I'd like a drink, even if you wouldn't."

By the time O'Rourke returned they had finished the cold chicken and the champagne.

"All the comforts of home, ha-ha." O'Rourke watched in fascination as Claudia returned the linen cloth and the china and silver to the hamper.

"That's very kind of you, Mr. O'Rourke." She took the plans from him.

"Not at all, Mrs. Beaumont. It was no trouble at all. Are you sure you don't want me to show you through once more?"

"Thank you, but there's no need. Mr. Joseph, why don't you walk Mr. O'Rourke to his car and then you can put the picnic things back in mine?"

Denbigh gave her a dark look. A moment later she heard the door slam and heard Joe stamping the snow off his shoes.

"I'm up here," she called.

He followed the sound of her voice up the winding center staircase. Claudia was standing before the fire in the room at the top of the stairs. Her clothes lay in a heap at her feet, and her skin was a rosy, burnished gold in the firelight.

She held her arms out to him. "I think you'd better come here. It's too cold to leave the fire."

The tweed of his jacket was rough against her skin, and she worked quickly at his clothes. His hair was wet from the snow and his tongue sweet with champagne. It was a fruity taste, almost like spices and lemon. They were beside each other on her fur, and she watched the fire in his eyes as her hands trailed lazily over his body. His skin was smooth, and she could feel the network of muscles beneath. She smelled the snow and the fire and tasted the wine and saw his dark hair against her skin as he bent to her breast. She closed her eyes and felt Philippe rising inside her. *Ma femme* echoed and reechoed in her head, and she drove her body relentlessly against his until there were no more words but only movement and sensation and a pleasure so explosive it was almost pain.

"Who is Philip?" he asked casually as if he were only interested in watching her pull on her silk stockings.

Suddenly she too seemed totally absorbed in dressing. "What do you mean?"

"Philip. Just now. You called me Philip. You said something in French, and then you called me Philip."

"I'm sure you're mistaken."

"It's not the sort of thing I'd be likely to be mistaken about."

"Well, I say you are mistaken. And you'd better hurry and dress. As it is, we won't get back to town until after six."

"You really prefer it this way, don't you? Sneaking, taking chances?"

"Perhaps I do. I don't know. I don't think about it. Why, Joe, are you dissatisfied?"

"I've been telling you that for two months, but you never bother to listen. I love you, Claudia."

"But I don't love you."

"Then what do you call this?"

"Making love is not love. Really, Joe, you surprise me. I thought you were *au courant*. Haven't you read Freud? You fulfill my sexual needs. It has nothing to do with love."

"It does for me."

"Well, Joseph, darling," she said, picking up her fur and heading for the door, "that's your problem, isn't it?"

The house was ready by mid-May, the tennis courts two weeks later and repairs to the private dock completed in another ten days. By the end of June Mr. and Mrs. Samuel Livingston Beaumont were settled on Center Island, a posh, pleasant enclave in Oyster Bay. A week later Joseph Denbigh sailed for Europe aboard the *Aquitania*.

"You might as well go," Claudia had told him. "I won't see you during the summer."

"You can find time if you want to."

"Perhaps I don't want to. Besides, the trip will be good for you. You know what they say about travel, Joe. So broadening. Don't you want to see where all your possessions come from, all those palaces and châteaus you raped?"

It was not Claudia's gibes that convinced Denbigh to go, but his faith in himself. She maintained she did not care for him, but he thought she did. Two months in the country with her husband would blunt the edge of her arrogance. By September she'd realize how much she needed him—and on his terms. Within a year he'd have the single trophy that had escaped him thus far—a beautiful impeccably bred wife.

Denbigh was even more sure of his success when he returned from Europe in October. He telephoned her immediately.

"Welcome home, Joe. How many châteaus did you buy?"

"Still the same sweet Claudia."

"Did you expect me to change while you were away?"

"Stranger things have been known to happen."

"Well, as a matter of fact, I have changed. Or at least I've made up my mind."

"About what?"

"I'll tell you when I see you."

"There's no one here now."

The phone was silent for a moment. "No, not now. I'll see you tonight. Sam's going to a race dinner. . . ."

"You'll never know how grateful I am for your husband's racing expertise. . . ."

"And you can pick me up at the Hallsbys'. Be downstairs at eleven." Claudia hung up abruptly.

She sounded exactly the same, Denbigh thought, but she said she had made up her mind. And she wanted to see him immediately. He'd been right after all. A summer without him had made a difference.

During the months he was gone Claudia had thought about Joe more than she liked to admit. It wasn't only the sex, though Lord knew that weighed heavily enough on her. Some afternoons, as she lay on the beach below the house stretching and basking in the summer sun, she could almost feel Joe's hands on her body. When Sam was beside her, she knew she could reach out and touch him and his response would be immediate and intense, but her thirst for Joe Denbigh could not be slaked by Samuel Beaumont.

But more about Joe than sex haunted Claudia that summer. She kept remembering a party he had taken her to. It must have been the end of March or the beginning of April because Sam was away on one of the first overnight races of the season. His absence had conspired with her boredom to make Claudia reckless.

"Take me someplace different, Joe. Someplace I've never been before."

"Aren't you afraid of being seen with me?"

"What if I am seen with you? Besides, if it's really different, there won't be anyone there who knows me."

"All right, Arthur Grashoff's giving a party tonight for Jimmy Walker."

"Who are Arthur Grashoff and Jimmy Walker?"

"Grashoff's an Englishman who's made a fortune in ginger ale and club soda. As for Jimmy Walker, if what they say is true, his name will be a household word in less than a year. Right now he's just a state senator, but he'll probably be the next mayor."

"Politicians! Joe, I didn't think you associated with such questionable types."

"Very funny, I'm sure. Anyway, Grashoff isn't a politician."

"The power behind the politician, perhaps. Is that another dream, Joe, like the one from the museum?"

"Do you want to go to the party or don't you?"

"Of course I want to go. I've never met a politician."

"Jimmy Walker's parties are hardly political."

"What does that mean?"

"You said you wanted to do something different. Why don't you see for yourself?"

If Lucinda and Polly had laughed at Joe's apartment, Claudia wondered what they would say about Arthur Grashoff's penthouse on West Fifty-eighth Street. From the looks of the furnishings the ill-gained profits of bootleg liquor were nothing compared to the money that could be made from the mixers that went with them.

Even without the small band in one corner of the living room the noise would have been deafening. A slight, dapper man threw an arm around Joe's shoulders. Claudia had never seen anyone treat him so intimately. "Joe Denbigh, just the man I wanted to see." He had a thin Irish face, and his sharp eyes took in every inch of Claudia as he spoke. She didn't particularly like the man's looks, but he was obviously an experienced appraiser, and she was glad she had worn the forest green crepe de chine that turned her eyes brilliant.

Joe introduced her to Jimmy Walker. "By next fall you'll have to call him Your Honor."

"It would be an honor anytime if Mrs. Beaumont would call me Jimmy." Before Claudia could answer, the guest of honor was dragged off to the dance floor by identical twins, blond, dimpled, and, from all appearances, drunk.

Claudia looked around at the rest of the party. As far as the women were concerned, there wasn't an unattractive face in the crowd, though in some cases it was difficult to tell under all the paint. And she had never seen so many lacquered fingernails in one room. She thought with a certain satisfaction that Sam was probably familiar with this kind of scene and would be furious if he had known she was here.

Jimmy Walker returned later in the evening and asked her to dance. If he was at all surprised at Claudia's presence, he didn't show it. She may have thought she was slumming, but Jimmy Walker was under no such misapprehension. She could read in those canny eyes that still made her uncomfortable that she was simply one more pretty woman in a room full of them.

Later, when Claudia went into one of the bedrooms to comb her hair, she found one of the prettiest of all. She had dark hair and huge black eyes in a perfect oval face. In anything simpler than the beaded crimson she wore, she would have been stunning, Claudia thought.

"I don't suppose you'd have some lip rouge I could borrow." The girl pouted at her image in the mirror. "I decided this color just doesn't go with my dress."

Claudia tried to hide her distaste. Even if she had the lip rouge, the idea of sharing it repulsed her. "Sorry."

"You a friend of Jimmy's? I never saw you around before."

"I only just met Mr. Walker."

The girl appraised her coolly. "He'll try to do something about that," Her words were muffled as she began to apply the unsatisfactory lip rouge. "Oh, don't worry.

I'm not jealous. I got over Jimmy a long time ago. Anyway, I always knew he'd never leave his wife. But we had a good time while it lasted. And I still like him—and his parties."

Claudia didn't know what to say to this strange girl, who had laid bare her life without a moment's hesitation.

"I don't suppose they're much for you, though," the girl went on. "You're probably used to a lot fancier than this. I guess that dark guy you came in with is your husband."

"Mmm." Claudia seemed suddenly intent on combing her hair.

"He looks just like Rudolph Valentino. It must be nice to be married—and to someone like that."

"I imagine you'll know for yourself in a few years." The girl didn't look much older than eighteen or nineteen.

"Not like that. Oh, maybe I can get some old guy with money or else some Broadway Charlie, but not someone like that with looks and class and everything. You sure are lucky. And you know, the funny thing, when you walked in here I thought you were going to be stuck up. I didn't think you'd even talk to me, but you're a regular kid all right."

Claudia wasn't sure what she had said to win the girl's approval, but she enjoyed having it. "Well, thank you. You're a pretty regular kid yourself."

Joe looked surprised when he saw them emerge from the bedroom in conversation. "I see you made a friend."

"Who is she—beside Jimmy Walker's former mistress?"

"You certainly did get chummy."

"Don't sound so shocked, Joe. After all, who am I but Joe Denbigh's current mistress?"

"You know I hate to hear you talk that way. You can be more any time you want."

"You know I hate to hear *you* talk *that* way. Anyway, I'm more interested in the girl. Who is she?"

"No one special. I think she's in the chorus line of

The Music Box Revue. Jimmy has a weakness for the theater."

"Well, I like her. I never knew a chorus girl before. She's interesting."

"Fine, you can have her to tea."

"Don't be such a snob. At least she's more interesting than Lucinda and Harriet."

"Just because something is different, Claudia, it doesn't necessarily follow it's interesting."

"Isn't that a dangerous statement for you to make, Joe?"

His eyes flickered in anger. "I'll take my chances."

Claudia supposed that was why she thought of the party so often that summer—because it had been different. She was bored and almost frightened. She had been married little more than a year, and it seemed her whole life was established. And she was as tired of the attempts to shatter the mold as she was of the mold. Like that weekend last July. The house party had gone on for two days, and no one had slept more than a few hours here and there between drinks. It was late, and Sam had insisted they all go for a midnight sail on *Mistress.* Somewhere around two A.M. Polly had gone to the bow of the boat, taken off all her clothes, and dived off in a great splash of phosphorescence and laughter. There had been a good breeze, and Sam had to come about quickly so as not to lose sight of her while Charles raced below for towels. Though everyone talked about the incident for the rest of the summer, Claudia found it as predictable as everything else. She guessed that was why she thought so much about Jimmy Walker's party. It had been unpredictable, like Joe.

There was one other thing about the party. She had succeeded in finding exactly the thing Sam would go to any length to protect her from. But Sam wasn't the only man in her life, and when she thought of Joe and that party from a different perspective, Claudia was less pleased with herself. She had known it all along, but the night Daddy and Mother drove over from Glen Cove for dinner, it came home to her with a new force.

Daddy had guessed something was wrong. Before

dinner they'd gone for a walk along the beach while everyone else was having cocktails.

"Is everything all right, baby?"

"Of course, why do you ask?"

"No reason. Actually, Sam more than you. You look fine—always do—but I can't say the same for him. He looks worried. And I'll tell you the truth, Claudia, I know I shouldn't meddle, but I can't help it: I watch you with him, and I don't like the way you treat him."

Stung, she stopped and faced her father. "Daddy, that's not fair!"

"Now, now, child, let's not get all worked up." He took her arm and continued along the beach. "I'm sure there's nothing to it, but all the same, appearances do count. I know there are those who say you're spoiled or selfish, but I've always believed you have a big heart. But I just don't see it with Sam. He worships you. When you're in the same room, he can't take his eyes from you, and when you leave, you can just see him wondering when you'll come back."

"Oh, Daddy, you're exaggerating."

"No, I'm not, Claudia. It's true. Sam adores you. And you . . . well, there's something wrong with the way you treat him. You're cold."

She kept her eyes on the sand as they walked. What could she possibly tell him? That she recoiled from her husband's touch. That she struck out at him and herself with a shabby affair that brought her nothing but sexual pleasure, self-hatred, and painful memories. If he criticized her for her coolness to Sam, what would he say about her warmth to Joe Denbigh? What would he say if he had seen them in this very house on that snowy afternoon last winter? She wouldn't be his *little girl,* his *baby* then. She'd be a whore, a tramp, a woman he could not love.

She threw her arms about his neck. "Oh, Daddy," she sobbed against his white dinner coat and resolved that moment she would break with Joe.

But that evening on the beach with Daddy was a long time ago, and now Joe was next to her in the backseat of his Bentley, and she knew it would not be easy. The moment she'd felt his mouth on hers even in that almost polite greeting she knew she had herself to fight as well as Joe. Her only hope lay in not going to his apartment. If she did, she knew he would take her resolve from her as easily as he lifted the evening cape from her shoulders.

She would not give him the chance. And she would not drink too much champagne either.

Denbigh told the chauffeur to drive home.

"Let's go out, Joe." He looked at her in surprise. "After all, it's a celebration. We haven't seen each other in months."

"Where would you like to go?"

"Well, it's almost our anniversary. Let's go back to that speakeasy—the one on the roof."

Anniversary, he thought. This *was* a different Claudia.

"You're awfully quiet," Joe whispered as they moved around the dance floor. "Aren't you glad I'm back?"

She smiled weakly. "Let's go outside, Joe. There's something I'd like to talk to you about."

"There's something I'd like to talk to you about, too. But first," he said when they were on the terrace across from the Metropolitan Building clock again, "I have something for you." He took a small velvet box from his pocket. Inside was a ring in which six perfect sapphires formed a small, beautifully wrought flower.

"It's exquisite, Joe, but of course, I can't accept it. How could I possibly explain it?"

"That's what I want to talk to you about. We can't go back to the way we were last winter. It's not right for either of us. You'll have to tell your husband."

"Tell him what?" She was busy preparing her own words and barely heard him.

"About us, of course."

She looked at him in surprise. "Don't be absurd, Joe. I came here to tell you I'm not going to see you again. I knew if I tried to tell you over the telephone, you wouldn't believe me, but you have to. It's over."

"You've said that before, Claudia."

"Perhaps, but I mean it this time."

"It isn't over. I love you." He pulled her to him, and she felt his lips against her ear. "And you love me. I'm part of you now. I'll always be part of you."

"No!" She took a step back, but his hands on her arms held her in place. "I don't love you. I never loved you. It was sex. That's all."

"That's more than you have with him."

"That's not true."

"I saw you, Claudia. I saw you every time you came to me. Look me in the eye, Claudia, and tell me what it's like with your husband. Tell me how you feel when he touches you."

Her voice was almost a shriek. "Stop it! Stop it this minute."

"I thought so." There was triumph in his voice and he was sneering as he dropped his hands from her shoulders. He had finally hurt in return, hurt her at her very core.

"Perhaps you're right. Perhaps I don't love my husband. But I don't love you either. And certainly if it isn't a case of love, you of all people, Joe, ought to be able to see the advantages of a proper marriage. What a fool I'd be to trade Samuel Livingston Beaumont for Joe Denbigh!"

He saw the disdain in her eyes, and for a moment Joe Daivone surfaced in Joe Denbigh. He remembered a man he had done business with a few years ago. The man had run a fashionable restaurant in the Forties. He had looked down his nose at Joe as he announced he had his own source of wine and spirits. The restaurateur had died in a car accident less than a month later.

Claudia's face held that same superior expression now, and Denbigh wanted to slap it till it bled. Then he remembered who he was, who he had become, and he knew there was no need for that.

It might take time, but he was not an impatient man. He'd have Claudia Trenholm Beaumont someday—and if he didn't, he'd have a revenge better than any physical one he might take tonight.

Sam sat in the darkened living room. When he had arrived home a little after midnight, he had gone from room to room, turning on the light, looking for Claudia. Then, when he saw she wasn't home, he retraced his steps, turning out each light until all that remained was a small circle of brightness from a single lamp in the living room. He poured himself a drink and snapped off the lamp. Then he sat down to wait.

Sam was usually adroit at keeping worry at bay. His response to any deficiencies he sensed in his marriage was to take some action. To sit and brood was useless. Worse than that, it was not masculine. And yet sitting and brooding was exactly what he was doing, and he was thinking as much about his own behavior as his wife's.

Sam prided himself on the fact that his conduct toward Claudia was beyond reproach. It followed logically from the fact that he was the stronger of the two. It was up to him to take care of her, to make allowances for her moods, and—for he always came back to the same point in the end—to have patience with her coolness. They'd been married only a year and a half, and Sam had learned through a book he had, uncharacteristically, bought, read, and hidden in his office that it took many women longer than that to begin to enjoy sex. He was willing to wait for Claudia, and in the meantime, he would be the perfect husband. His standards permitted nothing less. Yet tonight, just an hour earlier, he'd discovered a chink in his armor.

The dinner had been exactly like scores of others he'd attended in the last ten years. There was a pleasant air of conviviality, and Sam enjoyed the acclaim that went with the award. *Mistress* had taken first place again. It was not an exciting evening, but it was a satisfying one. Or so he'd thought until he found himself next to Chet Hallenbeck as they were getting their hats and coats. Sam and Chet had raced together, and against each other, and Sam respected Chet. His knowledge of wind and current was prodigious; his hand at the helm was uncanny. Chet Hallenbeck was a superb sailor. He was also a good friend of Anson Hagerty. To a man like Sam that said a great deal.

"Well, where to now, Sam, old man? Have to celebrate your victory."

"I think I've had enough celebration for one night. It's home for me."

Chet leaned conspicuously closer. "Even an old married man—especially an old married man—needs a night out now and then. The *Follies* are just letting out, and I've got a cute trick lined up. Come on, Sam. We'll make a party of it."

The invitation hadn't surprised Sam. He'd received dozens in the past. Until he was married, he'd accepted his share. Since then he'd declined good-naturedly, always careful not to sound priggish. What shocked him tonight was not the invitation, but his momentary entertainment of it. He had hesitated just long enough to allow Chet's eyes to light up in encouragement. Then Sam's cousin Graham Livingston had joined them, and Sam had accepted the offer of a ride home from him. Chet hadn't suggested they make it a threesome. Graham Livingston wasn't a man one wanted on a party.

He had not really thought of going, Sam reassured himself now. All the same, it was disconcerting. If he had never relied on others, Sam had always been a man who relied on himself. But if he could no longer trust himself, whom or what could he trust?

He heard Claudia's key in the lock and watched silently as she closed the door behind her and stood for a moment in the darkened foyer. Then she switched on the light, and he blinked against the brilliance.

"Sam, what are you doing in the dark?" Her voice sounded unusually shrill in her ears.

"Waiting for you. Who brought you home?"

"A few of us went to a speakeasy afterward. I think I'd like a brandy. Did Wilfred leave any out with your scotch?"

He poured her a finger of brandy, then filled his glass almost to the top.

"Don't you think you've had enough for one night?" She was sitting on the sofa, and as she leaned forward to take the brandy snifter from him, his eyes were drawn to the décolletage of her dress. The pale skin against the black chiffon seemed to command his attention.

"A man has to do something while he waits for his wife."

"Well, your wife is home now, so I don't see why you need another drink."

"Where did you say you went after the party?"

"Just some speakeasy on a roof on Fifth Avenue. I don't remember the name."

"Sounds like one of Anson's parties. Were Sky and Harriet along?"

She began searching in her evening bag for a cigarette.

"I asked who went along?"

"Really, Sam, you ought to go to these things in the first place. Then I wouldn't have to be cross-examined when I come home."

"I'm not cross-examining you, Claudia. I'm merely asking about your evening."

"Very well. The party was not very interesting. I went to a speakeasy on Fifth Avenue afterward. Joseph Denbigh had his car, and he dropped me here. Does that answer your question?"

"Joe Denbigh! Why did you come home with him? Why didn't you let Sky or George bring you home?"

"Really, Sam, this is getting absurd. Sky and George weren't there, that's why. Now if we've settled the great transportation issue, I'd like to go to bed. It was a long evening, and I'm tired."

"Who was there?"

"At the party?"

"You know what I mean, Claudia. At the speakeasy. If George and Sky weren't there, who was?"

There was no longer any need to lie. "As a matter of fact, just Joe Denbigh."

"You mean there were only the two of you!"

"Actually the place was crowded."

"That's not funny."

"It certainly isn't the serious matter you're making it out to be. Would you make such a fuss if I had gone with George?"

"Of course not. George is an old friend."

"Then let's say Denbigh is a new friend."

"Friend! My God, Claudia, that man is no friend."

"I've heard it all before, Sam. I've heard about his lowly background and his lack of breeding, and I don't want to hear it again."

"And I won't have my wife running around with a bootlegger."

"Now you're going too far. Just because the man isn't one of us—one of you—that doesn't make him a bootlegger."

"I happen to know he is a bootlegger."

"And I happen to know he's on Wall Street just like George and Schuyler and a dozen of the rest of your friends."

"Is that what your friend Denbigh told you?"

"Don't take that tone with me, Sam."

He walked to the bar table and poured himself another drink.

"I find your superiority a little out of place tonight, Claudia. Try to remember you're a married woman who has just returned from a speakeasy with a strange bootlegger. Try to remember, too, that I'm your husband. And his name isn't Denbigh. It's Daivone."

"What are you talking about?"

"The man's name is not Joe Denbigh. It's Joe Daivone. And until a couple of years ago he lived on Mott Street. That doesn't mean anything to you, does it, Claudia, because you don't know where Mott Street is. I'll tell you where it is. It's right in the heart of Little Italy."

"Little Italy! How disgraceful. You really are an incurable snob, Sam. Did you ever ask where my father was born? It wasn't on Washington Square or Sixty-ninth Street, you know."

"Your father has nothing to do with this."

"Why not? Isn't it exactly the same thing? I guess I

ought to be grateful you married me. Really, the Sheridans are all right, but the Trenholm money is so *new*."

"Now listen to me carefully, Claudia. In the time we've been married I've never given you an order, but I'm going to say this now. You will not see Mr. Joseph Daivone again. You will not dance with him, you will not speak to him, and you will certainly not go out with him alone."

It was almost enough to drive her back to Denbigh.

"I'll see whomever I choose, Sam."

"Maybe I'm not making myself clear. All right, you don't care about his name or that he was born in Little Italy, but think for a minute how he got from Mott Street to where he is. How did he get to a point in life where he can weekend at the Chesneys' and take *my* wife to a speakeasy? I'm going to tell you how and for once in your life you're going to listen.

"Denbigh is a bootlegger. He and his brothers—there are several of them—control all the bootleg traffic from Connecticut to New Jersey. About two years ago he decided to get out. Our friend Mr. Denbigh wanted more than money. He wanted respectability."

"I'm not sure we ought to blame him for that."

"What do I have to do to make you understand? Denbigh is not some fellow who made a little gin in his bathtub. He's a gangster. Do you think he got up one morning and decided he was going to control all the liquor that came into this area? It wasn't that easy or nearly that neat. There were a lot of other people in the same business, and now there are only Denbigh and his brothers. Do I have to get you newspaper clippings? Because I can, Claudia. I've seen a couple of them myself. There was one picture of a carful of dead bodies they pushed into the Sound off Stamford. Apparently the tide went out. That was just about the time Denbigh took over Connecticut."

Newspaper clippings again. "Are you saying he killed those men?" She could not put Sam's stories together with the man she had known for the last year.

"No, Claudia, he didn't kill them. He *had* them killed. Your friend Denbigh is a very important man."

"But I don't understand. Why isn't he in jail?"

"I just told you. He is a very important man. Some young fellow was convicted for those murders."

"How do you know all this?"

"Do you remember Denbigh's party? When I said he was Italian? I had mentioned his name at lunch one day, and one of the men knew the lawyer who'd changed his name for him. That was all I knew then. But after that party I started to ask a few questions." Sam didn't have to explain why he had begun to ask questions. Claudia had shown too much interest in the man for him to be uninterested. "That's when I found all this out. I saw no reason to mention it. I simply decided we'd stay away from the man. But of course, I didn't know you two were going to become such fast friends."

"We're nothing of the sort. I don't care what the man is. Joe Denbigh is of no interest to me. But I won't have you ordering me around and making a scene just because I go to a speakeasy after a party. What am I supposed to do, sit home and wait for you to return with another of your trophies? Perhaps I should make a scene about your dinner, Sam. Where did you go? Who brought you home?"

"That's different."

She stood up and drained her glass. "No, Sam. It's not different at all. I'm going to sleep. You can sit here and drink yourself silly until morning for all I care."

When she came out of her dressing room, Sam was sitting on the end of his bed. His glass was full again.

"Have you seen him before?"

"Have I seen whom before?"

"You know who I mean, Claudia. Have you seen Denbigh before?"

"I told you, Sam, I don't want to talk about it anymore. Besides, you're drunk, and I'm not going to stand here at three o'clock in the morning and carry on a conversation with a drunk."

He slammed the glass down on the night table, and she watched the liquid splash over her books and magazines. "Yes, I'm drunk, Claudia. But don't be so damned holier-than-thou about it because if you hadn't been running around town with that bootlegger, I wouldn't have been sitting here drinking for the last three hours. Now I asked you a question. Have you seen him before?"

"And I told you I don't want to discuss it." She turned her back to him, and the force with which he spun her around shocked her. She could feel his fingers digging into her arms. "Take your hands off me, Sam."

"Goddammit, don't you pull that ice goddess act on me, Claudia. And don't you tell me to take my hands off you. You're my wife, you hear that, my wife. The law says I have a right to your body."

She had never seen Sam so drunk, and it frightened her. She tried to take a step backward, but he held her firm. "Let go of me, Sam, let go." She began to struggle against him but only succeeded in throwing them both off-balance. They fell backward, and his weight pinned her to the bed. He was clawing at the lace bodice of her nightgown; then she heard something tear, and his hands were rough and insistent on her breasts. She could feel the terror rising as she thrashed against him, but he held her shoulders to the bed with one hand while he fumbled at his trousers with the other. She clamped her knees together; but Sam's own separated them, and she felt his hand beneath the satin skirt of her gown. Then he was savagely inside her, and she was nothing but a vehicle for his satisfaction. She turned her face away. Her mouth at least would be her own, but his lips found her ear. His words were slurred, but she knew them without hearing.

"Love me, Claudia. Love *me*." He shuddered and then sobbed.

3

Claudia turned sideways before the full-length mirror. She smoothed the peach-colored satin of her nightgown over her stomach. Flat. She took the material between her thumb and forefinger and held it away from her body. Grotesque. She could not believe she'd ever look that way.

There was a knock at the door, and Ellen entered. She was carrying a satin nightgown, almost identical to the one Claudia was wearing, but it was coffee-colored with beige lace. "This is badly torn, ma'am, but I think that shop on Madison Avenue, Emma Maloof's, will be able to mend it."

Claudia looked at the garment with distaste. She'd hidden it two months ago. How fitting Ellen should find it this morning. "Don't bother, Ellen, I'm tired of it."

"Tired of it! But you've hardly worn it. I'm sure it can be mended."

"I said I was tired of it, Ellen. Give it to one of the girls in the kitchen if you like. Send it to your niece."

"My niece, indeed. Now what would she be doing with a gown like this in a convent school?"

"I don't care what you do with it. Just get rid of it."

That night with Sam was vivid enough without memorabilia. It was ironic the way it had turned out. Sam had begun by telling her terrible things about Joe Denbigh, but in the year she had known Joe she'd never seen a trace of brutality. The only violence she'd known had come from her well-mannered husband.

Sam's manners, to be sure, had reappeared the following morning. The first thing she'd seen when she opened her eyes that day was Sam sitting at the window watching her. His face was pale in the harsh morning light, and there were black smudges under his eyes. She had never seen him look so tired.

"Claudia"—his voice was low and hoarse—"I'm sorry. It was the whiskey. You must believe that." When she said nothing, he walked to her bed and sat carefully on the edge. "Please forgive me."

She was out of bed in an instant. "I don't want to talk about it, Sam."

And they had not spoken of that night again, though it hung between them. For a month after that Sam had not touched a drop of whiskey, and when he did begin to drink again, it was with care. It was also with a purpose. Only after he had taken a drink did he dare approach her.

There was another irony to that night, one Claudia hadn't recognized until yesterday in the doctor's office. At least she had broken off with Joe. At least she hadn't gone to his apartment. It would be difficult enough to be the mother of Sam Beaumont's child. It would have been unbearable to be the mother of *either* Sam Beaumont's *or* Joe Denbigh's child.

Sam sat at one end of the long dining table, a plate of ham and eggs pushed to one side. Coffee and the morning paper were before him, but though he had turned to the sports page and worked his way through two articles, he had little knowledge of what he had read. When he looked up, he was surprised to see Claudia in the doorway. She rarely rose to breakfast with him, and for the last two months she had slept—or feigned sleep—until he was safely out of the house.

He watched her over the edge of his newspaper. "Good morning, Claudia. You're up early."

"I thought we might have coffee together before you left for the office." Her voice, her words, the chair she pulled close to his surprised him. There had been moments recently when she seemed to be considering a truce, but this sounded almost like the declaration of a peace treaty.

They were silent while Wilfred brought her coffee and retreated behind the swinging door to the pantry. "What are you up to today?" He seized on the familiar topic.

"I thought I'd have lunch with Polly."

His face darkened with suspicion. "I thought you had lunch with Polly yesterday."

"I lied to you, Sam. I didn't lunch with anyone yesterday. In fact, I didn't lunch yesterday."

"What did you do?"

"I went to Dr. Gettinger." His face expressed immediately what he dared not put into words. "I'm afraid you're going to be a father, Sam. I sound like something out of a Victorian novel."

He hadn't heard her last words. He was on his knees beside her chair, and his arms were around her. "Good Lord, Claudia, why didn't you tell me yesterday? Why didn't you call me from the doctor's office?"

"I don't know. I guess I had to get used to the idea myself."

"And are you used to it now?" He looked at her carefully.

"I guess I will be in a while." It wasn't entirely a lie. Sam's excitement was contagious. Perhaps this was a chance for a new beginning.

"How long do you have to get used to it? I mean when is it going to happen?"

"Dr. Gettinger says the end of June."

He was silent for a moment, and she could see his mind working. He might not be a brilliant banker, but he could count. "Oh, my God, Claudia, I'm sorry. I'm so sorry." He buried his face in her lap, and for a moment she thought Sam Beaumont was going to cry. Slowly, almost shyly, she stroked his fair hair. It was an unfamiliar gesture. "Why don't we just forget about that, Sam? That's the past, and after all," she continued, feeling very much like the heroine in one of the scores of plays that had shaped so much of her consciousness, "we have the future to worry about now."

He was holding her to him, and his words were soft against her hair. "My God, I love you, Claudia." They both were silent for a moment; then he released her as if he had suddenly thought of something. "Are you all right? What else did Gettinger say? Are you supposed to do anything? Or not do anything? I'll call him right now and make an appointment for this afternoon."

"Now, Sam, let's not get carried away. Dr. Gettinger said you can call him if you want, but I don't see the point. And as for everything else, I can go on just as I have been. I've never been very active, as you've often pointed out."

"All the same, I won't have you overdoing it."

"Don't be ridiculous. People have been having babies for years."

"We haven't."

"I guess that's true enough. Well, I promise to be sensible if you promise not to be ridiculous. Now you'd better be on your way. The world doesn't stop just because I'm . . . we're going to have a baby."

"All right, I'll leave, but I'll call you as soon as I get to the office."

"Don't be silly. Anyway, I'll be in my bath."

"Then promise you'll call as soon as you're out."

"I won't have any news in the next half hour, Sam."

"If you don't call me, I'll simply keep calling you."

"Very well, I'll call."

"Are you sure you ought to go out to lunch today? It's supposed to rain."

"Really, Sam."

"All right. Only you're going to have to cut down. I won't have you tiring yourself. And you'll have to give up all that charity work."

"I don't want to do that right now because I don't want to tell anyone just yet. If you tell people—especially people like Polly—too early, they get all worked up and expect the baby to arrive in two months. I'll tell them in March or April. I won't be able to go many places after that anyway."

"I guess you're right—about telling people, I mean. But it's going to be darned hard. I'd like to run through the bank this morning, handing out cigars."

"Don't you dare do anything of the sort. You may tell your father, but he's the only one. And no cheating.

I know you. A game of squash, a few drinks at the Racquet, and you'll all be toasting Samuel Beaumont, Junior."

"All right, I promise. Your secret is safe with me." He bent to kiss her good-bye. "On one condition. You call me after your bath."

Late that afternoon Sam stood on the street in front of the New York Bank and Trust Company, debating whether to stop by the Racquet. He feared Claudia was right. A game of squash and a few drinks were bound to wrest his secret from him.

"I said, 'is there anything wrong, Sam?' " He felt a hand on his shoulder and turned to find himself face to face with James Trenholm. "You were miles away. Is anything wrong?"

"No, sir, not in the least. I'm glad to see you. Very glad." Sam smiled as he shook his father-in-law's hand, and James could not help remarking how well he was looking. It was a definite improvement over the past few months.

"In fact, you're just the person I wanted to see."

"I am, am I?" James was surprised.

"Come have a drink. I have news, and we ought to celebrate."

"That does sound important. All right, I could use a drink. I'll send Henry along, and I'll walk home later —walk it off, as it were. Have to be careful at my age, you know.

"Now what is this momentous news, Sam?" They were seated in the corner of the small lounge of the club where Sam regularly lunched. It was almost deserted at this hour.

"Well, sir, you're going to be a grandfather."

"I can't say I'm surprised, Sam, not the way you were smiling all the way over here, but I am delighted.

"This is a day for good news. I almost forgot to tell you mine. Mrs. Trenholm and I had a letter from Katherine this morning."

Sam looked down into his glass. "She's coming home, I hope. I never could see her settled in California."

"Better than that, my boy. She's going to be married."

"That is good news. It calls for another drink."

James started to decline—one drink was enough for him this early in the evening—but he could see that Sam was genuinely pleased, pleased and relieved, and he didn't want him to think that he bore him any hard feelings about his older daughter. "Perhaps just one more. In honor of Katherine."

Sam signaled the waiter. "Tell me about it. Who's the lucky fellow?"

"We don't know much about him. He's a Texan of all things. Name's Whitely. Tom Whitely. People seem all right, not that I put much store in that sort of thing. That's Mrs. Trenholm's department."

"I imagine things like that are more important here than they are out west."

"Don't you believe it, my boy. Things like that are important everywhere. At least to some people. Well, Whitely's family's been in Texas for three generations now."

"Oil?"

"No, they're ranchers. Or Whitely's father and grandfathers were. Seems he's more interested in airplanes. What do you think of that, Sam? I guess I'm getting old. Twenty years ago I would have known it was the wave of the future. Now it just strikes me as a little crazy. Anyway, it seems Whitely wants to start manufacturing airplanes. That's how Kate met him. He wants Dick—that's Amanda's husband, you know—to go into this thing with him."

"I don't know the particulars, of course, but it could be a good opportunity. Are they going to live in Texas?"

"No. If he does go into this airplane thing, they'll settle in California. There'll be a lot of traveling, Kate says, but they'll live in California."

"I guess Kate likes it out there."

"Certainly seems to. At any rate, this Whitely does, and from her letter it seems Kate likes it wherever Whitely does."

"Well, I couldn't be happier for her, sir. Kate deserves the best."

"And now I really must be going." James stood up a little unsteadily. "I'm very happy for you, Sam, for both of you."

"Thank you, sir. Are you sure you wouldn't like me to get you a taxi?"

"No, thanks, my boy. I think I'll walk for a while."

By the time James reached Canal Street his breath was short, and despite the brisk November wind, he was perspiring heavily. He slowed his pace and tried to catch his breath. "Damnation," he swore at himself. "Can't even walk a few blocks anymore." By the end of the next block his heart was pounding, and he could feel his legs trembling beneath him. He stopped at the corner and leaned against a lamppost. In the darkening rush hour people pushed past him. Once or twice he was jostled roughly, but he seemed not to notice. A taxi stopped at the corner, and a young man jumped out. James clutched the door he had left open and climbed slowly into the cab.

"Sixty-ninth and Fifth. . . ."

"I can't hear you, Mac." The driver turned around, but there was nothing on the seat but a black homburg. On the floor of the car James Trenholm lay in a dark, crumpled heap.

"Are you sure you're up to going tonight?"

"Now you're not going to start that again, Sam. There's nothing very arduous about sitting in a theater for a few hours." She turned in front of the full-length mirror and examined herself critically. "Unless, of course, you're ashamed to be seen with me. Do you think I look fat?"

"Huge." He came up behind her and slipped his arms around her waist. "But I put up with you because it's all my fault."

"You must never tease about that, Sam. I am going to get fat, you know. Horribly fat and ugly."

"Not fat, Claudia, large. Large with child is, I believe, the proper expression. And I promise you are not going to get ugly."

There was a knock at the door. "Excuse me, madam," Ellen said. "Dr. Gettinger is on the telephone. He wants to talk to you, sir."

"That's odd." He turned to Claudia. "I did telephone him at his office this afternoon, but I didn't expect him to return my call at this hour."

When Sam returned minutes later, his face was pale.

"What is it, Sam? What did he tell you?"

"It's your father. They've taken him to a hospital."

"A hospital! What's wrong with Daddy?"

"They're not sure. They think it was a stroke. He's still unconscious."

"But what happened?"

"Apparently after he left me—I told you he said he wanted to walk—well, this just hit him."

"How *could* you have left him? Why didn't you make sure he got home safely? Why did you take him out drinking in the first place?"

"Now, Claudia, calm down. You must think of yourself, too. Why don't you lie down and—"

"I don't want to lie down. I want to see Daddy. Where is he?" He put his arm around her shoulders and began to lead her to the bed, but she pushed him away.

"Don't! Don't touch me! You did it. It's your fault he's in the hospital."

"Claudia, be reasonable. Your father had a stroke. . . ."

"I won't be reasonable. I won't! I want to see him, and you can't stop me."

"Your father is unconscious, Claudia. He won't know if you're there or not, and you have to think of yourself and the baby."

"I don't care," she screamed. "I want to see Daddy." She took a step toward the door, but Sam blocked her way.

"Claudia, please try to calm down. Think of the baby. Please think of the baby."

"I hate the baby," she shrieked. "And I hate you." She sank to the floor and lay there, sobbing. Sam picked her up and carried her to the bed. Then he rang for

Ellen and told her to call Dr. Gettinger and tell him to come as quickly as possible.

Wayne Gettinger was a handsome man in his fifties. His leonine head with its mane of gray hair, his tasteful dress, and his family connections conspired to make him a successful society doctor. Like many of his breed, he was not a bad doctor, but he tended to be an acquiescent one.

"Now, Claudia, what is all this hysteria? Your father is ill, certainly, but your making yourself sick isn't going to help him. I've known you all your life, and I've always thought you were a sensible girl. Don't change now. After all, you've got another generation to think of."

Her large green eyes stared up at him numbly. He recognized the mood. She would not give him the satisfaction of a reply, but she was listening.

"The pill I gave you will make you sleep. And I want you to stay in bed tomorrow." She opened her mouth, but he went on before she could speak. "I won't let your father have visitors, so there's no point in your going to the hospital. I'll keep Sam posted on all developments. Now, any questions?"

She shook her head.

"Good. Then I'll see you tomorrow." He picked up the black leather Mark Cross bag and turned to leave. Just as he reached the door, Claudia's voice, as small and frightened as a child's, called him back.

"Dr. Gettinger."

He walked back to the bed. "Yes?"

"Do you think it would be possible . . . I mean, I think I'd rest better . . . if I were alone. Do you think you could tell Sam that?"

She felt as if she were under a microscope as he looked down at her. When he spoke, his voice sounded older than his fifty-six years. "Yes, Claudia, I'll explain things to Sam."

Sam was in the library, pacing before the fire. He looked up expectantly as the doctor entered. His face under the tan he seemed to hold year round was whiter than his wife's.

"She'll be fine, Sam. It was only the shock of the news. There's nothing wrong with her—or the baby. Everything's in order. Which is more than I can say here. You look terrible."

"I'm all right, but you look a little tired yourself. Would you like a drink?"

"I'll have a brandy if you'll join me."

"Is she really all right?" Sam asked again as they sat on opposite sides of the fire, the brandy between them.

"She's fine, Sam. Just nerves. Some women tend to react more violently to everything during pregnancy. And then we mustn't forget that she and Mr. Trenholm are extraordinarily fond of each other. But she'll be all right. Plenty of rest and no excitement. I'm counting on you to enforce that."

"To the limit."

"I've given her a sedative, and she'll sleep tonight. And I've told her to stay in bed tomorrow." The doctor leaned forward and poured himself another finger of brandy. "As I said, Sam, it's merely a case of nerves. I shouldn't say merely. Frequently nerves are more diffi- cult to treat than physical ailments. The point is, you can do more than I can. I can give her a sedative tonight, but it's going to be the days and weeks ahead that will be difficult. I don't want to frighten you, Sam, but most miscarriages occur in the first three months of preg- nancy, and they can be emotional in origin. What I'm trying to say is that you're going to have to be consider- ate. Don't make any demands on her. In fact, it might be a good idea if you had your things moved into a separate room for a while. Until Claudia calms down."

"Of course, if you think it will help."

"I knew I could count on you, Sam. I told Claudia I'd be back tomorrow afternoon. By that time I should have some word from the specialist."

"How do things look?"

"It's too early to say, but confidentially, I'm worried. It was a serious stroke, and there's no telling how much damage was done. Of course, I didn't tell Claudia any of this."

"Of course not. How is Mrs. Trenholm bearing up?"

"As well as might be expected. For all the southern belle in her, Elizabeth Trenholm is a strong woman. She has Louisa there. That's some help. And Katherine should be home within the week. I had a wire sent this evening."

"It's a pity for her, too. She's planning to be married."

"There's no reason she can't be. Life goes on, Sam. Claudia's condition is proof of that."

The last leaf fell, the first snow covered Central Park, and still James Trenholm lay immobile in New York Hospital. Specialists replaced each other one after another, but the prognosis remained the same. Damage had been extensive, and there was little hope of recovery. James could neither speak nor move, and though Elizabeth swore his eyes lit up when she or one of her daughters entered the room, there was little reason to assume he recognized any of them.

On January 1, Miss Teddy, the nurse Sam had hired, wheeled James Trenholm into the small grille elevator that had been installed in the house on Sixty-ninth Street. She settled him comfortably in his room, then went to her own to arrange things. Miss Teddy looked around the large room with satisfaction. It was attractively furnished, and the four high windows faced south. It was fortunate the room suited her so well, for Miss Teddy expected to occupy it for several years.

"I don't understand why Tom can't come east," Claudia said, helping herself to the salmon mousse Wilfred held for her on a silver tray. "Daddy would have wanted you to be married here. You have virtually no family in California, Kate."

"What Daddy would have wanted is beside the point now."

"That's a terrible thing to say."

"It's easy for you to be indignant, Claudia. You haven't been living in that house for the last four months

—nurses and doctors constantly in and out and Mother and Aunt Louisa trying to convince each other Daddy's getting better. Well, I may have had to *live* with all that, but I won't be married with it. I'm taking the train west next week, and we'll be married at the end of the month."

"Couldn't Tom at least come east to get you?" Sam seemed to be addressing himself as much to his lunch as to Katherine.

"Tom doesn't have time to come east. Airplanes won't wait, he says. Besides, Tom doesn't like the East. He says easterners think they *are* America, but they aren't even part of it. Easterners, he says, are always looking east themselves. Toward Europe. Tom looks west. That's where the future is, he says."

"In China?"

"You know very well what I meant, Claudia."

"It sounds as if Tom has a good many ideas."

"There you go. Tom isn't you, Sam. He has his own ideas and his own way of doing things, and it's none of your business, yours or Claudia's."

"You can marry whomever you choose, Kate. I was merely thinking of Mother and Daddy."

"You were merely thinking of you, Claudia. As usual. It's so much easier for you as long as I'm home with Mother and Daddy."

After lunch Claudia went to her room to rest, in keeping with the doctor's orders, and Sam saw Katherine downstairs to where Henry was waiting with the old Brewster.

"I know you've been under a strain, Kate, but I wish you wouldn't argue with Claudia. The doctor said not to excite her."

"The doctor said that five months ago, Sam. There's nothing wrong with Claudia. Except that she's thoroughly spoiled."

"That isn't fair."

Katherine stopped in the center of the large high-ceilinged lobby. The floor was an oversized marble chessboard, and she turned to Sam and looked at him as if she were pondering how she had allowed her king to be checked and mated. When she spoke, she sounded very tired. "Oh, Sam, what a waste. What a terrible, useless waste." Then she was out of the lobby and into the car. As Henry pulled away from the curb, she waved once through the closed window. It was almost like a salute.

When Sam returned to the apartment, he found his wife stretched out on her bed. The shades were down, the room in half darkness. "Are you asleep?" He sat gingerly on the side of the bed and took her hand in his.

"No, I'm just resting."

"I'm glad to see you're being sensible."

"I warn you, Sam, if I hear one more word about my *condition*, I'm going to scream."

"Very well, we'll talk about my condition. Isn't it time I had my things moved back in here? Not that I minded separate rooms while you were ill, but now that you're feeling better, it would be nice to be back in our own room."

"Oh, Sam, must you? I've been sleeping badly lately, and I'm sure having you tossing and turning in the next bed won't help. And you know what Dr. Gettinger said about getting enough rest. Why don't we wait a little longer, just until the baby's born?" He said nothing, and she patted his hand. "Thank you, Sam. I knew you'd understand."

Sam stood in front of the nursery and looked at the rows of small red faces. He didn't feel at all the way he had thought he would. He felt none of the pride and joy he'd experienced that morning—it seemed years ago now—when Claudia first told him about the baby. He'd welcomed the idea then, welcomed the change it seemed to make in Claudia. The future had suddenly looked so promising. But then James had had his stroke, and everything had changed. Not everything, he thought, only Claudia. She'd become colder, more aloof than ever. He had tried, day after day he had tried, but there was no way to break down the wall she'd built around herself. She had taken herself away, and by doing that, she had taken the baby as well.

He looked at his son now. He felt no connection with the small bundle squirming in the basket before him. Everyone who came to visit said he looked exactly like Sam, but Sam didn't see it. If the child looked like anyone, he thought, he looked like that damned bootlegger. Sam knew it was an absurd thought, yet he hadn't been able to get it out of his mind ever since he had first seen the baby.

The door to Claudia's room was open. Harriet Mason was sitting on the end of the bed, and Schuyler was barely visible in the small chair surrounded by baskets of flowers.

"Ah, the proud father. Just in time, too. Is a martini cocktail all right, Sam? It will have to be. That's all we brought."

"Not another, Sky. You've already had two, and we're late."

"All right, Harriet. I'll just pour one for Sam, and then we'll be on our way."

"Don't let me hurry you."

"I assure you you're not, old man. Harriet is. Seems an hour is the very minimum in which my wife can dress for dinner."

"Did you see the baby on the way in?" Claudia asked when Harriet and Schuyler had left.

"Yes, and he wasn't crying."

"I don't think he has the energy after this morning. Your son kept the entire floor in an uproar."

"Isn't that supposed to be good for him?"

"Good for him, perhaps, but think about the rest of us. You'll simply have to have a man to man talk with Samuel Beaumont, Junior."

"I've been thinking about that, Claudia. I don't want to call the baby Samuel."

"But we decided months ago."

"That was months ago."

She thought of asking what had changed his mind but decided against it. "Besides," Sam continued, "I'm not named for my father. It isn't as if we'd be breaking a tradition."

"What would you like to call him?"

"We could name him for your father. James is a good name, and it would be a nice gesture. I think it would give your father pleasure."

"Would have given him pleasure," she corrected. "You know he won't know, Sam. He doesn't even recognize us. I'm sure of that."

"All the same, I think it would be nice to call him James."

"Whatever you say." It struck her as the final irony. Sam had taken her father's life, for surely the condition he lingered in was more like death than life, and with it he'd taken even the slightest justification for having lost Philippe. And now he wanted to name this child neither of them wanted—this accident of Sam's desire and her distaste—after her beloved Daddy.

4

The grass was still wet from the night's storm; but the sky had turned a brilliant blue, and the air was crisply clear. The bay shimmered in the early-morning sunshine, and across the Sound Claudia could see the sharp outlines of the Connecticut shore. Did she have a counterpart in Norwalk or Westport who sat on a similar terrace of a similar Georgian house and looked across the Sound at the outlines of the North Shore? Scores of counterparts, she imagined, for the feeling of uniqueness, so strong at twenty, had barely lasted the decade.

Last winter Claudia had turned twenty-seven. She had been married for five years. Anthony, her youngest child—and the last, she swore—was almost a year old. Diana had turned a noisy and tearful two a month ago, and Jamie was three today. Well, there was no point in dwelling on the last five years. They had passed, and that was that.

She stood and walked to the edge of the terrace. In the bay below two dozen small white sails crossed and recrossed each other. The juniors at the Sewanhaka Corinthian Yacht Club were racing early this morning. In a few years Jamie would be down there among them in his own small boat. Sam would see to that. Just as he had seen to the pony Jamie had found in the stables this morning. Claudia had argued Jamie was too young, but Sam had said nonsense, the sooner he started, the better horseman he'd be.

As she stood and watched the sails gliding through the bright blue water, she noticed two figures on the beach below. She poured herself another cup of coffee and settled back into the white wicker chaise. The couple on the beach turned and began to climb the hill to the house. Claudia watched as her husband and her sister advanced across the vast carpet of green running from the edge of the beach to the terrace. *Katherine's aging well,* she thought. Some of the hardness is turning to strength. In a few years people will stop saying she's pretty and begin calling her a handsome woman. She observed her sister carefully as she moved across the grass in long, easy strides. She'll be thirty soon, and she still has a superb figure, better than mine. Once again Claudia resolved there would be no more children. Three were more than she had ever wanted.

"You're up early," Sam said, brushing the wet grass from the cuffs of his white flannel trousers.

"It's too nice a morning to waste sleeping."

"Isn't it?" Kate agreed. "Did you see the race? It almost makes me wish I were ten again. You can collect all the trophies you want, Sam, but they'll never mean as much as those first ones. I can still remember that feeling the first time I single-handed it and won. I can still remember the summer you won that whole week of races. It was either 1909 or '10, I'm not sure, but I do know you were the youngest one in your class, and you won every race."

"I lost the second and the fourth. That was a darned good little boat. The first class boat I ever owned. She was a Herreshoft design, a Buzzard's Bay fifteen-footer, and she was a beauty. I wish they still made them. I'd get one for Jamie in a few years."

"Don't you think you're rushing it?"

"The earlier he starts, the better his chances."

"Sam's right, Claudia. It's never too early."

"I'll leave that to both of you," Claudia said without interest. "Would you like breakfast out here?"

"We've had breakfast," Sam said, "but I could use another cup of coffee. Would you like some, Kate?"

"If I have time. I thought Graham would be here by now."

"He arrived a quarter of an hour ago. He's in the

library. I told him it was more pleasant out here, but he insisted there were a few things he wanted to look over before he saw you. I must say, Sam, your cousin is certainly diligent."

"Graham is one of the best attorneys in New York. Katherine couldn't be in better hands. He didn't want to take the case at first. Divorce law isn't exactly his cup of tea, you know, but I was convinced he could do a better job than any of those fellows who make a practice of it. I'm glad he agreed to handle it."

"Thank you for convincing him, Sam," Kate said dryly. "I guess I'd better find out what news he's brought this morning."

Katherine walked through the small breakfast room bright in yellow and white chintz, through the large formal dining room, and across the great hall dominated by a large Manet and an even larger Canaletto from Tobias' collection. Nowhere in the huge house was there a touch of *style moderne,* Sam had pointed out happily the first time Katherine had come out for the weekend six months before.

Graham Livingston was standing in the dark book-lined library with his back to the door, examining one of a dozen ship models displayed in glass cases around the room.

"Quite a collection, isn't it?"

Graham turned to greet her. "I didn't hear you come in, Kate. Yes, it is. I think it's probably one of the best of its kind in the country. Look at this one. It's my favorite." He turned back to the model. It couldn't have been more than eighteen inches long, and it was an accurate replica of an old French ship of the line. "It was made by a French prisoner, taken during one of Napoleon's campaigns. I'm not sure which one. And I've never figured out how he came by the ivory. But look at the detail. Every plank, even the smallest spar, is a distinct piece. Imagine the diligence."

"It is beautiful."

Graham stood admiring the model for a few seconds, then pulled himself up with a start. "Ah, yes, well, now down to work." They sat across from each other in large club chairs on either side of the fireplace filled with purple and white irises the gardener had brought from the greenhouse that morning. Katherine watched as Graham shuffled the papers on his lap. Graham, like his cousin Sam, was a big man, but while Sam had the ability of a sportsman, Graham's bulk was best described as substantial. His appearance was an accurate reflection of his character. Graham's belief in standards was no less strong than his cousin's, but while Sam's seriousness was alleviated by his sociability and sportsmanship, Graham's was intensified by his devotion to his work. He approached the law with all the passion and energy Sam reserved for a regatta or a polo match. And their motives were identical. They pursued excellence for its own sake.

"Well, it's almost over now, Katherine. Another month, two at the most, and your divorce will be final. Though I must repeat I think you ought to reconsider. The financial settlement, I mean, not the divorce. Airplanes are big business now, and Whitely has made a fortune. You're entitled to part of it."

"I don't want Tom Whitely's money, Graham. I have more than enough for my needs, and it isn't as if I have to worry about children."

"That's true, of course, but from a legal point of view I hate to see you throw away your rights. And I hate to see you let Whitely off so easily."

"There's nothing you can say about Tom Whitely that I haven't said or thought myself, Graham. You think he behaved badly, but even you know only part of it. If I could ruin Tom Whitely—really ruin him, I mean—I would. I'd take every penny he has. I'd see him dead. But that isn't in my power. Or yours. And if I can't have that, I don't want anything. Certainly not a generous settlement that will ease his conscience—if he has one, which I very much doubt."

Graham looked at her in amazement. Her voice was even and she spoke quietly of seeing her husband dead.

Graham had been shocked when Katherine had first come to him about the divorce. He was not surprised about the divorce itself— that sort of thing was becoming all too common these days—but he was horrified at the reasons she produced. She had presented the evidence efficiently. Tom Whitely had been grossly and openly unfaithful almost from the beginning. Two months after the wedding friends began to whisper to Katherine that Tom had been seen here or there with other women. Kate dismissed the stories as vicious gossip until Tom made that impossible. He told her he was having dinner with a government official and returned home drunk, disheveled, and reeking of cheap perfume. When he went away on business and telephoned her at night, women's voices were clearly audible in the background. Often, after Tom returned from these trips, Katherine would go through his suitcase before allowing the maid to unpack it. She would not be humiliated in front of the servants. More often than not there would be a photograph in a cardboard frame from some cheap nightclub. Tom's taste was eclectic. There were slender blondes and voluptuous brunettes and even one very plain-looking redhead, or so Katherine thought. The only similarity was that the women were always flashily but badly dressed. And they always seemed drunk.

The picture Katherine painted for Graham that first morning in his antiseptic office shocked him. He looked down at the half dozen photographs in folders bearing names like the *Tropicana* and the *Café de Paris*. Nothing so sloppy had ever crossed that highly polished desk accustomed to carefully wrought contracts and watertight trusts.

"I can't believe it. How a man could behave this way . . . and then force it on you. . . ." His voice trailed off. He seemed more offended than his client.

After a moment Graham resumed his legal tone. "As for the practicalities. We can get a chap to sue in California, or now that you're back on Sixty-ninth Street, we can start proceedings here in New York. It appears you have the grounds. . . ."

"Appears!"

"As distasteful as these are"—Graham indicated the photographs before him—"they may not be incriminating in a court of law. And the rest is only your testimony, Katherine. If Whitely chooses to, he can contest that testimony, though, given his behavior, I can't imagine why he'd want to. But of course, Whitely is scarcely a predictable man.

"In view of his conduct it would be simple enough to hire a detective. . . ." Again Graham let his voice trail off. He was wishing he'd never let Sam talk him into taking the case. Surely Katherine deserved the best counsel she could get, but it should be one of those fellows who made a practice of this sort of thing.

"No, I don't want a detective. I won't stoop to Tom's level."

"Good. I agree. Just the same, if he decides to fight, we may need more proof. Did he ever treat you badly?" Graham looked again at the photographs on his desk. He smiled uncomfortably. "I mean violently. Did he ever strike you?"

"No, that wasn't Tom's style."

"What about verbal abuse? Did he ever humiliate you before friends or the servants?"

"Not exactly."

Graham looked at Katherine but said nothing. He knew he should encourage her to go on but he suspected he did not want to hear her story.

"I came home from the club one afternoon and . . . well, I found him with someone."

"In your house!"

Katherine nodded.

"My God!"

Kate could remember every moment. She'd been playing tennis at the club. The game had gone on longer than she'd expected, and rather than stop for a shower and a drink, she'd decided to drive home in her tennis things. In California, she had learned, one could do that. The point was she had been late. Not early, but late. She hadn't surprised Tom. He'd actually had to *wait* for her.

Kate had let herself in. Their staff was not large, and they were all in the kitchen at that hour. Katherine was expecting sixteen for dinner. She'd gone straight to her room. The door was closed, but there was nothing unusual about that. Carlotta had probably drawn the curtains against the late afternoon sun. Katherine had already begun undoing the buttons of her tennis skirt and her head was down as she opened the door. She seemed to sense their presence before she saw them. Then she lifted her head. There in her bed, not in Tom's but in hers, were her husband and a young woman. She had stood there, the glass door knob warm in her icy hand, the late-afternoon sunshine bright in her eyes. Unlike Carlotta, he hadn't even bothered to close the curtains.

When Tom saw she was not going to run, he laughed, and said, "Kate, I'd like you to meet Dorothy Devine. Dorothy's going to be a movie star, isn't that right, Dorothy?" He turned to the girl, who was holding Katherine's Porthault sheets modestly to her shoulders. "Dorothy, this is my wife, Katherine Whitely."

"You told me your wife was in New York." The girl was clearly confused.

"Did I? That must have been last week. I have trouble keeping track of her."

Then finally Kate had let go of the door and fled down the hall, down the winding flagstone staircase, out the front door, across the grass, and across the country back to the house on Sixty-ninth Street.

"You don't have to tell me the details now," Graham said quickly. "I don't think Whitely will contest your testimony about something like that. Though I hope we won't have to go that far. I don't want to bring any of this into the open unless it's absolutely necessary. And it won't be unless he contests the divorce."

"Tom won't do that."

Katherine could have explained her husband to Graham, but that would involve telling the rest of the story, the part that was even more humiliating than the incident with the film starlet. That was something she would never do.

Katherine had married Tom Whitely for a variety of reasons. He was attractive, he was forceful, and he was unlike anyone she'd known before. Most important, he was totally unlike Sam Beaumont. If she married Tom Whitely, she would not have to see Sam or be reminded of him in any way. They would live in California and lead a life that had nothing to do with the New York world of Sam Beaumont and her sister.

But the things that made Tom different almost immediately became precisely the problem. Tom's idea of fun was an afternoon spent roaming an airplane factory. His notion of a pleasant dinner party consisted of four men arguing the relative merits of triplanes, biplanes, and monoplanes. If the women present had an opinion about aviation worth hearing, it was welcomed. Otherwise, they were to sit in silence, look as attractive as possible, and ignore the fact that one of the men might still have machine grease under his fingernails.

Despite Tom's passion for the empire he was building and Katherine's complete lack of interest in it, their marriage might have worked. Kate was attracted to Tom, but it was not the sort of sentiment that demanded total possession. So long as he treated her properly when they were together, she would not have pried into his actions when they were apart. Kate cared more for the form of marriage to Tom Whitely than its substance.

Tom, though disappointed in the woman he married, was too caught up in the rest of his life to waste time worrying about her. He'd made a mistake, but it was a minor one. It was not as if the design for one of his planes hadn't panned out or a government contract had eluded him. Then at a dinner given in his and Katherine's honor he met Norma Selwegg. If Katherine had been a minor blunder, Norma would be a major redress.

Norma had, in addition to huge brown eyes and large, well-shaped breasts, an abiding interest in aviation. She came by it naturally. Norma was the only child of Effrem Selwegg, who had parlayed an early eccentric interest in flying machines into a multimillion-dollar industrial empire. Norma was attractive, but Effrem was irresistible.

Six weeks after Tom Whitely married Katherine, a month after he met Norma, he asked Kate for a divorce. "Never," she said quietly and turned back to the society page of the Los Angeles *Times*. For days Tom explained, begged, even threatened. Katherine simply refused to discuss the matter.

Had Tom Whitely known his wife better the reason for her recalcitrance would have been obvious. Katherine had left New York in failure. She refused to return the same way. Once again Katherine Trenholm would be the girl who simply could not hold a man.

Tom understood nothing of his wife's motives, but he knew a good deal of means and methods to a desired end. He had not got as far as he had by being a nice fellow. In fact, he had a certain reputation for ruthlessness, as his attraction to Norma suggested. If his plan worked, Katherine would be begging for a divorce in no time.

Tom convinced Norma to go abroad for several months. The divorce might be unpleasant, he said, and he didn't want her involved. Then he set out on the campaign that culminated finally in Katherine's bed with Dorothy Devine. Worst of all, Katherine knew it had been a campaign. At no time had she been able to convince herself Tom was a womanizer. She knew each time he flung another piece of evidence in her face that he did not want those other women. He merely wanted to get rid of her.

"I've told you repeatedly, Graham, it's simple. I made a mistake. And I want nothing to do with Tom Whitely or his money."

Again Graham marveled at Katherine's control. There she sat, cool and crisp, her arms and legs mahogany against the pale linen of her dress. She radiated health and normality, and yet try as he would, he could not drive from his mind the picture of Katherine finding her husband in bed with another woman. It haunted him. Graham was glad he left the certainties of the law infrequently. His world was complex, but this one was confusing—and dangerous, he suspected.

"Then that's it, Katherine." He took the signed papers and his pen from her. "There's nothing to do now but wait. And," he added with an uncharacteristic —and unsuccessful—attempt at humor, "we might as well wait on the terrace."

They found Sam and Claudia where Kate had left them on the side of the house overlooking the bay. Sam sat at a wicker table, poring over the drawings he had spread before him, and Claudia lay on the same chaise, staring out across the Sound. Kate went straight to Sam's side. "Are those the plans for the new boat?" She knew they were. "She's a beauty, Sam. Quite a bit larger than *Mistress,* isn't she?"

"Thirteen feet four inches larger to be exact. And faster, too."

"This one's going to bring in all the trophies, eh, Sam?" Graham dropped into the chair next to Claudia.

"My share, at least. Never forget, Graham, old man, that I'm a Mallory as well as a Livingston."

"I never knew that," Kate said.

"Well, not much of a Mallory, actually. My father's mother was part Mallory. Graham likes to joke about it, though. Whenever I do win, he insists it's my Mallory blood."

"Well, it certainly isn't your Livingston blood," Graham said. "And everyone knows the Connecticut Mallorys take home all the trophies."

Sam laughed. "Wait till *Revenge* is finished."

"*Revenge,*" Graham said. "You are serious about those trophies, aren't you?"

"I just assumed it would be *Mistress II,*" Kate said.

"Not this one. *Mistress* was a pleasure boat. This is a racing machine, a pure racing machine."

"All the same," Kate said, "*Revenge.* It sounds out of character. It's not a word I associate with you, Sam." All of them wondered for a moment whether *Mistress* was a word they associated with Sam. "Well, whatever her name, she looks as if she's going to be a winner. Have they started work yet?"

"They're pretty far along."

"I'd love to see her."

"That's not a bad idea. Why don't we all motor over to City Island this afternoon?"

"Not I, thank you. I've been living with those plans for months now," Claudia said. "And I don't think you ought to either, Sam. After all, it's Jamie's birthday."

"All the more reason to get away. There'll be enough noise and excitement from the children's party."

"I think he'd like to have his daddy here."

"Not his daddy, Claudia, his father. Daddy is all right for Diana, but Jamie's a boy. If he gets in the habit of calling me Daddy now, he'll be off to Yale and still calling me Daddy."

"Very well, I think he'd like to have his father here then."

"I will be here. I just won't be for a few hours this afternoon. What do you say, Graham, care to motor over and see the new winner?"

"No, thanks. I've had enough driving for one day. I think I'll stay here and enjoy your view. Maybe get in a swim this afternoon. That is, if Claudia doesn't mind." His pale eyes looked at her anxiously.

"Of course, I don't mind, Graham. We wish you'd come out more often. You probably wouldn't have come today if you didn't have some things for Kate. But you know you're always welcome."

"Oh, it wasn't just the papers for Katherine. I came to see you, too. I always like to see you—you and Sam and the children, that is." He stopped suddenly as if embarrassed at his outburst.

Claudia noticed that around his stiff collar—it was just like Graham to wear a stiff collar to the country simply because he was carrying some legal papers—his neck had turned crimson. She supposed it had something to do with his childhood, his "tragic" childhood people always said when they spoke about it.

Graham had been the only child of Sam's maternal uncle Graham Van Wyck Livingston and his wife, Mary Tyler Livingston. Mary had lost a son in childbirth, and a daughter had died in infancy. The arrival of Graham was an event. He was doted upon—too much so for his own good, more than one visitor to the Livingston home had observed. He had every toy money could buy and every indulgence two adoring parents could provide. Until he was six. Then at ten o'clock on the morning of July 2, 1898, Mr. and Mrs. Graham Van Wyck Livingston sailed for Le Havre aboard the French liner *La Bourgogne.* They had intended to take little Graham with them, but the child had had a sickly spring, and the doctor thought foreign climates might be dangerous. Little Graham had not minded his parents' departure since at the time the *Bourgogne* was being nudged out of New York Harbor, he was trying out an exact replica of the ship on the beach at Newport. The model was only two feet in length, but Graham Senior had seen to it that it was equipped with a miniature engine and all the accoutrements proper to one of the French Liner's finest passenger ships. Not only were there miniature lifeboats, but there were tiny steamer chairs in which lounged miniature passengers as well.

Two days later, at five A.M., as Graham slept quietly in his small bed, the model of the *Bourgogne* safe in playroom dry dock, the real *Bourgogne,* steaming sixty miles south of Sable Island at a speed of seventeen knots, perhaps a bit fast for the heavy fog, collided with the iron-hulled three-masted British bark *Cromartyshire.* Of the seven hundred and twenty-five passengers and crew aboard the *Bourgogne,* one hundred and sixty-five were saved. Of the one hundred and sixty-five, there were ten second class passengers, fifty-one from steerage, one hundred crew members and four subaltern officers. Not a single first-class passenger survived.

Graham returned to New York to live with two of his father's sisters. His Aunt Beaumont had offered to have him stay with her on Washington Square, but Amy and Edith, the Livingston spinsters, insisted it would be more appropriate for them to take their brother's child. Their younger sister hadn't protested for long. Sam was barely a year old, and she was not ready for another addition to her household.

Amy and Edith Livingston had been foremost among those who had disapproved of little Graham's upbringing. Their brother and his wife had spoiled the child horribly. Well, they would right that wrong. Like most childless women, Amy and Edith knew exactly how children should be reared. In a single year they turned Graham into a model of discipline. He never spoke unless spoken to. He never cried. He was admirably neat. He made no noise. And he never laughed.

It had been a crippling childhood, Claudia thought as she looked at Graham, so stiff and serious and out of place on that sun-drenched terrace. He was sitting in a wicker rocking chair, but Claudia could have sworn there was a desk in front of him.

"Then it's settled," Sam said. "We'll drive over to Minneford's this afternoon, Kate, and take a look at *Revenge*. I haven't been there for a while, and I'd like to see what they did this week." Claudia remembered Sam had in fact been out to City Island on the previous Wednesday but said nothing.

"Mummy, Mummy." A towheaded child, tall for his three years, came running across the lawn. "Did you see my pony? Isn't he wonderful? Isn't my pony wonderful?"

"Yes, dear, he's quite wonderful. Have you said hello to Uncle Graham?"

"Hello, Uncle Graham. Have you seen my pony? Daddy gave me the most beautiful pony for my birthday." Sam winced visibly at the term, but said nothing.

"No, I haven't seen your pony, Jamie. What color is he?"

"He's brown and white, and he's wonderful. Come see him, Uncle Graham."

"Don't bother Uncle Graham, dear. He's just got here, and I'm sure he doesn't want to go running off to the stables."

"No, I'd like to see him, Claudia." Graham turned to the boy. He was not especially comfortable with children, but he was no less so than with adults. "Let's go see your pony, Jamie."

"Will you come too, Daddy?"

Claudia saw Sam wince again. "Father," she said gently.

"Father," the child repeated. He was too excited about the pony to feel the customary sting at this rebuke.

The two men headed off toward the stable with the boy scampering between them. Claudia saw Jamie take Sam's hand for a moment, and then when the child dropped it to chase after a cardinal, Sam quickly put his hands in the pockets of his blazer jacket.

In fifteen minutes she saw the two men returning across the lawn with Jamie a few feet behind them. She could tell from the way he was scuffing at the grass and kept his head down that he'd been crying.

"What happened?" she asked as Sam and Graham dropped into chairs.

"Nothing happened," Sam said. "Where's Wilfred? Hasn't he brought out the cocktails? It's after noon."

Claudia turned to the child, who stood leaning against one of the pillars of the terrace with his back to them. "Go up now, Jamie, and find Miss Morris. Your guests should be arriving soon, and you'll want to tidy up." The child did not move. "Did you hear me, Jamie?"

"Yes," he mumbled.

"Yes, what?" Sam said sharply.

"Yes, Mother, I heard you."

"Very well, then go along, dear."

When they heard the door to the house slam, Claudia turned to Sam. "Now will you please tell me what happened in the stables?"

"You're making too much of it, Claudia. Nothing happened. I was teaching Jamie how to put on a bridle, and the pony began to act up. Jamie was excited, and a high-strung animal can sense that. Well, the pony was a bit snappish, and Jamie thought he was going to bite him. He started to run away, and when I insisted he come back, he began to cry. But I was firm, and he got the bridle on. Now everything is fine."

"Don't you think that lesson could have waited for another time?"

"No. No, I don't. Jamie has to learn how to handle animals. If you give in to his fear once, he'll never get over it. He'll grow up afraid of horses and then dogs and heaven knows what else. And I won't have that. He has to learn, and that's the only way. The first time he falls off, I'll make him get right back on, too."

Sam inched the Cord into the garage, where three other cars, including the old Rolls, stood in highly polished splendor. "I didn't think the drive would take that long."

"It was worth every minute of it, Sam. She's a beauty. When do you think she'll be ready?"

"With any luck we'll have her in the water by the end of August. That will give me a couple of months to get the kinks out up here, and then I think I'll take her down to Florida for a little practice this winter. We ought to be in top form by the Bermuda Race. That'll be her first big one. But I won't keep you in this hot garage talking about my plans. How about a swim? I think we deserve one."

"I'll be down in ten minutes."

A half hour later Sam lay on the warm sand at the edge of the water. His skin felt salty, and the damp wool of his bathing suit chafed against his chest, but he was comfortable. The icy water had washed away the heat and exhaustion of the long drive, and he felt at once relaxed and exhilarated.

The sun was low in the west, but it cast a warm glow over the beach. Suddenly Sam felt a shadow fall over him and then a few drops of water on his arm. He opened his eyes and saw a woman standing above him. She was nothing but a dark figure against the sun, and Sam couldn't make out her features. He knew it was Katherine, but in this light it could as easily have been Claudia.

"I thought you were asleep."

"I think I would have been in a minute."

"You're getting lazy, Sam. I outswam you by three laps."

He stood and handed Katherine her robe, and they started the climb back to the house. "I'm not getting lazy, Kate. I'm getting old."

"Aren't we all?"

"The funny thing is, I don't feel any older. Do you?" Kate was silent. "I'm sorry. That was a stupid thing to say. After what you've been through."

"I wish everyone would stop talking about what I've been through. I think it's Graham's favorite expression."

"All the same from what Graham's told me—nothing concrete, of course—you had a pretty bad time of it."

"Are you going to say, 'I told you so'?"

"You know I wasn't."

"I'm sorry, Sam. You've been wonderfully kind through this whole thing."

"Nonsense, I haven't done anything, but if there ever is anything I can do, Kate, you know you can count on me, don't you?"

They had reached the terrace, and she stopped and looked at him carefully for what seemed to Sam like a long time. "Can I really, Sam?"

"Of course you can." Suddenly uncomfortable, he turned from her and held open the door to the house.

"I think I'll stay out here for a while. Care to keep me company for a cocktail?"

"Thanks, Kate, but I'll pass this one up. I think I'll get in a nap before dinner. I told you I'm getting old."

At the top of the stairs Sam stopped in front of the door to Claudia's room. He was still thinking about Katherine. Or rather he was trying not to think about Katherine. He felt sorry for her. Acccording to Graham, she'd been through a tough time. Graham had implied that it was the kind of ordeal no nice woman should experience. Sam was determined to do everything he could to help her out now. She was welcome to stay with them as long as she liked. Kate hadn't taken a place of her own yet, and he had to admit the house on Sixty-ninth Street with its aura of long-standing illness was not the best place to recuperate from a bad experience. It was better for her to stay out here with them. Besides, Sam enjoyed having Katherine around. They had always got on well together. But wasn't that precisely the problem? Wasn't that what had hung between them a few minutes ago when Kate had looked at him so strangely? Katherine's divorce made things awkward, but Sam had to admit his marriage added an extra burden.

He knocked softly on Claudia's door. When there was no answer, he let himself in quietly. The room was in half darkness, but he could make out his wife's figure. She was curled childlike on one side, and her eyes were closed. He thought she was asleep until he noticed the table next to her bed. A cigarette still burned in the small china ashtray.

Sam let himself out as quietly as he had come in and went back downstairs. Katherine looked up as he stepped out on the terrace. "I thought you were going to take a nap."

"I changed my mind," he said and dropped into the chair next to hers.

Claudia moved about the dance floor of the Sewanhaka Corinthian Yacht Club, Graham's arm stiff around her waist. Poor Graham. He hated to dance, but he hated bad manners more. He had executed one turn around the floor with each of the women at their table. Claudia was glad she'd arranged a small party tonight. There were only five couples. Any more would have been more than Graham could bear, she suspected.

When the music came to an end, he looked relieved. "If you'll forgive me, Claudia, I'll head back to the house. I have some work I'd like to look at tonight."

"I think I'll go back with you, Graham. It's late, and I've had enough for one evening, too." They had reached the table, and she turned to Sam. "Graham's going back now, Sam, and I think I'll go along. We'll send the car back for you and Kate."

There was no surprise on Sam's face. "Don't bother about the car. We can get a lift with someone. You'll drop us, Sky, won't you?"

"Be happy to," Schuyler Mason said.

Two hours later the Masons' Chrysler pulled up in front of the house. "Come in and have a drink, Sky."

"I'd better not. Harriet may be waiting up."

"Nonsense, she left the party hours ago. She'll be asleep by now."

"You're probably right about that, Sam." Schuyler turned to Katherine, who sat between them. "Looks like you're the only lively one left, Kate. What's your secret?"

"Clean living," she said as Sam helped her from the car. She'd hoped Sam wouldn't ask Schuyler in.

"Come on, Sky. You need a drink for the drive home."

"Well, if Kate doesn't mind."

"Why should I mind? Anyway, I'm going to call it a night."

Sam was surprised at the wave of relief that swept over him. He hadn't realized how much the idea of a nightcap alone with Katherine had troubled him.

"She's really something," Schuyler said when they were alone in the library with a bottle of whiskey between them. "Katherine, I mean. Taking it like a trooper, isn't she?"

"She's a strong one, always has been."

"All the same, I was a little surprised when she decided to spend the summer out here. Do you think it will work out?"

"Of course—why shouldn't it?" But Sam did not give Schuyler a chance to answer. "How are things over at old man Winett's? Harriet says you're working too hard. Stayed in town all week, she said."

"And I was working, Sam. No question about that."

"I never thought there was, Sky. But why so hard? Or was that the way they taught you to do it at that southern gentlemen's school?"

"Only a New Haven man could call Princeton the South. Actually, I'm glad you asked, though, Sam. Something big has come up, and I wanted to talk to you about it this weekend."

"Can't listen with an empty glass." Sam poured more whiskey for Schuyler, then himself.

"I don't have to tell you what's going on these days, Sam. Every bank in town is setting up an investment affiliate. It's the wave of the future. Speculation. If you want to stay afloat as a bank these days, that's the way to do it."

"I get the impression this is not a hypothetical discussion, Sky. I get the distinct impression you're not talking about banks, you're talking about the New York Bank and Trust."

"When I talk to you about banks, I naturally mean the New York. The point is, Sam, the money today is in the investment business. That's true for the individual, and it's true for banks."

Sam laughed. "It sounds as if the bug that's going around the Street has bitten you."

"Don't be too quick to laugh. There's a lot of money to be made that way, a hell of a lot."

"I'm not sure I want to make a hell of a lot of money. What would I do with it? You know my needs are simple." Sam believed the statement.

"Damn it, Sam, this is 1929. You can't sit around and rest on your laurels or, rather, on the old Livingston and Beaumont fortune. For one thing it isn't going to be such a fortune at the rate things are going. Do you want to hear some figures? I saw these in the *Journal* the other day, and they stuck. In 1927 there were two hundred and ninety millionaires in this country. Last year there were four hundred and ninety-six, and at last count, a month ago, five hundred and eleven fellows had reached the mark. And it isn't just a matter of more men with money, Sam; it's a matter of more men with more money. The fortunes being made today make the old ones look like pittances."

"That's progress for you."

"You can laugh all you want, but I tell you you're going to be out-stripped. The economy is growing, and you have to grow with it, unless you want to be left behind."

"Exactly what is it you want me to do, Sky?"

"Well, as I said and as you know, Sam, the big news in banking is investment affiliates. Now if there's one thing you know about, it's banking. . . ."

"I always thought the general opinion, including yours, was that the one thing I didn't know about was banking. You fellows are always asking my advice about a new sloop or some horseflesh, but nobody ever asks me about banks."

"I'm serious, Sam."

"So am I, but go on."

"And if there's one thing I know about, it's investments. Now I've gone as far as I'm going to go with old man Winett. He's a stodgy old bird, and anyway he has a whole nest full of Winett heirs. I have a little capital, Sam. I don't have to tell you where from. It's Harriet's, of course. And there's another fellow at the office, Harris Harvey. I think you know him. Smart as a whip and no room left to rise at Winett, Barton. Well, between us we have enough to get started, but we need a bank. Not just any bank, of course, but a reputable bank with a big name."

"I take it that's where I come in."

"You won't be doing us a favor, Sam. You might even say we're doing you the favor. You give us your backing, and we give you profits, big profits."

"I'm sure it's a good idea, Sky, but it's not for us. I don't think Father would go for it."

"You could convince him."

"I don't know that I want to. You know what kind of bank we are. Old and conservative. Half our people still think of us as Beaumont Bank and Trust. Somehow I just don't see us with an investment house under our wing. Think of how it would strike old Mrs. Rhinelander."

"What does Mrs. Rhinelander have to do with it?"

"I was making a joke, Sky, but actually she has everything to do with it. Rhinelander means old New York. Just like the Schuylers and the Livingstons. . . ."

"And the Beaumonts."

"No, the Beaumonts are newer than the Livingstons, but you know what I mean. Old Mrs. Rhinelander would be horrified if *her* bank got mixed up in speculation."

"But that's where you make your mistake, Sam. It's not just the young hotshot banks that are into this thing. All the big fellows are, too. Old Charlie Mitchell at the National City doesn't think he's too good for an investment arrangement."

"I don't think we're too good for one, Sky. I just don't think we're right for one."

"You're making a mistake, Sam."

"It won't be my first."

"I wish you'd think about it."

"I won't promise to think about it because I know my mind is made up. This isn't for us. Not that it isn't the perfect thing for you, Sky. I respect your judgment, and I think you know what you're doing in this case. But I'll tell you what I will do. When you find your bank, when you begin to set things up, if you need more backing, you can count on me."

Schuyler looked at him in surprise. "Well, thank you, Sam. It isn't what I was asking for, but I can't say I'm not pleased. It's darn nice of you."

"There's nothing to thank me for. Not if this plan is half as good as you say it is."

"It's that good and better. You'll see. We're going to make a fortune."

After Sam saw Schuyler to the door, he stood for a while thinking of his friend. He wished he could have helped him. The offer of financial backing was generous, more generous than many men in his position would be, Sam knew. But it was not enough. Schuyler needed Sam's bank, and that was precisely what Sam was not willing to give. Committing the bank to a scheme like Schuyler's went against every tenet Sam had been raised by. Speculation was not only dangerous, but immoral. Of course, if Sam had bothered to think back beyond his father to his grandfathers and great-grandfathers, he would have realized that the sort of chance Sky wanted him to take was precisely the sort his forebears had taken to amass the vast capital that made it possible for Tobias and Sam and the New York Bank and Trust to be so smugly conservative today, but Sam did not question his own decision. He did not regret having to disappoint his friend.

Sam did not have to ask and Sky did not have to tell him why this scheme was so important to him.

Schuyler had been a poor boy among rich boys for too long. His wife's money had banished the genteel poverty, but not his acute sense of it. But, Sam supposed as he turned out the light in the entrance hall and started up the stairs, every man had his own set of problems.

He stopped for a moment in front of Claudia's door. He stood there thinking half of himself, half of Schuyler. No light shone under the door, and the house was silent. He could hear nothing but his own breathing, then his footsteps as he turned and walked down the hall to his own room. As the footsteps died away, Claudia, lying in darkness on the other side of the door, breathed a sigh of relief. She knew she had feigned sleep twice today, and she would have to let Sam come to her tomorrow, but that was tomorrow.

Farther down the hall, past Sam's room and a small sitting room, Katherine lay awake listening to Sam's steps as they passed her sister's room. She heard the door to his room close quietly, and she too turned toward sleep; but there was no sigh of relief. *What a fool, what a selfish little fool!*

5

Sam leaned back comfortably in the Rolls and opened the paper. He did not look at it immediately, however. He had other things on his mind this morning. It was a cloudy day, and there was a chill wind from the northwest. If the wind held, they could get in some good practice this weekend. It was the end of October, and he did not suppose they'd get in much sailing after next month. He could run down to Palm Beach and work on *Revenge,* but most of his crew would be up here. Well, they'd have to get in all the practice they could in the next month. Those three young fellows were coming down from New Haven this evening, and the other men were all in New York. There was plenty of time, he kept telling himself. Early spring would bring only minor trials. The Bermuda Race, *Revenge*'s first big test, was not until June.

Sam turned his attention to the front page of the *Times.* There was a two-column headline.

PRICES OF STOCKS CRASH
IN HEAVY LIQUIDATION;
TOTAL DROP OF BILLIONS

It looked as if it were going to be worse than *he* thought. The market had been sliding all month, and losses this past week had been especially severe. Sam saw no reason for real worry. He and most of his colleagues agreed the days of the big panics were long gone. The last one had occurred in 1907, and even that hadn't been as bad as 1893. No doubt about it, panics were ancient history.

A Washington dispatch in the *Times* and another in the *Wall Street Journal* agreed with Sam. According to Treasury officials, the market break was due to an excess of speculation. There was no basic weakness in American business. Pleased with his own judgment, Sam lit a cigarette and inhaled deeply. Things would be back to normal in a few weeks, and the market would be all the stronger for the shakedown. Just the same, he suspected some fellows were going to be hit hard. It was their own fault, of course, but Sam still felt sorry for them.

Miss Gelb, brown and mouselike in her brown dress with the white collar, brown pumps, and mousy brown hair, was at her typewriter when Sam arrived. She followed him into his office, took his hat and coat, produced a cup of coffee, and arranged three stacks of papers before him. She drew herself to attention at the side of his desk and waited for Sam's signal to begin the list of calls Mr. Beaumont had received thus far this morning.

". . . and Mr. Mason called three times. He wants you to call him as soon as you get in."

"Three times this morning?" Sam looked at his watch. "It's only a little after ten."

"He said it was very important, Mr. Beaumont."

Schuyler answered his own telephone. "Are you busy for lunch today, Sam?"

"All this rush over a lunch date?"

"I've got to talk to you, Sam. It can't wait."

"Well, go ahead."

"Not on the telephone."

"Then drop over here now. I've got a meeting at eleven, but if it's that important, I'll make the time."

"I don't want to be seen going to your office, Sam."

"You make the New York Bank and Trust sound like a bordello, Sky."

"If it were any other morning, I'd laugh at that, but this morning nothing strikes me as very funny."

"You mean yesterday's market drop?"

"It's worse than that."

"All right, Sky. Where do you want to meet?"

"There's a little Italian place on Tenth Street. . . ."

"You want to go all the way up to Tenth Street to eat spaghetti. Aren't you carrying this a little far?"

"Just meet me there, Sam. Please."

"Okay. Twelve thirty."

"Make it noon."

"See you then," Sam said, but Schuyler had already hung up.

Sam was on time, but Schuyler was waiting for him at a small table in the rear of the dark restaurant. "How did you ever find this place, Sky?"

Schuyler had no time for niceties today. "I'm in trouble, Sam."

"I take it it has to do with this mess in the market." Schuyler nodded. "Well, Sky, you never took me up on my offer of backing last spring. I see no reason why you shouldn't borrow some money now to cover your margin. I assume that's it. You're a little overextended." That was exactly the danger of speculation, but Sam didn't want to point that out now. From the way Schuyler looked, Sam guessed he was going through enough for the moment, and he didn't want to sound superior.

"More than a little overextended, Sam."

Sam was careful to keep his face blank. "Just how much is involved?"

"About three hundred and fifty thousand." Sam's face was still impassive. "But that's not the whole story. A month or so ago some fellows and I got up a pool."

"Who else was involved?"

"Anson, Charlie Gage over at Gage, Whitfield, and a couple of others you don't know. One of them has the columnist at the *Herald Tribune* on his payroll."

"What was your stock?"

"Union Carbide. We got the price way up there, and then this fellow over at the *Trib* did a couple of columns. For a while Union Carbide was the hottest thing on the Street. We were set to make millions."

"Then what happened? I take it you didn't make millions or we wouldn't be here now."

"Whatever it is that's been happening to everything this month. This pool came at the wrong time. I've been in two before, nothing as big as this, but they worked. We cleared out just as it hit the top." Schuyler's face flushed with pleasure at the memory.

"But this one didn't work, and you're out three hundred and fifty thousand."

"There's more, Sam. And not all of it is quite, ah, on the up-and-up."

"Pools aren't illegal, are they? I know a lot of people think they aren't ethical—and maybe this isn't the time to say this, Sky, but I'm not sure I don't agree with them—but surely you haven't done anything against the law."

"I didn't mean the pool, Sam. It was the money for the pool. When Union Carbide began to go up like that, it was too good an opportunity to waste. I had already put in every penny of mine or Harriet's I could get my hands on." Schuyler hesitated, but when Sam said nothing, he went on. "So I'm afraid I appropriated a few dollars from some of the firm's investors." Schuyler flashed his open, boyish smile. "Three hundred and fifty thousand to be exact."

Like father, like son flashed through Sam's mind. He shook his head as if to drive away the thought. Schuyler was his friend, his closest friend, he supposed.

"I'll pay you back, of course, Sam. With interest. What's been happening for the last month can't continue. You'll have your money back in six months, probably less. The thing is, I need the cash now. Without it I'll lose more than money. I can't go to Harriet's father, and I don't want to go to Anson. That would bring Harriet's family in again. If I went to Anson, Lucinda would find out, and eventually she'd tell her mother, and then old man Ardsley would find out and we're back to square one. We've been friends for a long time. That's why I came to you."

If another man might have found some irony in the form Schuyler's profession of friendship took, Sam did not. In fact, Sam would have been offended if Schuyler had gone to anyone else. The fact that Schuyler's actions hadn't been entirely on the up-and-up, as he put it, had nothing to do with it. If a man could not trust his friends with his mistakes, whom could he trust?

"Of course I'll give you the money, Sky. You knew that before you asked. We'll have a proper agreement drawn up just as if you were a little overextended on margin. That way there won't be anything questionable about it."

Schuyler sat up as if a weight had been removed from his shoulders. The haggard look that had haunted his eyes all through lunch was replaced by his usual optimism. "I knew I could count on you, old man. What a friend. I won't forget this."

"There is one thing I hope you won't forget, Sky. Let's just call it your momentary lack of judgment. The money comes without strings, you know that. I won't ask you for any promises because I know we don't need them. I know I can count on you to avoid mistakes like this in the future."

If Schuyler Mason wanted to tell Sam Beaumont to take his holier-than-thou attitude and his money and go straight to hell, there was no sign of it on his face. "You bet, Sam. You know that. This is the last slip old Schuyler is going to make. From now on it's the straight and narrow for me."

The two men emerged from the dark restaurant into the chill gray afternoon. "Feels like winter's on the way," Sky said ebulliently.

"I hope the wind holds. At least through tomorrow."

"Putting *Revenge* through her paces this weekend?"

"*Revenge* and the crew. I had some trouble getting those undergraduates down from New Haven on a home game weekend; but I threatened to find another bunch, and that did the trick. They may care about football now, but next spring they'll be begging for those big races."

"Well, I'd offer my services, Sam, but I'm not in your class."

"And don't you forget it, Mason. Three and a half

minutes to change a spinnaker. If I'd known it would take that long, I'd have arranged to get you on someone else's boat. When it comes to racing, old man, you're a secret weapon." Sam laughed as the Rolls pulled up in front of them. "Come on. I'll drop you at your office."

On the following Monday, October 28, Claudia drove into town with Sam. "Polly Chesney asked us for cocktails to meet some playwright tomorrow night. Apparently this is going to be Polly's artistic season. Next week she's having a dinner for a painter. I told her you couldn't make it tomorrow. Was I correct?"

"You were correct in telling her that. I don't mind Polly's parties in the country when Charles has something to say about them, but I can't stand her . . . what do you call them . . . her *soirées*. Are you going?"

"I thought I'd stop by for half an hour. I can go with Harriet. Schuyler isn't going either. Though if you and Sky want to come by later, we could all have dinner afterward. Harriet suggested it. She said she wanted to ask you something."

"Harriet wants to ask me something," Sam said in surprise.

"She was sounding me out. She wanted to know how you'd take it, what she wanted to ask you, that is. It isn't a favor, in fact, you might say it's an honor. I'm sure Harriet and Sky see it that way, but I must say I was surprised."

"Stop being so mysterious. What is it she wants to ask me?"

"Well, apparently Harriet's pregnant again. . . ."

"I didn't know that."

"She and Sky want to name the baby for you. Or Sky does, and she agrees."

"I wish they wouldn't."

"I knew you'd say that, but I didn't tell her. I thought that was up to you. Besides, she seems set on it. I wonder why. I know you and Sky are good friends, but that seems to be going overboard."

"I imagine they're trying to be kind."

"Kind?"

"Show their gratitude."

"For what?"

"I did Sky a favor. He needed some money, and I gave it to him."

"That's funny. Why didn't he go to Mr. Ardsley or Anson?"

"Because I'm his friend."

"Which means he didn't want Anson or the Ardsleys to know."

"As a matter of fact, he didn't."

"Which further means that it wasn't just a little favor. If Sky wanted to keep the loan quiet, there must be a reason."

"I never knew you took such an interest in business negotiations, Claudia."

"I don't, but I love mystery. What really happened?"

He hesitated for a moment. "You realize this is not to go beyond the two of us. Sky and I will never mention it again, and you're never to say anything to Harriet. I'm surprised Sky did."

"He may not have. Knowing Sky and Harriet, he said he wanted to name the baby after you because you were a good friend, and she agreed. But I'm not Harriet. I want to know what really happened."

"Nothing much. Sky got in over his head in a pool."

"A pool?"

"That's an arrangement where a couple of fellows get together and drive up the price of stock. They buy and sell among themselves—they don't really buy and sell, of course, they just make it look that way—leak some rumors, maybe get some columnist to write it up as a hot investment. That way they drive up the price artificially, and when it's hit the top, or what they think is the top, they sell fast."

"It doesn't sound like a very nice practice."

"I don't suppose it is, but it's done. Not all the time, but frequently enough. As I understand it, some men have made quite a bit that way."

"Then why did Sky come to you for money?"

"Pools don't always work the way they're supposed

to. Besides, it's been a rotten month for the market. Last week was a disaster."

"I didn't know that."

"A lot of fellows took a beating. If it gets too much worse, some men—the heavy speculators—will be wiped out for good."

"If everyone's in trouble, then I don't see why Sky was being so secretive about the whole thing. Why didn't he want the Ardsleys to know?"

"Well, Sky's situation was special."

"You mean Sky did something wrong in that, what do you call it, the pool?"

"He got too enthusiastic about it—invested some money that was not, strictly speaking, his."

"You mean he invested Harriet's money?"

"I'm afraid it was worse than that. He invested some of his investors' money."

"Without telling them? You mean he stole money from his customers or clients or whatever you call them?"

"He didn't exactly steal it, Claudia. He used it without their knowledge."

"He stole it."

"Well, he's going to pay it back."

"You gave him the money to pay it back."

"Yes, I did."

"But that makes you an accomplice."

"Don't worry, it's not illegal. I merely lent Sky some money. It's all been drawn up properly. No court of law could find me guilty of anything."

"That isn't what I meant, Sam. I'm sure you arranged it legally. But morally you're an accomplice. Sky stole money, and you're covering up for him."

"What would you like me to do, turn him over to the authorities?"

"He's a thief."

"You're being melodramatic, Claudia. I knew I shouldn't have told you."

"What about the people he stole from?"

"All the more reason to give Sky the money. That

way he can pay them back. Otherwise, they're out whatever he lost in the pool."

"They get their money back, Sky gets off scot-free, and you get a baby named after you."

"Not if I have anything to say about it."

"Name or no name, Sky still gets off."

"Would you prefer he go to jail?"

"I just don't think it's fair. He stole from other people, and you're whitewashing the whole incident."

"I'm not whitewashing anything. I'm certainly not justifying Sky's behavior. As I told you, if you're really worried about the people he took the money from, you ought to be glad I'm giving him the loan. That way the investors get their money back."

"And that makes everything all right."

"Why do you insist on looking at things in the worst possible light, Claudia? You could view this as a gesture that isn't going to cost us anything—not even the money since Sky will probably pay it back, though not as quickly as he thinks—and is going to be a great help to a friend, to say nothing of those people you seem so concerned about. Or you can see it as the great moral issue of the century. You can see me as a man who would like to help out an old chum or as a hardened criminal. And of course, you chose the latter."

His words stung her. He was right. She always looked at her husband in the worst possible light. He was merely being generous, and she was ready to indict him. "I'm sorry, Sam. You're right. There's nothing else you could do." She hesitated for a moment. "You know what you said before, not about Sky, but about the stock market?"

"You mean the way it's been sliding?"

She nodded. "That sort of thing doesn't affect us, does it?"

At any other time he would have laughed, but Sam did not find his wife amusing this morning. "No, Claudia. It would have to go awfully far to affect us."

She sank back into the deep upholstery with relief.

The days when she thought poverty would be fun were long gone.

Sam did not have to tell Schuyler Mason that he would prefer it if the baby were not named after him. He was never asked. Polly Chesney did not have her *soirée,* and the Masons and the Beaumonts did not dine together. Few people did what they had planned to do on the night of October 29, 1929.

Sam saw little of Schuyler Mason during the following winter, but each time he did, Sky was thinner, the lines around his mouth more deeply etched. Most of the men ruined in October, 1929, were ruined at a stroke. Schuyler had the rare misfortune to go downhill slowly. He lost his money immediately, but it took months to run through Harriet's and the children's in a vain attempt to recoup his losses. Others had known a quick and painless death. Schuyler had contracted a wasting disease. On March 15, 1930, Schuyler Mason did the only thing a terminally ill man can do. He shot himself in the head with the .32 automatic he kept in his dressing room. If Schuyler's life had been messy at the end, his death was impeccable. He had been leaning on his dresser, and as he fell backward from the impact of the shot, the gun dropped into the open drawer.

Schuyler's death meant more to Sam than the loss of a friend. It marked the loss of faith in friendship as well. Sam had known since October Sky would not pay him back, and the knowledge bothered him little. Three hundred and fifty thousand dollars was a considerable sum, but compared to what his friends were losing, it was negligible. Sam had been right. A lot of fellows had taken a beating, but men like Sam, men whose money was tied up in land and sound, conservative investments, had not been badly hit. Perhaps they had less ready capital around, but it made no noticeable difference in their lives.

Sam could afford to lose the money. He could not, however, afford the realization of what Schuyler had done with it. He had used half, as intended, to replace the money he'd appropriated. And he'd used the other half to try to save himself after the crash.

When he made the loan, Sam had asked for no promises. He had been sure Schuyler had learned his lesson. But Schuyler had apparently learned nothing. He left behind him a pregnant wife, three children, and one hundred and seventy thousand dollars in debts. Debts, of course, was the polite term. Harriet and the children could depend on Mr. Ardsley. He had sustained some losses last October, but he could still afford to take care of his daughter and grandchildren. Ardsley would save Schuyler Mason's family, but he would not save his memory or name. At least Sam did not think he would, and he was not going to give him the chance to refuse. Sam came up with one hundred and seventy thousand dollars, and Schuyler Mason receded into the past as one more casualty of the crash.

Sam learned of Schuyler's suicide early on the morning of the sixteenth, but it was not until late in the afternoon that he had sorted out the details of Schuyler's finances and set in motion the wheels that would right his friend's wrongs. Then, instead of returning to his own office, he left Schuyler's and went straight to the apartment. Claudia was alone in the living room.

"Did you see Harriet?" he asked as he dropped into a chair opposite her.

"I stopped by this afternoon. I didn't stay long. Mrs. Ardsley and Lucinda were there, and I left when Mrs. Mason arrived. She drove up from Philadelphia."

"How is Harriet?"

"Just as you'd expect. Though I must say she looks better than you. I've never seen you look so tired. Would you like a whiskey?" Sam nodded, and neither of them spoke until Wilfred had brought in the drinks and retired behind the pantry door.

"I'm sorry, Sam. I know how you felt about Sky." When he said nothing, she went on uneasily. "And I'm sorry about those things I said that time you gave him the money. You were right. Sky was a good man. One mistake didn't change that."

"No, he wasn't."

"What did you say?"

"I said Sky wasn't a good man. And he doesn't become one because he's dead. He never used the money to pay back those investors. Or at least he didn't use all of it for that. He paid half of them and used the rest for himself. Oh, I don't mean he spent it on himself, but he used it to try to save what was left. Except nothing was left. Not Harriet's money, not the children's, nothing."

"How awful. Does Harriet know how bad it is yet?"

"I don't know. With any luck she'll never know."

"What do you mean?"

"Old man Ardsley will take care of her and the children. I've no doubt about that. But if word got out, it would take more than money to live down what Schuyler did. I think Sky always felt funny about his own father. I don't know, maybe that's why he did what he did. To prove he was every bit as bad as people might say he was."

"You're getting awfully deep."

"You're right. There are no hidden reasons. Sky wanted money, that's all, wanted it enough not to care about anything else. But I wouldn't like his sons to know that."

Claudia looked at Sam as he stared moodily into his glass. "You paid off the rest of the money, didn't you?"

"Yes, I did, Claudia, and I don't want to argue about it."

"I think it was a fine thing to do, Sam. But I'm not surprised. I wouldn't have expected you to behave any other way." He looked at her in surprise but said nothing. "I called Alicia and told her we couldn't dine tonight. I knew you wouldn't want to. They won't have any trouble getting rid of the tickets. Everyone wants to see Cohan in *Gambling* these days. Why don't we have a quiet dinner here? You look as if you could use a rest."

"I guess I can."

Claudia leaned forward and laid her hand on top

of Sam's. Schuyler's death frightened her. She'd heard stories of men jumping from windows or shooting themselves, but she'd never dreamed it could happen to one of their set. Life was too short—and too fragile. Not that Sam would ever do anything like that. Sam was no coward. All the same she must stop making him miserable. For his sake and her own. She'd learned that much from Schuyler Mason's death.

But later that night after a light dinner and two brandies when Sam came into her darkened room and got into bed beside her—when she felt his body hard against her, his hands urgent, too urgent, under her nightgown, and his mouth avid on hers—she knew she had learned nothing.

6

"Are you sure you don't want to meet me in Hamilton after the race, Claudia? There are always a lot of parties and you like the yacht club. Any number of people have chartered boats, and they'd all love to have you. Kate's going with the Hallsbys."

"Alicia has asked me, but I'd really rather not, Sam. I was never one for long trips on anything smaller than the *France*. I might not mind so much if it were only a few people, but Alicia is turning it into a circus."

"Well, you don't have to go with the Hallsbys. There are plenty of other parties going down. Who's Chet Hallenbeck's wife sailing with? She never misses a race."

"Susan Hallenbeck never misses a race because she's afraid to let Chet out of her sight. If she could sign on as cook, she would. Anyway, she's going down with Chet's brother Porter and Claire, and Anson Hagerty will be with them. I am not cruising anywhere with a party that includes Anson Hagerty."

"Anson's not that bad. Anyway, Porter usually sees he behaves himself. And you like Claire. You might enjoy it."

"Joseph Denbigh will be on the Hallenbecks' yacht."

"You win, Claudia."

"I don't want to win, Sam—that's your department —but I don't want to go to Bermuda for the race either. Why don't you go and have a good time, and I'll stay here? We can say that Kate is my proxy."

"I just thought you might enjoy the sun."

"There's sun in Oyster Bay in June." She laughed, but Sam did not even smile.

Sam felt a hand shaking him roughly and he knew where he was before he opened his eyes.

"Come on, Sam. Your watch."

He was instantly awake and on his feet. Six hours on, six hours off—the alternating watches were no burden to Sam. Even at two in the morning he was immediately alert. He was into his sweater and oil-skin in a moment and left the other three members of his watch stumbling around below, trying to coax themselves awake with coffee. There would be plenty of time for coffee. Right now Sam was eager to check with the captain of the second watch, who was also the navigator.

"Did you get a good set, John?"

"The best, a three star fix, Fomalhaut, Vega, and Altair. She's all yours now, Sam," the navigator said as he dropped down the hatch, eager for his six hours' rest.

It was a clear night with an easy sea and a steady strong wind. The helmsman ordered a few minor adjustments to the sails, and Sam watched the two sleepy crew members spring to life.

They were a little more than fifty hours out, and it looked like a calm, emergency-free crossing. For the next six hours there would be little for Sam to do. Two men spelled each other at the helm every half hour, and each might require a minor adjustment to the sails. It would all go on smoothly with or without Sam's presence. He could go below and pore over the charts again, but the navigator had got a perfect fix. Sam had chosen to sail a few degrees farther west than the conventional course dictated, and they had picked up this strong, steady wind. Now that he had made his decision and as long as the breeze held there was nothing he could do except sit and watch the hull cutting through the white foam and the stars fixed and eternal overhead. There was nothing he could do except sit and watch and think.

He tried not to think of Claudia. What was there to think about her or his marriage that he hadn't been thinking for years now? He wasn't sure how or when it had happened, but they hadn't made a go of it. For the first few years he'd tried to fool himself. He would see an opening in the defenses she'd erected around herself and try to reach out and touch her, but she was never there.

Sam pulled himself up with a start. He was determined to drive Claudia from his mind. He forced himself to remember other races, worked his way back through the years recalling boats and crews and victories and losses long forgotten. He remembered one regatta—it must have been fifteen years ago. Europe was already at war, but all that seemed a long way off that sunny afternoon on Long Island Sound. He could not recollect the entire crew, but he did remember Katherine had been along that day. He had been tending the jib sheets, and he could still picture her as she leaned over to help him. There had been a strong breeze, and it had molded her middy to her. It was the first time Sam noticed Kate had breasts. At seventeen he found it was a sobering thing to notice about a crewmate.

Sam caught himself again. He was determined to think about races—not about his wife, or her sister, or himself. He'd do a tally. That would be the safest thing, and he began to count the number of races he'd won over the years.

Katherine crossed the lawn of the Royal Bermuda Yacht Club in her easy athletic stride. The terrace was empty except for Sam, slumped in a wicker chair at one end. His flannels were wrinkled, his shirt still damp, and a three-day beard bristled on his deeply bronzed face. Katherine thought he had never looked more attractive.

"Sam, you're in. How marvelous! Only one other boat is in. You must have done stupendously."

"It's good to see you, Kate, but let's not jump to conclusions. We may have come in second; but we still have to wait for corrected times, and *Revenge*'s rating is so darned high they'll probably have us coming in last by the time this is over." His words couldn't hide the pleasure in his eyes.

"Oh, Sam, you can pretend with everyone else but not with me. I know you've done a smashing job, and I know you know it, too."

He smiled. It was a very boyish smile. "I guess we did if I do say so myself. It was the second day out. We tacked pretty far west, probably farther than any of the other boats, and we found a bit of a breeze."

"You knew that's where the wind was. That's why you went that far west, isn't it?"

"I was only guessing, Kate."

"Nonsense. You knew it. What was your uncorrected time?"

"Eighty-six hours, twenty-seven minutes, and thirteen seconds."

"That's marvelous. The winning time in '28 was a little over ninety-six hours."

"Yes, but we had better winds this year. Anyway, I keep telling you, *Revenge* has too high a rating. They're going to kill us when they figure the corrected times."

"If *Revenge* is fast, it's because you designed her that way."

"Okay, I give up. There's no arguing with you, Kate. I'm the best sailor who ever lived."

"You're the best one I've ever seen." She had risen from her own chair and was standing over Sam's. "And I think the winner deserves a victory kiss." Kate bent over him, and instead of the polite touch of cheeks he'd expected, Sam felt Kate's mouth, soft and warm, on his.

"And now I think I'll let you get some rest before dinner. You look as if you could use it." Her voice was as cool as the breeze that ruffled the violet passionflowers at the edge of the terrace.

A current of anticipation pulsed through the yacht club dining room. Tomorrow night, after the results were in, the atmosphere would be celebratory. Tonight it was expectant—and therefore more exciting. Of the forty-two boats that had started, fewer than half were in. The rest would arrive during the night and the next day. Even before the race committee had begun to calculate corrected times or hear the protests, however, only four or five boats were considered to have a real chance of winning, and of those four or five *Revenge* and the schooner *Malay* were judged the real contenders. Spirits at Sam's table were high.

"This time you've done it, old man. I'm sure of it." Charles Chesney raised a glass to Sam.

"We won't know that till *Malay* gets in." Sam was finding it difficult to keep his own expectations in check when all his friends were giving rein to theirs.

Katherine recognized Sam's uneasiness. "Let's not be too quick to celebrate. Sam's time was superb, but *Revenge*'s rating is so low *Malay* can come in any time before two thirty-eight and still win." As Katherine spoke, the small native orchestra filed back onto the stand and took up their instruments. Grateful for the interruption, Sam led her onto the dance floor.

"Thanks for the note of caution, Kate. At least the two of us still have our wits."

"Do we?"

He blushed a little through his deep tan, but not at her double entendre. "I guess I can be straight with you, Kate. You know how much I want this. I just wish everyone would stop acting as if I already had it."

"Well, you stand a good chance, Sam. It's either you or *Malay*."

"That's just the point, me *or Malay*." They both knew second place would not be good enough for Sam.

They danced on in silence for a while until a gentle collision with another couple brought curt apologies on both sides. "The man can't even dance properly. He doesn't belong here, and he shouldn't be permitted in if you ask me," she said.

"Denbigh? I didn't know you knew him, Kate."

"It's hard not to know Denbigh these days. He goes

307

everywhere. I've met him at several houses, though I try to avoid him as much as possible."

"Has he ever bothered you?"

"Oh, no, we keep our mutual distance. I suspect Mr. Denbigh knows I'm not taken in by him."

"I've never understood why people put up with him. Why did the Hallenbecks invite him anyway? The man doesn't know a ketch from a yawl."

"He's a climber—one of the few with any money left. The attitude these days seems to be if someone held onto his money through last October, it automatically becomes old money. I doubt the Hallenbecks or anybody else remember who Denbigh was."

"Do you know anything about him?" Sam asked in surprise.

"Just what everyone else knows—nothing. But doesn't that say enough?"

He danced with her again later in the evening. Two more boats, neither of them *Malay,* had arrived. "Well, it won't be long now, Sam." She could feel the tenseness in his body as they danced. She took a step closer and whispered in his ear. "Relax. You're tight as a coil."

He became aware of his own body and, as he did so, of hers. At one turn she brushed against him; at another her head rested for a moment against his cheek. When she'd reached up a moment ago to whisper to him, her breath had been soft in his ear. He remembered the afternoon. Her mouth had been warm and yielding.

He took Kate back to the table and said good-night to the party. "But it's early, Sam. You can't call it a night," Charles implored.

"Early for you fellows, maybe, but not for me. I didn't get down here on one of those fancy motor yachts, you know."

"You're getting old, Sam. Your crew's still going strong."

"That's the crew, Polly. They only do the heavy work. I had to *think* all the way down here." Sam tapped his temple with his index finger, then turned it into a wave as he strolled out of the dining room.

He walked through the bar to a large desk near the front entrance. At this hour the room was empty except for an elderly black man who sat watch. Sam held out a two-dollar bill. "Raymond, get me a bottle of whiskey, a bottle of your real English whiskey."

"Yes, sir, Mr. Beaumont. Just take one minute, sir."

Whiskey in hand, Sam walked down to the deck and had the launch take him out to *Revenge*. He knew he would not be able to sleep with the possibility that *Malay* might arrive at any minute, but he'd be better off alone on his boat than back at the club. There were too many people too eager to celebrate a victory not yet his. And there was also Katherine.

The boat was deserted as he knew it would be. His crew would be celebrating long into the morning. They were sure they'd won, and even if they hadn't, second place would be considered a good show by most of them. He went below, took off his evening clothes, and got into a pair of old flannel trousers. The evening was unusually warm for Bermuda in June, and he did not put on a shirt. He poured himself a large glass of whiskey and stretched out in the cockpit, the glass by his side and the bottle within arm's reach.

The moon barely penetrated the low clouds hanging over the bay. Through the darkness Sam saw the lights of the yacht club. He could hear the music faintly across the water. Then the sound of the launch drowned out the orchestra, and Sam saw a light moving toward him. He hoped the boat was not heading for *Revenge*.

"Request permission to come aboard, sir."

"Kate, what are you doing here?"

"I must say that isn't a very warm welcome."

"I'm sorry. Here, let me help you." The dock boy steadied the launch alongside *Revenge* while Sam helped Katherine aboard. As she climbed into the cockpit, he noticed she wore neither shoes nor stockings. In the faint moonlight her legs looked very much like Claudia's.

"I knew you couldn't go to sleep while there was

still a chance *Malay* might come in, and when I saw you send Raymond for the whiskey, I decided not to let you drink alone. Dangerous habit, you know." She sat down in the cockpit and smiled at him. Sam was suddenly aware he was wearing nothing but trousers. His hand moved self-consciously over his chest.

"Excuse me, Kate. I'll just put something on . . ." He dropped down the hatch and made his way forward to a small cabin amidships. His back was to the cabin door as he searched for a shirt, and suddenly he felt Katherine's presence behind him. Her bare feet had not made a sound on the floorboards.

"You needn't be so formal, Sam." She took a step toward him.

"Kate, you shouldn't be here. Let me take you. . . ." She laid a finger on his lips to silence him. Her other hand was on his chest. It felt like fire against his skin.

"Please, Kate . . ." This time it was her mouth that silenced his. It was the fulfillment of that light, promising kiss she had given him that afternoon. His hands seemed to have a will of their own as he pressed her to him. He could feel that she wore nothing beneath the thin chiffon. The realization shattered his last reserve. His hands were swift at her buttons. In surprise he felt her fingers at his own. He was above her in the narrow bunk, and she clung to him, moving urgently, insistently in rhythm with him. *Finally, finally, finally.* It pounded in his head, a thundering echo of their movements.

It was only later that Sam realized what he'd meant, but the passions he had finally awakened were not his wife's. Making love to Katherine had been everything he'd ever dreamed making love to Claudia would be. He looked down at her now as she lay against him, her head on his shoulder, their bodies still molded together. Her figure, long and slender and pale where the lines of her sunburn came abruptly to a halt, reminded him of Claudia's. The fog of passion had passed, and Sam stood in the harsh light of his own judgment.

He sat up and placed his feet squarely on the cabin floor. His back was to her. "Kate," he said. It was almost a sob. "Kate, I'm sorry. I don't know how it happened. . . ."

She reached out and touched his back. Her fingers on his skin felt icy now.

"It had to happen, Sam. Don't you see that? It isn't as if we'd done something wrong. We've actually righted a wrong. Your marrying Claudia was wrong. Tonight proves that."

He seemed not to hear her. "But Claudia."

"If she were the wife you deserve, if she loved you half as much as I do, this would never have happened. But it has happened, and it's right, Sam. You know that as well as I do. And you know it will happen again."

He shook his head.

"Yes, it will. I love you, and you love me even if you refuse to admit it. I'll always be here for you, Sam. Whenever you want, wherever you want. But there's one thing. You must never touch her again. She's your wife. She has that much. But I want the rest. You must never go to her again."

Of course, he could never go to Claudia again, but it had nothing to do with Kate's demands. It had to do only with him and what he had done. If it had been anyone else, he could have forgotten with time and gone back to his marriage, but he could never forget it had been Kate, his wife's sister. Samuel Beaumont had his scruples. None of those easy show girls for him. Only Katherine, only Claudia's sister, would do.

"No, Kate, we can't undo tonight, but at least we can never repeat it. We can't do this to Claudia again."

"Do this to Claudia! Don't be a fool, Sam. What about what Claudia's done to you? If you won't admit what a rotten wife she's been, then at least think of Montreux. What do you owe her after that? And don't tell me you weren't married then. If it hadn't been for Montreux, she probably never would have married you."

"What are you talking about?"

"You mean she never told you!"

"Told me what?"

"What an idiot I was. Oh, Sam, we've both been such fools. Claudia ran off with that French fellow before you were married. They spent a week together in Montreux. She thought they were going to get married, but then he backed out—I don't know why, but I know he did—and that was when she decided to marry you. Only she told me you knew. But you didn't, did you? You thought Claudia was a sweet little virgin. You thought she'd spent her life just waiting for you to come along."

"Stop it, Kate. Claudia may be your sister; but she's still my wife, and I won't allow anyone, not even you, to talk about her that way. Besides, that has nothing to do with tonight."

He got into his trousers and the shirt she had never allowed him to put on and signaled for the launch. He watched as Kate dropped the chiffon dress over her bare skin. He realized how deliberately she had planned it all, but the knowledge didn't assuage his guilt. Nor did his fierce attraction to her lessen his hatred for her words or her need to say them. His guilt had made him sick and ashamed; his betrayal left him empty.

When the crew returned to *Revenge,* they found Sam in the cockpit with an empty bottle of whiskey. As they sat and talked and joked about the race and the evening, Sam walked to the bow of the boat. There he bent over the side and retched as he had never in all his roistering bachelor days.

"Hey, Sam, I thought you could hold your liquor," one of the younger crew members called. The other men laughed. They all agreed, Sam Beaumont was a good fellow.

The next day the times were calculated, and the protests resolved. *Malay* won by fourteen minutes and twenty-seven seconds, corrected time. But by then Sam did not care.

He had sworn to himself that night on the boat and during the days and nights that followed that he would not repeat his transgression, but he knew, even as he fought it, that he would. The first time had been the only impossible time. Even if he had resumed his intermittent and unsatisfactory relations with Claudia, which he would not permit himself to do, he would still have wanted Katherine. She was, he had discovered, everything he had thought Claudia would be. She loved him entirely. That night on *Revenge* her desire had matched his own; her passion and instincts had followed him at every turn. The memory still aroused him.

Just as images of Claudia still haunted him. Memories of Katherine and himself together invariably gave birth to visions of Claudia with another man, with scores of other men, and finally, in the end, with Joseph Denbigh. He'd been suspicious, even resentful of Jamie when he was born, but he had never really believed Claudia had actually had an affair with Denbigh. Now that he knew for certain that there had been one other man, he was sure there had been more than one. Images of Denbigh's hands on his wife's body assailed him. Visions of his own on Katherine's obsessed him. If Claudia had made a mockery of his love, Kate had inflamed his passion. He would go to her again.

He tried to postpone the day. He avoided her whenever possible. And he avoided Claudia as well. He began to stay in town. It was unusual for Samuel Beaumont to spend so much time in his office, but the summer of 1930 was an unusual summer. The Depression, a word the Hoover administration had coined because it seemed to hold less horror than the old term "panic," was changing the habits of many men and women.

All through July Sam dulled his senses with facts and figures and long, stifling nights in his office. Its conventional masculinity soothed him, if anything could be said to soothe him during those steamy nights. And then, just as he began to believe that perhaps he would win his battle after all, that he would not go to Katherine again, Katherine came to him.

Sam sat in his shirt sleeves, gazing out the open window at the lights of New York. Not a breeze stirred even from the river, and the air in the office was heavy with smoke and humidity. There would be a thunderstorm before the night was out.

When he turned from the window, he saw Kate standing in the doorway. He hadn't heard her enter the office, but he was not surprised to see her. She wore a dark dress of a thin material and the light from the outer office filtered through the folds of the skirt to reveal the lines of her body.

"The night watchman brought me up. I told him I was Mrs. Beaumont. Fortunate, the resemblance, don't you think?"

Sam said nothing.

"I must say, you don't seem happy to see me. And I've come all the way downtown on this dreadful night."

"Kate, what happened in Bermuda, it can't happen again."

"But of course it can. It has to."

"My God, Claudia is your sister."

"Claudia has nothing to do with this, Sam. I told you that in Bermuda. This is us. It always has been."

"Maybe everything you say is true, Kate. Maybe we should have married. I don't know. I don't seem to know anything anymore. Except I married Claudia and you're her sister. We've got to stay away from each other." Sam had stood instinctively when she entered, but he had not dropped the paperweight he had been turning absentmindedly in his hand. Now his knuckles were white as he gripped it.

Kate looked at his hands, then back at his eyes. He could not meet her gaze. "Sam," she began, then stopped. There was only one way to argue with him. She walked around the desk to where he stood. "Sam," she repeated. She put her arms around him and lifted her face to his. He responded exactly as she knew he would.

Sam continued to spend a great deal of time in town, but he no longer worked far into the night. Each evening, after calling Claudia to make sure she and the children were well, he would take a taxi up to Kate's apartment on Sixty-fourth Street, where she would have a cool drink waiting.

Kate had dismissed her old servants and hired a Japanese houseboy. He spoke little English and would not be likely to gossip with servants in the neighborhood. In any event, he had no idea who Mr. Beaumont was. He knew only that he liked his martinis very cold and very dry, his steak rare, and could go through several pairs of silk pajamas in a single steamy August night.

Evening after evening the electric fans whirred dully as they drowned themselves in tumblers of liquid as icy as the houseboy could make them, carried on a single desultory conversation that seemed to trail aimlessly, and made love with a passion that shocked as well as excited Sam. He was miserable. He had everything he had ever wanted and nothing the way he had wanted it.

Weekends in the country Sam kept his distance from her, but Kate didn't mind. She could watch Claudia with equanimity and a secret satisfaction. She knew what Monday would bring.

Even Claudia, self-absorbed and sunk in her own melancholy, could not help noticing the way Katherine looked at Sam, the way her eyes followed him, but she thought little of it. Katherine had always adored Sam. And if it gave her sister pleasure to be near her husband, Claudia did not object. She could not admit even to herself that she actually welcomed Katherine's presence in the house as a buffer between Sam and herself.

As the summer wore on, Claudia was surprised Sam no longer came to her room—surprised, but not disturbed. Relief was her only emotion. Like her gratitude for Katherine's presence, it was not something Claudia liked to admit to herself.

Once or twice, as she watched her sister with Sam, Claudia thought perhaps Katherine was the reason, but she dismissed the idea, almost as suddenly as she had accepted it. *She* might do something like that—flout convention, trample morality—but not Sam or Kate.

They were made from another mold. *More's the pity,* Claudia thought as she tossed in her solitary bed.

Outsiders observed the peculiar ménage at the Beaumont house every weekend and speculated. The men knew Sam Beaumont walked the straight and narrow, but each of them knew, too, that the most high-minded among them slipped now and then. The women simply assumed all men were alike—even Sam Beaumont. Lucinda Hagerty watched him across the table now. He looked tired and worried, seeming to lend support to her suspicions. Katherine was radiant. She had the sort of glow only an affair is likely to lend a divorced thirty-year-old woman. There was something in the way she carried herself that said she knew she was desired. And Claudia was simply Claudia, icy and aloof. Lucinda had seated her on Anson's right intentionally. She didn't mind placing her husband, whose weaknesses she knew to a fault, next to the most beautiful woman in the party. How much better to have Anson next to the ice goddess than someone less attractive but more available.

Lucinda gave a good deal of thought to her seating arrangements. Tonight, for example, she placed Sam and Katherine beside each other purposely. She'd noticed Sam, who had always got on so well with Kate, had begun to avoid her, and she was determined to throw them together to watch the results. Just as Lucinda had expected, Sam was miserably uncomfortable. Katherine was purely attentive. Even when Kate spoke to Charles Chesney on her left, she seemed to be listening to Sam.

Lucinda leaned toward Katherine now. "Claudia is so lucky to have you out every weekend, Kate. I've pleaded with Harriet, but she insists on staying locked up with Mother and Father."

"Well, after all," Charles said, "she is in mourning."

"Oh, Charles, you're so old-fashioned. I think you'd like to have us women practice suttee—throw ourselves on your funeral pyres."

"Not exactly, Lucinda. But I can understand how Harriet doesn't feel up to much yet."

"Of course, you're right. Poor Harriet. But then Kate is a different story. Aren't you, Kate? You're a free woman. In fact, Claudia ought to be grateful to have you every weekend, oughtn't she, Sam? I'm sure you could find more exciting ways to spend your weekends than with the old marrieds."

Sam looked up from his lobster blankly as if he couldn't understand Lucinda's words. "I'm afraid Sam's mind is somewhere else tonight," Katherine said. "He's worried about the storm. They're bound to cancel tomorrow's race."

"Don't be so sure," Charles broke in. "The latest report said it was supposed to veer out to sea."

"Not from the way it was blowing when we drove over," Kate said, and Lucinda turned to her other guests. Clearly, Sam Beaumont was farther gone than she'd thought.

Later that night Sam lay in bed, listening to the rain on the terrace roof below his window. He could hear the wind howling through the trees and, when the wind died, the waves crashing on the beach. It was sure to be a force 10 gale, if not worse. He was sorry to forgo the race, but more troubled at the prospect of spending a day in the house alone with Claudia and Katherine.

Sam heard his door open. He prayed Jamie had been awakened by the storm but knew his son would never come to him in the middle of the night. He would go to Miss Morris or Claudia, but not to his father. "Who is it?" he whispered. He knew without asking.

"Who do you think it is?" Her laugh was light and teasing. He saw a white robe. It fell silently to the floor, and Katherine seemed to be floating above him in the darkness. Her arms and legs were brown from the sun, and only the paleness of her body was visible in the blackened room.

She lifted the sheet and slipped into bed. Her skin was cool and smooth with talcum powder. She was above him in the darkness, and he felt her hair over his face like a gossamer web, thin but binding. "My God, Kate, not here."

"Why not here? You know she won't come in."

"But this house . . . our home. . . ."

"*Shhh,*" she whispered. He felt her hand familiar and deft between his pajamas.

"Please, Kate." It was a cry of agony. She silenced it with her mouth. He watched her moving above him in the darkness. She knew his pleasures, his needs, every secret corner of his desire. Her body was with his slowly at first, then faster and faster until his breathing was a moan, a moan he attempted to stifle while she silently prayed it would resound through every room in the house.

"Good morning, ma'am." Ellen set the breakfast tray down on the bed and began to open the curtains.

"Good morning, Ellen. Though I can't see what's good about it. Did the rain keep you up during the night?"

"Oh, it takes more than a little rain to keep me awake, ma'am. All the same, it looks like it's going to be a bad one. It's a shame, too, with that birthday party over at Mrs. Chesney's and Diana all excited about it."

"Maybe the children will be able to go after all. If it doesn't get any worse. Is Mr. Beaumont down?"

"He was down and out before I was up."

"Out? Where on earth could he have gone in this weather?"

"Cook said he wouldn't have any breakfast, not even a cup of coffee. She said he put on his oilskins and headed down toward the dock."

"In this weather!"

"Perhaps he just wanted to make sure everything was tied down before the storm hit."

Claudia pushed aside the tray and walked to the windows overlooking the Sound. *Revenge* drew too much water to be kept at their private dock, but Sam had bought a small sloop to take the children sailing. It was gone.

"He must be mad."

"You don't mean to say Mr. Beaumont went for a sail in this, do you, ma'am?"

"It looks that way, Ellen." Claudia remembered the few times she'd sailed with Sam. She remembered that storm on their wedding trip. "And knowing him, he'll be back in a few hours raving about how wonderful it was. I've seen him run out in the middle of a thunderstorm just to catch the following winds."

When Sam had still not returned by one o'clock, Claudia began to think there might be cause for worry after all. "There must be something we can do," she said to Kate. The sisters sat on opposite sides of the table, each toying with but not tasting her food. In the silences between their words they could hear the storm raging around the house. "We could call the Coast Guard and have them look for Sam."

"He'd be furious, Claudia. You know that."

"I suppose you're right. If only he'd left some word —where he was going or when he'd be back. Anything."

"He doesn't usually when he goes for a sail."

"But this is different."

Katherine looked at her sister carefully. "Why? Did you quarrel?" She prayed her sister would say yes. She could not bear to think her own actions last night, her own determination to push Sam as far as she could, had driven him to this.

"No. I meant the storm. If Sam's going to be foolish enough to go off in weather like this, he ought at least warn us."

They were silent through the rest of lunch. When Wilfred brought in the coffee, Claudia stood. "I'm going to call Charles. Maybe he's over there." Kate followed her sister to the telephone table in the little alcove off the entrance hall. Charles hadn't seen Sam, nor had Anson or several other neighbors. As soon as Claudia replaced the receiver, the phone rang again. Charles suggested she call the Coast Guard. "I wanted to, but Kate thought Sam would be angry."

"We'll worry about that later." Charles didn't tell Claudia he doubted they would have to worry about it at all. Sam was a good sailor, but a storm of this magnitude made a mockery of skill. He wondered why Sam had gone out. The thought triggered memories of Schuyler Mason. More than a thousand banks had failed in the last year. It seemed impossible the New York Bank and Trust could go under or Sam Beaumont be ruined, but it was a time of impossibilities.

Charles called Graham Livingston. He was Sam's lawyer, as well as a member of the family. Charles suspected Graham's presence would be necessary before long. "Who's with Claudia?" Graham asked.

"Katherine."

"I'll start immediately. It may take me a little longer in this weather, but I'll be there this afternoon."

When Sam left that morning, he wanted only to be out of the house, away from both Claudia and Katherine. He went, as Ellen had predicted, to make sure the boat was secured at the dock, but as he stood watching the Sound churned up by the wind and the waves crashing over the rocks at the entrance to the bay, he decided to take the small sloop out. He longed to exhaust mind and body in a struggle against the elements. He longed for danger. It was the only thing that would cleanse him.

And if the danger were too great, if the struggle conquered rather than cleansed him, well, that would be all right too. At least it was a way out—a final, complete, and clean end to it all.

The first half hour was exhilarating. Last night, the scores of nights with Kate seemed to be washed from him by the wind-lashed rain and spray. The sky was black and the sea menacing, but to Sam the horizon looked brighter than it had in months. Then the wind intensified, and the boat failed to respond to the tiller. With each gust it veered more into the wind until Sam was heading directly for shore and the nest of rocks marking the entrance to Oyster Bay Harbor. The only hope now was to shorten sail. He worked his way forward to the mast carefully. The wet decks were slippery, and the tossing of the boat made movement treacherous. In easier weather he could reef the mainsail almost in an instant, but now he had to move slowly or be swept overboard. His fingers worked rapidly at the halyard. If only he could bring the sail down before the wind made tatters of it or, worse, demasted the sloop. He heard a terrible sharp sound above the wind and knew he was too late.

The heavy fir beam that was once a mast lay across the boat, and the mainsail dragged in the water. Sam struggled to pull it out, but it had already filled with water and was too heavy to bring aboard. It had to be cut free, but that would take time, and the boat, pushed by wind and current, was coming dangerously near the rocks. He was close enough to hear the thunderous sound of the waves crashing up and over them. The noise was like an alarm calling him back to sanity. When he set out this morning, he had told himself he didn't care what happened. But face to face with the possibility of death, he wanted desperately to live. Claudia, Katherine, his betrayal, his guilt, no one and nothing mattered to him now but himself. He must survive.

He fought the tiller, but the sea was too strong. Like the trailing mainsail that acted as a sea anchor, he could slow his progress toward the rocks but not stop it. He felt the boat strike with sudden force and knew he had hit. His only chance was to try for shore. The sea was rough, but he was a strong swimmer. He grasped beneath the floorboards for a life jacket, but the fierce motion of the sea pitched him wildly about the cockpit. With each wave he felt the boat being lifted and hurled violently against the rocks. It was too late to dive free of them. The most he could hope for was to jump far enough from the boat so that it would not come down on him. The slippery decks and the motion of the boat made a foothold impossible. Just as he was about to leap, a wave lifted the boat and Sam was hurled into the rocks. He hit with force, and something in his ribs felt as if it had snapped. His arms and legs were scraped raw, but he was not aware of the pain. He knew only that he had to get clear of the boat.

It was beginning to break up, and huge pieces were crashing all around him. He saw the debris of his life swirling through the water. Charts floated past. He saw a child's life preserver caught on a rock. His hand, as he fought to push himself off, tangled in something. It was a small white sweater, identical to the one he was wearing. In one corner, stained with his blood, were his son's initials, JTB. It was the last thing Sam saw before another wave crashed over him. He felt a sharp stab of pain against his right temple. Then nothing.

The Coast Guard told Claudia they could not search until the storm subsided. By that time there was no need. A sail with Sam's numbers was washed ashore late in the afternoon.

Graham Livingston watched Claudia as she stood before the window staring out over the Sound. She seemed too completely in control of herself. *It was a bad sign,* he thought. "Perhaps I'd better call Dr. Gettinger."

"What for?"

"He might prescribe a sedative."

"Why?"

"It would help you sleep."

"I mean why did he do it, Graham. Why?"

"You mustn't think of it that way, Claudia. You mustn't think it was intentional." He was trying to convince himself as much as her. Sam had always been an adventurous sailor but not a reckless one. His choosing to go out this morning had been tantamount to suicide.

"Are there financial problems?" Claudia half dreaded there might be, half hoped there were. If Sam were merely another casualty of the Depression, it would mean she was not to blame.

"Not at all. The bank's still in good shape, and there's all that land."

"Then why, Graham?"

"Why?" Kate shrieked. She had been so quiet Graham had forgotten her presence. He turned to her now. Her face was white and her body trembling. "Why do you think, Claudia? Because of *you*. Because you're such a bitch. Because you did nothing but make his life miserable."

"Katherine!" Graham broke in. "We're all upset, but think of what you're saying."

"I know exactly what I'm saying, Graham. And so does Claudia. Don't you, Claudia?" Claudia, impassive again, turned back to the Sound. "Don't you?" Kate insisted.

"I think I'll lie down before dinner." Claudia's voice sounded like a distant echo in her own ears. As she started for the door, Katherine blocked her path. Graham heard the sound of her palm against Claudia's cheek and saw the bright crimson mark it left. "You killed him," Katherine screamed. "You killed him. And now you act as if nothing has happened. You go through life like a damned sleepwalker. You wreck everything you touch, and then you withdraw into your own comfortable little world. Nothing matters to you, does it, Claudia? It never mattered to you that I loved Sam or that you didn't care for him at all. You just went blindly ahead, spoiling everything. Are you satisfied now? Is Sam's death enough for you, because Lord knows his life wasn't. You took everything from him and gave him nothing. And if it hadn't been for me, he never would have had anything. If I hadn't come back to him——" She stopped and stood staring at her sister more in triumph than in regret. Kate hadn't meant to say as much as she had, but she was not sorry.

The room was silent for what seemed to Graham a long time. He watched in fascinated horror as the sisters stood facing each other barely inches apart. Slowly Claudia's face rearranged itself as if she had suddenly seen something. "Then perhaps, Katherine, I'm not the only one responsible for Sam's death." Her cheek, Graham noticed as she left the room, showed the distinct impression, angry and red, of her sister's hand.

7

"Now I don't say you have to wear black all the time or never go anywhere, but a country club dance, Claudia, don't you think that's indiscreet?" Elizabeth sat erect in the wicker chair, her back a good two inches from the chintz cushion. A lady had no need for such supports. The late-afternoon sunlight slanting across the terrace revealed an exquisite complexion almost enhanced by fifty-odd years of loving care. "Perhaps after the year is up, dear, but I still think it's premature for real social appearances."

"You mean in twenty-eight days I can dance on the tables, Mother, but until then I must not show my mournful face to the world."

"You know that isn't what I mean, Claudia. And I can't see why you'd want to go to the dance anyway. When Sam was alive, you always complained about the club dances."

"All you're worried about, Mother, is what people will say."

"People do talk. . . ."

"Let them!"

Elizabeth stood and picked up the large straw hat that lay at her feet. "I can see this conversation is getting us nowhere, dear. You're a grown woman and I daresay you'll do as you like. And now if you'll call for Henry. I ought to be getting back. I wanted to be home before your father has his dinner."

Claudia started to answer that it scarcely mattered when her mother returned. James had not realized she was gone and would not be aware of her return, but the truth was too cruel to bear reminding.

Wilfred was on the terrace before Claudia could call him. "There's a Mr. Denbigh to see you, madam."

Elizabeth saw her daughter pale. "Is there anything wrong, dear? Is he a friend of Sam's you'd rather not see?"

Claudia's mind was racing. How could she explain to her mother why she did not want to see Denbigh?

"I understand your feelings, Claudia. Each time you see someone you have to live through the ordeal again, but it must be done. Sam's friends cared deeply for him. Calling on you is a way of paying their respects. You must allow them to do that." Elizabeth turned to Wilfred. "Show Mr. Denbigh out here, Wilfred."

Her daughter's obvious discomfort only increased Elizabeth's ingrained sense of hospitality. "How do you do, Mr. Denbigh." She extended one perfectly manicured hand. "I'm Mrs. Trenholm. I understand you were a friend of my son-in-law. It's kind of you to stop by to see us."

Denbigh was more than her match. "Not at all, Mrs. Trenholm, it's kind of you to receive me." He turned to Claudia and took her hand as he had her mother's. "I was sorry to hear about Sam, Claudia. I would have come before this, but"—he hesitated for only a fraction of a second—"I was abroad for some time. How have you been?"

Elizabeth rushed in to fill the void left by Claudia's silence. "Claudia's been bearing up admirably, Mr. Denbigh. And of course, the children are such a comfort."

"Of course, the children." Denbigh seemed to be enjoying himself.

"Well, if you've been away for a year, I expect you have some catching up to do. And I really must be on my way. I do hope we'll meet again, Mr. Denbigh."

"I'm sure we will, Mrs. Trenholm."

"That's all right, Claudia. You needn't walk me to the car. Stay here with Mr. Denbigh. Wilfred and Henry will take care of everything." She touched her daughter's cheek with her own and was gone in a flurry of flowered crepe de chine.

"What are you doing here?" Claudia had prepared herself for Joe Denbigh's appearance any number of times since Sam's death. She would be polite but cool. Sam's absence did not change the way she felt about Joe. She had never loved him and had finally broken with him messily, vulgarly perhaps, but wisely. She did not want him back now, but back he had come. Characteristically, he had returned just when she had stopped expecting him.

Denbigh knew that—that, and one other thing. He had waited just long enough to allow her grief, or whatever it was she felt, to turn to restlessness.

"You aren't half as gracious as your mother, Claudia. Though I will say now I know where you get your looks."

"I have no intention of being gracious. I told you a long time ago things were over between us, and nothing has changed that."

"Don't be silly, Claudia. Of course, something has changed that. Your dear husband's untimely departure. You know, you may not believe me, but I am sorry. Not for you, but for him. You didn't give him much of a life and then this . . . this tragic death."

"You hypocrite."

"I always said we were alike."

"We're not in the least alike, and now will you please leave? I never would have seen you in the first place if it hadn't been for Mother."

"But that's just it. I can't leave yet. I might run into your mother in the driveway, and I wouldn't want her to think you'd been rude."

"You're worse than a hypocrite. You're vicious. And that absurd story about being abroad for a year . . . ."

"So you knew I wasn't abroad. I'm flattered,

Claudia. All the same, I couldn't very well tell your mother I was waiting until your year of mourning was up. You know I've always had great respect for the proprieties. But now the year is almost over I think it's time you started thinking of our future. I want to marry you, Claudia."

"I have no intention of marrying again, and if I did, it wouldn't be to you."

She saw the anger in his eyes, and for a moment she thought she had reawakened the old dark memory, but then he laughed as if nothing she said were to be taken seriously.

"Oh, you'll marry again, Claudia, and you'll marry me. And this time we start out as equals."

"We're not starting out as anything—least of all equals."

They had both remained standing after Elizabeth left, and now he took a step toward her. "You're wrong there, Claudia. I'm the only man you know who *is* your equal. I'm the only one who isn't afraid of you and the only one you can't walk all over. And you need that. And whether or not you know it, you like that."

They were standing only inches apart, and Denbigh could read the familiar haughtiness in her eyes, but there was another look there too, one he recognized equally well. She wanted him to touch her. Knowing that, he did not touch her but took a step back.

"I won't rush you, Claudia. If I've waited this long, I can wait a little longer. And time is on my side now. That and the fact you've been very bored for the last year—if not longer." She started to speak, but he went on quickly. "There's nothing to be ashamed of. You simply weren't meant for mourning. I don't imagine you could really mourn anyone, but especially not your late husband.

"Well, I've taken up enough of your time. I'll drive out again next week. Or perhaps I'll motor across the Sound from Connecticut and we can go for a cruise. In the meantime, if you want to see me before then,

I'll be in town all week. You do remember where to reach me, don't you?"

Joe Denbigh did not drive out the following week or for five days after that. Claudia had stopped wondering how she would dismiss him when he arrived and started wondering what kept him away.

He turned up on the first Wednesday in September. It was a perfect end-of-summer day, clear and crisp, but the sun climbing over Sagamore Hill across the bay promised it would be warm enough to swim in the afternoon. Claudia and Katherine were on the terrace when they first saw the large motor yacht pulling up to the dock below.

"Were you expecting anyone?"

"No," Claudia lied. "Perhaps they've mistaken our dock for someone else's."

Katherine stood and walked to the edge of the terrace, but Claudia forced herself to keep leafing through *Vogue*. "I don't think it's a mistake. Whoever it is has started up the hill." Kate raised a hand to shade her eyes. "My heavens, it's that Denbigh man! I can't imagine what he's doing here." Katherine turned back to her sister, who seemed to be engrossed in her magazine. "Or maybe I can. Do you know him, Claudia?"

"I did slightly—some time ago."

"I might have guessed it. And you're going to see him now. You're probably going to go out on that vulgar boat of his today. Is that the plan?"

"There is no plan, Kate, but what if I do? Sam's been dead a year. Isn't it time we all started living again?"

"Don't make me laugh, Claudia. You never stopped. I doubt you shed a single honest tear for Sam. I'm only surprised you waited this long to start running around with people like Denbigh. Or perhaps you didn't. Perhaps this has been going on for some time."

"Excuse me." His shoes had made no sound on the grass, and both women started at his words. "Perhaps I should have come around the front way."

"It is the usual approach," Kate said. "I'm giving Diana a riding lesson this morning, Claudia. We'll be back for lunch." Katherine disappeared into the house without so much as a second glance at Denbigh.

"Who is Diana?"

"My daughter."

"Ah, yes, the one who's such a comfort to you. I believe those were your mother's words."

"I wouldn't be insulting if I were you. You haven't been invited here, and I'm not at all sure I'm going to let you stay."

"Oh, you'll let me stay all right, Claudia." He looked at the door Kate had let slam behind her. "The irreproachable Mrs. Whitely doesn't approve of me. We've been introduced several times, but she continues to ignore me. I imagine she was shocked to see me here."

"Scandalized is more the word."

"Well, I didn't come to see Mrs. Whitely. I came to see you. As promised."

As promised a week ago, she almost said, but didn't.

"Here I am, and there's my boat, and it's a perfect day for a cruise."

"I have no intention of going on that boat or anywhere else with you."

"Of course you do, Claudia. That's what you and your sister were arguing about."

"What Katherine and I were arguing . . . saying is none of your business. And if you hadn't come sneaking up the back lawn. . . ." Her words drifted off. There was no way to end the sentence.

"If I hadn't come sneaking up the back lawn, I wouldn't have heard you arguing about me. Come on, Claudia. There's no way out. You know you're dying to go. You've been cooped up in this house much too long. Besides, if you don't go, Mrs. Whitely will think she talked some sense into you, and that would be insufferable."

"Really, you're impossible, Joe." The name slipped

329

out without her meaning it. "You come barging in here. . . ."

He took a step toward her. His hands were light but strong on her arms. "Stop it, Claudia. It's me. Joe. Remember. You and I know each other. Now why don't you just tell whoever it is you have to tell that you'll be gone for the rest of the day and we can get out of here?"

She turned away from him and started toward the house, then stopped for a moment with her hand on the screen door. "I must be home for dinner."

Her back was to him, and he permitted himself a smile at her imperious tone. "Whatever you say, Claudia."

The boat rode easily at anchor in a small cove some ten miles east of Claudia's own. The air was silent except for the sound of the waves slapping against the hull and an occasional rattle of dishes and hushed words among the crew below. The sun was still warm, though the breeze had cooled since they had sat on the afterdeck under the striped awning and picked at the lobster and champagne and strawberries Denbigh had so thoughtfully ordered. If it got any cooler, Claudia thought, she'd have to get up and put a robe over her bathing suit. She stretched lazily in the sun, her arms and legs as bronze and polished as the teak deck.

She sensed Joe change position next to her on the deck, then felt his finger tracing a lazy pattern on her shoulder. His hand was cool against her skin, his finger light over her collarbone, up her neck to her ear, gently over her cheek, back to her shoulder. She felt him toying with the strap of her bathing suit and caught her breath at the touch of his lips on her shoulder. She did not move a muscle, but she was sure he could feel her body straining to his.

"Well," he said. His body blocked the sun as he sat up. "If you have to be home for dinner, we'd best be away."

Claudia opened her eyes with a start. The sun was

behind him, and it was hard to see his face, but she thought he looked terribly pleased with himself.

The following week there was no fencing about the arrangement. She would be in town. They would dine together.

"I hope you're planning on taking me somewhere interesting, Joe. After all, in a sense this is my debut. I must admit, you came along just in time. I think I'm due for a great deal of amusing. The trouble, though, is that so few people are any good at amusing me."

"It's nice to know you appreciate at least some of my virtues."

"Are there others?"

"You'd be surprised."

"I think the word is bored. I'm not interested in virtues, Joe. Yours or anyone else's. I've had enough virtue for a while."

"Virtue—you!"

"You needn't sound so reproachful. Would you prefer me to go back into mourning?"

"Claudia, the last place I want you is in mourning." They were in the backseat of Denbigh's Bentley, and as he spoke, he reached an arm around her shoulder; but the movement was without desire, and he took his hand away a moment later to light a cigarette.

After dinner and the theater she demanded to be taken to Harlem. It was the first week of the new show and the Cotton Club was packed, but Joe had no trouble getting a table right on the dance floor. Claudia noticed no money had changed hands to accomplish the feat.

Claudia was glad they had arrived between shows. She was not in the mood for watching another performance. Couples moved slowly about the half-dark room in time to Duke Ellington's rendition of "Sugar Blues." She took a sip of her drink and felt the warmth spread. Her body moved slightly in rhythm with the music. She had never heard it so clearly, never felt the sensuality so sharply.

On the dance floor Joe's arms around her felt strangely familiar. She had forgotten how well he moved, how well they moved together. Through the thin satin of her dress she could feel his hand at the small of her back. She moved her hand from his shoulder to the back of his neck. Above the stiff collar his skin was warm and smooth. She leaned against him and let the music and the whiskey and the warmth of Joe Denbigh engulf her.

A single light burned in the living room. "Would you like a brandy?"

"No, thanks."

She was surprised at the refusal, more surprised still when she turned and saw he was standing in the foyer. "I'd better be on my way. It's been a long night, and I have an early appointment tomorrow."

"Then I won't keep you," she snapped. "Good night."

Outside in the hall Joe could not help smiling at the force with which the door closed behind him.

The following week Claudia called George Talbott. *Good old George,* she thought. "I need cheering up, George." George, of course, had tickets to just the play. He knew precisely the restaurant that would lift her spirits before and exactly the speakeasy that would amuse her after. Claudia thanked George for a wonderful evening and went to bed certain she had never had a duller time.

Joe called early the next morning. "Did I wake you?"

"As a matter of fact, you did."

"I know, but you were out entirely too late last night."

"How did you know?"

"I have my spies. Apparently Mrs. Beaumont is no longer in mourning."

"I'm not so sure after last night."

"Good old George was deadly dull, eh?"

"George Talbott is a very old and dear friend."

"I'm sure he is, Claudia, but then again I know how you feel about old and dear friends."

"Did you wake me at this hour to insult me?"

"Of course not. I called to tell you I was sorry I hadn't called all week. . . ."

"Oh, it wasn't that long, was it?" she lied.

"But I was in Albany."

"Albany. No one goes to Albany. Whatever were you doing there?"

"I can assure you a great many people go to Albany, only you wouldn't know any of them. But I'm back now, and I want to see you."

"I'm afraid that's impossible. I'm going to the country today." She hadn't planned to, but it would serve him right.

"Go tomorrow."

"I must get back to the children."

"Then I'll drive you out and you can invite me to dinner."

"I don't think that's a good idea. Katherine is still there."

"Then there's really no need to get back to the children, is there? With a nurse, and their adoring aunt, Mrs. Whitely, they'll scarcely be missing their mother." He lowered his voice a fraction. "Please, Claudia. It's been such a dull week without you."

"Well, I guess the children can get along for one more day."

"Of course they can. I'll come by for you at eight."

The evening was much like the one they had spent together the previous week, but this time Claudia was on her guard. As she moved about the dance floor of the Club Argonaut, she was almost stiff in Joe's arms.

"I think I'd better call it a night."

"But it's only twelve thirty," he protested. "And Texas Guinan's coming on again."

"I'm afraid I'll have to forgo that. After all, I have to get up early tomorrow if I want to get to the country before lunch."

Denbigh smiled at the repetition of his words but said nothing.

"Aren't you going to offer me a brandy?" he asked in the living room of her apartment. "Or are you afraid it wouldn't look proper? I know you only brought your maid into town with you—what's her name? Ellen?—

and she told me while I was waiting for you that she was going to Brooklyn tonight to see her family."

Claudia looked at him sharply.

"That's what happens when you keep me waiting." He laughed. "I'll get the brandies." He poured half an inch for each of them and sat down next to her on the sofa. With the back of one finger he traced the contour of her cheek. "You're the damnedest woman, Claudia. Even widowhood agrees with you." He laughed abruptly. "Perhaps I should say especially widowhood agrees with you."

"You're hateful!" She started to rise, but he pulled her back down next to him.

"Careful, Claudia, you're losing your sense of humor."

"I don't find anything funny in a statement like that."

"Perhaps not. Perhaps I was in poor taste. I apologize. From now on I'll treat you with more respect." His arm was around her, and he pulled her close. Their mouths were almost touching. "Is that what you want?" he whispered. "To be treated with respect?" But he did not give her a chance to answer.

His mouth on hers made her dizzy with wanting him. She felt his hand beneath the halter bodice of her dress, and her senses reeled.

He moved slowly as if deliberately holding her back. She fumbled hurriedly at his clothes, but he was painstakingly careful. The touch of his hand on her thigh above the silk stockings was maddening. Slowly he took the dress from her, then the chemise. And then there was nothing betwen them, nothing in the world beyond Joe Denbigh, wave after wave of him washing over her until she felt she would drown in the pleasure he gave her.

"When do you want to be married?" he asked.

She had gone to her room and put on a dressing gown, and Joe had put on his trousers and shirt.

"I don't remember anyone saying anything about marriage, Joe."

"I'm saying something about it now. There's no

334

reason for us not to marry. I love you, Claudia, and you love me. That's the simple truth."

"I don't love you, Joe." The line sounded familiar even after all this time, but she thought of the last year and last night with George, and her voice did not hold the old confidence.

She had never planned to marry Joe Denbigh, and she might not have but for two conversations that occurred at the end of a winter filled with him. It was 1932, and everywhere they went orchestras were playing "Night and Day." Claudia wasn't in love, and she wouldn't call herself happy—how could she be happy after the tragedies that had shadowed her life? she told herself—but she was no longer bored. Nevertheless, she did not consider the absence of boredom sufficient reason for marriage.

Two conversations changed her mind. The first was with Polly Chesney; the second with Katherine. Both, like her talk with Sam so many years before, took place on the beach in front of the Breakers in Palm Beach.

"Kate told me Joe Denbigh's coming down tomorrow." Polly, in brilliant pink beach pajamas, sat on a pile of pillows surrounded by an elaborate arrangement of parasols. "Well, I'm not surprised. I didn't think he could leave you alone for this long. When are you going to give in and marry him?"

"I'm not."

"You're being perverse, Claudia. Why won't you marry Joe?"

"Why should I?"

"That's the densest question. Why shouldn't you? You obviously care for him. I can't imagine your spending all that time with him if you didn't—not if you weren't married to him, that is. He has plenty of money —not that you have to worry about that, though it is unpleasant when only one member of a marriage has money. And to be perfectly frank, he's the most attractive and interesting man around. If I were you, I'd marry him in a minute."

"I don't mind spending time with him. . . ."

"You mean having an affair with him."

"Polly!"

"Claudia!" she mimicked the sound. "Really, we're not children anymore. Anyway, you're the last one I'd expect to worry about Joe's background. In fact, if I remember correctly, you were the one who championed his cause when we first met him. I wouldn't have expected you to marry him then—no matter how broad-minded you sounded—but that was a long time ago. I doubt if anyone even remembers it."

"You seem to."

"Well, of course we remember it, but no one cares anymore. Joe's accepted—everywhere. Even by Charles, and you know my husband is far from democratic in these matters. Remember how worried he was that summer when he thought his sister Sybil might marry Joe? You know what he said the other day? That he wished Sybil had married Joe Denbigh. I told you, of course, Sybil just started her third divorce. Well, anyway, so much for Joe's social acceptability. So why won't you marry him?"

"I just never thought about it seriously."

"Well, if I were you, child, I'd start thinking about it. You aren't going to be a *young* widow forever, you know."

A week later after Joe had returned to New York—Governor Roosevelt had announced his candidacy the previous month, and Joe insisted he had no time to waste sunning himself in Florida—she was on the beach again. Kate had just completed one of her energetic afternoon swims and was toweling herself vigorously.

"I see your friend Denbigh left this morning. Back to his political cronies?"

"You make it sound rather dishonest, Kate."

"I always thought politicians were."

"Joe isn't a politician. He merely takes an interest in politics."

"It just isn't a gentlemanly pursuit."

"What about Governor Roosevelt?"

Kate ignored the question. "But then no one ever accused your friend Denbigh of being a gentleman."

"If you dislike him so much, why do you keep talking about him?"

"Because you're still my sister and every foolish thing you do reflects on me. Are you going to marry him?"

"Why is everyone suddenly so interested in my marriage plans?"

"I don't care about you, Claudia, but I do care about having Denbigh in the family. It's unthinkable."

"Apparently you've given it a great deal of thought."

"You can't do it. It's bad enough you're seen everywhere with a man like that, but you can't really consider marrying him."

"Why not?"

"Because he's trash, that's why not. You know nothing about him or his background, except that he's a climber."

"As a matter of fact, I know a great deal about Joe's background."

"I wouldn't believe a word that man said if I were you."

"Oh, Joe didn't tell me about himself. Sam did."

"Sam! You're not going to tell me Sam approved of him."

"I didn't say he approved of him, I said Sam told me about him."

"What?"

"Just where he was born, how he made his money, that sort of thing."

"Then, if you know all that, you can't seriously consider marrying him. You know Sam wouldn't have wanted you to."

"I scarcely think Sam's preferences ought to determine whom I marry—if I do marry."

"If you don't care about Sam's memory, think about his children. You can't give Sam Beaumont's children a stepfather like Joe Denbigh."

"I can if I choose to, Kate. And I don't think it would be the worst thing in the world for them."

"For once in your life, Claudia, would you stop trying to shock everyone and think about what you're doing. You simply cannot marry a man like Joe Denbigh."

She agreed to marry Joe on March 3 after what the papers termed a "society beer party" celebrating 3.2 repeal. Katherine refused to attend the wedding. "Do as you like," Claudia told her. "We haven't attended each other's weddings so far. I see no reason to break tradition."

The wedding took place in the garden of Joe's house in Greenwich on May 29, the same day an exhausted and angry group of veterans marched into Washington to demand their "bonuses." The happy couple left immediately for two weeks in Bar Harbor. Joe did not want to leave what he called his interests any longer than that.

In the fall Claudia insisted on returning not to Joe's apartment but her own. "That's Beaumont's apartment," Joe said. "I won't move into his apartment."

"It isn't Sam's apartment. It's mine. I don't want to live in your apartment, Joe. I want to go back to my own. If you don't care about me, you might at least think of my children. It's not fair to them to make them leave their home."

"This has nothing to do with the children, and you know it, Claudia. It's between us—as always—and I don't like the idea of moving into your place. It looks as if I can't afford one of our own."

"Don't be ridiculous, Joe. Everybody knows you're a rich man and you signed away any right to my money. I'm sure you made that clear to anyone who was interested. If the money side of it bothers you, you can keep your place, too. Use it to entertain your political friends."

"These days it's bad taste to keep two apartments the size of ours. Don't you know there's a Depression?"

"Sorry, Joe, I keep forgetting what those visits to Albany and Hyde Park do for your conscience. Well, keep it or give it up, whatever you like, but I've already made arrangements to have our things moved back to my apartment. If you want me to have yours sent somewhere else, you'd better tell me now."

He was silent only for a moment. He might as well give in this time. Her place was larger, though certainly not more luxurious, than his. And no one could accuse him of using Claudia or her money. Everyone knew he had weathered the crash intact, even made money from it, and people were aware he had signed away any right to her fortune while settling a considerable sum on her and her children. Claudia was right about that. He had made sure it was common gossip.

"Very well, Claudia, we'll move back to your place, but don't be misled by your easy victory. It's not a sign of things to come."

"Why, Joe." She looked genuinely offended. "I hadn't thought of it as a victory. You have to have a battle to have a victory, and everyone knows you and I don't fight."

As the leaves turned, Claudia began to feel the entire presidential campaign was being run from her apartment. At least it seemed so when Joe was home. He was often out of town, and when he was in New York, he spent a good deal of time in the office he kept, no longer on Wall Street, but on West Forty-fourth Street. Conveniently close to the Harvard Club, Claudia said with a laugh.

She didn't know exactly what Joe was doing—the mysteries of political organization held no attraction for her—but she did know why he was doing it. Mere respectability was no longer enough for Joseph Denbigh. Even back in the days of Jimmy Walker, Joe must have known it would not be. He wanted something more, and more, Claudia knew now, was power—legitimate power. He had made the money, established the connections, and now he would be a power behind the scene.

And the scene had turned out to be the perfect one for Joe. If in the past he'd had little respect for most of the professional politicians he'd had to deal with, he had no such reservations about Franklin Delano Roosevelt. He was an aristocrat, well born and well educated, beyond reproach, yet there was nothing weak about the man. He was, simply, everything Joe Denbigh wanted to be. Just this once Joe's motives were clear to Claudia and she did not hesitate to goad him about them.

"I wish you'd turn that radio off, Joe. You know I can't stand that song."

> Once I built a railroad
> Made it run
> Made it run against time
> Once I built. . . .

Joe snapped the machine off. "I'm sorry if the music offends you, Claudia, but in case you don't know it, there's a depression. There are fifteen million unemployed men in this country."

Unemployed men. The phrase seemed to carry her back through the years. It was exactly a decade ago. *Right here in Paris there are thousands of unemployed men, and they can't feed their wives and children victory any more than the Germans can feed theirs defeat.* The words might be the same, but Claudia knew the difference that lay behind them. That afternoon in Paris Philippe's eyes had flashed with anger. Joe's now were cold. He'd step on each of those fifteen million to get where he was going.

"How could I forget the Depression living with you, Joe, darling? Why, sometimes I think you're going to put an end to it single-handedly."

But Joe would not be baited. He was too pleased with his progress to be affected by his wife's gibes. And when he introduced her to the candidate at a dinner where one paid several hundred dollars to eat some very bad chicken, he knew he had scored a point. Claudia was impressed.

The candidate was far more attractive than his photographs and entirely captivating, not at all like the politicians Joe occasionally brought to the house. While leafing absentmindedly through the paper, Claudia was struck again by a photograph of his wife. There was no doubt about it. People made the most peculiar marriages.

As October waned, the pace of Joe's activities quick-

ened. He left early each morning and was rarely home
before midnight. Claudia didn't mind. She enjoyed her
freedom—as long as it was built on a foundation of
security. It was pleasant to come home from a party or
a nightclub and find Joe waiting for her. He would
usually be in his bed with the early editions of tomorrow
morning's papers, a glass of milk on the night table by
his side. Unlike her first husband's nightcaps, Joe's were
not spiked with alcohol. Claudia suspected Joe did not
really like whiskey or even wine and took them only in
company when the situation called for it.

It was pleasant to know he was waiting for her, ready
for her. But one night, when, still dressed, she sat on
the side of his bed, she caught the unmistakable scent of
cheap perfume.

She sat up immediately. "God, you smell like a tart."

He laughed. "How do you know what a tart smells
like, Claudia?"

"I know what cheap perfume smells like."

"Well, I suppose I do. It was a smoker to raise
money, and you know there are always women there."

"Just how much did that cheap perfume cost you?"

He was still smiling complacently. "It didn't cost *me*
anything. I was doing the fund raising."

"Of course. Anything for the cause."

"It's a good cause."

"Hypocrite. The only cause you care about is your
own."

But Joe had already turned back to his papers. He
had not told her what the perfume meant, if anything,
and Claudia would not give him the satisfaction of asking. When she emerged from her dressing room, she did
not look at him. She removed her peignoir and got into
her own bed with her back to Joe. He could read the
lines of anger in it.

But most nights she returned home to a husband who
smelled not of perfume but of cigar smoke and whiskey.
After the perfume incident Claudia took to calling it his
political clubhouse smell. There was no question of
Claudia's accompanying him on these nights. In fact, he
rarely wanted her along even for the more genteel

political gatherings. When he got wherever it was he was going, Claudia suspected he would find her important, even necessary, but there was no need for Claudia in the rough-and-tumble of daily campaigning. Until that Thursday evening late in October. Apparently this party was important enough to Joe for him to want to display his trophy.

Claudia had finished saying good-night to the children and entered the living room just as Wilfred was taking Joe's hat and coat.

He looked at her print challis afternoon dress. "You'd better hurry, Claudia. We're already late, and at this hour the drive crosstown will take at least twenty minutes."

"What are you talking about? We have an hour, and Polly's just around the corner."

"What are *you* talking about? I told you about this cocktail party last week. It's very important."

"I'm sure it is, but I told Polly we'd be there tonight. If your cocktail party is so important, you can go without me and I'll go to Polly's. I don't feel like standing around with a bunch of your political friends. I hear enough of them when they come to see you. All they ever talk about are polls and who's taking what district."

"And what do that drunk Hagerty and that ass Charles Chesney talk about? Do you think your friends are more stimulating?"

"*My* friends. There was a time when you'd do anything to be accepted by those people."

"You're right. There *was* a time. And I *was* accepted. Why, one of you even married me. And now I'm interested in more important things."

"More important things! What's so important about this cocktail party? Has Mr. James T. Farley himself commanded our presence?"

"Don't be sarcastic, Claudia. Mr. Farley happens to be a very powerful man, but he is, after all, only a politician. The men at this party won't be politicians."

"More important than politicians! Goodness gracious! Is that possible? Who's giving this party anyway?"

"The name wouldn't mean anything to you. He's a professor at Columbia. He lives on Riverside Drive."

"You expect me to go to some tacky college tea over on Riverside Drive?"

She could see the anger flicker in his eyes. "It is not a tacky college tea. Some of the best minds in the East will be there."

"Why are you invited, Joe?"

"Very funny. These men are going to be important in Washington after the election—more important than the men who'll be making the headlines. They'll be the brains and the decision makers. They'll be running the government."

"And you're going to run it with them." She clapped her hands in delight. "It's beginning to come clear. Those heavy tomes I found on your desk in the library. John Maynard Keynes, indeed. You can't even get through a Hemingway novel." It was true. Joe couldn't stand the novels Claudia consumed at a rapid pace. "Tell me one thing, Joe. Where does it all end? You climb and climb, and where are you going to end up? In the White House perhaps? Do you see me as a First Lady?"

"I see you as late. Now go call Polly and tell her we can't make it, and then get dressed. And wear something conservative."

"Conservative. I don't understand. I thought they were all liberals." She saw his look of annoyance and laughed. "Very well, Joseph, darling, I'll wear something terribly bluestocking. Anything to help my dear husband along—if only I understood where he was going."

She thought about their conversation as she dressed in an understated black silk dinner dress. Claudia didn't know why she insisted on taunting Joe the way she did. She didn't love him, but she didn't dislike him. Or did she? Perhaps she resented Joe's hold on her. Marriage had not altered the nature of their relationship. She continued to want him—sometimes, perversely, when she liked him least. When they made love, he brought out something primitive hidden deep within her. Afterward Joe was always cool and Claudia embarrassed. She would come home wanting him and then afterward hate herself for the depth of her desire and the abandon of its fulfillment. If she had loved him, it would have been different; but she didn't, and it made her uncomfortable and vaguely ashamed.

Perhaps that was why she taunted him, as if she could get back in a civilized sphere what he had taken in a more primitive one. Certainly they rarely fought over issues. It was more a matter of wills. They seemed to be waging a war of attrition to determine whose will would triumph.

In the foyer of the apartment on Riverside Drive a man obviously hired for the occasion took their coats. Behind him Claudia could see a small living room crowded with people.

"Glad you could make it, Denbigh." Their host was beside them, small and round and flushed. Claudia thought he looked a little too jolly to be one of the best minds in the East. His wife was a spare, large-boned woman half a head taller than her husband. Her ugly print dress hung on her as if on a clothes hanger. Joe had said she was a psychiatrist.

"How nice of you to come, Mrs. Denbigh." Her voice was low and carefully modulated. She introduced Claudia to two men and a woman standing nearby, then drifted back to the foyer. Claudia took a martini from the tray of another temporary retainer in a short rented jacket and tried to concentrate on the conversation. They were talking about farms—not someone's polite estate in upstate New York, but farm problems in the Midwest.

Suddenly Claudia felt someone tugging at her skirt. She looked down to find a child, three or four years old, in Dr. Dentons and a flannel robe. It was extraordinary. She had never seen a child wandering loose at a cocktail party.

"My name's Abigail. What's yours?"

Of all the women in the room, Claudia thought, *why did she have to choose me?* "Claudia," she answered without bending down.

The child tugged at her skirt again. "Are you a friend of Mommy's?"

This time she merely smiled at the child without answering. Surely a nurse or some responsible adult would discover her presence and remove her. Claudia looked across the room to her hostess. She was talking spiritedly to another woman, and when she caught sight of Claudia and the child, she merely smiled at them.

"That's pretty." The girl was touching the delicate band of diamonds and sapphires encircling Claudia's wrist. Sam had given it to her for their second anniversary. "I want it."

"I'm afraid it's not for little girls to play with."

"Abigail wants it!"

"But Abigail can't have it." Claudia smiled through clenched teeth.

"Abigail *can* have it!" The child's voice was rising, but no one seemed to notice. Across the room her mother was still smiling at them absently.

Claudia tried to think of something to distract the girl. She remembered that as she had tossed things into the small evening bag, she had noticed an empty vial of *Nuit de Noël* Ellen had neglected to remove. The green tassel still dangled from the neck of the tiny black and gold bottle. Claudia stooped to bring her face on a level with the child's.

"I have something better than the bracelet."

"What?" she asked suspiciously.

Claudia took the bottle from her bag. Abigail snatched it from her. She tugged at the tassel a few times, then turned and scampered away.

Claudia straightened and found herself a foot away from a tall man in wire-framed glasses. Claudia noticed his evening clothes were well cut, far better cut than most of the men's in the room. He smiled at her.

"Apparently we have more than one psychiatrist here tonight."

"Far from it." Claudia laughed.

"You handled it well. Personally, she terrifies me. Last time she almost got my grandfather's pocket watch."

"You mean she makes a habit of that? Why doesn't anyone stop her?"

"And thwart Abigail's development. Perish the thought. The little thief is expressing herself. Or so her mother tells me. You're Mrs. Denbigh," he went on in the same tone. "I've seen your picture in your husband's office." *And been impressed,* his eyes seemed to add. "I'm Hadley Latham."

"Are you one of the best minds in the East?" He looked at her a little uncertainly. "According to my husband, that's who's here tonight."

"The best mind in the East." He laughed, turning his back to the party and enclosing himself and Claudia in a corner where they could go on talking without interruption.

Hadley Latham, Claudia later learned, was one of the best minds in the East. The youngest professor in the history of Harvard Law School, Hadley looked and acted more like a playboy. He came from a small town in central Massachusetts, but there was nothing of the small-town boy about him. He was a born raconteur and always in demand as an extra man. He carried himself gracefully, traced his ancestors back to the *Mayflower* and his fortune back at least three generations. Hadley Latham could have done nothing more than live on his income and rest on his laurels. Instead, he had carved a brilliant career before he was thirty and, were Roosevelt elected, was likely to walk off with one of a dozen much sought-after plums. He, like the candidate he supported, was everything Joseph Denbigh wanted to be. A week after the party Joe found Hadley Latham having drinks with his wife.

Joe had arrived home at six to discover the two of them in the living room. Latham looked suddenly uncomfortable. As Joe entered the room, Hadley seemed to be straightening his tie, smoothing his sleek brown hair, and fidgeting on the sofa all at once. Joe mentioned it to Claudia after Latham had left.

"He acted as if I had interrupted something."

"Don't be ridiculous, Joe. How could you have interrupted anything? Hadley came to see you, and I gave him a drink."

"And that was all?"

"What did you expect? To catch us *flagrante delicto?*"

"You forget how well I know you, Claudia."

"You're wrong there. The situation is different this time. If I found someone else, Joe, I wouldn't have an affair. I'd simply leave you."

"It's nice to know where I stand."

"Don't worry, I haven't found anyone else."

"Not even Hadley Latham? Things looked awfully cozy just now."

"Of course, they were cozy. He was passing the time waiting for you by flirting with me. Men always flirt with me. You ought to know that by now."

"And you always flirt back."

"Not always. Just when I feel like it."

"What were you talking about while all this flirting was going on?"

"Lady Chatterley's Lover."

"That piece of trash!"

"God, you get more bourgeois every day. And I thought your new friends might have some effect on you."

"You can be as sarcastic as you want, Claudia, the book is filthy. It wasn't even allowed in the country until a few months ago."

"Have you read it?"

"No, and I wouldn't have expected you to."

"Then you don't know me so awfully well after all."

"You can read what you like, Claudia. . . ."

"Thank you so much."

"But I won't have you seeing Hadley Latham alone."

She started to laugh.

"What's so funny?"

"You sound exactly like Sam. 'I won't have you seeing that Denbigh character alone,'" she mimicked.

Joe had remained standing after seeing Latham to the door, and now he crossed the room to where Claudia sat. He leaned over her and took her face in his hand.

"Remember one thing, Claudia, I'm not Sam Beaumont. *I* won't stand for your little tricks."

She wrenched her face away. "And I won't be spoken to that way."

"You'll be spoken to any damn way I choose to." He started for the door and then stopped. "One other thing. I knew you had read the book. I saw it on your night table. I'm going upstate for a few days. Have it out of my room before I get back."

"*Your* room. That's a laugh. I'll see that more than the book is out of *my* room before you get back."

Now it was Joe's turn to laugh. "You can have my things moved wherever you want, Claudia. It won't make any difference. If I want you, a locked door isn't going to make any difference."

When the election returns came in, Joe was euphoric. "You sound as if you had won yourself," Claudia said sleepily when Joe, just home from headquarters, awakened her to tell her the news. In terms of his plans for the future, she supposed, he had. Joe Denbigh was well on his way to being an important and respected member of society. There were only a few things missing, and those he planned to take care of in short order.

"I'm home, Mummy."

Claudia was in the kitchen giving the cook instructions when Jamie entered.

"I can see that, dear. Why don't you get out of your heavy things and then you can have your milk and cookies?"

As Jamie shrugged out of his coat she noticed the small St. Bernard's blazer jacket was short at the sleeves. She had ordered it in August. Did all children shoot up so quickly?

Jamie sat at the large table in the center of the kitchen.

"What happened at school today?" Claudia asked, only half listening for an answer.

"Nothing much." There was a pause. "Mummy."

"Yes?"

Jamie was carefully arranging the Arrowroot cookies

in a circle on the plate before him. "Am I going to have another brother or sister?"

Claudia glanced at the cook. She seemed to be absorbed in the fruitcakes she was wrapping in cheese-cloth, but Claudia knew she was hanging on every word. "I left the menu for Tuesday's dinner party on my desk, Clara. Would you get it please? . . . Now, Jamie, where did you get an idea like that?"

"From Uncle Joseph. This morning at breakfast. He said I shouldn't tease Diana because she was my little sister and I had to take care of her and soon I'd have another little sister or brother and I'd have to look out for him, too."

"Well, Uncle Joseph was wrong, Jamie. There'll be no more little brothers or sisters. I promise you that." The milk mustache on Jamie's face turned into a smile. "All the same, Uncle Joseph was right about one thing. You shouldn't tease your sister."

"She started it."

"And you're older and ought to know better."

Jamie's smile waned only slightly. The reprimand was familiar enough not to be taken seriously, and his real worry had been assuaged.

Not so for Claudia. She had been hiding from the problem for months. She had to face it. Till now she had been lucky—and careful. Ellen had said the church called it the rhythm method. Ellen also said, when discussing her sister's huge family, that it rarely worked. It had so far for Claudia, but she could not go on taking chances. Polly had told her about a new device. The best thing about it was that Joe wouldn't have to know. Although she would have to tell him to stop putting ideas in the children's heads.

"They're not ideas, Claudia; they're facts," he said when she confronted him that night. "Sooner or later the children will have to get used to the idea of more children in the house."

Claudia kept her back to him and continued brushing her hair. "Well, since it isn't sooner, there's no need to worry them about it now."

"I've been meaning to talk to you about that." Joe

put aside the papers he had been leafing through and took off the glasses he had begun to wear for reading. "Perhaps you ought to see a doctor. Just for a check-up."

"There's nothing wrong with me."

"I didn't say there was, but neither of us is getting any younger and I want children—as soon as possible."

"I don't see what the rush is."

"I didn't expect you to. All the same, why don't you make an appointment with Dr. Gettinger—or some woman's specialist if you like—just to make sure everything is in order."

"Are you beginning to worry you got a lemon, Joe?" Her laugh was deprecating.

"It's not something to joke about."

"Of course not, it's a very serious matter. Carrying on the Denbigh name and tradition is not something I take lightly."

"You can be as sarcastic as you like, Claudia. Just make sure you make an appointment."

"What about you, Joe? Aren't you going to see a doctor, too? After all, I have three children. In view of the facts perhaps we'd better worry about you."

"There's nothing wrong with me."

There was no reason to think there was, but she knew she had found a chink in his armor. "And there's nothing wrong with me either. I'll go to a doctor when you do."

"Stop being silly, Claudia. I told you to see a doctor, and I meant it. Now I don't want to discuss it anymore."

She knew she should not answer. She knew the sensible thing to do was lie about the doctor and keep lying about Polly's device. Perhaps by that time he'd come to believe there really was something wrong with one of them and they couldn't have children. But his orders and the tone in which he gave them annoyed her.

"I have no intention of seeing a doctor, Joe. And if you must know, I have no intention of having any more children, yours or anyone else's."

"That's ridiculous."

"Perhaps you see it that way. I see it as sensible."

He got out of bed and covered his silk pajamas with a matching robe. "This isn't an argument about an apartment or a book, Claudia. I'm serious about this. I want children, and we're going to have children."

"Correction, Joe, you're going to have children. If you want them so desperately, you can divorce me. I'm sure you can find someone else who'd be happy to bear your children."

"Stop talking nonsense. There'll be no divorces in this family."

"Fine. No divorces. No children. We're even."

"This isn't a joke, Claudia."

"I never thought it was."

He wrenched the hairbrush from her hands. "Goddammit, Claudia. You're going to have my children, and what's more, you're going to be a good mother to them."

"And how do you propose to achieve all that, Joe? I've heard of your usual methods, but I scarcely think putting me in a car and pushing me into the Sound off Stamford is going to make me much of a mother. . . ."

The swiftness of his movement shocked her. She felt herself being swept off the chair. Joe pinned her against the wall with both his hands. His eyes were black with rage and his voice was crueler than she had ever heard it. "That never happened. And no one is going to say it did. Especially not my wife. Do you understand that?"

She said nothing, and he shook her so hard her head banged against the wall. "Answer me, Claudia. Do you understand that?"

She was furious at her own trembling. She would not be intimidated by Joe Denbigh. "Do *you* understand there aren't going to be any more children? I'll be damned if you'll turn me into a cow to produce a bunch of urchins to inherit a made-up name."

Again his response was immediate and instinctive. The palm of his hand crashed against her face once, twice, a third time. The pain was explosive. Her head reeled from the blows, and through her blurred vision Joe's face, contorted with fury, looked like a gargoyle.

She tasted blood and could not believe it. Then she began to scream, and his hand fastened to her mouth.

"Be quiet. You'll wake everyone."

She heard her voice die, though she was not aware of willing it to. He held her that way, his hand over her mouth, his forearm pinning her shoulder to the wall, for several seconds. Then he released her and began to smooth the satin robe that his hands had disarranged. His voice was quiet, almost kind. "Go wash your face, Claudia. You're bleeding."

When she came back from the bathroom, he was standing in front of the window, looking down Park Avenue at the lights of traffic rushing toward him. He kept his back to her as he spoke. "I'm sorry, Claudia, but it had to happen. You had to be taught a lesson."

She had learned it well. The next morning, as soon as Joe left the apartment, she telephoned Graham Livingston.

"Graham, can I see you today?"

"I can stop by on my way home this evening, Claudia." As the executor of his cousin's estate Graham was accustomed to stopping by for Claudia's signature and other minor legalities.

"No, I want to come to your office. As soon as possible."

"I'm free at three."

"Can't you see me before that?" Her voice was impatient.

"Of course, if it's that urgent." He told her to be there at eleven.

Before she got into her bath, she examined her face carefully. To her surprise, there was no swelling, though when she pressed her fingertips against her cheeks, it felt tender. At the corner of her mouth where she had bled there was a minute red line, as if she had been out in the cold and her lips had chafed and cracked.

Strange there was no marked physical scar. She was sure the emotional one was indelible. She had thought that once before—after that awful night with Sam. With time she had learned to live with that, but this was different. That night with Sam had been an accident. He had been drunk. He had sworn to her the next morning when he tried to apologize that it would never have happened if he had not been drunk, and she knew it was true.

She knew no such thing with Joe. She had seen a new side of him—violent and unrelenting—and it terrified her. She knew now it had always been there and always would be lurking ominously just below the surface. The knowledge of it was too much for Claudia. She could live with a man she didn't love or respect, but she could not live with a man she feared. She would have to get free of Denbigh. If she didn't, she knew now her will would be overcome by force and she would be broken.

Claudia arrived a few minutes after eleven, and Graham's secretary showed her into his office. She had not been there since the reading of Sam's will.

Graham offered her a cigarette from a large silver box. "Well, Claudia, what can I do for you?"

"I want a divorce."

Graham's face was impassive, but his hands toyed nervously with a fountain pen. Would there be no end of messy problems from these Trenholm girls? Graham was fond of Claudia, but for the moment he wished Sam had never married her. First they had forced him into handling that shameful affair of Katherine's, and now Claudia was about to involve him in another sordid case.

"I'm not that kind of attorney, Claudia. You know that."

"You handled Kate's divorce."

"That was a special favor. Sam asked me to."

"Well, if you can do a favor for Kate, I should think you could do one for me. I'm sure Sam would have wanted you to."

She did not appear to see the irony in her words, and Graham did not call her attention to it; but he knew everything about Claudia's second marriage would have offended his cousin.

"You know I'll do anything I can to help you,

Claudia, but for proceedings of this sort it's generally advisable to have a specialist in the field."

She slammed her glove hand on the top of his desk. *"Generally advisable. Specialist in the field.* I'm asking you for help, Graham, and you sit there and give me legal platitudes. You have to help me. You're the only one I can turn to."

Graham had never seen her so distraught. She was usually cool. That was one of the things he admired most about Claudia, her composure.

"If you don't want to handle the details, Graham, you don't have to. You can turn that part over to anyone you like. I'll leave that to you. But you simply have to take care of Denbigh for me. For one thing you have to get him out of the apartment. Immediately. I won't spend another night under the same roof with that man. I can't." Her voice had risen steadily as she spoke, and Graham thought she was more than upset. She was frightened.

"Let's try to be calm, Claudia. I take it from the immediacy of your demands you and Denbigh have quarreled. You don't have to tell me about it," he went on quickly, "but we ought to look at the larger picture. Does a single quarrel necessitate a divorce?" Never having married himself, Graham believed implicitly in the sanctity of marriage.

"It wasn't just a quarrel, Graham, it was . . . it was. . . ." She began to sob quietly. She could not bear to tell Graham what had happened last night. She had been beaten by her husband. It was brutal and common and vulgar. It was the sort of thing that did not happen to people like them, and she could not admit to Graham it had.

Graham's hands fluttered over his desk in discomfort. "Please don't cry, Claudia. Everything is going to be all right. I promise you. I'll take care of everything. Perhaps it would be better if we started at the beginning and took things step by step. You say you want a divorce. I'm afraid you'll have to go away for some time. Divorce is difficult in New York State."

"Katherine didn't have to go away."

"Katherine was fortunate." He smiled uncomfortably. "I mean unfortunate enough to have grounds according to New York law. Adultery." Graham's voice had dropped almost to a whisper as he spoke the last word.

Claudia was silent for a moment; then her face brightened. "Then I'll get an annulment. Didn't the Lapworth girl get an annulment? That would be much better. It would be as if the marriage had never happened. And I could go back to being Mrs. Beaumont."

"Claudia, the Lapworth girl's marriage lasted fewer than forty-eight hours. The grounds for annulment are generally that the marriage has never been"—Graham coughed—"consummated."

"Are those the only grounds?"

"I believe there are one or two others—I told you, you needed a specialist for this sort of thing—but they're not often used."

"What are they?"

"Well, if, for example, Denbigh had married you under false pretenses. If there was something that affected your marriage he hadn't told you about before."

"I don't understand."

"Children, for example. If Denbigh refused to have children, had never intended to have children, and kept that knowledge from you until after the marriage, he would have married you under false pretenses and you would have grounds for annulment."

"But that's wonderful. We'll just say I refused to have children."

"Claudia, if you refused to have children, Denbigh would have to bring the action against you."

"Oh." She looked thoughtful for a moment. "Then you'll just have to convince him to, Graham. The last thing Joe wants is a scandal. You'll simply tell him if he doesn't have the marriage annulled, I'll make one. I assure you I can. And he knows it. Tell him I want no money, nothing from him, only to have the marriage annulled. Tell him if we do it that way, there'll be no scandal, and he'll come through like a perfect gentleman. But if he won't do it that way, tell him I'll make a scandal he'll never forget."

"Claudia, I don't think threats are the best way to go about this."

"It's the only way. You see, I know something about his past he doesn't want known. Even if I can't prove it, I can make enough fuss to start people wondering. His political friends won't like that. You don't have to make it sound like a threat, Graham. Just explain my position. You have to. There's no one else I can turn to. You will help, won't you? It's not only for me, you know. Think of the children. We'll all be better off without Denbigh."

Graham wanted to tell her she should have thought of that before she married, but there didn't seem to be much point in arguing. He knew he'd do what she wanted.

"Here's Denbigh's telephone number." She handed Graham one of Joe's cards. "He should be at his office now. You can see him today—and tell him I'll have his things packed and sent wherever he wants tonight."

When Denbigh arrived at Seaburn, Seaburn, Nolton, and Livingston at six that evening, it was deserted except for Graham and three clerks in a large fenced-in outer area. One of them showed him into Graham's private office.

Though annoyed at the summons, Denbigh had agreed to come. Livingston managed Claudia's affairs and kept delicately out of their personal life. For the past eight months the two men had treated each other with formal deference. If Graham chose to intrude now, the matter, in his eyes at least, was serious.

Joe hadn't expected Claudia to tell anyone about last night—least of all that cold fish Graham Livingston—but since she had, he would have to take care of the matter before it mushroomed out of control. He had two plans. The first was to convince Livingston Claudia's tale of a beating was an exaggeration. She had become hysterical, and he had slapped her once to quiet her. If Graham did not believe the story, Joe would simply order him to keep his nose out of other people's marriages—but he didn't think that would be necessary.

Graham stood when Joe entered. "Sorry to have to drag you down here at this hour."

"Not at all," Joe said affably and took the cigarette Graham offered.

"Mrs. Beaumont, excuse me, Mrs. Denbigh came to see me this morning, Mr. Denbigh." Joe managed to muster a look of surprise. "She has asked me to speak to you on her behalf." Calmly, logically, Graham ticked off the points. He was careful to keep any hint of a threat out of his words. Claudia wanted her freedom. It was unfortunate, but these things happened. The important thing—they all agreed, Graham was sure—was to do things quietly, in a civilized manner. There must be no scandal, no nasty newspaper publicity. Denbigh would not want to subject his wife to that, nor could he want it for himself. It could only impair his political effectiveness, and even a staunch Republican like himself—Graham permitted himself a wan smile—knew how important Denbigh had become in the Democratic organization.

"I think it will be better for everyone this way, Mr. Denbigh. I think it's decent of Mrs. Denbigh, since it is she who wants her freedom, to bear the onus of the proceedings. With any luck the entire action can be taken care of in a matter of weeks."

Claudia had him this time. She could prove nothing, but she could open a chapter of his life he could not afford to have revealed. He had covered himself carefully, nothing could be traced to him, but the idea that his own wife would suggest it could would be scandal enough to destroy everything.

"You can tell my wife I agree to everything she asks." Joe stood. "And I wish you'd tell her one more thing, Livingston. I would tell her myself, but you've made it clear she doesn't want to speak to me." His tone was tinged with quiet sadness. "Tell her she's making a mistake—one she'll be sorry for someday."

Graham had never liked Denbigh, but he couldn't help feeling sorry for him now. He obviously cared very much for Claudia. Perhaps Claudia was making a mistake by throwing such a love away. It never occurred to Graham that he was being asked to carry not a last plea for reconciliation, but a threat of ultimate retribution. Someday, Joe swore to himself, Claudia would pay as she never had before.

8

"Are you sure you're dressed warmly?"

Jamie regarded his mother with nine-year-old reproach.

"I assure you we're both properly insulated against the elements," Graham said.

"Well, I'm sure I don't know why you'd want to go out to look at birds in weather like this."

"It's the best time to look at birds, Mother. There are no leaves on the trees."

Graham smiled at the boy's tone. In the last two years he had become an integral part of his cousin's family. After her break with her second husband Claudia had retreated to the house in the country. It was as if she had gone into mourning again. More than once, when he had driven out to confer about some legal matter, Graham thought he had been right that morning in his office. Something had frightened Claudia, and she seemed to be wary of the world. Her life had become quieter, and Graham as a result had begun to occupy a larger place in it. He not only managed the family's legal and financial affairs, but had come to take a considerable personal interest in Claudia and the children. He was especially fond of Jamie. At times Graham saw flashes of himself in the boy. Jamie even looked a little like himself.

The boy and the man set off across the field that led to the marshy lowland. Each wore a pair of binoculars around his neck and carried a small pocket guide and a notebook.

At the edge of the water Jamie spotted a family of grebes. There were four chicks swimming about, and two others rested on the mother's wings. "Pied-billed grebe, right?"

"I think so. Let me check." Graham wasn't humoring the boy. He had never been a serious bird-watcher, and these expeditions were more for Jamie than for Graham. "Does the bill have a black band?"

Jamie tiptoed a few steps closer to the water. "The mother does. I can't tell about the chicks."

"Well, if the mother has, that's good enough for me. You're right again, Jamie."

The boy quickly began scribbling in his notebook to hide his pleasure.

They tramped on for another hour, stopping often to observe and make notes. As usual, Graham tired first. "I don't know about you, old man, but I could use some warm refreshment." They headed for a dry field above the marsh and found some logs to sit on. Graham poured a cup of cocoa for each of them from the thermos jug he carried.

"Well, how's school these days?"

"Okay," Jamie said casually. Graham recognized the tone and the sentiments it was designed to hide. A country day school with its emphasis on competitive sports was not a pleasant place for a child like Jamie. "I wish we lived in town all the time. Then I could go to a different school."

"You might not find it better, Jamie. Anyway, you'd miss the country—and all your birds."

"We could come to the country on weekends. And if we lived in town all the time, I'd see more of you, wouldn't I, Uncle Graham?"

"I suspect you see quite enough of me already. I'm sure your mother thinks I'm underfoot all the time."

"Oh, no, Uncle Graham, Mother likes to have you around." Graham stared into his hot chocolate and said nothing. "Could we move back to town for all the time, do you think?"

"Well, I know your mother has thought about it, Jamie." Graham suspected Claudia was beginning to feel restless. "But she hasn't made up her mind. I thought you liked it out here."

"It's all right, but I'd rather be in town. I could come see you whenever I wanted then, couldn't I?"

"You certainly could. I tell you what, Jamie, why don't you convince your mother to come into town next weekend and I'll take you to a matinee? Would you like that?"

"Thank you, Uncle Graham." Jamie would like a matinee, just as he liked bird-watching, but he had more in mind. "Uncle Graham, why can't you come live with us?"

There was a brief silence, only a missed beat in the conversation. "I'd love to, Jamie, you know that, but it's impossible. It just isn't done."

"What if you married Mother? It wouldn't be impossible then, would it?"

"Where do you get your ideas?" Graham laughed uncomfortably.

"Well, it wouldn't, would it? She married Uncle Joe, and he came to live with us. I didn't like him, but it would be different with you. It would be fun to have you live with us, Uncle Graham."

"That's very flattering, I'm sure, but I think your mother might have something to say about it."

"She'd like it, too. I know she would. She always says how good you are, and anyway, don't ladies always want to be married?"

"I don't know about that, Jamie."

In January, 1935, there were still enough people with enough money for a charity ball at the Waldorf to attract two thousand philanthropists eager to see and be seen. Half of them bobbed around the floor now to Emil Coleman's muted strains of "You're an Old Smoothie," while the other half drank, talked and watched.

"What a surprise to see *you* here, Graham," Lucinda Hagerty said. "I know you always give your money to good causes, but what have we done to deserve your presence, too?"

Graham looked decidedly uncomfortable.

"Now let me guess. It's Claudia's influence, isn't it?" Her eyes swiveled to Claudia. She was a widow and a divorcée, and she ought to look hurt and deflated, yet Claudia was simply stunning. Her blond hair, longer now, was drawn back in a sleek chignon, and her skin was pale alabaster against the simple black satin gown.

"I think Anson's calling you, Lucinda." Claudia nodded across the dance floor to where Anson, drunk as usual, was gesticulating wildly, but Lucinda would not be distracted.

"If you're turning over a new leaf, Graham—under Claudia's influence, of course—I'm going to put you on all my lists. Everyone's still cutting back, and it's simply impossible to muster a decent turnout for anything."

"Oh, no, Lucinda," Polly Chesney, the chairman of the ball, cut in. "I found him first. If you're supporting any charity balls this year, Graham, you must come to mine."

Claudia laughed and stood up. "Well, Graham, I leave you to the victor—whoever she may be. I've had enough for one night."

Graham stood immediately, as all three women had expected him to. "I'll see you home, Claudia."

Graham followed her into the white living room. As well as he and Sam had got on together, he had rarely visited while his cousin was alive. Now the apartment felt comfortable and familiar.

"Brandy?" she asked.

"I'll get them." He handed Claudia a glass and sat down across the coffee table from her.

"Now I've got you into it, Graham. After tonight Polly and Lucinda and everyone else will be hounding you to turn up everywhere. You're going to be the most sought-after extra man around."

"I think you're overstating it, Claudia. At least I hope you are."

"You'll see." She laughed.

"Well, it won't work. I only went tonight because you asked me to."

"It was kind of you, Graham, but then you always are. I can't thank you enough for all the time you spend with Jamie."

"You don't have to thank me, Claudia. I enjoy doing things with Jamie. All the same." He hesitated for a moment, then rushed on. "I think Jamie would like a father. More than that, I think he needs one."

"Much as I'd like to oblige my son, I have no intention of marrying again."

"Isn't that a little drastic, Claudia? You're still a young woman."

"I'm not that young, Graham. Not young enough to make another mistake, at any rate."

"Perhaps the second time was a mistake." He spoke haltingly. She never referred to her second marriage. "But surely your marriage to Sam, you don't regard that as a mistake. It may have ended tragically, but surely there were happy years."

"You were there the day Sam . . . the day Sam died, Graham. You heard what Katherine said."

"Katherine was overwrought. We all were."

"All the same, she was right. I made Sam's life miserable, and that's one mistake I don't plan to repeat."

"But it might be different this time. You and Sam were both young and probably starry-eyed romantics. Perhaps those aren't the best prerequisites for marriage. And you remarried too soon after Sam's death. You were lonely. But this time, Claudia, you could marry for companionship and respect and . . . well, more mature values. You need someone to take care of you and the children."

"I don't see why, Graham. We're perfectly well off. Sam left us a great deal, and you manage everything beautifully. I don't see why we need anyone else."

"I wasn't speaking about anyone else, Claudia. I was asking you to marry me. I know you don't love me, Claudia, but I flatter myself that you feel some friendship and affection for me. And the children like me.

363

Jamie has even said he'd like it if I were around all the time.

"I'm not a demanding man. You know that. You wouldn't have to change the way you live. I'd just be around more. That would be enough for me." He was silent for a moment as if searching for words. "You see, I never used to mind being alone, but for the past two years I've got accustomed to you and the children. I look forward to the time I spend with you. Listen, Claudia, I'm not very good with words beyond a legal contract, but I guess what I mean is I love you, and I'd like to take care of you and your children. I know that isn't a very romantic proposal, but it's a sincere one."

"I don't know what to say, Graham."

"You might consider saying yes. I know it wouldn't be the way it was with Sam, Claudia—I know you don't love me—but perhaps it might work out for the best precisely *because* you don't love me. The excitement at the beginning might not be there, but then neither would the disappointment."

She looked across the table at Graham. His eyes were pleading, and his face was flushed with embarrassment. She wanted to reach out and touch him, but she couldn't. She did not think she had ever touched Graham Livingston except on a dance floor.

"I don't want to shock you, Graham, but I think I'd better tell you something about Sam and me."

He looked away from her quickly. "You don't have to tell me anything you don't want to."

"But I want to, because I want you to understand something. I'm terribly fond of you, Graham, and I don't want to hurt you; but I can't marry you. Not because I loved Sam so much and it went wrong, but because I never loved him. That's what Kate meant that day. I married Sam for all the practical reasons you're talking about, and then I found I couldn't live in that kind of a marriage. I guess Sam found the same thing."

"I'm not Sam, Claudia."

"But I'm still me. I'm fond of you, Graham, and grateful to you, but I can't marry you."

He stood and hurried to the foyer, and she followed him.

"I hope this won't make a difference between us, Graham."

"Of course not," he said. But they both knew it would.

Jamie heard the front door close and scampered down the stairs. He stopped in the entrance to the east sitting room. "Oh, I thought it was Uncle Graham."

"Don't be rude, Jamie. Come in and say hello to Mr. Talbott."

"Hi, Jamie." George shook the small hand offered him. "What are you doing inside on a day like today? I passed a bunch of boys playing hockey on the pond on the way over. Aren't you a hockey player?"

"I thought Uncle Graham was coming today." His words were almost an accusation to Claudia. "I wanted to show him my new bird book."

"Well, I guess Uncle Graham couldn't make it after all."

"Would you like to show me your book, Jamie?"

The boy looked at George suspiciously. "Do you know anything about birds?"

"I like duck hunting."

Jamie dismissed him with scorn and turned back to his mother. "Will you call Uncle Graham and ask him when he's coming out?"

"Perhaps next week, dear."

"I mean today. He might still come out this weekend."

"I said I'd call him next week, Jamie, and I don't want to hear any more about it." Claudia's voice was more impatient than she intended, possibly because she was as relieved at Graham's absence as Jamie was disappointed.

The boy went straight to the upstairs telephone and called Graham's number. "Uncle Graham, aren't you coming out this weekend? You said you were."

"Jamie, how are you?" Graham asked uncomfortably.

"Are you going to come out or not?"

"Well, I had planned to, but something came up. The fact is, Jamie, I have a lot of work to do this weekend. Kind of like having a lot of homework." Graham laughed weakly, but the boy did not even smile.

"Are you coming next weekend?"

"I'm not sure. It depends how things go. I've let a lot of work pile up, Jamie."

"You don't work all the time, do you, Uncle Graham?"

"I tell you what, Jamie. I'll do my best to get out next weekend. Now I don't promise I can, but I'll do my best."

Jamie stood watching as his Aunt Katherine helped Diana mount the chestnut gelding. "It's just as much my horse as Diana's," he said sullenly. "Why does she always get to ride first?"

"You must learn to share your things, Jamie. You don't want to be a selfish little boy, do you?" The distaste in Katherine's tone was barely veiled. It was peculiar that she cared more for Sam's daughter than either of his sons. She would have expected to dislike any daughter of Claudia's and adore Sam's sons, but of the three children Diana seemed most like Sam. She had his soft hazel eyes, and she even held herself as he used to. Katherine could spend hours watching her practice the small jumps she was beginning to learn. She loved the way she sat proudly atop her horse.

"But I want to ride him now," Jamie whined.

"You didn't want to till I did," Diana taunted. "And besides, he likes me better." Diana was right, and they all knew it. She was better with ~~horses~~ than Jamie would ever be. The animal could sense Jamie's fear as well as he could Diana's affection and natural command.

Jamie turned his back on his sister and aunt and amused himself making imperfect "smoke" rings with his breath in the chill February air. But the game wasn't much fun if there was no one there to admire his prowess, and he finally drifted back to the house.

Jamie found his mother reading in the sunroom.

His little brother, Anthony, sat at her feet with an army of brightly painted soldiers. She looked up absentmind-edly as he entered. "Did you have a nice ride, Jamie?" Claudia returned to her book without waiting for an answer.

"Why doesn't Uncle Graham ever come to visit any-more?"

"I wouldn't say ever, dear. He just hasn't been here for a while. I'm sure he'll come again, soon."

"Mother."

"Yes?" Claudia's voice was impatient. She had read the same paragraph three times now.

"Who are the Lindberghs?" He noticed he had finally got her attention.

"Why do you ask, Jamie?"

"This morning Miss Morris and Ellen and even Wil-fred were all talking about some people called Lind-bergh. They said they had a baby, and it was kidnapped a long time ago, and it was an awful thing, and now some man was going to be punished for it." Claudia made a mental note to speak to the servants. They ought to know better. "Why is kidnapping so awful? What does it mean? Is it like dying—like going away the way Daddy did?"

"Well, not dying exactly, dear, but perhaps a kind of going away. . . . Why don't you get your book and you can read with me until lunch?"

"I bet they miss their baby, don't they?"

"I'm sure they do, Jamie."

"I bet they'd do anything to get it back, and I bet they'd be ever so nice if it came back."

"Now, Jamie, I want you to forget all about it. And I don't want you talking about it to Diana." She went back to her book, and Jamie wandered around the room, touching things. "Jamie, stop picking things up that way. That's exactly how you broke that ashtray last week. And I don't want to have to scold you again."

Jamie looked at his brother who was totally absorbed in his soldiers. "Come on, Tony, let's play war." With-out waiting for his brother to agree, Jamie began to rearrange the soldiers.

A small fist struck him. "They're my soldiers."

Jamie pushed the hand away and continued aligning his forces. Tony's face contorted in six-year-old anger while his fists pounded at his brother. Jamie pushed him away, and the child fell backwards with a wail of protest.

"Now see what you've done, Jamie. Tony was playing quietly until you disturbed him. Now I want you to take Tony to Miss Morris and then get cleaned up for lunch. And I won't have you invading my sunroom until you learn to behave like a gentleman."

Claudia sighed as she watched Jamie leave the room, dragging a tearful Anthony behind him. In the last two years she had tried to spend more time with the children, but somehow it never seemed to work out. She simply wasn't suited to motherhood and she knew it. All the same, she thought as she returned to her book, she'd have to make more of an effort. Perhaps she'd take a walk with Jamie this afternoon and let him show her some of his birds. But of course, this afternoon was impossible. She had promised to attend that tea for the new hospital wing. Well, perhaps tomorrow. Tomorrow she'd go for a walk with Jamie.

He debated whether or not to take his panda. Miss Morris said big boys did not sleep with panda bears, and Jamie usually tried not to, but he thought he'd like company tonight. More company than just the birds. He was wondering, too, if he could slip into the kitchen and get some cookies without being noticed.

He started out a little after three. The panda was in his schoolbag—in case he ran into anyone—along with several handfuls of cookies. He wandered around the marsh for a while, but the birds weren't much fun without anyone to show them to, and anyway his feet were wet and he was beginning to shiver. He headed for the woods behind the Petersen house. They were the largest woods in the neighborhood, and they'd never find him there.

By seven o'clock Jamie had finished all his cookies, but he was still hungry. He was cold, too, and afraid of the dark. The birds weren't such good company at night. He hugged the panda. At least he'd had the sense to bring him.

By nine he had decided to head home. He had planned to stay the night, but he hadn't counted on the cold and dark or the chill loneliness and strange night sounds of the woods. Nine o'clock was almost as good as tomorrow morning, he reasoned. They'd be just as glad to see him now as they would tomorrow morning. The only problem was the woods looked different at night—just as they sounded different. Jamie could not seem to find his way out. Then there was no hope of finding anything through the tears that blurred his vision. He slumped down on a bed of pine needles and hugged the panda. By the time he slipped off to sleep the panda was soaked with tears.

The police did not begin to search immediately. Thanks to Bruno Hauptmann's lurid trial, the word "kidnap" was in the forefront of the national consciousness again, and the detective and his assistant first searched the house thoroughly and questioned all the servants. Nothing was amiss. No one had remarked anything unusual. Wilfred did seem to remember seeing the boy wander off sometime this afternoon. He hadn't paid much attention. The child often went hiking through the fields and marshes to look at his birds.

Finally, the search teams started out, but it was slow work. In the morning they formed a cordon and began to sweep the woods. Jamie's blue jacket was bright against the winter brown of the forest. He was asleep, the panda still clutched to him.

They took the child directly to the hospital. "In cases like this, Mrs. Beaumont," the police chief explained, "it's best to keep the boy under observation for twenty-four hours."

Within three Jamie was running a fever of 103 degrees. The young resident on duty told Claudia it might be pneumonia, but it was too soon to tell. Claudia was not about to accept the word of a young, unknown doctor. She called Graham, and he promised to find Dr. Gettinger and drive him out immediately.

Double pneumonia was Dr. Gettinger's diagnosis. Both lungs were affected.

Claudia had always thought of Jamie as a tall child, but he looked suddenly tiny in the long hospital bed. It was almost as if he had shrunk during his night in the woods. His face, crimson against the white sheets, was covered with a film of perspiration. She took the small hand that lay motionless above the sheets, and he shivered.

"It's the chills, ma'am," the nurse whispered.

He opened his eyes slowly. "Mummy." The voice she had so often found grating sounded small and hopelessly weak in her ears.

"Yes, dear, it's all right. Mummy's here now."

"Will you stay with me? You won't go away and leave me here, will you?"

"No, darling. I'll stay with you." She brushed back the hair plastered to his forehead. He was burning up, but his skin felt clammy.

"Mummy." His voice broke in a horrible racking cough. It was too much for a child. "I knew if I went away, you'd like me better when I came back. You like me better now, Mummy, don't you?"

She was fighting to hold back the tears, and her voice was a sob. "I love you, Jamie, and I've always loved you. You didn't have to run away for that."

"But I did." He coughed again. "So you'd like me better when I came back. You and Uncle Graham. Do you think now he'll come visit again?"

"I'm sure he will, Jamie. He's here now. The doctor said you can see him tomorrow."

The child had heard all that was necessary. He closed his eyes, and soon the small hand relaxed its grip on Claudia's.

Graham was waiting for her in the day room. He looked tired and haggard under the harsh hospital lights. The sight of him released all the pent-up emotion of the last twenty-four hours. Claudia sank against him and began to sob. "Oh, God, Graham, it was all my fault. Jamie didn't get lost. He ran away. He thought it would make me like him better, make both of us love him more." Through sobs she told him the story of Jamie's question about the Lindbergh baby.

"It wasn't all your fault, Claudia. I shouldn't have stopped coming out to the house. I was thinking too much about me—about us."

She stopped crying, and Graham dropped the arm he had put around her in comfort. "We both were, Graham, but I've learned my lesson this time. When Jamie pulls through this, I'll marry you and we'll make a real home for him."

"No, Claudia. You don't have to sacrifice yourself for Jamie. You were right. Things were well enough as they were. I can try to be a father to Jamie without forcing you to be a wife to me. And I promise I will. We've both learned our lesson."

The convulsions started that night. Dr. Gettinger explained they were a normal symptom of pneumonia in children, but each time Claudia saw the small body contort and the back arch high in the air, she thought her heart would break. The fever abated each morning but climbed progressively higher every evening. On the fifth day the convulsions stopped, but the fever reached 105 degrees. On the sixth, 105.5. He continued to cough up great quantities of a brownish red phlegm. When Claudia tried to wipe it from his chin, the nurse reprimanded her. It was highly contagious, she said.

Jamie no longer recognized Claudia as she stood by his bed. Dr. Gettinger tried to convince her to go home and get some rest. Her presence did Jamie no good and herself considerable harm if appearances meant anything. Claudia was adamant. She arrived early each morning and stayed until the nurse forced her to leave at night.

As she sat in the chilly hospital room—fresh air and good ventilation were essential, Dr. Gettinger had explained—on the afternoon of the sixth day Claudia reached out to smooth the hair back from Jamie's damp forehead as she had so many times in the past week. His skin felt like fire. "I'm sure his fever's gone up again." The nurse took a step toward the bed and felt the boy's face. Then she summoned the doctor.

"I expect the crisis will come tonight," Dr. Gettinger said. "All we can do is try to hold the fever down and hope. The night nurse will sit with him, and I'm staying in the country so I'll be on call all night. Now I suggest you go home and get some rest, Claudia. I won't let you stay with Jamie, and you're not doing anyone any good sitting out there in the day room."

But Gettinger knew it was hopeless. At eleven o'clock that night he found her, as he knew he would, alone in the day room, staring with unseeing eyes at the drab green leaves of the hospital wallpaper.

"Now we must be cautious . . ." he began, but she saw the expression on his face and did not allow him to finish.

"You mean he's all right." Her voice sounded like a prayer in his ears.

"Let's not be premature, Claudia. It's too early to tell, but I think the crisis has passed. The fever's down a little—not much but a little, and that's unusual at this hour—and he seemed to be resting more comfortably. We'll know more tomorrow, but . . . well, I'm optimistic."

She called Graham as soon as she got home. She thought Jamie would want to see him when he came to. He agreed to leave early the next morning and go straight to the hospital.

Claudia barely had the energy to get out of her clothes and into a nightgown. She felt almost as helpless as Jamie as Ellen helped her off with her things, and she fell into a deep dreamless sleep. It was the first time in a week she slept through the night.

Claudia arrived at the hospital before eight. She wanted to be there when Jamie awakened. Dr. Gettinger was just coming out of the boy's room. He had not seen Claudia and had not assumed his professional mask. His face was naked in grief.

"No," she began to moan. "No, no, no. . . ." Her cries echoed like a dirge down the hospital corridor.

Book Three

1940

1

Claudia tossed the *Times* aside in annoyance at the five-column headline.

RAF BOMBS BERLIN AND 20 TOWNS:
LIGHT LONDON RAIDS TEST DEFENSE:
NAZI-LED DRIVE IN EGYPT FORESEEN

The country was not at war, but the country was clearly war crazy. Headlines screamed of foreign battles, and the rest of the paper was full of arguments about national defense and pictures of young men—*not men,* she thought, *boys*—registering for the draft and being trained to fight. Even the social pages talked of nothing but benefits for war relief.

The mail was just as bad. This morning there had been requests from the British Book Fund for Soldiers, the French Foreign Fund for Shortwave Broadcasts, Chinese Relief, and British War Relief. The verbal requests were even more plaguing. An hour before a woman Claudia had not seen in six years had called and asked her to serve as co-chairman of a special fund-raising program for Polish refugees.

Claudia answered all the requests for money generously. The demands on her time that she had thus far eluded were getting more difficult to turn down. Polly Chesney had accused her more than once during the past summer of being unpatriotic. Claudia pointed out the term was somewhat inaccurate since America was not at war, but Polly had merely shook her head in disapproval and said Claudia knew exactly what she meant. Harriet Mason was even worse. "I tell you, it's our salvation, Claudia. Finally, there's something for us poor old widow women to do." Claudia felt certain Harriet would emerge from the war furor with a new European husband. Well, that was fine for Harriet, but the only husband, European or otherwise, Claudia had ever wanted had passed beyond her grasp long ago. And if she couldn't have him, she wasn't going to settle for anything less. At least she had learned that much. In the years since Jamie's death Claudia had made a life for herself—quiet, uneventful, and most of all, safe. There had been a time when she wanted excitement. Now all she wanted was the security of hurting no one and knowing she would not be hurt in return.

Wilfred knocked discreetly at the door. "There's a Mr. Van Nyes to see you, madam."

Claudia could not believe it. She hadn't seen Harry Van Nyes since she'd left Paris seventeen years ago. Of course, he'd be home now. The war intruded again.

Harry's appearance startled her. Claudia had watched time take its daily toll of most of her old friends, so there seemed to be no obvious aging. She remembered Harry as a boy. Now she was face to face with a middle-aged man. She brushed his slightly worn cheek with her own.

"Harry! It's so good to see you. It's been years and years."

"I must say you don't show them, Claudia. You don't look a day older than when you left Paris."

Claudia wondered if Harry was as shocked by her appearance as she was by his. "A blatant lie, but one I never mind hearing."

"Well, then barely show them. You're looking well."

"So are you. The gray is very *distingué*. And you don't look quite American. Not quite French, but not quite American either."

"The expatriate life—that man-without-a-country look."

"But you're home now."

"Actually it feels more as if I'd left home. But there was no choice."

"Now I don't want to hear a word about the war, Harry. I want to hear about you."

"Don't worry, Claudia, I have no war stories. I got out early in May before the Germans marched in."

"Harry Van Nyes, do you mean you've been home all this time and haven't come to see me until now?"

"I haven't paid many calls, Claudia, but I was sure I'd see you at one of the benefits. It seems when it comes to raising money for the war effort I'm the next best thing to a Frenchman, Englishman, or exiled Pole."

"I contribute, Harry, but I don't go to the parties."

"From what I hear you don't go anywhere."

"I guess I don't get out much since Jamie. . . ."

"I heard, Claudia. I'm sorry . . . about Sam too. . . ." His voice trailed off. How did one say he was sorry to hear about her son's death and her husband's and her father's and mother's? Three years ago James had finally relinquished his tenuous hold on life, and Elizabeth, as if wearied from her husband's long struggle, had followed six months later.

"It's extraordinary being here with you after all these years." Harry changed the subject. "I've felt peculiar coming home because New York has changed so much, but here in this house it seems nothing has changed. It's almost as if I'd never been away."

"The house is comforting, isn't it? Kate wanted to sell it after Mother and Daddy died, but I couldn't do that. I knew Daddy wouldn't have wanted me to. So I sold the apartment—but of course, you never saw the apartment—and moved the children in here. It's too big for us, and it's impossible to find decent servants; but I'm determined to hold onto it."

"Holding onto it is one thing, Claudia; holding up in it quite another. According to some of your friends, you've become a recluse."

"That's just Polly and Harriet exaggerating."

"That's what I thought at first. I couldn't picture the Claudia I remembered as a recluse, but after all these months without running into you anywhere I'm beginning to think they're right. They say you refuse to go to their parties, and Polly says you could have remarried a dozen times if you'd wanted to but you won't give anyone a chance. You're foolish, Claudia. You're not a woman who was meant to live alone."

"You haven't changed a bit, Harry. I haven't seen you for years, and without a moment's hesitation you're wading into my personal life—a little indelicately, I think."

"In other words what they say is true."

She thought of her life since Denbigh. There was Graham, of course, but Graham didn't count. She had never, even during that brief uncomfortable period, thought of Graham as a man. He was a lawyer, a trustee, an adviser, a friend, a member of the family, but he was not a man.

Other men had shown interest, but no one had managed to penetrate her defenses. She remembered the architect who had designed the Chesneys' new country house. It was two summers ago now. Polly had decided the old house was passé. She wanted something modern, something *functional*. Charles said with a staff of eight every house was functional, but Polly overrode him as usual and called in a young architect who had just returned from two years' study in Germany. Polly turned the young man into an architect-in-residence. Geoffrey Turnbull had to be on hand every moment that summer to consult with Polly about the details of the house, to go over the blueprints, and to serve as an extra man. The arrangement afforded mutual satisfaction. The young man was attractive and well bred, with beautiful manners. Polly Chesney for her part put no limitations on the house. She wanted it to be as modern and as expensive as possible. It was Turnbull's first big job and would be sure to bring him more work—if this cursed Depression ever passed.

By the end of the summer Geoffrey Turnbull had completed the plans for Polly Chesney's house and fallen hopelessly in love with her friend Mrs. Beaumont. He knew there would be problems—she was ten years his senior, a widow with two children, and had a fortune while his family had lost everything in the crash—but he was sure, as only a man in his twenties can be, that he would overcome them.

Claudia had never for a moment thought of marrying Geoffrey Turnbull, but she had, one hot August night when he had driven her home from Polly's and they had gone for a swim, considered an affair with him. As she sat on the beach in the sultry, breezeless night and listened to his stories of life at the Bauhaus and holidays in Berlin, she began to emerge from her cocoon. He had kissed her, and she had let him. His body felt young and strong, and he tasted faintly of whiskey and tobacco and salt water. It was a taste she associated with masculinity, and for a moment she felt as if this boy might save her from drowning in the long years of loneliness. Then—she didn't know what it was, perhaps the sight of the house over his shoulder after he had kissed her a second time, perhaps the thought that he was only a boy after all—the moment passed, and she retreated into the safe world she had built for herself.

"It doesn't matter whether it's true or not, Harry. For years now people have been telling me how to live my life, and frankly I'm tired of it. I've lost a husband and a child, and if I choose to live a quiet life, I don't see why anyone should object."

"Stop feeling sorry for yourself, Claudia. There are women all over Europe today who have lost more than you, and they go on fighting."

"I'm sure they do, but there's nothing I want to fight for."

"*That* is exactly my point. They're fighting for life, and you're throwing it away."

"Aren't you being a little melodramatic, Harry? Just because I choose not to go out much, I wouldn't say I'm throwing my life away."

"Well, I would, and now that I'm home I intend to do something about it. Tomorrow night not only are you going to write a fat check for the cause of the Free French, but you are going to a large and vulgar cocktail party to convince others to write equally fat checks."

"I'll give you the money, Harry, but please no parties. The only thing I'm more sick of than war talk is war parties. I did go to a few at first, but there didn't seem to be much point to it. Even if I didn't find the idea of a party in honor of war offensive, I can't stand all those people sitting about trying to outdo each other with 'inside' information. None of them really knows what's happening; but someone invariably starts to argue it's our duty to get into it, and that's the time I write my check and go home."

"Don't tell me you go along with Lindbergh and that group."

Lindbergh. The name still sounded like an accusation.

"I don't go along with any group, Harry. I simply don't believe in war. Besides, to be perfectly selfish about it, I have a son."

"Surely he can't be that old."

"Of course not. Tony is only twelve, but these things always last longer than anyone expects."

"Did it ever occur to you, Claudia, if we don't fight now, there won't be much of a world for Tony or anyone else to grow up in?"

"I've heard it all. This is going to be the war to right all the wrongs. The war to end war. Wasn't that what the last one was for? And how much good did that do?"

"This is different. Hitler is different. The world's never seen anything like this before."

"Wasn't that what you said about the Boches twenty-five years ago?"

"Maybe I did, and maybe I was wrong. But I'm not wrong this time. I know enough about what's going on in Europe to know that."

"Really, Harry, I know you feel strongly about France, I'm sure you have many friends you're concerned about. . . ." Claudia's voice trailed off, and for a moment she seemed unable to go on. She realized that since Wilfred had announced Harry, she had been thinking of Philippe. She had sat there making polite conversation, but all she wanted to do was ask about

Philippe. *Did he still see him? How was he? Was he even alive?* Claudia knew with a shock that every time she had tossed away a newspaper filled with war news it had been as much in fear for Philippe as it had for more disinterested convictions about the war.

What a fool she was! After all she had lived through, how could she still think of Philippe? How ridiculous could she be to grieve at her age for a young love—a young love who had thrown her over without a second thought? Claudia still winced when she remembered that morning in Philippe's hotel room.

She pulled herself up. She might make a fool of herself in her private dreams, but she wouldn't behave like a child in front of anyone else. She would not ask Harry about Philippe. "I'm sure you're concerned about France, Harry. We all are. But I don't see that our concern has to go as far as war. Surely we can help without getting into it ourselves."

"Ah, yes, all aid short of war. That's the cry, isn't it?"

"You can ridicule me all you want, Harry, but you won't convince me we ought to go to war."

"It doesn't matter whether I convince you or anyone else, Claudia. We're going to be in this before long no matter what anyone says."

"If you're so sure of that why do you bother proselytizing?"

"I'm not proselytizing. I'm merely trying to raise funds for the Free French. They, and England, can't hold on forever while we debate the pros and cons of doing what we have to do. They need material support, and if I thought it would help, I'd go to a hundred cocktail parties and force you to go to every one of them with me. Starting tomorrow night, Claudia, you're my secret weapon. I'm sure you can get through to any number of men who wouldn't give me a penny."

"Oh, Harry, I couldn't. I said I'd contribute, but I couldn't ask anyone else to."

"You won't have to. All you have to do is stand there and smile. Surely you can smile for a good cause, can't you, Claudia?"

"Harry, you're impossible."

"I prefer to think of myself as dedicated. And before long I plan to have you the same way."

"I agree to tomorrow night, Harry, in honor of your return, but I make no promises beyond that."

"Come tomorrow night, Claudia, and we'll worry about the rest after that."

The party proved to be much as Claudia had expected. She knew perhaps a third of the expensively dressed men and women who jostled each other in the carefully decorated living room of Mr. and Mrs. Justin Daniels' apartment. Ten years before she supposed she would have known everyone. Or more to the point, ten years before half the people in the room would not have been invited. And she supposed too ten years before the people she did know would have reacted to the idea of Justin Daniels much as they once had to Joseph Denbigh. But they had gone to Joe's parties and ended up by accepting him, and now they were permitting Daniels to give parties for them and they'd end up accepting Daniels and his overdressed wife. Poor Sam, he wouldn't have liked the turn the times were taking.

The air was heavy with smoke, and as Claudia moved about the room, she picked up snatches of conversation above the tinkle of ice and glasses.

"It's moving day, Eleanor, the Willkies are coming." The girl in the violet dress laughed as she repeated the campaign slogan. Once again Claudia wondered how some women could spend a great deal of money on clothes and still manage to end up looking cheap.

The girl was talking to an older man who did not seem to be in the least offended by her attire. "I only hope we can get him out before he gets us into this damn war. I tell you, the man may be an aristocrat, but he's no gentleman." Claudia knew from his tone that the man had been saying the same thing for several years.

She saw Polly and Charles Chesney crossing the

room toward her. Polly might laugh at Mrs. Daniels, but she wouldn't miss one of her parties.

"Surprised to see you here, Claudia," Charles said.

Polly dispensed with greetings. "Where's Oren Root? I heard he's here, and I must meet Oren Root."

"Polly's given up artists this year in favor of politicians," Charles said.

"Who's Oren Root?"

"Honestly, Claudia, you're impossible. I know you never leave that tomb of yours, but don't you even read the paper? Oren Root practically *made* Willkie. And don't say, 'Who's Willkie'?"

"If he practically *made* Willkie, why is he here? I thought Willkie was going to keep us out of the war."

"He's not here for the French, Claudia," Charles said. "He's here for the votes. People like Daniels get people like you and me here to raise money, and Root simply takes advantage of the situation."

"Stop lecturing, Charles," Polly said impatiently. "Are you going to find Root and introduce me or not?"

"Yes, I'm going to introduce you to Root. Coming, Claudia?"

"I think I'll bypass this one. Anyway, I like Roosevelt." She saw the look of surprise on their faces. "Even if he's not a gentleman."

Harry was standing with a small group before the fireplace. "I tell you, it's going to mean change, big change. The last war was the beginning of our era. This one will be the end of it. But it has to be fought."

"How do you mean 'the end of our era'?" Anson Hagerty was not ready to relinquish anything so satisfactory as *his* era, even if he did not understand what it meant.

"Harry's probably right," Claudia broke in. "Remember how our parents used to complain the war had changed everything? If there is a war—and I hope Harry's not right about that—we'll probably end up saying the same thing. We came of age with the last war. We'll probably get old with this one."

"You are full of surprises tonight, Claudia." Lucinda turned her searching eyes on her. As if hunting for a flaw, they took in the carefully arranged blond chignon, the simple crepe dress with the draped bodice, the single strand of pearls. "First you turn up here and then you wax positively philosophical. Is that Harry's influence?"

"The party is Harry's influence. I'm not sure about the philosophy."

"Ah, that's why you're here—for Harry. And I assumed it was for the marquis."

Claudia could feel herself begin to tremble. Her hands were as icy as the glass she held. She turned to Harry. "The marquis?" Her voice sounded unnaturally loud in her ears, even above the noise of the party.

"Didn't I tell you, Claudia? I'm not the attraction tonight. I'm merely an attendant prince, as it were. We're expecting an authentic Free French representative."

"You know very well you told me nothing of the sort."

"Oh, well, I'm sure I meant to. I imagine you remember Philippe de Boissevain."

Claudia turned her back to Lucinda so only Harry could hear her words. "It was a terrible thing to do, Harry. Perhaps you thought you were being amusing, but I assure you there's nothing amusing about it."

"I was merely trying to be kind, Claudia."

"I don't thank you for it."

"Kind to Philippe. You really ought to see him. He's been through so much."

"Who hasn't?" Her voice was still a whisper, but her words were sharp with anger.

"I mean the war."

"Has he been wounded?" She asked the question without meaning to.

Before Harry could answer, she saw him across the room. His face was lined, and the skin across his cheekbones tightly drawn, but only the hollows of his face revealed how thin he had grown, for the uniform, dramatic, almost dashing, was designed to camouflage the ravages of war.

His eyes swept the crowd over the elaborate coiffure of Mrs. Justin Daniels. Then he was across the room in three strides, and they were only inches apart. Impossible as it seemed, she could reach out and touch him.

"Hello, Claudia."

Her memories had been of his eyes—dark and liquid under thick lashes—but it was his mouth that struck her now. It was thin and deeply sensual.

"Hello, Philippe."

His hand was warm against her icy fingers.

"I'm glad you came." He lowered his voice. "I was afraid you wouldn't want to see me."

The memory of their last meeting flooded back. She took her hand from his.

"I didn't know you'd be here."

He had released her hand, but his eyes held hers.

"Would you have come if you had?"

Before she could answer, Mrs. Daniels was between them. "I'm sorry, Mrs. Beaumont, but I must steal the marquis for a moment. I particularly want him to meet the Bowens."

"Please don't leave," he said quietly. "I'll get away as soon as I can."

Claudia merely stood there. The thought of leaving had never crossed her mind.

She watched him as he moved about the room. He smiled easily, shook hands, answered questions, thanked people for their help. He seemed completely at ease, while she could not stop trembling.

Then they were outside the apartment in a taxi threading its way through the noisy evening traffic. In front of the grille elevators in the lobby of the Plaza Hotel, Philippe explained he had to turn some things over to the Count de Rochefleur and then they could have dinner.

"Would you like to come up? The count is De Gaulle's personal representative here. You might enjoy meeting him."

"I think I'll wait here."

Philippe smiled. It was a real smile, not the formal

one he had been using so effectively all evening. "You've become cautious, Claudia. I didn't think it was possible."

She laughed for the first time since she had seen him and preceded him into the elevator.

The count's appearance was unimposing, but his manner left no doubt about his own sense of importance. He was polite but abrupt. Clearly there were more important things on his mind.

Claudia wandered about the sitting room of the suite while the two men spoke in rapid French, their voices quiet and confidential. There was nothing of Philippe in the room, no traces of his past or the man he had become. The only signs of life were the overflowing ashtrays, the newspapers and magazines scattered about, and Philippe's kepi and gloves on a table beside the count's civilian things. It said a great deal about the times but little about Philippe.

Where was the boy she had loved? She had thought him a man then, but she saw the two of them now as such children. Was there anything left of those children in the two distant people who had met tonight? In her fantasies she had known the answer, but in Philippe's presence she began to doubt it.

"I have enjoyed meeting you, Mrs. Beaumont." The count spoke in French, and it took Claudia a moment to realize he was addressing her. Her face must have shown surprise, and Philippe explained the count was taking the ten o'clock train to Washington. He bowed politely over her and was gone.

"Now that's taken care of, where would you like to dine? I've only been in New York a fortnight, so I'm afraid you'll have to decide." Without thinking he had passed his hand over his eyes as he spoke.

"Perhaps we'd better forget dinner. You don't look quite up to it."

"Please don't leave, Claudia." The alarm in his face, the urgency in his voice startled her. She must be careful not to read too much into it. It was wartime; he was lonely; he did not want to dine alone. It was no more than that. Well, she could do as much for the cause as

386

Harry or Polly or any of them. She could dine with a war hero. "Very well, I won't leave, but I don't think you're up to a night on the town."

"We could have something sent up." She hesitated and saw him smiling. "And you were the girl who loved giving people something to talk about."

She could hear her own voice of years ago as clearly as his. *Then isn't it lucky I give the American community something to gossip about, Kate?* "We could have something sent up," she agreed.

"Would you like a whiskey while we wait? The count left some ice."

His hand touched hers as he gave her the glass. She withdrew it as if startled, but if Philippe noticed, he pretended not to.

"Tell me what you're doing over here." She tried to make her words impersonal as if there were no other questions behind them. *Why are you here with me now? Why did you ask Harry to bring me tonight?*

"What I've been doing is exactly what you saw me doing tonight. Going from party to party begging." *Would you have come if you had known I'd be there? Do you still hate me after all these years? Could you still love me after all these years?*

"Surely not begging."

"I don't mind. It's the most useful function I can serve these days. Collecting money, support, anything for the *cause*." He pronounced the word with a faint touch of mockery, but she knew he was ridiculing himself rather than the war.

"I thought you didn't approve of war." She could still remember his anger that first day at Les Deux Magots. She had spoken of glory and honor, and he had taught her neither existed in battle.

"I don't approve of war, but my disapproval won't make it go away. And in the meantime we need all the money and matériel we can get."

"And when you've got enough, will you go back to France?" *Will you go back to your wife?*

She means, will I go back to Simone? "There's no France left, Claudia, only Vichy, and I won't go back to that. Of course I had planned to at first. Most of us who got out at Dunkirk planned to return through the south. . . ."

"Dunkirk! You went through Dunkirk!"

"Unscathed as you can see."

"Somehow I can never picture you in the army, and somehow you always are." It was her first reference to the past, and she cursed herself.

"Not always, Claudia."

They both thought of the years between, the years that had made them strangers.

"And I wasn't in battle this time. Not even a new scar to show for it."

She wished he did not sound so cavalier about the war. It was not like him, or at least not like the Philippe she had known. "Not in battle. What do you call Dunkirk?"

"An evacuation."

"But you had to be with troops to be evacuated."

He heard the concern in her voice. Was it merely the proper response everyone made to the war, or did she really care what happened to him?

"I was with them for less than a week. I had been posted to the Deuxième Bureau in Paris. Technically that's intelligence, but I was given the crucial task of protecting our national art treasures. That was all they would trust me with."

"I don't believe it." He still used jokes to hide from her everything that was important to him.

"It's true. I served as minister of culture in the Popular Front government back in '36." *What were you doing in '36, Claudia? Harry told me your husband was dead. He said you married again, but it lasted less than a year. Was there someone else by '36?* "Not only does that qualify me to take charge of all those treasures, but it makes me clearly suspect to the Deuxième Bureau. They're not fond of Leon Blum or his followers. We're all one step away from Reds as far as they're concerned." *Bolsheviks, your beloved daddy used to call them.* "But with Hitler at the door they'd accept anyone's services, even ours—in noncritical positions, that is. So there I was drawing up contingency plans to save the Louvre."

And where was your wife? "That's a long way from Dunkirk."

"They needed a messenger—someone expendable— to send to the First Army in the north. But by the time I got there very little of the First Army was left. Half of them were surrounded by the Germans at Lille; the other half were being evacuated with the BEF. I got out with them. On a London fire float of all things."

He seemed to sense the question that was coming and stood suddenly. "Here, let me freshen your drink."

The absence of his eyes watching her every response gave her courage. "And your family? Did they get out, too?"

She thought she detected a missed beat in his movements at the sideboard; but his back was to her, and she could not read his expression. "My wife and son are with her family in the unoccupied zone. They're quite safe there. Her family is strongly Pétainist." There was no mistaking the note of distaste in his voice.

He handed her a fresh drink and sat down. His face was perfectly composed, but she saw his hand touch his scar.

"Mother's there, too. Father died two years ago. I guess I ought to be grateful he missed all this. Vichy would have pained him, but he never could have turned against Pétain—or followed De Gaulle. The upstart, he used to call him. They all do."

Claudia thought he looked relieved at the knock on the door. Of course, he'd be relieved. Philippe did not want to talk about his wife. It was poor strategy.

The talk through dinner was halting and impersonal. They discussed the war, of course. America would be in before long, but in the meantime, the Free French and British had to hold on. He did not agree with De Gaulle on many points, but De Gaulle was the only rallying point for a reasonable Frenchman. She might as well have been with Harry Van Nyes.

"Would you like a brandy?" The table had been removed, and she was across the room from him. He felt as if she were across an ocean.

"No, thank you. I really must be going." It had gone on too long. There was nothing left.

"I'll just get my hat and coat," he said.

"You needn't see me home. I can get a taxi downstairs."

"It's no trouble."

Impersonal, polite, meaningless words. Their sentences brushed against each other, then backed off apologetically.

He took her coat from the chair where she had tossed it two hours before. She was aware of him close behind her as he dropped it over her shoulders. She felt the years of loneliness and abstinence welling up within her. His lips were at her ear. "Claudia, my God, what are we doing? Have we become strangers?"

She whirled around and took a step back. She must keep a distance between them. "There is no *we*, Philippe. There hasn't been for seventeen years. You saw to that."

"Are you really so sure? Is it so easy for you to place the blame?"

"I wasn't the one who married before the winter was out."

He slumped into a chair, suddenly tired again. "No, I was the one who did that. And you're not going to let me forget it. Or my wife in the unoccupied zone."

"One would hope you wouldn't have to be reminded of her."

"My wife and I have led separate lives for some years now."

And you've had your women, I suppose. "How convenient for you. Really, Philippe, the next thing I know you'll be telling me your wife doesn't understand you. Isn't that the usual approach?"

He was on his feet barely inches from her, and she could read the familiar anger in his eyes. "My wife understands me perfectly, Claudia. She understands I've never loved her. She understands I loved someone else when I married her and I've gone on loving someone else ever since. That's why we live apart."

"Surely you're exaggerating. If you had loved someone else, you would never have married your wife."

"Why did you marry Beaumont?"

"That was different. You were already married."

"And you had already left me. Why, Claudia? How could you run away after Montreux?"

She took another step back as if the word were a caress. "Don't talk to me about Montreux!"

"If only you'd stayed."

She had said the same thing to herself a hundred times. "For how long? A week, a month, a year?"

"Let me show you something." He took a soft leather bill fold from his pocket. In a hidden compartment was a worn piece of paper. It was yellow with age, and as he opened it, the paper parted along the folds. "Frau Schwarzburgen forwarded this to me. It came to the chalet the day we left."

She took the paper from him gingerly as if it might contaminate her with some disease. Above the prefect's ostentatious signature were a few lines in formal French. Their papers were in order, and they could be married at their earliest convenience. That afternoon, if they wished.

"Oh, Philippe." She sobbed. "I'm sorry. If only I hadn't been such a fool, such a cowardly fool." His arms were around her, folding her to him, and his words soft and consoling in her ear. "It was my fault, Claudia. I never should have let you go. But it doesn't matter anymore. I've found you again. That's all that matters."

She started to say something, but his mouth on hers drowned the words. They'd had enough words, more than enough for one night. They had talked and talked and said nothing to each other. And now she was in his arms again, and everything was clear. They were together. They had never really been apart. She had no doubts now.

The image of Simone de Chauvres—Simone de

Boissevain—flashed through her mind. She didn't care. She was tired of being safe. Philippe was here, and she was in his arms again. That was all that mattered.

They seemed to be moving slowly back through time. She was no longer a thirty-eight-year-old woman but a nineteen-year-old girl, and Philippe's hands on her body told her it was as fresh and desirable and miraculously yielding as a young girl's. He was not the stranger of a few hours ago, but her own Philippe, dark and strong above her in the narrow bed.

She touched his eyes, his mouth, the scar, fainter now than she remembered it. She felt his hands tangled in the web of her hair and his mouth on hers, speaking their own wordless language. Her flesh seemed to have a memory of its own recognizing, responding, following him as if there had been no years between, and she was like a flower opening to him, and he was with her, inside her, part of her, all of her.

"As soon as the war is over, I'll get a divorce. It isn't easy, but with money and the right connections in the church it can be done."

"And of course, Simone has both." She had not pulled away from him, but her voice sounded as if she had dressed and moved across the room.

She saw him flinch as surely as if she had slapped him. "I'm sorry, Philippe, but let's not talk about divorce. It sounds so tawdry. Just another wartime affair."

"We're not that, Claudia."

"Isn't that what everyone thinks? We're different. We're special."

"I don't know if we're special, but I do know this isn't just a wartime affair. And you know it, too."

She wanted to believe it so much she was afraid to. She wanted it to last so desperately that to talk of its lasting would be tempting fate.

"I know it, darling, but"—she forced a laugh—"we're too old to make plans for after the war."

"Ah, yes," he murmured. "Too old." His mouth

moved from her eyes to her mouth to her throat. "Absolutely ancient. The two of us, you know, darling"—his head came to rest on her breast—"we're quite beyond love."

2

"We'll have coffee and brandy in the library, Wilfred."
Claudia caught herself. She had almost said in "Father's
library." Strange how after all these years it was still
James' library. She supposed if there were another man
in the house, it would become his library. The irony of
Daddy's library becoming Philippe's was not unpleasant.
Claudia couldn't believe after all these years Daddy
would still mind.

It was their first night alone in the weeks since they
had found each other again. Every night there had been
some party or dinner to raise funds, someone to see who
might help the cause, some appearance Philippe must
make. Claudia resented every demand on him except her
own. Surely after all these years they should leave him
to her. But they would not leave him to her, so she went
along and soon became knowledgeable in matters of the
cause. It was not as simple as it might seem, for in the
autumn of 1940 for the French both at home and
abroad there were many causes. Claudia discovered that
one night at 21. A short, balding man stopped at their
table.

"Boissevain! I didn't know you were in New York,"
he said in French. His greeting held all the warmth of a
wartime reunion in a foreign land.

Philippe introduced the man to Claudia and the
others at the table.

"Have you seen Fournet?" the man asked Philippe.
"He was behind me a moment ago. I know he'll want to
see you."

At that moment Claudia saw a man with a round face and a mane of white hair brushed back from a receding hairline approaching their table. When he and Philippe saw each other, each looked quickly away. The man called Fournet changed his direction and did not pass their table. Claudia was certain he and Philippe had cut each other because of her.

"That Fournet," she said when they were alone in the taxi, "is he a relative of your wife?"

"No."

"A friend then?"

"They've met occasionally."

"And that's why he cut you and you turned away. Because of me?" Claudia wasn't certain what she was annoyed about, but there was something in her position she did not like.

Philippe laughed. "I hate to disappoint you, darling, but none of that had anything to do with you. You may be the most important person in the world to me, but I doubt Pierre Fournet even noticed you. I know that's hard to believe, but in this case it's true."

"Then why did he avoid you?"

"I prefer to think we avoided each other. Fournet is the recognized head of the French community in New York. That's the way the magazines describe him. He is also a zealous Vichyite. That's why we didn't speak. It's a shame. I used to like Pierre."

"Do you mean you won't even speak to an old friend because of some political disagreement?"

"This is more than a political disagreement, Claudia. Either you stand against Hitler or you might as well stand behind him. And that's exactly where Vichy stands."

It had taken only a few conversations like that one for Claudia to become familiar with the landscape. The Vichyites were reprehensible, not to be spoken to. The anti-Vichyites, who were nevertheless willing to break the British blockade to send food to France, were misguided. They were to be argued with. The supporters of De Gaulle, no matter what their individual views, were to be tolerated as a means to an end. And so it went.

Claudia might be persuaded to see it all as a childish game if Philippe had not taken it so seriously.

She watched him now moving about the library. He stopped before a collection of silver-framed pictures on the Regency library table. Among photographs of the children and James and Elizabeth was a picture of Sam on *Revenge*.

Philippe was shocked at the wave of jealousy that surged through him. The man had been dead for ten years. And Claudia had never loved him. He knew that now. Still, the man's very existence clawed at Philippe. He had been a big man, fair, and, from his stance at the helm, graceful. His hands on the wheel looked large and strong. They were the same hands that had touched Claudia, his Claudia. Philippe despised the man—and was ashamed of himself for it.

Claudia crossed the room and laid a hand on his arm. She could not very well remove all traces of Sam—after all, the children must have photographs of their father about—but she wanted Philippe to know Sam did not matter, had never mattered. Yet how would she have felt if she had found a photograph of Simone in Philippe's hotel room that first night? Their love was too intense to admit other people—even the shadows of other people.

"If you're going to Washington, I'm going, too." Beneath the covers Claudia moved closer to Philippe. She was not looking forward to the ride home in the bleak January night. If only she could stay here in the apartment Philippe had been lent by friends, if only she could spend a single night with him. It seemed little enough to ask, but it was precisely what she could not do.

She remembered the argument she'd had with Katherine a few weeks before. Kate had come for lunch on the last day of the children's holiday. The sisters were alone in the downstairs hall after watching Tony and Diana, looking small and glum in the backseat of the big car, drive off.

"I feel so sorry for them every time they go back after

a holiday. Once they're there, I know they like it, but there's always that moment when I want to run out and snatch them up and tell them they don't have to go back."

"I never knew you had such a strong maternal streak, Claudia. Anyway, if they don't go back, they'd only be in the way. The holidays must have been a terrible hardship for you with Tony and Diana home. So inhibiting to have one's children around in the middle of an affair."

"I don't know what you're talking about, Kate."

"Oh, come on, Claudia, everyone knows. Even if they don't talk about it to me, they do to each other."

"And just what are people saying?"

"About what they do in cases like this. The details vary, but one tawdry affair is pretty much like another. They say he has a wife in France. Tell me, Claudia, how do you like being the other woman? Well, it's none of my business. You can do as you like so long as you don't involve the children. I don't think Sam would have liked your involving the children in something like this."

"My, aren't we fastidious?"

"When it comes to Sam's children, yes."

"But not when it comes to Sam or your own sister."

"It's a little late for you to play the victim, Claudia."

"Are you sure you want to go to Washington?" Philippe's voice in the darkness called her back to the present.

What a foolish question! Of course, she wanted to go to Washington if he was going. She wanted to go wherever he was going. Her one fear was that he would be recalled to London and she would not be able to follow. No matter how imperfect things were now—the sneaking about in the middle of the night, the gossip, the gnawing knowledge that across an ocean there was a woman who had a legal claim to Philippe, one she might not relinquish—at least they were together. But that could change at any moment. Claudia never forgot that the whim of some officer in London could take Philippe from her without warning. Time after time he reassured her it wouldn't happen. "I may not be much use here, but apparently they think I'm better off here than back at headquarters."

"Of course, I want to go to Washington if you're going."

"People may talk."

"People *will* talk."

"What happened to all that caution of a few months ago?"

"I left it at the Plaza."

"I'll get you a room on a different floor."

"It won't fool anyone."

"Then at a different hotel."

"It still won't fool anyone."

"Shameless hussy."

She could feel the laugh run through his body, and she turned to him. She would have to leave soon, but for the moment there was time.

America was still not at war. The President had been given a third term on the promise that America would not go to war. *"I have said this before, and I will say it again and again. Your boys will not be sent to fight in any foreign war."* But representatives of foreign governments jockeyed with representatives of crucial industries to get a foot in the door of the right offices, and the once-quiet halls of the imposing federal buildings erupted in noisy activity as the nation raced toward war.

Claudia had never cared much for Washington. It seemed to her a southern town moving at a northern pace. Now the pace had quickened, and the city was a madhouse. Restaurants and nightclubs were packed. Taxis were impossible to get. If she had not valued privacy more than convenience, she would have come down in her own car with her own driver, but in this case the difficulty of getting around was more than compensated for by the pleasure of her newfound freedom. With the children back at school and anyone who might take an interest in the comings and goings of Mrs. Samuel Beaumont at a safe distance, Claudia reveled in anonymity. The madness of the city only contributed to it. If the hotel maids found the traces of two people in her suite and no sign of occupation in Philippe's room, it made no difference to them. There was more to worry about in Washington in February, 1941, than the comings and goings of a Free French major and an obscure, exquisitely dressed woman.

Claudia stood under the hotel marquee now as Philippe queued up for a taxi. The line behind the doorman was long, and Philippe's uniform made no difference. There were three Japanese officers in front of him and a very important-looking British admiral.

She felt the cold, damp wind cut through her chinchilla coat. She was still uneasy about the evening ahead. It would be a large dinner party and, Philippe hoped, an important one for him. He had spent the week they had been in Washington trying to get through to a variety of congressmen instrumental in something called Bill No. 1776. It was, he explained to Claudia, the President's lend-lease program.

"Surely the President doesn't need your help on that," she said with a laugh.

"There's a good chance that in order to get it through, they'll limit aid to Great Britain, China, and Greece. The real point, of course, is to keep it from Russia, but nobody seems to remember the Free French in this."

"But aid to England is aid to the Free French."

"Tell that to the general. Anyway, it's my job to recruit anyone who has any influence on that bill."

"And that's where tonight comes in?"

"That's where tonight comes in. The dinner's being given by an industrialist—airplanes—but there'll be plenty of government men there."

"The invitation said Selwegg. Is that the airplane man?"

"There are two of them. Selwegg and a younger one, his son-in-law, I think. Whitely's the name."

"Tom Whitely?"

"That's the one. Do you know him?"

"I've never met him, but I certainly know of him. Tom Whitely was Katherine's husband. It was years ago and only for a period of months, but they were married. Perhaps you'd better go to this dinner alone."

"If you'd rather."

Claudia could read the disappointment in his face. They seemed to have little enough time as it was. "I don't mind meeting him," she said. "In fact, I'd love to meet him. I've always been curious about Kate's husband. But as Kate's sister I'd probably be something of a liability."

"I doubt very much, Claudia, you'd ever be a liability, but in this case, there's no problem. Whitely was the one I gave your name to for the invitation, and if he didn't recognize it then—and I'm pretty certain he didn't—he doesn't know who you are. Or doesn't care. Besides, Whitely isn't the one I'm worried about. It's all those government types."

"I promise to be on my best behavior with all those government types, though I warn you if they're as bad as that representative from Illinois I had to dance with last night, it won't be easy. I wouldn't have minded his stepping on my feet all night if he hadn't told those terrible jokes while he was doing it. How many planes do you think you'll get for our efforts?"

"Not a single one. Just a little goodwill."

"Well, you'd better hurry and get the planes—before *my* goodwill runs out."

The idea of Kate's being married to this large, balding man with a protruding abdomen that clearly proclaimed he thought any sort of physical exercise an absurdity amused Claudia. And Whitely's wife, small and round like a soft Kewpie doll, was as unlike her sister as any woman could be. If Whitely had married his second wife for practical reasons—and after meeting Mrs. Whitely's father, Effrem Selwegg, Claudia suspected he had—the marriage had clearly succeeded. Claudia couldn't help feeling a little sorry for her sister.

Mrs. Whitely had moved off to greet the other guests, and Claudia stood with Philippe and Tom Whitely pretending to listen to their talk of B17s and B25s. Suddenly a word from a conversation between the two women standing behind her caught her attention. Had they really said "Denbigh" or was it her imagination? And if they had, so what? Surely there were scores of Denbighs in the world. *But not in Washington,* Claudia thought.

"She's a Guest on her mother's side," one of the women said. "And I can tell you her mother wasn't happy about the match. Though what could the poor woman do? From what I've heard the girl was simply head over heels in love with him. Despite the age difference. He's almost twice as old as she is."

"He was married before, wasn't he?"

"I think I heard something like that, though he never talks about it, and he's not the sort of man one wants to ask personal questions. Delightful as he is, there's something forbidding about him."

"I know what you mean. There's an air about him. A kind of"—the woman laughed self-consciously—"raw power. Perhaps it's the trait of self-made men, but whatever it is Joe Denbigh has it. Maybe that's what the little Guest girl saw in him."

The two women drifted off, and Claudia forced herself to focus on Philippe's conversation with Whitely. She did not dare think about Joe.

"I think I have just the man you want to meet, Major. Dollar-a-year man in the National Defense Commission. He doesn't have much of a title, but don't let that fool you. And he's from New York so he's close to Representative Golden. I don't have to tell you Golden is one of the sponsors of seventeen seventy-six. The point is Denbigh's on the ground floor as far as military preparedness goes. He's influential in who gets the steel and who's going to get the butter and carries a lot of weight about what can be spared—and for whom. Now's as good a time as any for you to meet him. He's right over there."

Of them all Joe seemed to have changed least. He was still darkly handsome, though when she saw him standing next to Philippe, Claudia no longer saw the similarity. Denbigh hadn't put on a pound, but compared to

Philippe, he looked fat and contented. The years had been kind to him, and the coming war was no threat.

"How are you, Claudia?" Joe interrupted Whitely's introduction. "You're looking well."

His words were polite and impersonal. He indicated no more than that they had known each other in the past, but it was enough. She knew Philippe had picked up the current between them. She stood in the hot glare of both men's gazes.

Gratefully Claudia saw Mrs. Whitely heading toward them. "Dinner everyone. Tom, will you take Mrs. Beaumont in?" Mercifully, Claudia was seated far down the table from Joe.

She thought she had escaped him, at least for the evening, but as she was standing alone for a moment in the foyer waiting for Philippe to finish a last word with someone from the War Department, she felt Denbigh beside her.

"Your friend Major Boissevain is coming to see me next week, Claudia. I'm not sure I got his first name correctly. What was it? Philippe?" He did not give her a chance to answer. "I must say I'm surprised, Claudia. Not shocked, but surprised. I see I underestimated you. But then you always underestimated me, too. Perhaps it was one of our problems."

"I scarcely think this is the time or the place. . . ."

"I scarcely think this is the time or the place for that tone. After all, we go back a long way together. That's why I'm glad the major's coming to see me rather than some stranger. I wouldn't want him to have to ask favors from a stranger, and I feel as if he and I are old friends. We have so much in common."

In the taxi on the way home she asked Philippe if Denbigh were as important as Whitely made him seem. "Surely that man from the War Department, the one you were talking to before we left, would be a more direct route."

He took her hand in both of his. He had drawn off the glove and was stroking her fingers as he spoke. "Don't worry about it, Claudia. This isn't a personal matter. Denbigh and I are only going to talk about planes."

Philippe asked no questions and said nothing more about Joe, but later, in the darkness of her hotel room, Claudia sensed an unspoken anger. There was an edge to his passion and a certain fierce desperation in his movements, as if he were using his body, their bodies, to obliterate something in his mind.

Denbigh's secretary put her through immediately.

"Good morning, Claudia. I was expecting your call."

She ignored his words and tone. "I must talk to you."

"I was expecting that, too. I take it you want to talk to me without your major."

"You're not making this easy for me."

"Is there any reason I should?"

"Can I come to your office today?"

He paused as if looking over a calendar. "Today's rather tight, Claudia, but . . . I have an idea. Why don't you stop by my apartment this evening? We'll be able to talk privately. My wife—I did mention I married again, didn't I?—is in New York this week."

Claudia hesitated. She thought of Philippe and all his talk of the cause. She thought of some anonymous officer in London scrawling an order: *Recall Boissevain.* "I'll be there at six," she said dully.

Joe answered the door himself and showed her into the living room. She recognized a few paintings and one or two pieces from his apartment in New York and the house in Connecticut, but now they were blended with impeccable style. Joseph Denbigh had come a long way.

She started as he went to take her coat from her. "What I have to say won't take long."

"Let's be civilized, Claudia. You can't stand there talking to me in a coat. Why don't you sit down and I'll make us each a drink and then you can tell me what all this is about?" He took the coat from her shoulders.

"You know perfectly well what all this is about. You can't refuse to help Philippe because of me."

As he handed her a drink, he shook his head as if something were very sad. "You still haven't learned, have you, Claudia? I can do whatever I want, and in this case it's poor strategy for you of all people to tell me what I can and cannot do."

"But what Philippe wants is important, more important than our personal feelings. Certainly you can't let your hatred for me stop you from helping a good cause."

"There are a good many good causes these days, Claudia. It's merely a matter of priorities."

"Surely the Free French are high on your list of priorities."

"My, my, the major has made a convert of you, hasn't he?"

"You have to help him! I'll do anything you want if you'll only promise to help him."

"I thought you might. That's why I suggested you come here rather than my office."

She felt as if someone had run an icy finger down her spine.

"You really love him that much, Claudia? You'll go to any length to help him—and his cause, of course. We mustn't forget his cause."

"Yes!" She was defiant now. He might force her into anything, but he would know why. He would know it was out of love for another man and contempt for him.

His laughter was cruel and mocking.

"What do *you* know about it?"

"I know you, Claudia. You're too selfish to love anyone. At least to love anyone that selflessly. But I do think you love the drama—the idea of sacrificing yourself for your love. And it would be a terrible sacrifice for you, wouldn't it? You couldn't bear to feel my hands on you again, so familiar and knowing, could you?"

She turned away from him. His eyes on her were like a touch.

"Well, don't worry, I won't force myself on you. Oh, you're still desirable, I'll give you that. But who wants to make love to a sacrifice? Although"—he leaned toward her and began to toy with a stray wisp of hair that had escaped her hat—"I'm not entirely sure it would be a sacrifice for you. I have some vivid memories. Do you remember that night in Bar Harbor—"

She jumped up from the couch and took several steps away from him. "I didn't come here to discuss our past."

He laughed. "More's the pity. I enjoy reminiscing. About some things, that is. You're a bitch, Claudia, but there aren't many women who can hold a candle to you—in or out of bed."

"You're vulgar."

"And I thought I was being complimentary."

She stood for a moment in the center of the room, trying to get her bearings. "What are you going to do about Philippe? Will you help him?"

"I haven't decided yet. Of course, I have to hear his case."

"Then you won't let what happened between us influence your decision?"

"I didn't say that. I only said I hadn't made up my mind. That's one of the reasons I didn't take you up on your offer. It was an offer, wasn't it, Claudia? I want to be free to deal with your major, and I wouldn't be if I had accepted favors from his mistress."

His handsome features composed themselves into a sneer, and she wanted to strike out at him; but she knew it was the one thing she could not do. If she had won nothing for Philippe this afternoon, at least she hadn't lost him anything. And perhaps she had achieved something after all. Perhaps Joe would be satisfied with his humiliation of her and not find it necessary to make Philippe pay as well.

Denbigh's office was small and very neat. On the desk were two phones, a leather-framed blotter, a handsome pen and ink stand. There were no papers. This was not the office of a civil service bureaucrat. This was the office of a decision maker, a man who traded in other men.

Denbigh stood as Philippe entered. The two men shook hands across the desk rather like boxers before a fight.

"Good of you to come see me, Major." The words were hearty, but the tone was cool.

"It's good of *you* to see me, Mr. Denbigh." A straightforward approach, Philippe reasoned, would be best. Denbigh knew he held all the cards. "I know you're a busy man, and I'll get straight to the point. As a representative of General de Gaulle and the Free French I'm naturally interested in the fate of the seventeen seventy-six."

"As we all are, Major."

"Specific amendments to the bill are, of course, of special interest to us. . . ."

"You overestimate me, Major," Denbigh broke in. "I'm not a congressman. I have no influence on what is or is not included in seventeen seventy-six. Of course, if you want to talk specifically about planes or matériel, I'm willing to listen, but even there I'm afraid I can't be much help. I'm merely one of Mr. Knudsen's lesser functionaries. All we're concerned with here at the Advisory Commission is getting the guns and planes out. We have nothing to say about where they go."

"I understand the purpose of the commission, Mr. Denbigh, but I also understand your influence in Washington in general and on certain members of Congress in particular."

"I'm afraid you're not listening, Major. I told you, my job is simply to help transform a peacetime economy into one ready for war. I have no influence on where military matériels go or on legislation determining that."

"Surely, you're being modest, Mr. Denbigh. You could, if you chose to. . . ."

"But perhaps I don't choose to."

"I can understand your fear of arming Russia, but the Free French—you can't have any reason for not sending a few planes directly to General de Gaulle rather than channeling them through the English."

Denbigh seemed to be measuring Philippe, as well as his words. When he spoke, his tone was friendly. "I suggest you ask Mrs. Beaumont my reasons."

Philippe was taken back. He had expected sparring, but he had not been prepared for open warfare. Denbigh had challenged him as surely as if he had slapped him. Philippe struggled to drive thoughts of Claudia from his mind. This was not the time for personal vendettas.

"We were speaking of the Free French."

"*You* were speaking of the Free French, Major. I've said nothing about them."

"But surely our cause is yours."

"Is it? I'm not at all certain you and I see things alike."

"I was not speaking of you and me, I was speaking of all of us, Americans, British, Free French. I was speaking politically, not personally."

"That's admirable of you, Major, but perhaps I'm not up to your standards. You see I often find it hard to isolate issues so clearly."

It took all of Philippe's determination to keep from getting up and walking out of the office. He had known men who wielded power for their own pleasure and personal ends, but he had never seen anyone apply it so blatantly.

"Perhaps I could clarify the issue for you. The Free French. . . ."

"I didn't say I didn't understand the issue, Major. I said I sometimes have trouble separating it from other concerns. If you're interested in what those concerns are, I suggest again you ask Mrs. Beaumont."

Philippe's fist tightened on the arms of his chair. "Mrs. Beaumont has nothing to do with this."

"She has everything to do with it. You don't really believe you and I could have a conversation that didn't concern Claudia? Or didn't she tell you? Claudia was my wife. That's right, Major, your mistress was once my wife. It makes a difference, don't you think—our both knowing her so well." His voice seemed to hold and caress the word "knowing."

Philippe was still gripping the arms of his chair, and he felt sure if he looked down, he would see the marks of his fingernails had torn the leather upholstery. "Now General de Gaulle would like—"

"Ah, yes, General de Gaulle. You and Claudia are

both so single-minded, so devoted to the cause of the Free French. You did know Claudia came to see me, didn't you? I see from your face you didn't. I'm sure she meant to tell you, Major—eventually. Don't misunderstand me. She came entirely on your behalf. You know how determined Claudia can be, and she was determined to help you. In fact, she was willing to do anything to make sure I did. Absolutely anything."

The dam exploded. Pure physical hatred surged through Philippe. He was on his feet without knowing it. Denbigh was just beginning to rise when the force of Philippe's fist against his jaw sent him back into his chair.

Joe's first instinct was that of the killer. Then his cunning took over. He had achieved his end. He would not now be caught scuffling in his office. How much better to have Boissevain removed by guards. He pressed a button on his desk.

The major was still standing above him. Denbigh could hear his shallow breathing, more from anger than exertion. He looked startled—as much by his own action as the lack of response to it, Denbigh suspected.

"It's a shame, Major," Denbigh said as two uniformed guards came through the door. "I was prepared to cooperate with you—in the end." He smiled as he rubbed his chin. "If only you had been patient."

Outside the vast marble building the snow had turned to an icy sleet. Philippe walked briskly without destination. He crossed block after block as if in a daze. He could not believe he had hit Denbigh, though his gently throbbing hand told him he had. How had he done it? He wasn't a violent man. He prided himself on his rationality and self-control. The fury he felt toward Denbigh mingled with a deep shame. He had endangered the entire French cause for a personal whim.

Philippe said nothing to Claudia of his meeting with Denbigh, and she did not ask about it. She suspected from Philippe's silence things had not gone well, but he continued his dogged pursuit without the aid of

Denbigh. At this very moment he was struggling to win over an influential Virginia senator.

Claudia turned off the radio. No matter which program she dialed, it always turned into war news sooner or later. The trees in the park below were shadows in the dusk. She began walking around the suite, turning on lights. Philippe would be back soon. He must not find her brooding in the dark.

The knock at the door was not his. She knew that even before she opened it and found the Count de Rochefleur.

"Forgive me for intruding, Mrs. Beaumont; but Major Boissevain was not in his room, and I thought I might find him here." He did not have to explain why he thought that. There was little room for personal secrets in wartime.

"I'm expecting him any minute. Would you care to wait? I was just going to call down for some tea."

"No, thank you, Mrs. Beaumont. If you'll ask the major to call me when he gets in. I'm in Room"—he looked at the key in his hand—"Four Thirteen."

"I'll have him call as soon as he gets in. I trust there's nothing wrong." It was a politeness she uttered without thought. She had not expected the count to talk to her about their affairs, but then she saw the look on his face. "There is something wrong!"

"Not at all," he lied.

Claudia's mind raced ahead to the worst she could think of. "He's being sent back to England."

"Mrs. Beaumont, I really think I'd better speak to the major. . . ."

"But you can't, you can't send him back to England."

"I have nothing to do with it."

"He's been working so hard here. He's done so much."

"Too much, apparently."

"What do you mean?"

"Mrs. Beaumont, perhaps you'll forgive me if I speak plainly. The major is no longer useful here because of an unfortunate incident with a Mr. Denbigh, a man with rather important connections, at least so far as we're concerned. I don't know the details of the situation, but I know the major well enough to know it was entirely out of character. I'm not suggesting the incident itself had anything to do with you, but I have noticed a change in the major in the last months."

"Are you suggesting I interfere with the major's work?"

"I'm suggesting there are times in a man's life when he must be free of ties."

"I don't agree with you."

"I didn't expect you to. Nevertheless, I'm not sure you're the best judge in this case."

"I think I'm an excellent judge when it comes to the major. I'm sorry if I've interfered with his work, but there's more to life than the cause."

"Don't be smug, Mrs. Beaumont. You may be doing him more harm than good."

"By giving him something to care about besides his work?"

"As I said, there are times in a man's life when he ought not to care. It can make him bold when he ought to be cautious. It can also—and perhaps this is more dangerous—make him cautious when he ought to be bold."

"What do you mean?"

"In wartime, in order to survive, one has to live in the present, not the past or the future."

"I assure you, I'm well aware of that, Count."

"Well, then as long as we agree, Mrs. Beaumont, there's no problem. I'll be on my way now. Please tell the major I'll be waiting for his call. It's important that I speak to him immediately."

Philippe looked tired and dejected when he returned from his meeting with the Count de Rochefleur.

"They're sending you back to England, aren't they?" He nodded.

"And it's all because of me."

Philippe's smile was wan. "It isn't because of anyone, least of all you, darling. There's a war going on in Europe. In wartime people get shifted here and there as a matter of course."

"It's because of Denbigh. The count said it was. Denbigh implied things about me and you got angry, isn't that it?"

"He told me you had been married. It was a long time ago, Claudia. It has nothing to do with us now."

He did not trust himself to talk about it. What had happened with Denbigh was his fault, not Claudia's, but the knowledge of her and Denbigh tortured him. And the idea of her going to him filled him, each time he thought of it, with the same rage that had made him strike out that afternoon. It was not something they could discuss.

They had been sitting side by side on the sofa, and she stood and walked to the window overlooking the park. It was a moonless night, and the glass threw back an image of the room. She could see her own face pale against the darkness and behind her Philippe staring off somewhere in the middle distance. Absorbed in his own thought, he was no longer watching her. She turned from the reflection to the man.

"Philippe, about Denbigh. . . ."

"There's nothing to say about Denbigh. It's over."

But not the repercussions, she thought later that night as she listened to his even breathing beside her. And now they'd take Philippe from her. It was unfair! But just or unjust, Claudia knew one thing. Her punishment was self-inflicted.

Why had she married Joe? From boredom? For sex? She thought of his taunts that afternoon in his apartment. Now with Philippe's body warm beside her, her attraction to Joe made her sick with disgust. She cringed in shame at the memory of their intimacy. And now she would pay for it.

They were taking Philippe from her. He said it wouldn't be for long, but she knew he was lying. The chances of his returning before the end of the war—and who knew how many years away that was?—were small. And what if he never returned? Images of London charred and destroyed by the blitz marched through Claudia's mind. Without meaning to, she uttered a cry. In half sleep Philippe turned to her, his

411

arm forming a protective circle holding her to him. She laid her cheek against his chest. In the stillness of the night she could hear the steady beat of his heart. The sound grew louder and louder until it sounded like a succession of bombs.

3

March 28, 1941

My darling,

It has been fifteen days since I left you. It feels more like fifteen years. The days on board ship were long and empty. How they dragged without you! The days here in London have been long and busy. And how they drag without you! Though, of course, I'm not in the least without you. You're with me everywhere. The other day I shocked one of the secretaries by talking to you out loud right in the corridor of Carlton Garden. I must be careful or I'll become known as the mad major.

I doubt, though, that I could be more mad than half the men running around headquarters. For every serious officer dedicated to driving the Germans out of France there are two opportunists out to turn the war to their profit. The jockeying for position and what little power exists is scandalous. After all your worry you'll be happy to know the greatest danger I run in London—the remnants of the blitz notwithstanding—is that of being stabbed in the back by a fellow officer who thinks I stand one office closer to De Gaulle than he does.

The most surprising thing happened to me yesterday—although why I feel that people from one's past turning up in unexpected places in wartime is surprising I can't imagine. I was on my way home from headquarters when the sirens sounded, and

I headed for the nearest shelter. The usual crowd assembled as the warning continued, and I didn't pay much attention to the white-haired fellow next to me. I probably wouldn't have recognized him, but fortunately, he recognized me, even after all these years. I hadn't seen Herr Schlosser since he was last in Paris in '31. At that time he was teaching economics at Heidelberg and was on summer holiday.

Schlosser was an active member of the Social Democratic Party and wrote several books and pamphlets against the Nazis. He was in Germany until '39, and I needn't tell you the sort of time he and his wife had. He was in a concentration camp for a year and a half. Then one morning for some inexplicable reason he was simply released. Such, apparently, is the order of the New Order. They were fortunate to get out just before the war broke out, and they've been in England ever since.

The point, darling, of this lengthy story about a man of whom you've never heard is that Herr Professor Schlosser and his wife need an American sponsor. He has had an offer to teach at a small college in one of your northern states—is there a place called Williams?—but the offer comes without personal sponsorship. It seems anyone at the college who has the means to sponsor him—ten thousand American dollars, according to Herr Schlosser—has already pledged himself for a refugee, and the ones who are free simply don't have the means. (I suspect American universities don't pay their professors very well.)

When Herr Schlosser told me his story, I immediately thought of you. Of course, I said no more to him than that I would poke around among American friends. The fact is Herr Schlosser and his wife would be no burden to you. You need only fill out a few forms and pledge the $10,000, which, in view of the promised position, is only a formality. Of course, if you chose to take Wilhelm and his wife under your wing for a few days when they arrived, it would be more than kind of you.

I realize I'm asking a lot of you, darling, but only because I know you will want to help. If you can imagine the ordeal these two good people have been through, you will see it is the least we can do.

I know what your answer will be, and I am wildly envious of Wilhelm, for he will be with you in a matter of weeks. With any luck I won't be far behind. Until then, remember I love you and am with you always.

All my love,
Philippe

After a battery of physical and psychiatric examinations that assured Claudia she would be harboring neither disease carriers nor a madman and madwoman, Herr and Frau Schlosser arrived. The process of investigation and acceptance had taken not weeks, as Philippe predicted, but months. In August Claudia drove in from the country to meet their ship and took them back to Oyster Bay for two weeks rest before they made their way north to a new life.

Her houseguests were quiet, considerate, and not in the least troublesome. Herr Schlosser read and walked in the garden. His wife, who had trained Olympic swimmers only to be banned from the 1933 Olympics for political reasons, spent her days improving Diana and Tony's styles. The Schlossers were a peculiar couple, Claudia thought, as she sat at the water's edge watching Hilda with her two children. Why had this strong young woman who treated her body almost as an instrument married that quiet, bookish man? Even if Claudia could give credence to the cliché that opposites attract, she could not account for Hilda's choosing a man twice her age. Psychiatrists might inquire after a father complex, but Claudia doubted it. There was nothing paternal or filial about the Schlossers' relationship.

Claudia stood and motioned to the children to come

in. Predictably Tony began to swim out to the float. "Just one last dive," he called.

Moments later he emerged from the surf, shaking water from his body like a rambunctious puppy. Diana, a year older, walked straight and tall in a not unsuccessful attempt to emulate Frau Schlosser.

"Up to the house now, children. Uncle Graham's coming for lunch, and I don't want you to be late."

Hilda sat next to Claudia on the sand. "I expect the adults have a moment to rest." Hilda's English was perfect, if heavily accented.

"As long as you like. Lunch won't be till one, but I thought they'd had enough water."

"I don't think they will ever have enough. Anthony is a sea otter. And Diana is a born swimmer. I have watched her coordination. She is a very good athlete. She told me she takes after her father in this."

"Well, she certainly doesn't inherit it from me. It's kind of you to take so much time with them."

"Not at all. I enjoy it. It is you who are kind to us. Without your help and Monsieur Boissevain's we would not be here. It is amazing. One does not see a friend for years, and then suddenly one meets him and he becomes one's salvation. Of course, we have always had a high regard for Monsieur Boissevain. Ever since before the last war. I was not in Paris then, but my husband was."

"Was Herr Schlosser teaching in Paris?" Philippe had never explained his friendship with Herr Schlosser, and Claudia simply assumed it was that of a gifted student and encouraging professor.

Frau Schlosser looked at her in surprise. "Wilhelm teaching in Paris before the last war! Good heavens, no. He and Monsieur Boissevain were students together. I believe my husband was a year or two behind."

This time it was Claudia's face that registered surprise, and Frau Schlosser understood immediately. "My husband's appearance is misleading. Four years ago, when they came to take him away, there was not a gray hair on his head. He looked like a young man in— how would you say it?—the full bloom of life. When I met him at the railroad station a year and a half later, I almost did not recognize him. His hair was completely white as you see it now. He was never a heavy man, but he had lost more than thirty kilos—seventy pounds. He was—and remains—a sick man. His kidneys—you will excuse me—were ruined by frequent beatings across the lower back. The floggings were done to music. There were tortures of which I will not speak. But worst of all, my husband was taken away with a colleague. They had known each other since boyhood, had grown up together, served in the last war together, worked in the party together. They hanged the other man. Or rather they forced my husband to hang him. It is something he never speaks of, but I know he lives with it every day.

"You must excuse me. My husband would not want me to tell you these things, but I feel they must be told. People must know. You have been more than kind to us, but there are many others who have not had our good fortune. They, too, must be helped. Perhaps if you and your countrymen know how things are at home, they will begin to help."

Prodded by the woman's fervor, Claudia's horror turned to indignation. Hilda was right. People could no longer sit by in silence. Something must be done.

December 7, 1941, was an anticlimax for Claudia. She had already been at war for almost a year. Despite his assurances that London was safe and he was in no danger, Claudia worried constantly about Philippe. And the pebble of indignation Hilda Schlosser had tossed into Claudia's sea of indifference had sent significant ripples through her life. After the Schlossers went off to New England, Claudia agreed to sponsor another family. It was then that she was approached by Sylvia Miller, head of a small, still purposely unnamed group dedicated to helping victims of Nazi persecution.

"The point is, Mrs. Beaumont, you can reach people we can't. The refugees we help are of all religions. The Schlossers, for example, are Catholics from South Germany. Herr Schlosser was jailed for political rather than religious beliefs. We've helped Germans, Poles, Czechs,

Hungarians, every group that's been overrun by Hitler and his troops. A good many of our refugees are, of course, Jewish, but many are not. We've been fairly successful so far in finding sponsors and volunteers among Jews. With your help we can branch out and make this the nondenominational effort it ought to be."

Sylvia Miller saw Claudia's hesitation, but she had wrung aid—and dollars—from drier stones than Claudia. "You've done so much already. The Schlossers. The Feldmanns. And still, it's only a drop in the bucket for what must be done. We wouldn't ask too much of your time, Mrs. Beaumont, but we'd be grateful for whatever you could spare."

Claudia began slowly. She enlisted a few more sponsors, raised a small amount of money, recruited a few volunteers, and by the time Pearl Harbor shocked America into action she was spending three mornings a week in the small office on Forty-eighth Street.

Right now she was sitting in Sylvia Miller's glass-enclosed cubicle. Mrs. Miller had gone to Washington for the week and asked Claudia to watch over things while she was away. Like others before her, Sylvia Miller recognized that Mrs. Beaumont was good at getting people to do what she wanted. Mrs. Miller also knew the trait was likely to make Claudia a good administrator.

"Would you close the door behind you please, Victoria? I'd like to get some work done, and the noise out there is distracting."

"Certainly, Mrs. Beaumont." The girl looked at her with admiration. She was young and idealistic and impressed by Claudia.

Claudia took Philippe's letter from her handbag. She wanted to re-read the last paragraphs. She couldn't believe they were true.

So you see, darling, you have nothing to worry about. Far from sending me off to battle, the powers that be here at headquarters laugh at the idea of my manning anything more dangerous than a desk. I am, Colonel Fontaine recently informed me—not without a certain malice, for the colonel is close to seventy—simply too old.

There is, however, a slight possibility I'll soon be leaving Carlton Gardens. Rumor has it now that America is at war the general is eager to post a few more officers to Washington as his personal representatives. Of course, nothing is certain yet, but it seems just as unreasonable to expect the worst as the best. So with any luck, my darling, I'll be with you before spring. Until then, remember I love you and am with you always.

All my love,
Philippe

Claudia looked through the glass partition separating the small private office from the larger one where most of the volunteers worked. Victoria Newell was telephoning possible sponsors. Her face was intense, and her mouth worked rapidly, but like an actress in one of the old silent movies, she made no sound. Another girl and an older woman were filling out forms, and at the far end of the room an elderly couple sat huddled in fear and confusion. The young Vassar graduate whose German went no further than translations of Goethe was trying to communicate with them. The pantomime was eloquent through the glass partition, but Claudia watched without seeing it. It was a shameful thought, but she would welcome Pearl Harbor if it brought Philippe back to her.

"Claudia, I wish you'd leave those things alone and listen to me."

"I'm perfectly capable of listening to you and sorting at the same time, Kate."

Katherine gave her sister a disapproving look. In her flannel trousers, cashmere sweater, and pageboy hairdo she seemed almost as young as her children. The three of them sat cross-legged on the floor, boxes of old Christmas ornaments between them. Not only did she look almost as young as they, Kate thought, but she acted as irresponsibly as they did. "It's just like you,

Claudia, to go off this way. Of course, you couldn't do the normal thing, the acceptable thing. You couldn't work for the Red Cross or volunteer in some hospital. You have to sign up with that peculiar foreign group. First you were forcing your friends to sponsor the strangest people, and now you're filling the house with heaven only knows what sort of trash. If you keep this sort of thing up, you'll have Diana married to some Jew in no time."

"*Yucch.* . . ." Diana said to the fragile crystal angel she was wrapping.

"That is not a very ladylike sound, Diana, or a very Christian sentiment," Claudia reprimanded.

"Well, if not to a Jew then," Kate continued, "to one of those brooding Poles, and they're all Catholics."

Claudia saw the look her daughter and sister exchanged but thought nothing of it. "I don't think we have to worry about Diana's marrying anyone yet. She's only fifteen."

"Almost sixteen, Mother."

"Fifteen," Claudia repeated. "Diana is still a child, and even if she weren't, it wouldn't stop me from helping these people in any way we can."

"Ah, yes, Claudia must do her duty as she sees it."

"It wouldn't hurt you to help, Kate."

"You can move those people into your house, Claudia, but you won't convince me to."

"I haven't moved anyone in. In this case, I've merely invited a few families for Christmas. They're alone and frightened in a foreign country. It would be cruel not to have them here to share Christmas with us."

Tony looked up from the line of nutcracker soldiers he had arranged. "Mother"—his tone was sharp with adolescent reproval—"Jews don't celebrate Christmas."

For a moment Claudia looked nonplussed. "You see," Kate raced in, "you're so busy playing Lady Bountiful you haven't even stopped to think of what's good for those people."

"I don't think a decent dinner and a few small gifts are going to undermine anyone's religious beliefs." As she stood and straightened her trousers, Claudia felt the stiff paper of Philippe's letter crinkle against the soft wool of her pocket. "I think what we're doing is the only decent thing to do." She touched the letter. As soon as she was alone, she would read it again.

December 12, 1942

My darling,

I can't tell you how proud I am of you. Your letters make it sound as if you're merely doing a little conventional "charity" work, but Frau Schlosser has written me differently. She says you're absolutely tireless in rounding up new sponsors and volunteers. She also reports you've sponsored three more families yourself. What you're doing is wonderful, darling, and I couldn't be more proud of you.

It was always the same with Philippe's letters. Every time her interest began to flag, every time she thought she'd done enough for *those* people, as Katherine called them, Philippe's encouragement and approval sent her right back to the small center on Forty-eighth Street. Once again she'd be cajoling friends into sponsorship and filling the house with people she felt sorry for, but had no real interest in. She supposed it was one way to stay close to Philippe during the long, lonely months. She turned back to his letter.

We seem to be doing little except hanging eagerly on every word from North Africa. Of course here at headquarters there was a furor over Darlan's assassination, but since the little that was left of the French fleet was scuttled before the Germans got to Toulon, the consternation has died down. After three and a half years of war a single casualty has little meaning. I never believed I would write such words, but I never believed the war would drag on so endlessly. I guess, like everyone else, I didn't learn much from the last war.

I'm reluctant to even mention the good news— I've disappointed you so many times in the past—

but I can't keep it to myself. Because of rumors of an important conference in the near future and the general's uneasy feeling about General Girard (Darlan's successor), he wants to make sure his interests are represented in the planning of that conference. There are only three of us here who could possibly be sent to Washington. I'll say no more for fear of tempting fate. Until then, remember I love you and am with you always.

All my love,
Philippe

Claudia had read through the form several times, but the information hadn't sunk in. The family was from a small town in Poland. Their name was Wolkewich. Strange how she now took the most extraordinary names for granted. She could master the succession of consonants without an intervening vowel with ease, and the Cohens and Levys were as common to her now as Smiths and Jones. But to get back to the Wolkewich family. . . .

Claudia heard the front door slam. "Diana," she called, "would you come in here please?"

The girl entered the library reluctantly.

"How was the skating?"

"Okay." Diana shifted her weight from one foot to the other impatiently.

"I didn't think you'd stay out this long. It's dark."

"We went back to Sally's afterward."

"Oh, you went skating with Sally?"

"I told you I was, Mother."

"If you're going to lie, Diana, you ought to at least take the trouble to substantiate your lies." She saw Diana's face assume a stubborn, hostile expression. "Sally called here around two. She wanted to know what you were doing this afternoon. So do I. Where were you, Diana? And with whom?"

"I went to the movies."

"With whom?"

"Just some kids."

"Then why did you tell me you were going skating with Sally?"

"I thought I might, and then I just changed my mind."

"What did you see?"

"Road to Morocco."

"Who else went?"

"Ann Whimple and Sue and Jean Carrier."

"Then you won't mind if I call Mrs. Whimple and Mrs. Carrier and ask them where their daughters were until this late hour. I'm sure they were worried, too."

"Um . . . well, they went straight home. I didn't."

"I'm tired of playing games, Diana. Where were you this afternoon?"

The girl was silent.

"I'm waiting for an answer."

"I was with Kurt Mueller."

"Who is Kurt Mueller?"

"If you paid any attention to all those people you pretend to care so much about, you'd know. His father is Dr. Mueller."

"The political refugees from Mainz."

"They all have titles for you, don't they, Mother?"

"Don't be impertinent, Diana. I deal with a great many people. I can't be expected to remember all of them. And I'm not the one on trial here. Why did you lie to me?"

"Kurt doesn't think you'd let me see him."

"He may be right, but not for the reasons you might think. Unlike your Aunt Katherine, I have no prejudices against these people." Diana looked at her mother skeptically but said nothing.

"Tell me something about him. I'm still trying to remember which one he is."

"He was here for Thanksgiving, Mother. You even talked to him about colleges."

Now she remembered. The boy was right. She hadn't approved of him at all. His looks and manner had reminded Claudia of a picture of one of those Hitler Youths. If the stories of children turning in their parents were true, she wondered why that aggressive, muscular youth had not reported his parents. Besides, he was much too old. He had said if they were in Germany, he would be at the university now.

"How old is Kurt?"

"Oh, I'm not sure. . . ." Diana toyed with the knitted cap in her hands.

"How old is he, Diana?"

"Twenty."

"Well, to begin with, he's much too old for you."

"He said you'd say that, but the real reason is that he's German. That's what you have against him, isn't it?"

"That's ridiculous. If I helped his parents get into this country, I'd scarcely hold it against the boy for being German. I have nothing against Germans or any nationality, Diana, only against Nazis. I trust Kurt doesn't fall into that category. I'm sure he's a very nice young man, but he's simply too old for you. And I should think he'd find you and your friends too young." She saw Diana begin to toy with the cap again. "You weren't with any of your friends, were you? You were alone with Kurt."

"Yes."

"And you didn't go to the movies at all, did you?"

"No." Diana's tone was growing progressively more defiant.

"Where did you go?"

"We went to Kurt's house. He doesn't have the money to go anyplace else."

"I take it Dr. and Mrs. Mueller were out."

"What if they were?"

"Then you're a very foolish child, as well as a bad liar, Diana. And I want to know exactly what went on this afternoon."

"Nothing went on this afternoon, but what if it had? Does that make me not a nice girl, Mother?"

"You're a child, Diana, and I won't have you having dates, to say nothing of going to boy's houses alone with them."

"When can I start, Mother? When I'm sixteen or seventeen? When did you start? And don't tell me just two Christmases ago, when that Major Boissevain was here. You didn't really think I didn't know, did you? If I hadn't guessed for myself, I would have known from the gossip. . . ."

The palm of Claudia's hand silenced her. It had been a light slap, but it was enough to bring tears to Diana's eyes.

"Everything Aunt Katherine says about you is true. You're cruel and selfish and hateful. God knows why Daddy ever married you."

"Your father was a very good man, Diana, but I'm a little tired of this saint you and your aunt have constructed. If your father were here to discipline you, I have no doubt you'd find him a good deal more strict than I am. I'm only concerned about your welfare, just as he would be."

"You don't give a damn about me."

"I won't have you cursing, Diana. And I won't have you running around with twenty-year-old boys. And as for your lying, I'm afraid I'll have to punish you for that."

"What are you going to do, keep me from that dull old dance tomorrow night? Go ahead. I don't care. There's nobody there I want to dance with anyway."

"That's fine. Then you won't miss going. Now you'd better hurry and change. Dinner is in half an hour."

Claudia was not surprised to find Katherine waiting for her when she returned home the following evening.

"How could you do it, Claudia? This is the biggest dance of the holidays."

"According to Diana, it isn't much of a sacrifice. Anyway she lied to me, and I will not tolerate lying."

"At least in anyone else."

"Diana has to learn right from wrong, Kate."

"And you're going to teach her. If it weren't so tragic, I might be able to laugh."

"What do you suggest I do, encourage her to go sneaking around with that Mueller boy?"

"Of course not. I'm as opposed to him as you are. But don't say I didn't warn you. I told you a week ago in this very room that if you insisted on filling the house with those people, something like this was bound to happen."

"I can't wrap Diana in cotton for the rest of her life. She'll have to learn how to conduct herself around all kinds of people. Anyway, I have nothing against the boy," she lied. There was nothing concrete. "I don't even know him. He's simply too old for Diana. And I will not have her going off alone with young men and then lying to me about it."

"And if you keep her from the dance tonight, it gives her the perfect excuse to keep pining over him. She'll never get over the boy this way."

"For heaven's sake, Kate, she's only fifteen. She'll get over him."

"I almost forgot, we all get over things but Claudia. Only Claudia can be really hurt. Only Claudia has feelings."

"My feelings have nothing to do with this. I'm only interested in Diana's welfare."

"You've never given a thought to anyone's welfare but your own. I care more about that girl than you do."

"Only because she's Sam's."

"Whatever the reason, at least I care, Claudia. You've never had time for her. You've never had time for any of your children. You've always been too busy taking care of yourself."

The recrimination stung. Behind Katherine on the library table was the silver-framed picture of Jamie in short pants. It had been taken the year before he died. "Perhaps I haven't been a great success as a mother. . . ."

"A great success! You've been an abysmal failure. You're a rotten mother, and you were a rotten wife. That about sums up your life, Claudia. Unless we're going to rate you on being a mistress. Perhaps that's where you win all the prizes."

Claudia regretted letting down her guard. She should have known better with Katherine. "At least that's more than we can say about you, Kate. Apparently you didn't make Sam any happier than I did."

It had been, to say the least, an unusual Christmas Day. Katherine left immediately after dinner. "I wouldn't have come at all if it weren't for the children."

Diana wanted to leave with her aunt, but Claudia insisted she stay. "We have guests," she told her daughter.

Graham, though he clearly hadn't enjoyed the day, had played host with customary reserve to a group of thirty. They came from four countries and a variety of backgrounds and spoke several dialects and languages. The only common characteristics were a certain wan, undernourished appearance and an expression of fear.

The last family was finally leaving. A girl of about eight, who had said nothing all day, clutched a doll blissfully to her. Katherine had argued a rag doll would be more than sufficient, but Claudia had insisted on a small Madam Alexander baby. She was glad now she had. The child, holding the doll fiercely, half hid behind her mother's skirt as the woman tried to thank Claudia. She spoke no English but pronounced her words in that slow distinct way designed to make an unknown language intelligible.

Claudia accepted the thanks while trying to ease the family toward the door. She was tired. Suddenly the woman's hands clutched at Claudia in thanks. Her arms, visible beneath the short sleeves of someone else's cast-off dress, were covered with an angry red rash. Without meaning to, Claudia recoiled. The woman, seeing her error, drew back and offered a final, wounded thank-you.

In February, 1944, Sylvia Miller had a heart attack. She was in the cluttered office of a clothing manufacturer whose sudden and impressive success could be traced to the thousands of uniforms he had turned out for the United States government. As the man affixed his careful signature to a check for one hundred thousand dollars, Mrs. Miller keeled over quietly into a rack of WAC uniforms. The next day Mr. Miller explained his wife could no longer continue her duties in the League of Friendship, as it was now called, and Claudia, by consensus of the directors, ascended to the presidency.

The organization was more elaborate than the one Claudia had joined two and a half years ago. In addition to the volunteers, who now numbered twice as many, there were two professional secretaries and a full-time social worker.

Claudia was busier than she'd ever been, and she supposed it was good for her. At least Philippe's letters said it was. Time after time he praised her for all the good she was doing and told her he was glad she had something to occupy her while they were apart.

Occupy her, indeed. Did he think she thought of him less simply because there was more to do? She thought of him all the time. While she was raising funds, recruiting sponsors, interviewing refugees, he was in the back of her mind. When she was tired of wheedling money out of unpleasant people and bored with the by-now familiar tale of misery and hardship, only the thought of Philippe and his admiration kept her going. And his letters, of course.

She placed the last one with the others. The drawer was almost overflowing. Soon she'd have to start another. At first, when she hoped Philippe might return in a matter of months, she had stored his letters in a carved mahogany box meant for photographs. But they soon outgrew one box and then another and were now overflowing the drawer. Almost three years of letters. Almost three years of loneliness.

She took the last one from its envelope. She'd read it once more before she put it away.

April 11, 1944

My darling,

Just a note since things are terribly hectic here

at headquarters. The place is rife with speculation about the coming invasion, and everyone is working round the clock. Excitement runs so high it isn't even dampened by the knowledge that while France is being liberated, many of us will be left behind at our desks. As you know, I've never believed in the glory of battle, but this is one operation I'd give a good deal to be part of. I tell you that, darling, only because I know it is impossible, so there's no need for you to worry.

To steal a bit of the illustrious prime minister's thunder, I can't help thinking this is not merely the end of the beginning, but finally the beginning of the end, which means the beginning of our future. It seems impossible the war will end and we'll be together again, but I know now it will. I feel sure that within the year I'll be able to hold you in my arms, and after that, darling, I promise you we'll never be apart again. Until then, remember I love you and am with you always.

All my love,
Philippe

4

Claudia applied the lipstick carefully. She had to look perfect today. After all, it was, as Katherine had said, although in her mouth the words took on a venomous edge, a momentous day. Every hair was in place, but Claudia began to comb again. There would be photographers and a crowd, and she wanted to look her best. Today she must be worthy of Philippe's love and pride.

She walked to the full-length mirror. Was the gray Molyneux suit too girlish? After all, she was no longer in the first blush of youth. No, the skirt was short, but still longer than the War Regulations Board would like. Was it too stylish and flamboyant? After all, the war was not quite over, though everyone knew it would be any day now. Paris was once again the City of Light. The morning paper had shown pictures of lights going on all over the city. Claudia had to admit she was surprised at some of the women in those photographs. They wore muttonchop sleeves and full skirts. Hadn't the couturiers heard of shortages?

She decided the suit was all right. Not too gay, not too somber. Exactly appropriate for the occasion.

Claudia unlocked the small marquetry box on her dressing table. Inside was the letter from the Swiss prefect Philippe had shown her that night at the Plaza. It no longer made her cry to read it. With it was a photograph Philippe had carried. They both looked so young. They were standing under a huge oak tree with the chapel behind them, and Philippe's arm was around her. That had been his father's touch. "Don't

be so stiff, my boy," he'd thundered at Philippe as
he focused the camera. "You're not expected to stand
at attention when there's a beautiful woman beside
you." She wondered if there'd be a St. Hubert's Hunt
again when the war was over. Claudia took the last
object from the box. It was a plain gold band folded
in a piece of writing paper. There were a few lines in
Philippe's familiar hand.

> My darling,
>   I bought this in Montreux, but I waited too
> long to give it to you. Still, we've had more than
> most. I love you and am with you always.
>
>   All my love,
>   Philippe

She knew the letter by heart. It was as familiar as
the gold band on her third finger. She'd read the letter and tried on the ring a thousand times since the
Count de Rochefleur had brought it to her just after
the invasion of Normandy. It would be a year soon,
but the night was as vivid to her as if it had been
yesterday.

She had come home from a small dinner tired but
pleased with herself. She had enlisted two more sponsors.

"There's a gentleman waiting for you in the library,
madam. A Count de Rochefleur," Wilfred said.

Claudia was surprised. She hadn't seen the count
since that day in Washington when he had told her
Philippe was recalled to London. She prayed he'd come
to see her about the League of Friendship. *There's no
reason to assume it has anything to do with Philippe,*
she told herself, but the moment she saw the count's
face she knew it did.

He stood and bowed when she entered. "I'm sorry
to disturb you at this hour, Mrs. Beaumont. I would
not have come if it hadn't been important."

"It's Philippe!"

"The major is dead."

The words echoed off the book-lined walls and

thundered through her brain. *The major is dead. The major is dead. The major is dead.*

"But how? I don't understand. He said he wasn't to be part of the invasion." Her voice was quiet. She was still sure it was a mistake. Philippe could not be dead. Not when the end was so near. And he had sworn to her he was in no danger.

"He was a very important part of the invasion, Mrs. Beaumont, but few people knew it. The major volunteered to serve as a contact with the underground forces in France. He was dropped behind the German lines two days before the invasion."

"Then you don't know he's dead. You merely don't know where he is."

"The Germans picked him up immediately. We suspect there was a leak. He showed great courage, Mrs. Beaumont. He held out for twenty-four hours, and that is what is required in his position. He provided time for plans to be changed."

"He held out for twenty-four hours! Are you telling me the Germans tortured Philippe for twenty-four hours?"

"Please, Mrs. Beaumont, I'm not telling you anything of the sort. The major was picked up by the Gestapo. He was very brave. He did everything necessary and died a hero's death. You must be proud of him."

"Proud of him! I don't want to be proud of him! I want a living man, not a dead hero!"

"Please, Mrs. Beaumont," the count repeated. "It will do no good to become hysterical. The major gave his life courageously for a great cause. He would want you to think of it that way. He'd also want you to carry on your work for that cause."

"How did he die? The least you can do is tell me how he died."

"I have no details."

She looked at his eyes. "You're lying."

"Mrs. Beaumont, you're excited now—understandably. Perhaps we could talk some other time. In the meantime, I wanted to leave these things with you. The major gave them to me when he was posted to

London. He asked me to give them to you in the event he did not return." He handed Claudia a large sealed envelope. "I'm sorry, Mrs. Beaumont. The major was a man of honor and courage. A great man. You have my deepest sympathies."

Little good that would do her, the count thought when he was safe outside the house. But what would do her any good? Surely she hadn't really wanted to know how Philippe had died. He had seen the reports from their informant and could piece together the rest. It was not something a woman ought to know about.

Gestapo headquarters outside Arras was in a small, handsome château. Philippe sat in a straight-backed chair in the center of the brightly lit room. On the wall behind the officer white squares on the age-darkened walls revealed where paintings had been removed. Philippe wondered whose collection in Germany they had enhanced. During his last session—was it an hour ago, two, only a half? His sense of time was disoriented—he had tried to fill the white squares with paintings. First he diverted himself with Brueghel; then, when the pain grew more intense, he had summoned Goya. The faces of the wounded soldiers mirrored his agony. Finally, mercifully, he had passed out.

It couldn't be too much longer now, he thought. They had picked him up just before dawn, and it had been dark the last two times they had brought him in for his session. Two more hours to go, four at the most. Then his twenty-four hours would be up, and they would simply kill him. He was of no value to them after twenty-four hours.

He wondered which it would be this time. There was no order to their methods. He saw the field telephone on the desk. The electrodes again. At least it wasn't the ice water.

"Stand," the younger officer barked in German.

"There's no need to be rude, Sergeant," the captain said. "Boissevain is, after all, an officer and a gentleman, and we're not barbarians."

They did not permit him to remove his own clothing. The first time he had found it an indignity. Now he no longer cared. He watched numbly as they removed his trousers, then undershorts. The sergeant attached the electrodes carefully. They were meticulous, these Gestapo. They ordered him to sit again and strapped him to the chair so his body would not wrench forward when they sent the charge. In his exhaustion and dull agony it seemed to Philippe it was happening to someone else, but the pain, he knew, would be his. He saw the captain's hand move toward the telephone. An explosion of pain convulsed his body, and the force of the shock lifted him and the chair off the floor. Perhaps it wouldn't take as long to pass out this time. The white square on the wall turned crimson as another spasm shot through him.

The captain's voice came to him dimly as if from a great distance. He did not try to make sense of the words. What the questions were made no difference. The only thing that mattered was the few seconds' respite they would give him.

Philippe looked at the ceiling. At least they had not shipped that back to Germany. In one corner cupids cavorted through a sun-dappled garden. They were fat and pink and absurdly lewd. From the corner of his eye Philippe saw the captain's hand move toward the crank on the phone. The pain exploded within him. Had that bestial cry been his?

In another corner of the ceiling a shepherd flirted with a maid. The boy's face was that of a pretty child. Philippe thought of his son. He would have changed a great deal by now. He'd be almost twenty. He tried to conjure a man's face out of the boyish countenance he remembered; but the sergeant's face leered before his, and then his fists crashed against Philippe's head in a gratuitous assault. He felt his neck snap, and the room swam around him.

He tried to concentrate on the ceiling again, but his vision was blurred. Directly above him a bland Adonis wooed a voluptuous blond Venus. He thought of Claudia. As if the captain had read his thoughts, two more spasms shot through him, convulsing his body and lifting it off the floor. The face of the Venus was too round, the body too full-blown. Again the pain, and for a moment the ceiling turned back. *Just a little longer*, he told himself. He tried to bring the Venus back into focus, but the figure was dim. His memory sharpened the picture. He could see Claudia looking back at him, her green eyes clear, her mouth partially opened, her arms held out to him. The pain shot through his body, then echoed a second time, a third, a fourth. He could no longer distinguish Claudia's features. She was a soft blur that seemed to be hovering over his head, beckoning him to follow her away from here. The captain's guttural sounds came to him dimly—like Frau Schwarzburgen coming to wake them in the morning. The perspiration was wet and cold on his face, and he felt as if he were rolling over and over in the snow with Claudia, and then the snow turned to a sharp, searing fire, and Claudia's face became a red flame that consumed them both.

For a month after Rochefleur's visit Claudia did not leave the house. She sent the children to the country with Katherine and passed hour after hour locked in her father's library. The count's words still echoed through it. *He held out for twenty-four hours.* No matter where she turned Claudia could not escape visions of those twenty-four hours. Every story of Nazi atrocities returned to haunt her. She tried to drive the images from her mind, but pictures of Philippe undergoing every torture were more vivid than the surroundings she moved through like a sleepwalker. She saw his face contorted in agony, his mouth open in a silent scream, his body broken, bleeding, maimed beyond recognition.

Ellen, the only servant Claudia had kept in town, shuttled silently in and out with meals Claudia left untouched. More than one morning Ellen found an empty brandy bottle among the overflowing ashtrays in the library. She clicked her tongue disapprovingly but reasoned that if it helped the poor woman sleep, there was no real harm to it.

Several women from the league came to see her. They were appalled at her appearance. Even in the most frantic moments Claudia had always been impeccably turned out—her skirts never wrinkled, her cuffs never soiled, and her perfectly understated make-up never faded. Now her hair looked dirty and tangled, and she wore an old silk dressing gown stained with brandy and marred by cigarette burns. She received them but answered their questions in monosyllables. To their pleas that she return to the office, that they needed her, that hundreds needed her, she said nothing. Finally, the rebuffed women decided to send the full-time social worker. Claudia would not see her.

At the end of July Katherine came into town for the day. She was appalled at what she found. "Go upstairs, and put on some clothes. I'm taking you to the hairdresser."

Claudia touched her hair uncertainly. "Would you like a brandy, Kate?"

"No, and you're not going to have one either. You can play the madwoman of Sixty-ninth Street for everyone else, but I won't buy it. Damn it, you got through your husband's death, and you can get through your lover's."

"I don't want to get through it," Claudia said quietly. "There's nothing to get through it for. I don't care about living if Philippe isn't alive."

"Rubbish."

"I'm not going to fight with you, Kate. Just go back to the country and leave me alone."

"If you don't care about your children or the spectacle you're making of yourself, what about your precious league? All that good you've been telling me you do. Surely the league can't go on without you."

"I don't care about the league."

Katherine whirled on her. "Of course not. You've never cared about it or anything else but yourself. All those poor souls you kept lecturing me about. You never gave a damn about any of them. All you cared about was how good you looked playing the Angel of Mercy.

"I told you once, Claudia, the only thing you were ever any good at was being a mistress. I was wrong. You're a failure there, too. You never loved your precious Philippe. If you had loved him—the flesh-and-blood man that existed, not some romantic picture of yourself being in love with him—you'd care about what he died for. But you don't, and you never did. All you care about is playing the bereaved widow, the woman lost to love. Just the latest in a long line of Claudia Trenholm's starring roles.

"You're a fake, Claudia. I've always known it, and now everyone else is going to see it too, and I can't wait. You never cared what Sam thought. Well, I only wish your Philippe were alive to see you for what you are. That would be the best retribution I could wish on you."

Katherine had not meant to be kind, and her cruelty achieved what none of the urgings of more well-meaning friends could. If she went on as she was, Claudia reasoned, she would be lending credence to Katherine's words. But her sister couldn't be right. If she were, it made a mockery of Claudia's life. If she hadn't loved Philippe, then everything she had done was meaningless.

The next morning Claudia was in her office at the league by ten. She looked neat and crisp in a navy linen suit and a dark straw hat. The women in the office agreed that except for the weight she had lost, she looked exactly like the old Claudia.

She called a meeting for eleven o'clock. There she explained to her staff in her simple, straightforward way that they must redouble their efforts. The end of the war could not be far off. As France and the rest of Europe were liberated, there would be more and more displaced souls in need of homes, care, and comfort. It was up to them to provide as much as they could for as many as they could. There was not a moment to waste. They would start a drive for new volunteers, additional sponsors, and more money immediately. Step by step she outlined the strategy of the drive and the responsibilities of each member. The women looked at one another with relief. It was good to have a leader again.

The drive had been a success, the league had achieved great things, and now Claudia was to receive an award for their work. Ellen stood in the door to Claudia's bedroom. "There's a man from the *Tribune* on the phone, ma'am. He said he wants to set up an appointment for an interview."

"Tell him to call back tomorrow, Ellen. I haven't time today."

She couldn't be late. One didn't keep the First Lady waiting. Claudia wondered if she'd be seated next to Mrs. Roosevelt or somewhere down the dais. She had never received an award before, and she was not sure of protocol. One of the First Lady's aides had instructed Claudia that a real speech was unnecessary. All she need do was thank the First Lady and say a few words about the need for more help and more money. The important thing, he had told her, was to publicize the fine work the league was doing —and must go on doing.

Katherine, when she heard about the award, had been appalled. She refused to attend the lunch where it would be presented. "It's vulgar, Claudia. There'll be pictures of you in all the magazines and newspapers and a lot of publicity."

"Do as you like, Kate. You don't have to come if you don't want to."

"That's right. Nobody will miss me. This is your circus. You'll be in the limelight, and won't you just love it?"

Claudia smiled at her image as she gave her hat a final adjustment. "Vulgar," Kate had said. Wait till she saw the article in *Time* magazine or, better yet, the one in *Life*. If they used the pictures they had taken of Claudia at home with Tony and Diana, Kate would be furious. Well, let her be. Times had changed and if Katherine wasn't willing to change with them, so much the worse for her. Mother used to worry about having their pictures in *Town and Country*, but that was twenty-five years ago. Publicity wasn't the shameful thing it used to be. Why, she knew a dozen women, two dozen, who would pay to get the attention Claudia did through her work in the league. Not that she had done it to get attention, of course, but all the same, there was no reason she should avoid publicity that went along with her work. Besides, it was, as Mrs. Roosevelt's aide said, important to make people aware of how much still had to be done.

The room was warm. There were too many people and too many spotlights focused on the head table. From the number of newspapermen milling about with cameras, Claudia knew the aide had organized well. The league would get a good deal of mileage out of this.

Her eyes combed the room. There must be thirty tables, perhaps more, and there were ten people at each table. Had all these people come just to see her receive an award? Three-quarters of them were women who, she supposed, had nothing better to do. For the rest—a few government types, representatives of other charities, religious leaders—this was business.

The waiter removed her untouched lunch, and she felt the aide behind her. He bent to whisper to her. An intense young man with horn-rimmed spectacles, he repeatedly reassured Claudia there was nothing to worry about, though she had given no sign of worrying. "It'll be about five minutes now, Mrs. Beaumont. Just keep calm. And don't let the lights throw you. We're hoping to get some newsreel coverage out of this. Now remember, nothing elaborate. Just thank Mrs. Roosevelt, and I guess you'll want to thank all the people who have worked for the league and sponsored refugees, that kind of thing. Just make sure you say there's still a lot to be done. Okay?" He was gone before she could answer.

Then she saw the First Lady stand, adjust the microphone, and begin to speak. "An outstanding achievement . . . humanitarian effort . . . compassionate . . .

still much to be done ... in gratitude for all she had done so far."

Claudia heard the burst of applause. It was her signal to stand. As she did, the applause mounted. It was warm and encouraging.

She walked the few steps to Mrs. Roosevelt, took the plaque, shook the strong, almost gnarled hand, murmured a word of private thanks, then turned to face the room. Hundreds of faces were turned to her expectantly.

From a table somewhere in the middle of the room a face jumped out at her. He was a man in his fifties. Beneath the dark hair, graying at the temples, the slender face was attentive. For a moment she seemed to forget where she was. It was Philippe. But of course, it wasn't Philippe at all. Philippe had been dead for almost a year. The face turned to the woman next to him. His profile in the gloom beyond the bright lights was Joe's. She blinked against the glare of the spotlights. The face swam back into focus. It was no one she knew, but he was watching her, waiting for her to speak, and while he was waiting, he was admiring her. His expression seemed to say, "A fine woman, and so attractive, too."

She began to speak. His expression did not change. "A rare woman, that," his face seemed to say. His approval felt like a ray of sunshine. She basked in it, and her cheeks grew rosy.

The last of her words emerged from the microphone, reverberated through the room, and died. She heard the applause start up again and swell until she thought she would drown in the warmth and admiration of a room full of strangers. Katherine had said it was vulgar, but it was not vulgar. It was almost like being loved.